If I Fall

NEW CASTLE 2

LYDIA MICHAELS

Romantic Suspense
IF I FALL

Content Warning

This romantic suspense novel contains graphic scenes of violence, which may not be suitable for sensitive audiences.

For more details, please visit https://lydiamichaelsbooks.com/content-warnings/

For Schultz.
xo,
Elmer

JADE AWOKE IN HER APARTMENT, immediately realizing something was terribly wrong. First, she was in her bed. She usually crashed on the couch. Second, she was completely nude. And third, her abdominal muscles were sore and her thighs, sticky. She frantically tried to piece together the events of the previous night but remembered nothing subsequent to saying goodbye to Jeremy.

The scent of sex lingered on her flesh. Her tender insides churned as wooziness had her stomach rising and falling with strange cramping. An excruciating ache resonated between her temples, threatening enough that she had to focus on not vomiting. Had she been in a car accident?

After staggering out of bed, she scanned her surroundings for any explanation as to how she got there. Had Jeremy come home with her? No, she specifically remembered him leaving the bar. And sleeping with Jeremy was something she'd never forget. Right?

They'd eaten dinner at Paprika's after the wedding rehearsal. Jeremy sat with her the majority of the evening and when the dinner ended, they met at The Pink Lounge for another drink. Subtly flirting, she made every attempt to let Jeremy know it could be his lucky night. But, always the gentleman, he politely ignored the implication of an open invitation to her bed.

Jade frowned. They definitely didn't do anything last night. Why was she so disoriented? Last night was too fuzzy after only a few drinks. Gaping holes cut apart her memory, telling her something wasn't right.

Kat had texted her, reminding Jade to pick up the rings from the jeweler. It was around that time that Jeremy said goodnight and things got fuzzy. But why? She'd been fine.

So fine that when he asked if she was okay to drive she laughed. After only three drinks over the course of five hours, she was barely buzzed—or so she thought.

The fringed edge of her memories showed glimpses of her straw twirling in her empty cocktail. Then ... nothing.

No blur of time passing. No memory of paying her tab, nothing of the ride home, or talking to anyone else at the bar. Nothing—until morning.

"What the hell happened last night?" She

rubbed her head, her fingers tangling in a massive knot of blonde hair.

The muffled chirping of her cell phone played. Ignoring the pain in her skull, so intense it caused her vision to momentarily blur, she searched for her cell. Her foot connected with something sharp and she stumbled. Squinting down at the jagged object, she frowned.

Why were her car keys on the floor? A few inches to the right sat her lip gloss.

The ringing continued as she frowned at the objects scattered across her bedroom floor. Her purse was flipped inside out, gutted, and lying on the carpet next to her wallet. "What the fuck?"

Taking a shaky step forward, she toed her wallet, flipping it over. It was completely empty. Even her library card was gone.

On buckling knees, she dropped to the carpet. Limbs weak, she briefly considered if there had been a car accident. Perhaps she was suffering a sort of delayed amnesia from bumping her head? Sweeping aside the dust ruffle, she spotted her phone next to a dirty sock, a hanger, some dust bunnies, and more items that belonged in her purse.

Using the hanger, she fished her phone within reach. It spun across the dusty hardwood floor toward the carpet as the incessant bleating suddenly ceased. She zoned out, staring at it in her palm.

Her phone wasn't where it belonged—more evidence that something was horribly wrong. Cell phone, keys, purse... It seemed silly, but all those belongings had a home. Fear crawled up her spine like little spiders.

Her cell chirped and she released it, dropping it onto the carpet. Bleak emptiness settled over her. Her thoughts teased like distant whispers. A million suspicions came to fruition as she sat, paralyzed, and naked on her floor. Her fingers closed over the swollen folds between her legs and it hit her like slow sifting sand eventually strong enough to bury her alive.

Rape.

I. Was. Raped.

A scream built in her mind, pounding to break free, but only a whimper slipped past her lips. Suddenly freezing, her arms protectively curled around her belly as her body trembled. An impotent fury gripped her so tightly, her limbs vibrated in an attempt to contain it.

Rocking and gasping, she whimpered in the silence.

A wave of nausea dragged up from the pit of her stomach and she dry heaved hard enough to draw the flesh covering her back muscles painfully taut. Chills prickled her skin as she sobbed in the silence.

Her jerky gaze dropped to her body, appraising the parts she could see. A bruise marred her thigh in an ugly shade of yellow. *What the fuck happened to me?*

What should she do? She was a medical professional. Trained in emergency situations. But she couldn't find a single logical thought in her head because this was not about a patient. This happened to her.

"Hello?" she cried, but no one answered. "Hello!"

Pushing her legs to stand, she leaned against the wall and shuffled toward the bathroom with the grace of a newborn calf. Nothing looked out of place, yet everything seemed off. Oddly, her laptop sat on the breakfast bar completely untouched. Wouldn't a thief be interested in that?

She turned and froze, the blood rushing from her limbs and her grip slipping on the wall. The front door was not just unlocked, but standing open.

Without consciously taking a step, she flung forward and threw both hands at the hard surface, slamming it shut. Hands violently shaking, she locked the knob and jerked the deadbolt home.

Panic sent a spasm of tremors racing up her spine. Every bit of her world was violated—her home, her body, and unquestionably, her mind.

Her face pressed into the cool door as she sobbed and gasped, but no matter how many times she asked why, no explanation followed. The best she could do was wash away the filth.

The shower faucet squealed as scalding water rushed down the drain. Stepping under the steaming spray, she winced. A million hot, welcome, prickling needles burned her skin.

Blotchy, red hives rose to the surface as she scrubbed her body. As she washed her shoulders, her fingers nicked a tender spot of raised, raw flesh and she vomited. That flick of her fingers over tender skin syphoned the last of her strength and she crumbled to the floor in a sobbing heap. She hissed as her fingers abraded a cut. Tilting her chin at an awkward angle, she studied the angry welt on her shoulder, trying to figure out how it got there. It hurt, hot like scalding poker, tender like a fresh scrape, and deep enough to send another sweep of nausea through her.

"Oh, fuck." Another sob forced its way past her ragged throat and aimed for the drain.

The force of retching brought her to her hands and knees. As her tender stomach emptied its contents, she stared dispassionately as bile made its way down the drain. Unable to form one coherent thought, she leaned her arms and cheek against the cool tile and caught her breath.

The water cooled as she continued to weep. Her fingers and toes pruned, discoloring as ice formed in her veins. This wasn't happening.

One

"NOW, MOMMA?" Young Mia's whisper echoed over the guests' hushed chatter and the organ music.

"Not yet, babe," Kat, Mia's mother, repeated for the thirteenth time while flattening a trembling palm over the ivory satin of her wedding gown. "Kiki has to go first."

Mia turned her anxious grin on Jade, who she adoringly referred to as Kiki since she was able to first talk. The stuffy air in the back of the chapel took crinoline to a new level of unpleasant. In the small, stuffy space the itchy material grated over Jade's already sweaty skin. Sunlight filtered through the glass, adding another layer of heat to the sultry air. Jade fiddled with her flowers and dabbed the perspiration beading at her brow before it melted her makeup. God, she was a wreck.

"Okay, Jade, it's your turn." The uppity wedding planner offered a tight lipped smile.

Jade wanted nothing more than to jam that clipboard right up her haughty ass. Thank God all this planning would be over tomorrow. Although, if there was nothing to plan things might get a little too real for her to handle.

"Take it slow and smile," the woman added.

Fluffing her chocolate taffeta gown, Jade took a deep breath, anxious to exit the compact foyer and breathe something other than recycled air. The tall, wooden doors parted and a gust of welcome central air chilled her clammy face. August in Pennsylvania, as usual, meant highs near the hundreds and humidity thick enough to kill a bridesmaid. Really, what was wrong with an autumn wedding?

Nerves thinner than a spider web, she slowly stepped out of the sweltering vestibule, onto the burgundy runner and froze. A sea of cheery faces stared as she choked on the scent of her Casablanca lilies. As her grip tightened on the bouquet a pin stabbed her finger through the floral tape and she clenched her teeth, hissing in a breath.

The organ music faded into a white noise, suffocating her in deafening silence. At the pulpit, Tyson, Kat's groom, tilted his head to the side, his dark brow creased with a look of concern.

Focus, Jade! Focus! Just breathe.

The creak of timeworn wooden pews echoed

in the woozy blur of sounds and she swayed, her hollow smile wilting as the expectant organ cords thrummed, urging her forward. Exposed and yet somehow claustrophobic, she broke into a full body sweat, a trickle of perspiration racing down her spine.

Too many people. Is he *here?*

Jeremy stepped into the aisle, his worried gaze locking with hers. His brow creased as his palm uncurled in a silent plea for her hand. Across the distance separating them, Jade mentally clung to his invitation like the last lifeline she had left.

Jeremy.

He was so strong. A week ago he was her highest priority. That towering, muscular body, all bronzed sinew, and well-sculpted muscle, had consumed her thoughts, depleted her battery supply, and fed countless fantasies. But looking at him now, she only recognized security. Jeremy was safety.

Taking a wobbly step, she moved sluggishly toward that outstretched hand. The reverberation of music bloomed with each careful stride as she neared the front of the chapel. So long as his gaze held hers she didn't need to acknowledge all the strangers watching them.

This wasn't her. She wasn't some weak little woman who needed a man to guide her every step of the way. She was strong, damn it. She was smart and independent and knew how to make shit happen—until...

Oh, fuck, was she lost forever? She hated the

paranoia that set in after...

She just hated it. This wasn't her. But, regardless of her denial and what she knew of the woman she had always been, right now, in this moment with a hundred strangers staring her down with expectation, she did *not* feel strong. She felt terrified. And the urge to run and hide under the bulk of Jeremy's protective body was swallowing her whole.

With quickened breaths, she loosened her fists strangling the bouquet and reached for him. His steady fingers trapped her trembling ones as he offered her a comforting squeeze. Sweet relief stole a good deal of her tension as he led her the rest of the way to the altar.

His hold loosened and she was once again on unsteady ground. Jerking her gaze to his, panic pierced her lungs and her throat constricted around a plea begging him not to let go. His secure touch fell away as her stomach dipped, bile rising in her gut.

Do not get sick! Do not get sick!

The lump of unwelcome emotion clogging her throat grew like a gigantic pill she couldn't gulp down. Her stare followed Jeremy as he took his seat and she winced as her neck twisted, chafing raw flesh of her shoulder. The newly acquired wound reintroduced itself with a sharp hiss of shame and her composure faltered, tears welling in her eyes.

They'll think they're happy tears. No one knows. Deep breath... Deep breath...

She was trapped in a steady attempt to piece back the events of the last few days in order to make sense of her unwanted reality. But there was no making sense of anything. The only thing she knew about the other night, the unwanted brutality her body had unconsciously endured, was that the brand burned into her shoulder would never match the pain forever scored into her heart.

A tear slipped past her lashes and she quickly brushed it away. Why? How many were there? *Who did this to me?*

Blinking through tears of panic, she focused on Mia making her way down the aisle. Prettier than an *Anne Geddes* portrait, her best friend's four-year-old sprinkled the runner with rose petals as guests hummed at the majestic promenade.

The music shifted as pews creaked and guests stood to watch the processional. The double doors opened, painting a white silhouette around Kat and her father. Her simple, ivory gown sparkled in the sunlight as they took their first steps.

Emotion swept through Jade with the force of a brush fire. This was Kat's moment, which was why her best friend knew nothing of Jade's inner turmoil.

"Please be seated," the reverend announced as Kat reached the front.

Aged wood groaned under the heft of guests taking their pews and Jade's attention zeroed in on the unrecognizable faces, looking for any familiar detail that might trigger a memory from the other night.

Nothing.

She recognized almost everyone, aside from a few of Tyson's much older relatives. But none of the faces satisfied her memory. This wasn't normal. Something from that night *had* to come back to her.

"And now a reading from the Gospel of Luke."

Jade blinked at Kat who sent her a wide-eyed, expectant look. Her mind scrambled to interpret what the look meant—*Oh, the reading.*

Passing her flowers to Tyson's sister, Gloria, she stepped up to the podium. Glancing at the scripture, she took a deep breath and tried to still her fingers from shaking.

Her heart pounded in her chest like caged lightning. Licking her suddenly dry lips she dabbed her damp hairline with the back of her hand as her vision rippled. A wave of dizziness had her gripping the podium for balance.

She opened her mouth, but no words came out. Her eyes drifted to each man, tall, short, dark, light, blond, bald, and brown hair. *Is he here? Is he watching me now?*

She looked back at the reading. The words scrambled across the page, lacking sense and clarity, nothing more than faded hieroglyphics. She tried to swallow, but her throat couldn't force the motion. Saliva gathered in her mouth.

Her knees shook as everyone stared at her expectantly. She couldn't do this. She couldn't stand there in front of all those strangers—

A hand closed over hers and squeezed, jerking her out of her frantic thoughts and ripping her stare away from the guests. Her gaze flung from the jumbled reading to dark green eyes. Jeremy.

His skin was warm, his hold firm and strong. A familiar sense of security allowed oxygen into her lungs.

"A reading from the Gospel of Luke," he announced, tone unshakably strong.

She stared at his hand, still holding hers. Soothed by the deep baritone cadence of his voice, she concentrated on the rhythmic thrum of each word as it wove past his lips.

When he finished the reading, he angled the microphone away and whispered, "I think you need to sit down."

Holding onto her hand, he led her to his pew. Kat's brow creased with concern, but the bride's attention was quickly pulled back to the ceremony as the reverend announced it was time for the vows.

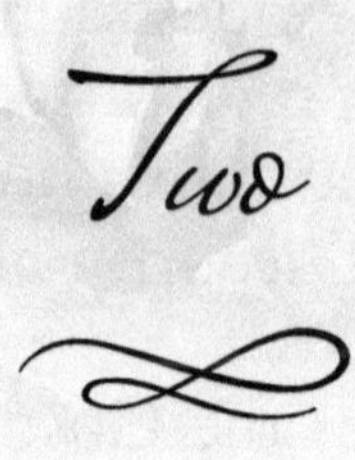

JEREMY NODDED TO GLORIA, who was now holding two bouquets, and ushered Jade to a pew. Her delicate perfume softened the stale, paper-scented air of the chapel as she stiffly sat. Her hands were clammy and cold as ice. Did she have a fever? The temptation to trace his fingers over her brow and check was strong, but he resisted, seeing as how many people were currently watching them.

The ceremony was almost over. Once the guests were distracted he'd get her some water and find out what the hell was going on. They sat in forced silence, the minutes ticking by at the speed of centuries. And then it happened. The mother of his child became Mrs. Tyson Adams.

Tyson was a good man, a friend, and a great stepfather to his daughter, Mia. Sitting in on Kat's marriage to another man had not been anticipated, but with the passing of time, he couldn't regret the way things had turned out. As much as he loved Kat for the incredible mother she was to their daughter, he'd never been *in* love with her. He was glad to see she was finally getting the happy ending she deserved.

Jade was another unanticipated part of his current life. She'd matured from a beautiful girl into a stunning woman, one that exuded confidence. He worked hard to maintain an appropriate level of friendship with Kat's best friend, but lately, his control was slipping.

The other night he had to literally drag himself away from the bar after she shamelessly invited him to her place for a nightcap. Truth was, he was dying to take her to bed. Jerking off to mental images of her sexy mouth, those playful glances she tormented him with on a daily basis... It was getting old and he was running thin on patience. Every soft tinkling of laughter from her lips sent blood rushing to his cock. If everything went according to plan, he'd wake up wrapped around her body tomorrow morning.

It was only a matter of time until they found themselves in a tangled mess of naked limbs and sweaty sheets, and he'd hoped—now that Kat was officially married to Ty—that tonight would be the night. But looking at Jade now, with her skin paler than usual and a gleam of moisture coating her skin, it seemed his plans might be postponed.

For months, he fought his desires out of re

spect for his family, Kat and Mia. It wasn't that sleeping with Jade was a bad thing. On the contrary, the experience would probably be earth shattering. But his daughter adored Jade and he didn't want to mislead his impressionable little girl.

As a new father trying to make the right impression on an observant four-year-old, he avoided the complications of dating. When he needed to get laid, he looked for company in the next town.

His situation with Mia was still new and delicate, their relationship just starting to become natural. He also didn't want to jeopardize the comfortable rapport he shared with Kat and Tyson by sleeping with Kat's best friend.

He should leave well enough alone, but even now, as he held Jade's delicate hand with her dainty white-tipped nails, he couldn't seem to stop the ache from forming in his pants. He wanted her with an intensity he'd never wanted anyone.

She was a temptress, from her sun-bleached hair to her generous curves all the way down to her sexy feet that carried more feminine grace than most women could muster in their entire lives. He longed to kiss every square inch of her body under a pile of sex-warmed blankets and fantasized about it daily.

His dick throbbed in a constant state of arousal every time she was near. Even now, sensing she wasn't feeling well, he shifted uncomfortably to hide the erection pressing up on his zipper.

Yes, his control was definitely dwindling.

Running his thumb over the soft flesh of her

wrist, he accepted she was ill and that their moment would eventually come, but not tonight—no one was coming tonight.

"You may kiss the bride."

Jade's hand pulled from his as she applauded with the rest of the guest and awkwardly rose from the pew. Her typical agility seemed off. He eyed her as he clapped, wondering if maybe she and the other bridesmaids had a few drinks before the ceremony, but he didn't smell alcohol on her breath.

As the recessional started, Jeremy placed her hand in the crook of his elbow, escorting her from the chapel. Jade blinked thick, golden lashes at the bright August sky as they stepped into the thick heat. Voices faded, replaced with the hum of insects lulling over the grass.

He didn't give her a chance to fall in line with the wedding party. "Come with me."

"What?" She tugged back on his arm as he ushered her toward the doors. "We have to—"

"Jade." He leveled his tone with authority and gave her a stern look. The last thing Kat needed was Jade making a scene by falling over or getting sick.

With a sigh, she let him lead her out of the church.

Three

LEADING HER TO HIS JEEP, Jeremy opened the passenger door. "Sit."

Despite her shaky mood, she couldn't help but smirk at his bossy tone. Somehow he made surliness the sexiest thing in the world.

The heat from the leather seat burned through the material of her gown and a trail of dew trickled between her breasts. Trapped in the sweltering car, she lowered the window. He climbed behind the wheel and turned the key.

"We're leaving?" They couldn't leave. Kat would skin her alive.

"Are you drunk or sick?"

"*What?*" Startled that he'd think she was drunk at two o'clock in the afternoon on her best friend's wedding day, she scowled at him. "I'm fine."

And maybe she was fine now. For the first time

in hours, she felt like she could breathe again. But oh, God, she'd made a complete scene during the ceremony.

"You're probably not the only one wondering if I'm drunk." Moaning, she rubbed her hands over her face, wishing he wouldn't look at her like that—like she was crazy. *Pull yourself together!*

Jeremy gave her a reassuring pat on the knee and she instinctively jerked her leg away, her spine drawing tight as a bow. The car filled with uncomfortable silence as he frowned at her. Watching her closely, he said, "Maybe you caught a twenty-four-hour bug."

Thinking she'd rather be assumed sick than drunk at her best friend's wedding, she grabbed the excuse. "I... I don't feel well. Do you think Kat's upset I ruined the reading?"

"You didn't ruin anything."

"Yeah, right," she scoffed. "I saw everyone staring. I couldn't even walk on my own. It took everything in me not to puke on the Rabbi." The part about almost throwing up was true. "What kind of maid of honor am I?"

"Reverend," he corrected.

"Whatever." Tears prickled as she replayed the humiliating production. *Do* not *cry in front of him.*

"So you got a little stage fright. So what? You don't always have to be perfect, Jade."

A rude noise vibrated in the back of her throat. "I'm *far* from perfect. My life's an absolute disaster."

"Do you want to talk about it?"

Groaning through a spike of nausea, she exhaled roughly. "I can't."

"Jade, at this point I'd like to think that we're friends. You know you can trust me. If something's wrong and I can help, you know I will. You don't have to be embarrassed in front of me. We all get sick and we all have stressful shit to deal with in our lives."

Lost in her thoughts, visions of the other morning tortured her tired mind. She could barely tolerate the weight of her own skin. "Can you turn on the air?"

He adjusted the dials and Freon scented air chilled her damp flesh.

"Why don't we sit here until the guests clear out? I suppose you have to get pictures and stuff. I can wait with you and after that, if you're still not feeling well, I can take you home. How's that sound?"

That sounded wonderful and at the same time impossible. "I have to go to the reception. Kat spent the past ten months planning for today and I need to be there. I can't blow it off."

"You wouldn't be blowing it off. If you're sick, you're sick."

Tears flooded her eyes. *What if I am sick? Really sick?*

"Hey. Are you all right?" He twisted closer, eyes creased with concern. "Whatever it is, we'll fix it. Do you want me to go get something? You look like you're gonna throw up. Should I get Kat? Or a trashcan?"

"No!" Kat couldn't know. It was her wedding day and she deserved everything to be perfect. And she'd never forgive herself if she puked in front of Jeremy. "I'm fine." She blotted her eyes and cheeks. "I just need to pull myself together and not think about it."

"It?"

"Nothing. It's nothing. I'm okay. Please... Let's just wait until the guests leave and then go back inside. I'll be distracted once I'm busy doing maid of honor stuff and I'll be better."

She smoothed the wrinkles from her gown and lowered the visor to fix her hair. *Shit.* She was a mess.

Once all the guests were gone they returned to the chapel. Kat wore an expression of relieved concern. Determined not to spoil her friend's day, Jade pasted on a convincing smile and tried to be her usual self. "Hey, *Mrs. Adams.*"

Rather than smile at the new title, Kat frowned. "Are you okay?"

She rolled her eyes and stuck with the lie. "Yeah. My stomach got really upset all of a sudden."

"Do you want me to see if someone can run to a drugstore for some medicine?"

"No. I'm all right now. Probably just cramps or something."

Her gaze remained concerned. "Are you sure?"

"Totally." Jade waved away her concern. "Enough about that. How's it feel to be married?"

Kat glowed, her smile so genuine and beautiful. "It feels *really* good."

Despite the nightmare in her head, Jade's heart couldn't help but feel happily full for her friend. Kat deserved this day and a lifetime of joy with Ty. They were perfect for each other in every way.

"You okay, Jade?" Tyson asked as he slid an arm over his wife's shoulders.

"Yeah. I think the meal I ordered last night was a little dodgy. Whatever was wrong, it passed." There would be no more detracting from their special day. "Let's get the pictures done so we can get to the fun part."

The remainder of the day dragged in intervals of picture taking, toasts, dancing, eating, and bride maintenance. Miraculously, Jade managed to keep her emotions in check throughout it all.

As the florescent lighting replaced the romantic glow that had filled the reception hall, she collected the bride and groom's personal keepsakes in a neat pile to make sure they had plenty of mementos from their wedding day. Jeremy emerged from a door marked STAFF ONLY and casually headed in her direction, his broad build capturing her full attention.

He sure did make himself at home.

But a man who carried that much confidence in his stride didn't give people a chance to question his authority. He winked at her, sending a shiver of excitement up her spine as he continued toward Kat's parents.

Jade turned and stared as he brushed aside Mia's toppled curls and pressed an affectionate kiss to his daughter's cheek. His adoration for Mia was another check in the 'why Jeremy is sexy' column.

"Can I get one of them?"

Startled but the unfamiliar masculine voice, Jade turned. A man she didn't recognize pointed to the bagged slices of cake she held in her arms. It took her a moment to recall he was the DJ, but she continued to stare at his outstretched hand, giving no verbal confirmation that she heard his request.

His mouth crooked into a half-smirk. "I know a little thing like you isn't hoarding all that cake for yourself. What do you say we share?" He reached forward and she jerked out of reach, stumbling back a step as the confections tumbling to the ground.

She flinched again as Jeremy's deep voice boomed behind her. "Can I help you?"

"I just wanted to get a piece of cake."

Jeremy eyed him accusingly as he scooped up a bag and grasped her hand. She tensed and he immediately let go, placing his body in front of hers, but no longer touching her. He tossed the bag at the DJ who caught it against his chest. "You have your cake, now go."

The DJ rolled his eyes and stalked off.

The concerned look was back in his eyes when he turned to face her. "You okay?"

Taken aback by his intrusion, she ignored her

response to the stranger, and focused on his territorial interception, trying to play down whatever just happened. "Really, Jeremy, he was only asking for cake."

He narrowed his eyes, which always seemed a bit more perceptive than most. "He may've asked for cake, but that's not what he wanted."

His gaze held hers, suspending time as her desire manifested in every cell of her being. "And what *did* he want?"

He smirked, the soft expression suddenly replaced by a mask of complete control. "Something I don't think you were offering."

She sobered. Was this how she'd gotten into trouble? Was she a tease? Someone who sent out signals, making men think they were welcome to things she wasn't willing to provide? She hadn't been flirting. She hadn't even looked at the DJ the entire evening!

"Jade?" He was frowning again. "Why don't I load the rest of this stuff in Ty's car and then I'll take you home?"

She nodded, once again distracted by the dark shadows in her mind. As he walked away, her mind jerked to the present. *Take me home?* Oh, no. Was he finally offering what she'd dreamt of for the past year and...

No, no, no, no no... She had to delay this. Somehow push him off without scaring him away completely.

She was so totally infatuated with Jeremy, but even he couldn't touch her at the moment. The thought of anyone's hands on her made her want to curl up and die. She shivered, quietly slipping outside to get some air and calm her nerves. Soon enough, he appeared again and escorted her to his Jeep.

The pale blue glow of the moon lit the interior of Jeremy's Jeep as it fought for a place in the sky amongst the rolling clouds. Every now and then a silver flash of lightning flickered in the distance. Classic rock played quietly from the speakers on the dashboard and the air-conditioned breeze softly tickled across her skin.

As they neared her apartment, his hand slid from the gearshift to her knee. This time he didn't close his fingers over her knee, he simply brushed the material of her gown covering her leg with the back of his knuckle. But it was enough to make her stop breathing.

What was that? Was he sending her a silent confirmation that he wanted to get laid? She subtly drew her body closer to the door and kept silent.

Not since she was a young teen and first discovering boys, had she wanted someone as much as she'd wanted Jeremy over the last few months. But the gentle tug at her insides was overshadowed by shame—her body was no longer her own in some intangible sense.

Although they'd known each other for years and spent a lot of time together since he returned from Iraq, never before had he brazenly showed such blatant physical interest. Always so polite and reserved, maintaining healthy boundaries, she'd longed for this moment, longed for proof that the chemistry was mutual.

Her instincts told her they shared something beyond friendly sentiment, but one never knew with Jeremy—still waters ran deep and all that philosophical jazz. There were so many mixed signals, so many moments she'd hoped he'd ease a little closer or touch her in some slight way. So why couldn't she just compartmentalize her trauma and use this for the incredible distraction it could be? She wanted to, but no matter how she tried to pretend today was normal and she was unbroken, she couldn't.

Her heart melted every time she caught a glimpse of him with Mia, so kindhearted, but serious, soft-spoken, yet stern. He smiled easily, but never needed to be the funny guy or the center of attention. Fiercely loyal to those he loved, he would do anything to protect his friends.

He glanced at her, his hand still resting on the console between them, but now his fingers were open and his palm was up. "Why are you sitting all the way over there?"

She casually moved her back to the center of the seat. "I just ... moved when the car turned."

The corners of his mouth turned up and he lifted his hand in invitation. Her heart pounded hard against her ribs as she stared at it. Her fingers slowly lifted and rested in his, intertwining. Warm skin, slightly calloused at the pads of his fingers, cradled the weight of her smaller hand as he tightened his grip. It felt so good yet so terrifying.

His thumb moved in a slow pattern over the back of her hand. The smooth, seductive weight of his touch offered a degree of peace, blurring her recent urge to withdraw. So many fantasies founded on a treasure of innocent embraces shifted into possibilities, making it all the more painful to accept she wasn't prepared. Any other night she would have been ecstatic, but she wasn't herself right now—maybe she'd never be herself again.

As they turned onto her street, she pulled her hand away and clasped her bag on her lap. The horribly nostalgic scent of a stranger on her flesh filled her memory, so real she could swear she was breathing it in. Taking a deep breath, she rolled down the window, but her stomach lurched and she swallowed back a sob.

Irrational fear quickened her breathing. Her home no longer called to her the way it once had. What had always been a sanctuary was now a scary place of untold nightmares that attacked her in her sleep.

He put the car in park. "Can I walk you in?"

Always an openly affectionate person, intimacy now seemed outside of her ability. Fragile, and battling so many unpredictable emotions, she feared turning him away might spoil the only chance she'd have with him, the chance to finally get the one thing she wanted. Jeremy.

Maybe she was overreacting. Maybe he just wanted to see her home safe.

Safe. That word no longer applied to her apartment. Everything was different now, cold and tainted. Shivering, she let out a long breath, exhausted from the mere exercise of thinking so hard, searching for explanations that wouldn't come. Her head eased back on the seat as she shut her eyes.

"Jade, I wish you'd tell me what's bothering you. You haven't been yourself all day." The warmth of his hand returned to hers and she stifled the jolt of fear. "Why don't I walk you up?"

Her mind was a maze of questions and doubts, a frightening labyrinth she couldn't escape. She hadn't slept in thirty-six hours. Weary, her lips tightened as she fought to contain her turmoil. Despite her efforts, a tear slid past her lashes.

"Hey." The leather seat creaked as he shifted his body. "Why are you crying?"

She couldn't open her eyes and her lips were pressed too tight to form a response.

He left the car and opened her door. Reaching across her waist, he unlatched her seatbelt and pulled her into his arms. She sucked in a ragged breath, too weak to pull back, but her muscles internally locked as he cradled her to his hard chest.

"Shh," he soothed as he pressed her face to his shoulder and he ran a hand down her back.

The familiar scent of his skin met her nose and she repeatedly told herself this was Jeremy. He was not the bad guy. He was the safe guy. The good guy. The friend who would probably throw his own body between her and harm without a single second of hesitation. Slowly her muscles relaxed.

His large build cocooned her smaller form, delivering a sense of security. She clung to his strength, needed it in that moment. His grip tightened, grounding her to the now in a way that reminded her the past was over. His hold settled her, anchored her. Jeremy was safe. But she still needed to keep reminding herself of that.

Tension tied her in knots that kept coming undone, unraveling. The coherent woman inside of her was tangled in a web of chaos no one else could see. The fact that she was fighting an unseen enemy all alone broke her. She lost the battle to her tears and let out a jagged breath that turned into a ragged string of snotty sobs.

She desperately longed to tell him what happened, but shame crippled her words, letting only sobbed syllables escape as her body quaked. She was losing it.

"Jade, baby, you have to calm down. I can't help you unless you tell me what's wrong."

Her thoughts spiraled. "I..."

She sobbed. Her humiliating attempt to communicate was choked off by a strangled moan. It seemed everything she worked to hide over the past few hours in order to participate in Kat's wedding was now demanding escape.

"I c-can't..." Breathing hurt. Pain constricted

in her chest as she sucked in one serrated breath after another. "I can't ... s-s-sleep here."

His steady fingers brushed a strand of hair away from her damp cheek. When he turned her face so he could see her, he was wearing a confused frown. "Where? Your apartment?"

Unable to offer an explanation, she wept harder. Placing his hands on her shoulders, he took a slight step back. She wanted to hide in his shelter, but Jeremy always preferred to face things head on. "Jade." Under other circumstances, it might have been funny how he kept trying to pull back only to have her grip him closer. "Jade, I want to talk for a second."

She clung to him, not wanting to let go. No matter how much she tried to stop crying, she couldn't. Sniffling and gasping, she simply apologized again and again. "I'm sorry. So sorry. I ... know this isn't... your pr—" She gasped. "—problem."

"Honey, look at me." He gently wrenched her away from his chest, his finger tipping up her chin. "Whatever's going on, you need to tell me." His green eyes showed emerald under the moonlight, heavy with concern.

Incomplete breaths tumbled in and out of her lungs. "I'm scared."

His gentle caress tucked a wisp of hair behind her ear and he pulled her back to his chest. His warm lips pressed to her temple. Her breathing slowed as his lips traveled to her cheeks and eyes. "Shh. It's okay. I'm here. You're okay." His kisses weren't sexual. Rather, they were protective and soothing.

Emotions taut, her nerves threatening to sink her deeper into hysteria, a sort of drowsy calm washed over her, quieting her mind. Tipping her face to the side, he gently brushed his lips over hers, tracing yet barely touching, softer than a butterfly's wing.

"It's okay," he whispered.

Her damp lashes lifted slowly as his feet shifted. She looked up at him, wondering what this was. Her body trembled, not with fear but longing. She didn't want to sleep with him tonight, but *this,* the way he was touching his lips to her face and sheltering her body with his, *this* she wanted.

His mouth tenderly closed over hers and her heart thundered in her chest. Her jagged emotions couldn't keep up with all the twists and turns her mind was taking. Slow and sensual, the delicate caress of his lips grew bolder, drawing her away from numb exhaustion to teetering hysteria and into something she knew she couldn't handle.

Shivers raced up her limbs, down to the tips of her toes, as he gradually traced the seam of her lips with his tongue. His unique and familiar scent of heated skin and something incredibly male filled her senses.

Her instincts took over. Slightly parting her lips, she pressed into the kiss and he made a sound of satisfaction. Easing her into a state of passivity, he kept each caress slow, lulling her into a sedate corner where only pleasure could touch her.

Easing away, one slow pull at a time, he drew back. "Do you want to stay at my house?" he whispered. "Just sleep, nothing more."

Reality, fantasy, and temptation became an indecisive disaster in her head. She nodded lazily, still unable to open her eyes. Tucking her legs back into the vehicle, he gently shut the door. Pressing her cheek into the soft leather of the seat she let her mind rest in preparation for whatever conversation they'd have next, and she hoped it wouldn't be about why she couldn't have sex with him.

The drive was silent, but her thoughts were calm, focused only on the memory of his lips against hers. Savoring the absence of demons, she kept her eyes closed and let the soft hum of the engine calm her into a restful state.

The click of the seatbelt jolted her. The engine was quiet and Jeremy was lifting her out of the Jeep. "Go back to sleep. I've got you."

She tensed, but as he pulled her snug against his broad chest she relaxed. His keys jingled as he unlocked the door and a rush of cool air hit her skin as they entered the house.

She'd never been to his home. It was a new house, built by Adams Construction, on the property once owned by Jeremy's father and it still smelled of fresh paint. As much as she wanted to see it, she didn't want to interrupt the moment.

Her body barely jostled in his solid hold as he ascended the stairs. Easing her down, her back pressed into a soft mattress and she curled onto her side. Two nights of insomnia had taken its toll, making coherent thought as impossible as opening her eyes. And behind it all was the incredible sensation of feeling safe and protected.

The slide-click of opening and closing drawers vaguely registered. The mattress dipped as the heat and weight of his touch glided over the catch of her gown. He placed a tentative hand on her shoulder and paused.

"Jade, honey?" he said in a thick whisper. "I have a T-shirt and shorts here for you. Do you think you can get yourself changed the rest of the way?"

She peeked at him through drowsy eyes, too exhausted to care.

Gaze dropping to the ground, he mumbled, "I ... uh... I'll go get you some Tylenol and a glass of water while you change." He stood and left the room, his movements stiff.

Light seeped from the hallway, slicing through the darkness. She sluggishly sat up and pulled her gown off her shoulders, letting it fall to a heap on the floor.

The shirt swallowed her, gaping around her arms and neck, but she didn't care. Climbing under the warm covers, drowsily scanned the empty room. She was in Jeremy's room. In his bed. This moment was nothing like all the various ways she'd fantasized.

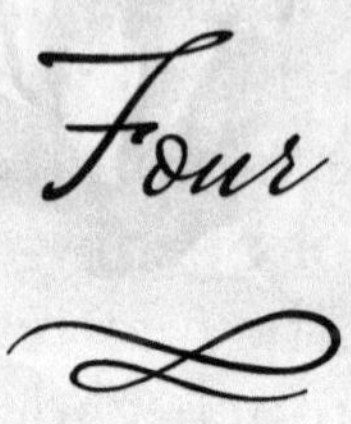

Four

JEREMY RETURNED from the kitchen to check on Jade and found her in a tiny heap beneath his comforter, breathing softly. Placing a glass of water and two small pills on the nightstand, he studied her.

He didn't think she drank a lot at the wedding, but he was sure crying like that would give anyone a headache. Something was majorly wrong and he was pretty sure not even Kat knew her best friend was going through something big. This was not the Jade Shultz they knew. But why the secrecy?

Picking up her gown from the floor, he awkwardly folded it at the foot of the bed. She didn't even take up a quarter of the mattress. Brow pinched, he tucked a ribbon of flaxen hair behind her ear.

Don't look at her like that.

His gaze traveled over the contours of her body. The shorts he'd left for her were still folded on the comforter. The thought of her in his bed, without pants, made his throat instantly dry. His blood grew so thick he sensed it throbbing through his—

Time to go.

Placing a kiss on her temple, he breathed in her delicate scent. She was in his bed, but certainly not the way he'd anticipated. Standing, he reached for a pillow. He was couch-bound tonight. Grabbing the jeans draped over the hamper, he crept out the door and headed downstairs.

When his gaze hit the sofa he grimaced. It was a good size but far too small for a man his size to sleep comfortably. He glanced at the ceiling. No, he couldn't sleep with her until he knew why she was so upset. Tossing his pillow on a chair, he turned down the hall and slipped through the basement door.

His body was primed and thrumming with energy and he needed an outlet. Stripping off his rented tux, he flipped on his stereo and winced, quickly dialing down the volume. In his briefs, he approached the weight bench. Not quite the same rush as fucking a beautiful woman, but it should take the edge off. Hopefully, this would just be a temporary fix, because he still intended for Jade to return to his bed—under better circumstances.

As he worked himself into a sweat, his mind crawled over her strange behavior today. One of Jade's most appealing qualities was her sassy confidence. He preferred seeing her that way, but there was something ... delicate about seeing her vulnerable. As a trained security professional, he got a rise out of protecting those in need of protecting. So, holding Jade and giving her a safe haven in his arms... It lit somewhat of a fire inside of him.

The question was, what the hell did she need protecting from? Maybe he'd finally talk her into a security system. She shouldn't be afraid to stay home alone when she'd lived by herself since college.

He dropped the barbells on the carpet. Did someone break into her place? Was that what this was about? If so, she better have filed a fucking police report. He'd get to the bottom of it tomorrow for sure.

Flipping off the music, he made his way back up the stairs and to the second floor. Jade still slept, her body in the same position it was when he last saw her. Slipping into the bathroom, he grabbed a towel and turned the faucet on cool. A quick rinse and he'd return to the living room.

Glancing between his legs he grimaced at the thick hard-on pointing to his bedroom, to the woman on the other side of the wall sleeping in his bed.

"Fuck." He fisted his cock and stroked, not sparing the time or consideration to do more than get himself a little relief so he could sleep.

His mind filled with flashes of blond hair, green eyes, and soft lips. What would her mouth feel like, wrapped around his cock, those lips stroking slow and tight? He grunted and tightened his fist, stroking faster.

Her short, curvy little body bouncing hard on his cock. Her big eyes staring up at him as he fucked her full tits. "Shit."

He tugged and pulled his flesh, his palm flattening on the tile wall as his breath soughed through the steamy air. His eyes pinched shut as he imagined her coming on his dick, the walls of her pussy clamping around his flesh, milking his release.

"Yes," he growled, pumping his fist fast.

The base of his spine tingled as his balls drew up tight. A ribbon of come shot past his clamped fingers onto the wall. He panted, slowly releasing his hold and catching his breath.

Once he had himself under control and no longer seeing cross-eyed, he rinsed away the evidence. Yes, he could definitely be patient if that's what she needed right now, but after a year of tempting offers and not so subtle flirting, he really needed her to tell him why they were suddenly waiting. He wasn't sure he'd ever wanted a woman to the degree he wanted Jade. And he had every intension of having her.

JADE AWOKE from a nightmare to the sound of screaming. Panicked, her eyes darted around the unfamiliar room. She twisted awkwardly, her limbs tangling in the sheets as her hyperventilating gasp choked off her shrill cries. The door burst open and there, looking disheveled and fierce, stood Jeremy, aiming a handgun directly at her.

Eyes wide, she whimpered and scurried back the headboard.

His eyes scoured every nook and cranny of the room, landing on her in a hard scowl. "*What the hell happened?*"

The events of the previous evening came hurtling back to her. Kat's wedding, driving home with Jeremy, crying, Jeremy kissing her, him carrying her to his bed. Well, *a* bed. He'd apparently slept somewhere else.

"Jade!" He did something with the gun that made it click before he lowered it. "Why were you screaming?"

It was a dream. She'd only had a bad dream. For a moment, she thought a faceless man was chasing her. Shutting her eyes, she sighed and smiled. Dreaming meant she'd slept.

"What the hell is so amusing? It sounded like someone was murdering you up here."

He was so cute, all serious and prepared to blow away whatever frightened her. How close was that gun that he had it locked and loaded in the time it took her to belt out a scream? She hoped he kept it in a secure and safe place when Mia visited. She'd mention that to him later.

"*Jade!*" he snapped, demanding her attention. "What happened?"

Okay, funny time over. "Um, I had a bad dream, then I woke up and I didn't know where I was." She gave him an apologetic grin and his shoulders relaxed with a huff.

"You didn't want to sleep at your apartment last night so I brought you here."

"I know. I remember, now. I was disoriented when I woke, that's all. But the good news is I slept. Where's your bathroom?"

He made an awkward nod and hitched a thumb over his shoulder, rapidly dismantling the gun in the next second. "Through that door. When you're finished, come down for breakfast."

It wasn't a question, or at least wasn't one

where he was going to wait around for an answer. Shaking his head, he turned and disappeared down the hall.

After freshening up, she searched Jeremy's cabinets. She told herself she was looking for a new toothbrush, but really, she was searching for clues about the man.

Unfortunately, her search revealed nothing interesting, just some over the counter medicine, shaving cream, a razor, toothpaste, floss, after-shave, and regrettably, a partially used box of con-doms. She tried not to think about who was using Jeremy's condoms. Finding an unopened princess toothbrush—probably purchased for Mia—she brushed her teeth.

The delicious scent of coffee and bacon greeted her at the bottom of the steps. Wandering through the unfamiliar home, her nose guided her toward the kitchen.

The house was nice, simple. It was clearly a bachelor pad, white walls adorned with mis-matched picture frames surrounding utilitarian furniture. It seemed too vacant, lacking in per-sonal belongings.

Rumpled blankets hung off the couch. In the corner, a toy chest overflowed with dolls. A door in the hall was slightly open, leading to carpeted steps. Jeremy worked from home, doing some-thing with computers. That was probably his office.

Entering the small, eat-in-kitchen, she grinned as Jeremy spooned scrambled eggs onto a plate.

His bed head was gone, replaced with damp blond spikes, and he now wore a shirt. *Pity.*

"Perfect timing." He carried two plates to the table.

"Smells delicious." Sliding onto a chair, she kept her eyes on her food and slowly picked up her fork. Sneaking a glance at him, he squared off a bite and shoved it into his mouth as if he were alone. The awkward silence stretched as she slowly nibbled at her food.

This is weird. Just say something. Comment on the weather, or Mia, or the fact that you're still wearing his shirt.

Here she was, at Jeremy's house, wearing his clothes, after sleeping in his bed. As she used the last bite of her toast to shovel the remaining crumbs of egg into her mouth, she looked up and stilled. He was watching her.

"What?" She self-consciously wiped her mouth.

"I'm glad you like my eggs. It's one of the few things I can cook."

"I was starving. I can't remember the last time I ate."

"Didn't you eat at the wedding?"

"I, uh, didn't have much of an appetite." She took a sip of her coffee and immediately regretted it. Grimacing, she swilled the bitter mix around in her mouth for a second, contemplating anywhere other than her stomach to put the putrid brew, and haltingly swallowed.

"Sorry about the coffee. Here, try adding some

sugar." The bowl slid across the table. "Did you sleep well?"

"Mmm, like a rock. Thanks for letting me crash here. Your bed's really comfortable."

He didn't reply, so she assumed it *was* his bed. Were they going to talk about her disgraceful outburst last night, or more importantly, the kiss?

"You didn't have to do that, you know." She tipped her head toward the den. "I could've slept on the couch." *Or you could have shared the bed...* She quickly recalled how skittish she'd been each time he touched her yesterday. Now, in his kitchen, wearing his shirt, she felt braver.

He mumbled something and stood, taking their plates to the sink.

"I'll do the dishes. It's only fair since you cooked."

"I'd rather talk than worry about the dishes right now." He returned to his seat, all humor gone from his expression.

Shrinking under his scrutiny, she played dumb. "About what?"

"About what's going on with you."

It was probably a good idea to talk to someone about what happened and Kat was off limits until her honeymoon was over. She took a deep breath and stood.

"Fine. But if we're going to have some drawn-out conversation at least let me make some decent coffee."

She dumped the remainder of sludge down

the drain. It looked more like syrup than coffee. When she lifted the filter trap she identified the problem. "Holy shit, Jeremy. How many scoops do you use?"

He negligently lifted one broad shoulder. "I don't know. I guess it."

"Well, for future reference, you only need four heaping scoops." Then, for some stupid reason, she added, "Can't expect your lady friends to hang around if your coffee sucks."

He grunted. "I don't bring lady friends to my home. It's a place for my daughter, no one else."

Then what am I? "Oh." Restarting the coffee cycle, she returned to her seat without making eye contact.

"Why are you acting so different lately?"

Silently examining the surface of the table, she shrugged. She wanted to tell him, but it wasn't easy to find the words. Her somewhat pleasant mood wilted, her yummy breakfast curdling in her belly.

How did one confess something so horrid? Words darted through her head, simple and un-attached to emotions because if she didn't vocalize them, they weren't real. But the longer she fum-bled for an explanation for her recent behavior the more their meaning set in.

Sinking into her chair, she searched her brain for the right words. *Rape. I was raped. Drugged. I think someone drugged me. Someone broke into my house. Or, no... Someone took me home after...*

Fuck. She didn't know what exactly happened to her, but she hated it. Hated imagining it. Hated trying to fill in the ugly fucking holes. She let out a frustrated breath. She couldn't explain because there was no simple explanation. And the complicated ones made her physically ache to rip off her skin and scream like a lunatic. "I don't know."

"Something's bothering you, Jade. I've known you since we were kids and I've never seen you lose it like you did yesterday."

"I had a bad day." True and concise.

"Why? Kat's been your best friend since I can remember. You get along great with Tyson from what I can tell. You seemed happy for them at the rehearsal—"

"I am happy for them," she interrupted.

"Then what's going on?"

"I don't know."

She did know, but she wasn't sure how to frame the reason for him. If she told him, would he launch into a full blown rage, insisting she go to the police, and everyone, including Kat who was currently preparing for her once in a lifetime honeymoon, would be devastated by the disgusting news? Or would he question her, not believe her? Maybe blame her? No, he wouldn't blame her. But for some reason, she felt to blame.

"You can tell me. Whatever it is, I'll keep it between the two of us."

Scooting a grain of sugar over the tabletop with the tip of her finger, she turned phrases over in her mind hoping one slipped out. *I was raped. Someone drugged me. Can you teach me how to use a gun? I'm losing my mind.*

This time when the term rape echoed through her head it jarred something loose in her chest. A painful ache climbed up her back, pressing through her breastbone and her lungs tightened.

Leaning closer, he stilled her fingers and gently gripped her hand. "Tell me."

The contact flustered her. She didn't normally get flustered by men and found it irritating. But then nothing was the way it was before...

"I can't." The truth of that statement added to her aggravation.

"Why?"

Just say it.

"Jade?"

"Because I don't know!" she snapped. Letting out a frustrated breath, she apologized. "Sorry."

His eyes were vacant of anything other than concern. "What don't you know?"

"I don't know what's happening to me," she muttered.

"Are you sick?" he quietly asked.

A humorless laugh slipped past her lips as her vision blurred. Was she sick? She could be. Suddenly nauseous, she pulled her legs to her chest and rested her cheek on her knees.

In a barely audible voice, he asked, "Is that it?"

A tear slipped from her eye and she quickly grabbed the baggy collar of his T-shirt and blotted it away.

"Have you talked to a doctor?"

Overwhelmed, her feet dropped to the floor. This wasn't Jeremy's problem. She'd thought she could talk to him about this, but she was wrong.

With what she hoped was convincing assuredness, she said, "I'm not sick."

What if that was a lie? What if she had contracted AIDS or some other sexually transmitted disease? She was such an idiot for not going to the hospital. She knew better. She worked at one and knew rape protocol. Jesus fucking Christ, that word!

He tilted his head. "Well, then what?"

Gazing toward the door through a wall of an unshed wall of tears, she gave him all the information she could offer at the moment. "I'm just dealing with some things right now and I have to deal with them on my own." She stood, accepting that she, unfortunately, needed to leave.

He stood as well and frowned. "What're you doing?"

"I have to go, Jeremy. Thank you for letting me stay last night, but I have to get back to ... my life." The thought of her apartment made her cringe. Maybe she'd stay at Kat's tonight since her and Ty wouldn't be there.

He took a hesitant step forward and she sent him a staying—pleading—glance, praying he wouldn't make her exit more difficult than it already was. How tempting to simply pretend life was a-okay and waste the morning in his home, in his bed.

But everything was different now. She was a risk factor and until she understood the full consequence of what happened, she couldn't proceed. Not with him or anyone for that matter. More resentment bubbled up inside of her. The inferiority of being physically smaller than the opposite sex set fire to her inner rage and made her want to hit something.

His concerned frown morphed into an intense scowl. "What the fuck, Jade?" He tugged the drooping collar of her shirt away from her shoulder and she instinctively shoved him away. On the tail of being the physically weaker sex realization, she lost it. "Get the fuck off of me!"

But he was too big, too strong, and too in control. He jerked the collar down, exposing the burn. She met his eyes and her lip quivered, her heart plummeting into her feet.

There was something familiar about it, something that pissed her off beyond its link to recent events. She glared at him and yanked herself out of reach. "Back off," she snapped, covering the wound.

It had become an unattractive scab, resembling some kind of fancy symbol. Clearly not just a scrape. The detail of the burn—she was now certain someone had branded her—was put there for a reason. A fucked up reminded that some sociopath had touched her and she'd never fully wash that truth away.

"What the hell is that, Jade?"

"Mind your own business." She adjusted her

clothing.

"Did you do that to yourself? Why?"

"It's none of your business!" She turned to escape the inquisition and he grabbed her wrist in a startlingly tight grip. Without thinking, her fist shot out and connected with his nose.

His hold broke. "Goddamn it!" He cupped his face and her eyes went wide.

The instinctual reaction took her as off guard as it apparently took him, but she wasn't the one bleeding. "*Ohmygod!*"

"What the *fuck*, Jade!"

"I'm sorry! I'm *so* sorry. I can't believe I just did that. I don't know why I did that. Here, sit down. I'll get some paper towels."

She rushed to the counter and yanked the roll of paper towels off the rack, filling his hands with a wad. Racing back to the sink, she wet another gob of paper. She winced at the agitated way he glared at her over the stained mess.

"I'm sorry. Here." She removed the dry towels and replaced them with the damp ones. "It's not that bad. I don't think it's broken. It's just bleeding. Tilt your head back."

She pulled the blood-soaked paper away from his face and wiped away the mess. He looked furious so she gave him a nervous smile. "S-see, it already stopped bleeding. Aside from a little pain and wounded pride, I'd say you're as good as new."

He reached for his glass and took a sip as he continued to grimace.

Jade nervously rambled while cleaning up the soiled paper towels. "Yup, looks like your run of the mill anterior nosebleed, which really is the most common kind of nosebleed." She tossed the used towels in the trash. "It comes from the front of the nose. Capillaries, or very small blood vessels, inside the nose break and bleed, causing the blood to flow and eventually clot."

Life she couldn't do, but nursing was as natural as breathing to her.

She moved to take the last towel he blotted at his face and examined him carefully. It really wasn't a serious injury.

Standing in the space between his knees, she twisted to grab a clean towel from the table to wipe a missed spatter as she continued to babble. "This wasn't a posterior nosebleed, which occurs most often in older people who..."

Her gaze met his and she shut up. His shoulders were slowly moving up and down as he breathed deeply. He appeared to be holding onto his control by an overtaxed thread.

He was either going to kiss her or strangle her. And being that she'd just punched him in the face, her money was on the latter. Swallowing, she nervously laughed and hastily untangled her legs from between his.

He lunged so fast she gasped. His body blanketed hers against the table as his hand cupped her ass, lifting and sending chairs skidding across the kitchen floor, his mouth crashing against hers.

His tongue shoved between her lips as she

gasped, probing, demanding control of the kiss, as he pressed his hips into the cradle of her thighs and backed her to the table. Her eyes widened. He was rock hard.

A sense of victory washed over her, fast and only slightly blurred by unwelcome emotions. She wasn't sure how this happened, but dear *Gawd*, the man could kiss. Her legs tightened around his trim hips and her fingers flew into his hair, tugging hungrily.

Gathering the hem of her shirt, he yanked it upward. "Lay back," he growled between kisses, as he shoved her more onto the table.

Her hands tightened in his gorgeous, sun kissed blond hair as his mouth traveled down her neck. Breathing fast, his fingertips skated along the soft flesh of her belly to the underside of her breast. He whispered her name in a husky voice, pulling her legs around his back as his mouth devoured hers.

This was not the man who kissed her last night. This was a man on the brink of losing control, a wild animal free of its cage. And she wanted more—

Her mind fractured in two as strong fingers closed around her nipple. Her inner hedonist reveled while some deeply devastated part of her cringed and her body locked up.

No! You're not going to freak out!

For a year, she'd prepared for this very moment and she wasn't going to ruin it. He ground himself into her sex and she gasped, fighting back the voice screaming in her head. Her conscience recoiled, as she forced all the fear away, refusing to acknowledge the timid shrieks building in her mind. If she could just let go, maybe the fear would go away.

Stop. Get off. I can't breathe. "Don't stop," she hissed, as his hips continued to rock and her mind rapidly unraveled.

"Can you come like this?" The denim of his jeans abraded the thin silk barrier of her panties.

Sure, she could come. *I think I can come.* Concentrating on her body's natural reflexes, the precarious tease of pleasure evaded her. His tongue stole deeper into her mouth as his grip tightened. Frustration built as her body lacked any typical response.

What the fuck? Work, damn it!

"I want you to come," he whispered, cupping her breasts and dragging his thumbs over the engorged tips as he ground his erection against her panties.

So do I!

Eyes squeezed tight, she anxiously waited for that tip of pleasure to send her over the edge, but the elusive orgasm wouldn't come. Tears stung her eyes as flashes of the other morning clouded her mind.

No! Put that shit away!

If she burst into tears he'd think she was insane and that would definitely scare him off. Biting her lip, she regrettably did what she promised to never do. She had to. It was the only way to hide the fact that she was broken and possibly dying on the inside. Forcing out a sensual moan, she gasped and gasped again.

His lips kissed up her neck as she panted and cried out in artificial bliss. Her thighs clenched around his hips as she made her muscles tremble. Her performance was award-winning but came with an expensive chunk of her pride.

She didn't fake orgasms—ever. The fact that she'd faked one with Jeremy made her insides curl into shriveled bits of foregone self-worth. More secrets between them...

Easing back, he stared at her with drowsy eyes. Her legs slid down his hips as he lifted her to his chest. Carrying her to the living room, he carefully adjusted their position as he sat on the couch.

Focusing on anything other than how fake she was, she tried to be herself—someone she was rapidly losing. "Well..." She laughed nervously. "That was new."

A deep chuckle rumbled through his muscled chest as he kissed the top of her head. "Do you object?"

"Yes, I highly object to any earth shattering orgasms before ten in the morning." God, she was such a fucking phony. If her track record didn't make her throw up, her lies might.

They sat in silence for a several long moments. The burn of his stubble lingered on her cheeks. She stared at the pile of toys in the corner, so normal and appropriately chaotic. Blinking in the silence, she swallowed. It wasn't going to go away. What happened to her couldn't be buried or forgotten—even if she couldn't ... remember.

She wouldn't be able to hide it from him forever, especially if this was the direction their relationship was heading. She'd waited so long for him to get his hands on her and she'd ruined it. Their first kiss was over her tears. Their second was on the tail of her assault and battery outburst this morning. And she'd just faked an orgasm. Stunning firsts all around.

Her hatred needed a target, but she only could aim it at a blank spot, so she turned her anger on herself. Ignorance was impossible, even when she knew very little about what she actually suffered.

It was over. Why couldn't she just forget what happened and get on with her life?

Shutting her eyes, she accepted that wasn't going to happen. There would be no going back to the girl she was a few days ago. She liked that girl, admired her confidence, took pride in her independence, and drew pleasure from her sexual assuredness. But now that girl was gone, and here she sat, on the lap of a man she lusted after for a solid year, a scared, helpless, sexually frustrated girl who couldn't find her way home.

A tear rolled down her cheek. She couldn't do this. It was too hard. She'd rather not have him at all than chance ruining the hope of having something great with him.

This would be the last time she let herself get close to him—at least until she made some sense about what happened and figured out how to cope with the aftermath. It wasn't what she wanted, but she couldn't involve him, couldn't bear showing him this filthy blotch on her soul.

She didn't want him to know this sniveling person she'd become. She wanted strong Jade back. That was who she'd always been—that was the only person she wanted to be.

Six

"THERE YOU GO. That's the last one," Dr. Lily Bishop, Jade's good friend and co-worker, taped a piece of cotton gauze to Jade's arm. She'd been pricked, swabbed, and asked to pee in a cup, all under the assumption of wanting to make sure she was at the top of her game after a night of drunken, wild sex.

"And how long until the results are in?"

The paper-covered exam table crinkled under her weight as she fidgeted. Lots of new habits— fidgeting, sleepless nights, constantly looking over her shoulder for a dangerous stranger she wouldn't recognize, faking orgasms from Jeremy Larson—yup, the times they were a-changin'.

"Well, I gave you the rapid screening. I'm sure I could pass along a request to Derek at the lab to speed things along, but either way, you should have your results somewhere between forty-eight hours and a week. However, if anything comes back looking suspicious, it could take up to a month for further testing.”

“Wonderful.”

Lily placed a label on a vial of Jade’s blood. “Now, I’m going to pretend to play along with your fib, because it’s not my business, but I’m also going to remind you I’m here if you want to talk.”

“Don’t wanna talk,” she mumbled, as she pulled the sleeve of her scrubs down to cover the gauze.

“You know, you really should have an exam as well if you suspect your body may be at risk of infection.”

Swallowing back her ever present nausea, she drew in a deep breath. “Well, let’s just say I had too much to drink and can’t remember if we used a condom. How long would it take for something to show up?”

“Symptoms can show up anywhere between two days and two years. Your blood work will rule out a lot, but it’s still important to have a physical exam to be sure.” She placed her hand on her arm. “Jade, I’m not going to lecture you. You’re an adult, but this whole scenario seems to have holes. I’m trained to know when my patients are lying to me. You’re my friend and I want to help you. I promise complete confidentiality, no matter what the case is.”

She looked at the woman who’d worked with her since her internship. She was stunning, even in scrubs and a lab coat. A mixture of Spain’s spice and Italy's sensuality, this beautiful, willowy creature was a successful doctor to boot. She was, hands down, the best OB/GYN Jade ever knew.

She took a deep breath and sighed. "Do I have to change into a gown?"

Lily's professional smile held a hint of satisfied pride. "Not if you promise you've been keeping up on your monthly breast exams."

"I have."

"Then just drop the drawers."

A minute later, Jade found herself scooting to the edge of the table, where she was warned to expect a little pressure. It was a typical page in the long list of joys that came with being a woman.

"Jade?"

"Yep?" Her mind was slowly disassociating from her lower half.

"When was the last time you had intercourse?"

"Um..." She swallowed hard. "I guess I would have to say Thursday night."

"Have you noticed any spotting or bleeding?"

"No. My cycle isn't due until the end of the month."

"I wasn't referring to your cycle. There's some inflammation around your cervix. It seems to be bleeding from even a light touch. That's okay, I just wanted to know if you're in any pain or had any noticeable hemorrhaging."

"No," she croaked as a tear rolled into her hairline. She still felt tender but it was difficult to tell if that was emotional scarring or physical injury. Life rapidly become heavy and far too real.

There were no words to explain the degree to which she'd been violated. Desecrated. Chills covered her body in a swoop of discomfort that swallowed her whole.

Removing the speculum, Lily patted her knee. "You can sit up."

Wiping her eyes, she adjusted her top to cover her lower half.

"Ok, sweetie here's the deal. I found no early symptoms of any noticeable STDs that would be evident at this point, but that's what the blood screening's for. However, you have a bruised cervix. It's nothing dangerous or anything that won't heal, but I am going to recommend that you refrain from intercourse for about three weeks and don't use tampons during your next cycle." She smiled. "And next time, try not to be so rough."

In a failed attempt to match her levity, Jade choked on an "Okay" and a sob flung past her lips. Her fingers covered her mouth, but it was too late. She burst into tears.

"Oh, sweetie, come here." Lily pulled her into a nurturing embrace, which only made Jade cry harder. "Shh, shh, shh. It's okay. I told you, it's not a big deal. I see it a lot and once your blood work comes back you'll realize all of these tears were likely for nothing."

She had to stop doing this. Pulling back, she scrubbed her palms roughly over her face and forced her composure into place. Nodding quickly, she said, "I understand."

Lily's manicured brows drew together. "Jade,

are you sure that I'm the only person you should be talking to? If something happened, something involving your body without your permission, you have rights." Lowering her voice, she asked, "Did someone do something to you?"

Sucking in a deep breath, she met her friend's intense stare and shook her head, lips pursing as more tears fell. "I can't remember."

Lily stilled. "What do you mean, you can't remember?"

"I've tried ... *for days!* But it isn't even blurry. It's just ... *blank!*"

"Okay." The doctor nodded, glancing around as if the answers were written on the walls. "We need to talk about this, but I want you to be calm. Why don't you get dressed and then you can start at the beginning. I'm going to—"

"You can't tell anyone!"

"Of course not. Jade, I told you, we share doctor-patient confidentiality, under *all* circumstances. Plus, we're friends. You can trust me. We're just going to talk, but we'll have more privacy in my office. Maybe it'll help you to remember."

Jade relaxed a little, but not enough to clear her blurry vision. She nodded and released the death grip she had on Lily's lab coat. "I don't... I don't want to talk here." This was her hospital too. She didn't want to chance anyone seeing her upset and asking questions.

"Okay. Then we'll go to my place. Let me just tell the nurse I'm leaving for the day."

Two hours later Jade was curled up on Lily's couch, pouring the last drop of wine from a bottle of red.

"Did you call the cops? Even if you don't want to report the rape, your personal items were stolen."

"Only the stuff in my wallet. He didn't take anything else and my laptop and iPad were in plain sight. I called all my credit card companies. They weren't used."

He'd only used her. Shakily, she reached for her wine glass.

"Do you think it could have been this Jeremy?" Lily kept her expression neutral, but Jade spotted the assumption in her eyes. Jeremy was the last man she saw that night. But it wasn't him.

"No. Jeremy's a good guy. Plus, he's fiercely protective of his friends. Besides, I'm fairly certain Kat did an extensive background check on him before she let him back into Mia's life."

"Why would she do that if he's completely trustworthy?"

"It had nothing to do with his character. Kat's just crazy. Besides, I know Jeremy. I trust him. He wouldn't hurt me."

"You're sure?"

"Yes."

"Okay. What do you remember about the bar? Was it full or empty?"

"It was sort of full, but it was a Thursday night. Bars are usually busy on Thursdays regardless."

"What about the people there? Was the bartender a man or a woman?"

"A man. I don't remember much else, except that Jeremy left around 9:04 p.m."

"Right, because of your text from Kat. When he left, did he pay the tab?"

She thought for a minute. This was where her memory fizzled. "I think so. I don't remember signing anything. I should ask him, but I'm trying to avoid that."

"Maybe you should go back to the bar to see if it jogs your memory. You could also contact your bank to see if you paid the tab and, while you're at it, check the time on the receipt."

"That's a good idea about the bank, but I can't even go into my apartment without losing it. I doubt I could walk into that bar. Thanks, by the way, for letting me crash here tonight."

Lily gestured, putting up a hand. "No problem. But what if the bartender remembers something? If you want, I can go with you for moral support."

"What if I find something out I don't want to know? Like, what if this is all my fault? Or what if it *was* the bartender?"

"It doesn't matter if you were running around flashing people and offering to blow the entire bar. The moment someone has sex with someone whose judgment's too impaired to give consent, they're committing sexual assault. None of this is your fault, Jade. Drugged or just plain plastered, they're in the wrong, *not* you."

"I must've been drugged. It's the only explanation that makes sense. I only had a couple drinks and I was fine when Jeremy was there. How long does it take for drugs like that to take effect?"

Lily eased back, holding her glass to her chest as she crossed her arms. "Well, it depends. With Rohypnol, the sedative effects appear approximately thirty to forty-five minutes after the drugs ingested. The effects can last between four and twelve hours. Different doses and body types make it difficult to know exactly."

"Will something like that show up in my lab results?"

"Its compounds will show up in urine for at least five days. We might've missed that window, but if you give me a sample of your hair it can be traced for up to a month after ingesting even a single dose."

"Do you think that's what I was given?"

She tilted her head. "I think it's a good possibility. It's easy to get. It can incapacitate victims, preventing them from resisting sexual assault. It can produce anterograde amnesia, which means individuals may not remember experiences following the introduction of the drug. But there are plenty of other drugs out there that do the same."

Jade definitely wanted the lab to take a sample of her hair. She hesitated to go to the police because her experience with victims at the hospital didn't give her much hope. There was so much exposure and shame and she'd yet to see any real consequence for the predators, even when they were caught. Even if by some miracle she figured out who hurt her, she didn't expect him to ever know the pain she now lived with.

That was the fucked up truth about sexual assault. There was no justice, hardly ever any outside witnesses, and the penalty could never match the crime. If she had her way, it would be an eye for an eye. Either that, or rapists should have their dicks cut off. Maybe have predator tattooed across their face. But the reality was, most convicted rapists served less than six years. The length of time she'd carry the consequence of some sick fuck's actions... It was a life sentence.

Perhaps she'd speak to someone at the police station eventually, but for now, she was more worried about finding her own peace. That seemed a more realistic goal than any sort of blind revenge.

JADE AWOKE in yet another unfamiliar room to the sound of her cell phone ringing. She blindly fumbled around until the ringing stopped. As she drifted back to sleep the ringing started again. Holding the phone close to her face, she squinted at the screen but didn't recognize the number.

"Hello?" Too much wine and too many tears left her voice sounding like she'd swallowed a fist full of razorblades.

"Jade?"

"Who's this?"

"It's Jeremy. Why aren't you answering the door?"

"What door?" She was so not a morning person.

"The door to your apartment."

"Oh."

Wait, what?

Sweeping the knotted clump of hair from her eyes, she bolted upright. "Are you at my door?"

"Yes. I've been knocking for ten minutes." He sounded irritated.

"Why?"

"Because I wanted to see how you were today and I brought you coffee."

Aww... he brought me coffee. She smiled. "Who made the coffee?"

"I bought it." He exhaled into the phone. "Jade, do you think you could let me in?"

This is exactly why you need to get your life back to normal! Look what you're missing.

She sighed. "I'm not there." There was a long moment of silence. *Still going. Silence. Nothing, but crickets.* "Jeremy?" She looked at the phone but they were still connected. Why was he being so—

"Where are you?" he growled.

"I spent the night at a friend's."

"What kind of friend, Jade?"

She hadn't done anything to deserve that tone. "A co-worker. Jeremy, look, it's nothing you have to worry about. Dr. Bishop's a—"

"It's fine," he interrupted. "I'll just see you around."

He didn't sound fine, he sounded pissed. "Jeremy, wait a second—" The phone disconnected. *Son of a bitch!*

Despite her frustration, the idea of a jealous Jeremy did delicious things to her insides. She smirked and fell back on the bed, savoring the simplicity of normal boy girl politics over the much more complicated adult man woman bullshit. "He likes me."

Jeremy observed everything but only spoke when there was something important to say. It was interesting to see his usually unfailingly confidence waver because she couldn't recall ever seeming him anything but self-assured.

They really were polar opposites. She was elegant but sometimes clumsy and clever but never shut up. Her life was a constant string of blunders and social fails, but her sense of humor made it easy to laugh at herself. She had a good heart and always apologized when she inadvertently upset someone else.

She didn't like to wallow in sorrow, which was why she preferred her usually bubbly personality to her recent one. Her sense of humor might not cure cancer, but it often relieved a bit of the pain for her patients. Laughter was amazing medicine, and perhaps the one thing she hadn't allowed herself to enjoy since her *ordeal*.

As she showered and dressed her mind drifted around thoughts of Jeremy. And Thursday night. Back and forth, back and forth.

She growled. Part of her was grateful for the blackout. Not knowing what happened to her was its own form of torture, but recalling the actual assault could be worse. Torn between wanting to know and wanting to hold onto her ignorance—and her remaining shred of sanity—she weighed her options.

She wanted to put the whole, gory fiasco behind her. Involving the police might only drag things out, though she should let them know a predator was in the area. Staggered by the thought, she stilled.

What if he was doing this to multiple women? She suddenly had a responsibility to notify the cops, regardless if it led to more embarrassment and a fruitless search with little evidence—she couldn't stomach the idea of someone else suffering what she'd suffered.

Her shoulders slumped as a new weight bore down on her. There was a dark humiliation that came with rape. Despite being victimized, she couldn't shake the nagging sense of guilt. It was wrong to feel responsible for someone else's crime, but as irrational as the emotion was, it lingered.

This is probably why survivors seek therapy. I should probably look into that.

She wasn't mentally prepared to go down that avenue, at least not yet. But once the idea of speaking to a professional crossed her mind the more inevitable the outcome seemed. Spending an hour in some cold office, gushing over a trauma she couldn't remember and desperately wanted to forget... The idea held zero appeal. But the hope of getting over this and coming out normal? That was what she wanted most.

She was procrastinating. Not the healthiest choice, but the reality of the situation was daunting. She didn't want to be a statistic or a victim. She wanted to be herself—a *survivor*. Whole. But the truth was someone did something to her that forever changed her and the old her, the fearless, worry-free girl she was a few days ago... She died the second someone stole something she couldn't get back.

She needed to face this whether she wanted to or not. Denial might be the only defense mechanism she had at the moment, and even that was wearing thin.

Eight

JADE PULLED into Jeremy's driveway and was relieved to find his Jeep parked by the back of the house. Not sure if she should knock at the front or the back door, she hesitated. After building up her confidence, she decided to take the first step confronting this thing they were flirting with—be it a disaster or just an accidental hook up. Grabbing the caddy of coffee, she headed toward the backdoor.

Yellow siding, trimmed in white, wrapped the house. The small rear deck was cluttered with flats of flowerpots. A grill, a Barbie bike with training wheels, and two Adirondack chairs, one for a child and one for an adult, furnished the patio.

He'd said his house was only for him and Mia. The truth was adorably evident in every object she passed.

She tapped lightly on the screen door. Music

played from somewhere within the house, so she knocked a little harder and waited. When he didn't respond, she shifted her purse and the coffee and opened the door.

"Jeremy?" Following the obscenely loud music toward the hall, she pushed the cellar door open. "Jeremy?"

Metal clanked over the music as she took a hesitant step down the stairs. A long desk filled the corner with four computers resting on top. There was an empty office chair and files neatly piled by a modem. Descending two more steps, she peeked under the drop ceiling and sucked in a sharp breath.

An outdated sound system, with speakers the size of mini fridges filled the far corner next to a weight bench. Facing the wall, barefoot and in only his jeans, Jeremy pulled his body off the ground with a bar attached to the ceiling. *Holy back muscles, Batman!*

His knees bent, calves curling behind him as he pulled his weight off the ground in one graceful lift. His arms bulged as veins stretched under his damp flesh. Dew coated his skin, his musky scent filling the air.

Her stomach cartwheeled at the whoosh of his breath coming through his teeth as he exerted himself. *Dear Lord!* Tendons and sinew pulsed and twitched at his shoulders and down his back —*Come to Momma.*

She carefully placed the coffee on the edge of the desk, tempted to run her fingers over his bunching muscles and write her name in his glistening sweat. Every swell of brawn tightened with each repetition. A spattering of jagged scars disappeared beneath the waistband of his jeans. He probably looked incredible in his military fatigues.

Prepared to make herself comfortable and enjoy the show, she grinned. Jeremy released his grip on the bar and dropped to his feet with a grunt of force. He turned and froze.

Biting her lip, she gave diminutive finger wave. "Hi."

His expression remained blank as he reached for a remote on the weight bench and muted the stereo.

Silence.

"I like that song."

"Don't you knock?" He breathed heavily as he mopped the sweat from his neck with a hand towel.

"I did knock. You didn't hear me."

"Maybe I didn't want to be disturbed."

"Maybe I didn't care," she teased, trying to lighten the mood. It didn't work.

"Are you on your way to a shift?"

She frowned then followed his gaze. She was still in her scrubs from the day before. "Uh, no. I don't go in until tomorrow at three."

"Ah, so you came here right from your sleepover." He turned, tossing the towel into a laundry basket.

If he wanted to be a jerk and make assumptions, fine. "That's right."

"What do you want, Jade?"

Okay, he didn't like being baited. "I brought you coffee." She pointed to the caddy on the desk. "You know ... an olive branch, for not being home this morning."

He looked at the coffee but made no move to retrieve it or even say thank you.

"Jeremy, about last night—"

"I have work to do, Jade." Snatching his shirt off the weight bench he yanked it over his head, successfully ruining her view. *Well, if he was gonna be a dick...*

"Look, Jeremy, I don't know what you think happened—"

"I don't care, nor is it any of my business. Like I said, I have work to do, so if you could just go out the way you came in..." He walked right past her, as if she were invisible, and sat at his desk.

Bristling, and a little hurt, her smile faltered. "God, I never realized you could be such an asshole." Snatching her purse off the floor, she took the stairs.

What a douchebag! He didn't have all the details and who was he, anyway, to act like she wasn't allowed to sleep out? He had no claim on her. For *a year* she'd done everything to get his attention. Just because he finally felt ready to make a move did not entitle him to some sort of claim over her.

By the time she reached her car she was trembling. With shaky hands, she jabbed the key in the ignition and gripped the wheel.

She had nowhere to go and she didn't want to

go home. Maybe her olive branch had actually been a desperate attempt to avoid returning to her apartment.

She needed a plan B. Kat was on her honeymoon, Mia was at her grandparent's, and Lily was sleeping. Her frustration doubled as her vision blurred. *Fuck this.* Letting out an aggravated growl, she turned the key and flinched at the sight of Jeremy standing in front of her car.

What the hell was he doing? Rolling her eyes and lacking the energy to argue, she put the car in reverse. Before she took her foot off the brake, he stalked to her door and opened it. "I'm sorry. Come back inside."

"Not if you're going to be mean to me."

"I won't be mean. Please."

She hesitated, letting out a frustrated huff, and put the car in park. He held out his hand.

She followed him back inside, wanting to be done with the misunderstandings. "Look, I don't know what's going on with us, but you should know, Dr. Bishop's a woman. I only slept there because I didn't want to go home."

"You could have mentioned that over the phone."

"Why bother when you already assumed I'd wake up with one man and spend the night with another? There's a jerk here and I'm pretty sure it's not me."

"I was wrong to make an assumption. Sorry."

Was that a real apology? She supposed so. "I'm

sorry I teased you and let you believe Dr. Bishop was a man."

Eyes on his coffee, he folded back the lid. "What's this new aversion you have toward your apartment?"

Rather than answer, she sidled closer and slid her arms around his shoulders, smiling up at him. "I don't like when you're mad at me."

"You're avoiding my question."

"Just for a little while longer. Feed me and then we'll talk." She hoped this time she'd be able to get some words out.

His fingers teased along her arm. She liked that they had reached a point where they could invade each other's personal space. So long as she remembered it was Jeremy she liked it very much.

His pupils darkened, swallowing the green of his irises and deepening the color to a rich pine. "Do you want to go out to lunch?"

"I thought you had all that pesky work to do."

"Smart ass."

Smiling, she glanced down and sighed. "I need to change."

"We can stop at your place."

That's what she was afraid of. Maybe if he went with her she could get in and out without a total mental meltdown. While she was at it, she could grab some personal items to get her through this little nomadic spell. Chances were she'd be staying at Lily's again—or Jeremy's. But Lily's was probably the sensible choice.

When they pulled up to her apartment, her stomach cramped painfully. *You can do this.*

"Do you want me to come up with you?"

Grateful he offered before she had to ask, she masked her fear with a grin. "If you don't mind. It'll only take me a minute to change and grab some stuff."

As they took the stairs, she focused on ordinary things in an attempt to convince herself her home was unchanged. The lip of loose carpeting in the hall still needed to be tacked down and the stack of her neighbor's bills littered his doormat as usual. She was fine until she faced her own door.

I don't want to go in there.

Her tongue lay heavy in her mouth, weighted by the taste of fear, as she took a deep breath and turned the key in the lock. *Get in and get the hell out.*

"I'll just be a minute."

Keeping her gaze on the floor, she darted into her bedroom. Filling a bag with clean scrubs, some toiletries, and pajamas, she went about her task like a person retrieving a quarter from the bottom of a swimming pool.

"How long have you lived here?" Jeremy's voice echoed from the open living room.

She entered the living room. "Um, about two years. Ready?"

"Wow. That was fast."

"Yup. Let's go."

Tilting his head, he jerked his chin in the direction of her duffle bag. "Are you taking a trip?"

She slung the bag over her shoulder. "No, I just like to be prepared. Come on." Cutting off further questions, she turned and hustled to the hall.

When he stepped over the threshold she slammed the door and locked it, giving the knob a jiggle to ensure it was secure. "Okay, let's get out of here."

She quickly led the way back to the car.

~

Fury had him gripping the steering wheel hard enough to snap it off the column. Who the fuck was with her? He grit his teeth as the man took Jade's arm and led her to his car.

He glanced at his Rolex. Ten minutes. They'd been inside her home for less than ten minutes, not long enough to do anything significant.

Shutting his eyes, he calmed his anger by picturing her naked body in his arms again. The scent of her silky hair, the taste of her skin. She was so fucking soft, so warm.

What would it be like to have her awake? Would she grab him? Fight him? His cock stretched and pulsed in his jeans.

Hearing her breath quicken as she tried to fight him off... His eyes closed on a guttural groan. She would need to be subdued, held down. He'd pin her to the bed or the floor and stare at her, waiting until she submitted, accepting that he was ultimately stronger. Oh, she'd be helpless—again. But this time it would be her choice.

His palm pressed over his zipper and he groaned. He wanted to feel that moment of acceptance with her. That specific point when she gave over to his authority and became his, not because he drugged her, but because she chose to go peacefully. Eventually, it would happen.

Opening his eyes, he scowled as the guy slid a feminine print duffle bag into the back of the Jeep. His lip curled at the inconvenience of another man in her home. But she hadn't been home. She'd been hiding.

Don't you like your bed anymore, Jade?

THEY DROVE in silence until they reached a small restaurant called The Honey Pot. Jade's mind continuously debated if this was a date or just friends having lunch. It was difficult to tell because the dialogue flowed easily and there was a familiarity she didn't usually share with dates.

"It's good to see you're finally doing something about that body of yours," she teased over lunch.

He arched a brow. "Is that so?"

She shrugged, taking a bite of her Cobb salad. "Yeah. I mean, you're so scrawny. If you ever need a spotter..."

He laughed. "I'll remember that."

For dessert, she ordered a colossal slice of cake. Placing her fork on the edge of the smeared, empty dish she groaned. "*That* was amazaballs."

"Amazaballs?"

"Totally."

Chuckling, he rolled his eyes. "You, uh, missed your mouth a little there."

Pausing, she slowly lifted her pinky and dabbed the corner of her lips. "Did I get it?"

"Not even close."

She rubbed her fingers under her lip. "Now?"

"Maybe this is a job for a napkin."

"Where is it?" She bunched up her napkin.

His shoulders shook as he silently laughed. "It's just a little spot right there on your cheek."

She swiped the napkin over her cheek. "Gone?"

A smile broke across his face and she growled. "Oh, for the love of fuck."

Reaching into her bag, she removed her phone and opened her camera to the selfie setting and—*oy vey*—her entire cheek was covered. Scoffing, she dabbed her napkin in the glass of water and quickly cleaned her face. "Jerk. How long was that there?"

"Pretty much since the first bite."

"Thanks for telling me!"

"I did tell you."

"Yeah, when the tab arrived. The waitress probably thinks I'm a complete slob." And this wasn't the first time she'd worn her food without realizing. Toddlers had better table manners.

"Oh, stop. It was cute."

Her embarrassment fizzled as she met his gaze. "Cute?"

He shrugged one negligent, muscled shoulder. "Adorable."

"Well…" She folded her napkin and sat back. "If you're going to call me nice things I suppose I can forgive you."

His eyes smoldered as he watched her, tiny golden flecks showing like fiery embers in the green. The moment intensified and he cleared his throat, breaking eye contact to reach for his wallet. Oh, to be that wallet, tucked tight against his fabulous ass, warm and constricted.

"Do you want to come back to my place? We could watch a movie."

His place seemed just the place her body wanted to be. "Sure."

When they returned to his house he handed her the television remote. "I gotta run downstairs and check my messages. I'm waiting for a client to get back to me. Why don't you check Netflix?"

"Okay."

He paused and sent her another look like the one he'd sent her just after lunch. Her breath held as she both feared and hoped he'd kiss her. "I should only be a couple of minutes."

As soon as he left, she exhaled. When he looked at her like that her entire body tingled. There was definitely some building chemistry between them. As much as she wanted him to make a move, she was also glad they were taking things slower than they had the other morning.

She made herself at home and got cozy on the couch. Once she found a movie, she cued it and paused at the opening credits, waiting for him to return. A couple of minutes to Jeremy were more like a half hour to the rest of the world. Passing the time, she edited his Netflix account, changing his name to Herby Butt-Muncher and the emoticon to a fancy little girl. She was practically dozing off when he finally returned.

"Everything okay?" she asked, scrubbing her face to wake herself up.

"Yeah. Sorry, I had a complication with a file."

This was probably a good time to inquire about his career. He went to school while in the military and got a degree having something to do with IT and security, but she wasn't exactly sure what his job entailed. "What exactly do you do, Jeremy?"

"I write and break codes."

"Like computer codes? Who do you work for, the government?"

"Right now I work for myself, but there're a few government companies bidding for me to come on full time."

Impressive and so very Jason Bourne. She didn't think there were any government agencies in New Castle aside from the social security office. "Would you have to move again if you took one of those jobs?"

He sat beside her and pulled her close as if it were the most natural thing in the world. "That's one of the negotiations I'm working on. I won't leave Mia again." Because he'd already missed the first three years of her life while in Iraq. She didn't want to talk about the war.

"So what kind of coding do you do? Are you a spy?" she teased and he laughed.

"No. I look at encrypted software within global networks and find out where people are most vulnerable to threats. I rewrite the codes, encrypting them further, so my client's assets are protected."

"Ah, very double o'seven." She had no idea what he was talking about. "And people—*normal* people—need this service, because...?"

"Because they want to protect their portfolios. I have a few lawyer clients, people who are big in the stock market, and some small business owners. It's really a form of insurance. I look at how they store their data, find the weak points, and encrypt the files so they're stronger."

"Huh, that's pretty neat." She could tweet. That was the extent of her computer savviness. "And you enjoy this?"

"Well, I was always good with numbers. It's second nature."

"Did you do that kind of stuff in Iraq?"

"No." His eyes abruptly turned distant. "In Iraq, I was part of combat."

Until he was wounded. The little she knew about his time at war she learned from Kat. Jeremy had returned home after an honorable discharge and some time in the south. Kat said he'd gone through some physical therapy, but Jade didn't know much about the extent of his injuries. This morning she'd noticed some more light scarring around his torso, but nothing major.

"Then you went to Texas."

"Right." His gaze studied her for a moment. "You want to talk about this?"

She shrugged. "Not if it makes you uncomfortable."

Stretching out his legs, he pulled her close and sighed. "I was shot with a buddy of mine. He never made it home. I stayed at a rehab facility in Dallas for a few months while I got my affairs in order. After seeing so much death and gore I... It isn't something anyone wants to remember. That's when I knew I wanted to come home and be with my daughter."

"I'm glad you came home."

"Me too." Several minutes passed in silence, him staring at the wall while he ran his fingers slowly over a strand of her hair.

Admiring the size of his other hand and the bulk of his muscular thighs, the temptation to kiss him grew. Pressing her knees together, she steeled herself for the inevitable and broached the subject they'd danced around for the past several months.

"Jeremy, what's going on with us?"

His attention flicked to her, the side of his mouth kicking up with boyish charm. "What do you mean?" He knew what she meant.

"I mean, what is this?" She gestured between the two of them. "*Us.*"

Capturing her fingers, he brought them to his

lips and kissed the tips. "I'm not sure, but I know I like it."

"I like it too. I'm just not sure what to make of it. I mean, you've been home for a year now and never made a move until the other day. Why?"

"I ... needed to see that Kat was taken care of first. I know she was with Ty when I returned and I know he'll always take good care of her, but I needed to make sure I had a role in their lives. In Mia's."

She not only understood but respected that. Jeremy was a good dad and Jade loved Mia enough to make her happiness a higher priority than her own. "So, Kat getting married was some sort of green light for you?"

"The things she didn't have, in a way I took them from her. I didn't want to steal anything from this monumental time of her life. I'm glad she got the happy ending she deserved." He twisted to fully face her. "Whatever happens between us, Jade, I want it to be ours. I know Kat's your best friend, but it's a little weird because she's also the mother of my daughter."

"She knows how I feel about you."

He smirked. "How *do* you feel about me?"

Her heart skipped as his gaze devoured her mouth as if he held his breath for her answer. "Um ... you're okay."

"Just okay?"

She shrugged. "I like you."

"Like or *like* like?"

She laughed and shoved him. "What are you, twelve? It's a heavy like, okay?"

"Well, I'd hoped." He spared her a cocky smile. His expression was light, but his eyes gave away a hint of insecurity, making her believe it mattered more than he was letting on.

"So, what exactly are we doing? Are we dating?"

"I guess it's whatever we want it to be. I'm not interested in a relationship that isn't monogamous though. Last night, when I thought you spent the night at another man's house, I wanted to wring your neck and hang the bastard by his balls."

Her face heated. Possessiveness could be a nuisance, but when a man was territorial, that was a whole different ball game. Knowing he wanted some sort of claim to her made her insides all warm and gushy.

"I'm okay with monogamy, so long as it's equally honored."

"Good. Also, I don't want Mia to know anything—at least for a while. I don't want her to get ahead of herself with assumptions about the future."

"I agree. I don't want her to get hurt or be angry because something didn't go the way she expected." She loved that little munchkin.

"I also don't plan on having a hollow relationship, Jade. I expect you to be open with me and honest. That means you have to trust me with some of your secrets. Whatever was going on with you last week, I hope it's better now, but from here on out I expect you to talk to me about your problems."

Her smile faded as she glanced at her lap. "It's over," she whispered, now taking his words seriously.

She would go to the police after her next shift, tell them what she knew, and stop dwelling on the negative events of her life. *This*, right here with Jeremy, discussing their future, this was what she wanted.

"Will you tell me what happened?" His warm fingers dragged slowly over her jaw.

She shut her eyes, proud when tears didn't come rushing to the surface. Taking a deep breath, she asked, "Is that a condition to us being together?"

"No, but I'm curious. Something obviously upset you. Badly."

"Look," she sighed. "Maybe, down the road, I'll be ready to talk about it, but for right now I'd rather not. I think—if you can respect that and give me time—we'd be better off. Like I said, it's over. I'm safe and in a few days I'll—hopefully— never have to think about it again."

He tensed. "What's in a few days? And when was your safety ever in question?"

Shit. "See? Questions like that make me have to think about it and that's what I want to avoid."

He frowned and she sensed he wasn't going to let it go. This had been the best day since her ordeal and she didn't want to spoil it. Ignoring his frown, she scooted closer and reached for his jaw. "I have a better idea..."

He caught her wrist. "I'm not easily distracted, Jade. If you're in danger, I want to know. I may be able to help."

She let out a frustrated breath and sat back. "Fine."

A version of the truth was still the truth. Crossing her legs under her body she folded her hands tightly in her lap.

"Someone stole my credit cards. They never had a chance to use them because, as soon as I found out, I canceled them and I don't want to sleep in my apartment because I'm not sure if they were stolen inside my home or from my purse while I was out." It was a minor fib.

He scowled. "Someone might've broken into your *apartment*?" Okay, he was outraged. *Exactly why he will never know the whole story.* "And you've been going back there?"

"Well, as infrequently as possible—"

"Did you even call the cops? Or have the locks changed at least?"

"No, but—"

"Jesus Christ, Jade! Why didn't you tell me about this? Do you know how lucky you are that all they got were your credit cards? You could have been—"

"*Stop!*" Jade held up her hand and gave him a look that communicated one more word and she was leaving. "I didn't tell you so I could get a lecture and I'm not pretending to be any form of lucky. You have no idea how seriously I'm taking this. You want to help me? Change my locks. I don't need or want anything else, and I *certainly* don't need a speech on the dangers of the world."

His nostrils flared as his jaw twitched. "Fine, but you aren't sleeping there until the locks are changed."

"*Fine.*"

"And you aren't sleeping at Dr. Bishop's either."

"*Fine.*" She huffed indignantly and crossed her arms over her chest. "But I'm also not putting you on the couch in your own home. We'll just have to share your bed."

A slow smile crept across his face. In a husky voice, he said, "Fine."

Ten

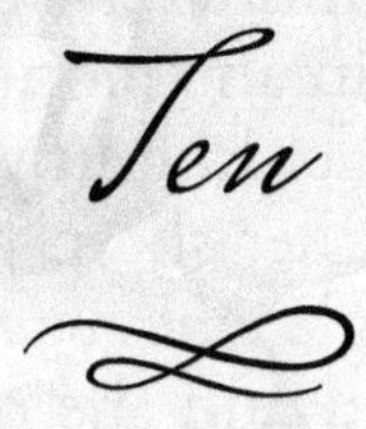

JADE WAITED in her pajamas while Jeremy showered. A part of her wished she'd packed something a little sexier to sleep in instead of her sheep pajama bottoms and a tank top that said *Bahhh!* across the boobs, but she figured—unless he was into farm animals—her pajamas would keep things kosher between them.

Pulling back the covers, she quietly climbed into the queen size bed. The water shut off. Pulling the blankets to her chin, she lay as if she had an iron rod up her ass. A second later, he walked into the room with a towel slung low around his waist. Averting her eyes but peeking through her lashes, she glimpsed the spattering of scars above his left knee.

Drawers opened and closed as she stared at the ceiling and panic set in. What if he expected sex? Little did he know, her private parts were staying safely tucked away in her sheep pants. It wasn't just that she was waiting on lab work. Sex could really hurt her—in more ways than one.

She was living in an emotional madhouse and wasn't prepared to let him in yet. There would be no *flocking* around her sheep pants on this night. She tried not to giggle. *You're such a dork.*

The bed dipped and she quickly scooted farther under the covers and turned to her side facing the door. He shut off the light and the room was bathed in darkness. His heavy arm cinched around her waist, dragging her flush to his front.

Oh, God. This was going to require some major self-restraint because he was definitely aroused.

"You're suddenly quiet," he whispered next to her ear, smelling of soap and mint.

"Mm-hm." Goosebumps prickled up her arm as his knuckles brushed the underside of her breast.

"Having second thoughts about sharing my bed?" His fingers teased as he playfully brushed his lips over her earlobe.

Her belly swooned. *Be strong!* She nervously shook her head, the sound of her hair scratching across the pillowcase overly loud in the shadowy silence.

"What's the matter? Cat got your tongue?" He gave her hard nipple a quick pinch.

She moaned and reflexively pressed her bottom firmly against his arousal. She had to stop. She could *not* fool around with him.

His fingers trailed upward between her breasts and followed the collar of her shirt to her shoulder. Chills of excitement chased across her spine as he gently pulled the thin strap down her arm. As the fabric rasped against her skin, exposing one breast, her breathing hitched.

"Is this okay?" The backs of his fingers dragged across the tight bud of her nipple.

She nodded, when, in fact, she needed this to stop before things got out of hand. Tomorrow she'd talk to Derek at the lab and once she knew everything was okay, she and Jeremy could—*Shit*! —She forgot about her bruised cervix!

How long did Lily say? Two weeks? Three? The mere thought of her battered insides hit her like a bucket of ice water. Traces of someone else, proof of mistreatment and abuse.

Her body stiffened and she could no longer feel his caress or make sense of his words. Her ears buzzed as her breathing quickened. Her throat locked around some ball of emotion trying to get out and she suddenly had the urge to scream.

"Your skin's so soft."

His smell enveloped her, familiar and grounding. Teetering between delirium and arousal, she couldn't stay in one place long enough to find her balance.

The sound of his even breathing and soft whispered words made his touch all the more alluring. Her body relaxed into his heated caresses. Dear God, and the things he was doing to her nipples alone. Applying the slightest pressure to her shoulder, he rolled her to her back and her heart raced as the heat of his mouth closed over her nipple.

It felt good. Tender. Then his weight settled over her and her eyes closed and something changed.

"*I can't sleep with you!*" she blurted and he froze.

Lifting his head he blinked those striking green eyes at her. His damp hair was mussed from the pillows. "Do you want me to go to the living room?"

"No, that's not what I meant. I mean that I, well, I can sleep with you, I just can't *sleep* with you."

He chuckled and gently chafed his five o'clock shadow across the tip of her breast. "Okay. Do you want me to stop what I was doing?"

Why did he have to ask such difficult questions?

"I can keep things under control, Jade. I'm in no rush. I can keep the game in the north court."

She moaned, as he brushed his lips suggestively across her breast. She wanted to fool around within the bounds of Lily's rules, but she was afraid she might freak out. There was a very strong probability she was losing her mind.

"We can still enjoy ourselves." He pulled her other strap down her other arm, fully exposing her breasts.

His sense confidence was something she craved, but her stupid issues were getting in the way. She didn't want to stop him. Especially because this was how she wanted him, confident, authoritative, *hot*. Saying no could give him the wrong message and mess up all future hook ups.

"Remember the other day, when I made you come?" His voice rumbled as he licked the outline of her areola.

Guilt crashed over her. She should have never faked an orgasm with him, but she didn't want to give the impression she was frigid or suffering some form of post-traumatic stress. She just wanted to be normal, damn it!

"We managed just fine while keeping ourselves half-clothed. Let me make you feel good again, baby." His hand drifted to the apex of her thighs and she reflexively arched her back, her heart racing. "Is that a yes? I'll tell ya, I had planned to let you get some sleep, but then I saw these sexy pajamas and I couldn't resist. I must have a fetish for sheep."

She laughed causing his hand to press more firmly against her sex. "Maybe you were a naughty farmer in a past life."

So long as there was no penetration they should be fine and she *really* wanted to have an orgasm with him so she could erase the memory of the fake one.

"Or maybe it has to do with the sexy woman in my bed wearing cartoon barnyard animals. Can I keep going? I promise I won't pillage your flock."

His fingers found the niche of her pussy and he applied the perfect amount of pressure. Jade's panties dampened and her knees drifted farther apart, the allure of normal experiences arousing her more than anything else.

"Yes," she answered in a hoarse voice sounding nothing like her own.

"Good girl." His mouth latched onto her nipple, causing a sob of pleasure to escape her lips as his fingers rubbed over her pajama pants.

He was so controlled and so in charge. All her fantasies didn't do him justice. She never knew what to expect with him. Sometimes he was tender and drugging, while other times he was forceful and firm.

His mouth tugged at her sensitive breasts as his body moved over hers. The ridge of his cock delved into the dimple of fabric between her thighs. Running her fingers over his defined shoulders, she clung to him, as his mouth worked up her throat to her ear.

The pleasure built and with each pulsing wave, her desire grew. It was going to happen this time. Digging her heels into the mattress to meet his blunted thrusts, she moaned as his teeth gently tugged at her ear and his fingers pinched her flesh.

The pressure grew as their pace increased. The friction against her clit, coupled with his licking, kissing, nibbling, and moaning had her panting, begging he keep going. He worked his way back to her breast and held them together in his large hands.

"I could spend days here."

Lacking any obvious inhibitions, he bent and

sucked hard on her nipples, plumping her breast, massaging, all the while grinding his arousal against her core. The pleasure left her dizzy.

Brushing his lips to her nipple, he growled. "You're so fucking hot." His lips crashed against hers in a frantic kiss.

Senses on overload, her body continued to peak. He gave a deep, long moan into her mouth, his tongue dueling with hers as his body trembled. Dampness seeped through her pajama pants.

She called his name, moaning deeper each time it passed her lips. It had to be him, this spell he wrapped around her, so safe and secure. His touch and need, subdued by their juvenile petting and grinding was so erotic it threw her right into sweet release. Her leg muscles locked as he rubbed over her, finishing himself, and shattering the last of her control.

Victory!

As waves of ecstasy crashed through her veins her mind rejoiced. She wasn't broken. She wasn't frigid. She was still a functioning woman capable of sexual response—when the man was the one she wanted.

Trembling, they looked at each other, breathing hard, eyes glazed, shaking from the aftermath of their joint orgasms. *We're amazing together.*

Smiling, he softly kissed her. "That was incredible."

Immensely relieved, she smiled. "You have no idea."

Eleven

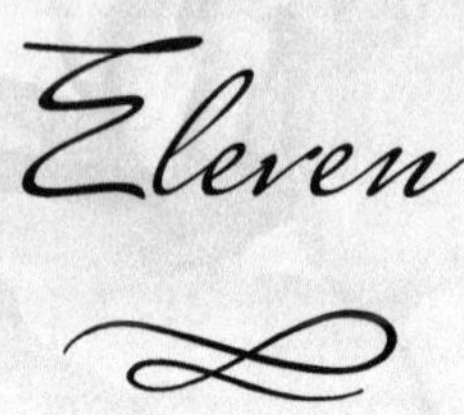

JADE AWOKE to the sound of a car pulling out of the driveway, the rumble of the engine resembling the familiar hum of Jeremy's Jeep. She frowned as her hand drifted to the cool side of the bed. Groggily, she squinted at the clock. 10:06.

Deciding to take a shower, she searched for a towel. She was developing new ticks like singing loudly when she was alone or humming to mask the deafening silence. Using a heavy hand, she opened and closed closets, the noise a comfort, as though it might scare off an intruder.

With every passing day, she accepted more of her emerging quirks, as though her brain could only process at a certain pace. Perhaps it was survival instincts, only allowing so much introspection in at a time.

Belting out a few bars of Jack Johnson's *Ba-*

nana Pancakes—he should totally ask me to do a duet with him—the water heated her skin. As the washcloth brushed over her shoulder, she winced.

Angling her chin close to her shoulder, she held her sopping hair out of her eyes and analyzed the mark in a detached sort of way. The scale of space her ordeal held in her mind was enormous. Even without the memories, she'd never forget. The mark on her skin promised that much.

It seemed like progress to lock the emotions tied to the event in a mental box. That way they weren't so scary to face. Acknowledging her fears was terrifying in itself. Nothing would take away what had happened. Nothing.

The idea of a stranger touching her was... Words failed her. It was a total mind-fuck, a vortex of unanswerable questions that would drive her to insanity faster than anything else. So she pushed the thoughts into the shadowed recesses of her mind and continued to sing.

As she combed out her tangled mane, making a mental note to pick up conditioner, her phone beeped. There was a missed call from Kat. Thrilled to talk to her best friend and see how things were going on Lover's Lane, she quickly twisted her hair into a bun and called her back.

"Jade?"

Her familiar voice filled Jade with a sense of peace. "May I please speak to Mrs. Adams?"

"God, that sounds so weird!" She laughed. "How are you?"

"I'm good. How are the Keys?"

"Oh, mygosh, Jade, it's so much fun here. Last night I actually threw up from drinking too much!"

"No way! That's so unlike you."

"I know! Tyson was not happy. Where are you? I called earlier and you didn't answer. Did you cover someone else's shift?"

"Uh, no. I'm actually at Jeremy's ... sitting on his bed."

"*What?* How did this happen? You aren't supposed to do anything fun until we get back. Start at the beginning. I want to hear everything! Oh my God, you and *Jeremy*! I knew you two would eventually hook up. I can't believe this. *Tyson!*"

Jade jerked the phone away from her ear. "Whoa, settle down, Kat. We haven't even slept together—"

"What? Why not? Jade, you've been pining after him for a year. And I know Jeremy's no virgin."

"Okay, let's try to steer the focus away from how you know that and settle down a bit. First of all, we didn't sleep together, but we definitely did some first class fooling around. I, uh, I can't have sex right now anyway. I, um, I have my period," she lied.

She normally told Kat everything, but there was no way she was spoiling even a minute of her best friend's honeymoon.

"Oh, that sucks. Did you spend the night at his house?"

"Yeah."

"So are you guys, like, an item now?"

"Well, we talked about it and we want to see where things go. We agreed not to see other people and we aren't telling Mia. Yet."

"That's a good idea. Mia gets really attached and you're already up there with Santa and the Easter Bunny in her eyes. The idea of you and her father would be like... I don't know, Cinderella joining the family."

Tyson's deep baritone mumbled in the background. Kat briefly muffled the phone and explained the situation to him at an inhuman pace. "Tyson said Jeremy's a good guy, but you already knew that. Anyway, are you going to work today?"

"Yeah. I have to go in at three. Why?"

"Oh." She sounded disappointed. "Well, is Jeremy with you?"

"No, he went out. What's up?"

"Nothing, it's just that Gloria has Trixie and it turns out Darrel's dog allergies aren't immune to beagle fur after all. I was wondering if you or Jeremy could take her for the rest of the week, but then I thought about you working doubles and that's too long for Trixie to be left alone. I mean, you could stay at our house if your lease doesn't allow dogs, but again, with your schedule... Jeremy's really the best choice. Besides, I'm sure Mia misses her and she'll be with him tomorrow night so—"

"Kat." The girl could ramble for days, worrying herself into a seizure. "It's okay. Give me

Gloria's number and between Jeremy and me, we'll work something out."

"You're sure?"

"Yes, it's fine."

"And like I said, you can stay at our place if it's easier. You have your key, right?"

"Yup, and I may just take you up on that." She thought about crashing there two nights ago but didn't have an excuse. This was perfect.

"Thank you so much. We really appreciate it. I miss you."

"I miss you too."

With everything going on in Kat's life, Jade was sure she had no idea just how much that was true. She longed for the moment her friend was back and life resembled normal again.

"Okay. Ty's yelling at me to get off the phone. We have reservations for a couples' massage and then we're heading to the airport for our flight to Jamaica. I love you."

"I love you too, babe. Be safe and call me when you get to Negril."

"I will. And have fun with Jeremy! Bye."

By twelve o'clock Jeremy still wasn't back. After an hour of television, claustrophobia set in. Retrieving her latest issue of *Cosmo* from her car and a glass of water from the kitchen, she dragged one of the beach chairs off his back deck and placed it in a sunny patch on the lawn.

Tall sycamore trees offered a bit of privacy. There wasn't a neighbor for at least a quarter mile. Looking around one last time to make sure she was alone, she hiked up her shorts and stretched out her legs.

Somewhere in the middle of the *40 Girlie Moves that make Guys Melt* article, gravel crunched and Jeremy's Jeep pulled in the driveway. She shaded her eyes from the sun as he walked around the corner holding a tool kit.

"Well, that's a nice sight to come home to."

Self-consciously, she stood and unrolled her shorts to cover her thighs.

"Don't cover those beautiful legs on my account." He swaggered closer and placed a soft kiss on her mouth.

Her body hummed with pleasure. "Where were you?"

"Your place."

She stilled. "What? Why?"

"You said you needed a new lock, so I installed one. You left your keys by your purse so I borrowed them. Here's your new key."

She took the keys, not quite understanding her irritation. "Wow, I didn't realize you were in such a hurry to get rid of me." But that wasn't it. She was more annoyed that someone went into her home while she was unconsciously oblivious—again. It didn't matter that it was Jeremy.

His brows lowered. "No hurry, I just wanted you to feel safe in your apartment."

"Oh." Was that all? Well, perhaps he could replace her memory too while he was fixing things. Then she'd be good to go. "Thanks." He did her a favor, after all. There was no reason to be bitchy about it.

"Did you have lunch?" He picked up a small toy Mia must have left in the grass.

"No, I would've made something, but I didn't know when you were coming back."

"I left a note."

"Where?"

"On the fridge. Said I was going to run some errands and I'd be back around lunch. I guess you didn't get it. Sorry."

"That's okay. I kept myself busy." She followed him into the house.

"Doing what?"

"Nothing much. Took a shower, watched some TV, talked to Kat."

He gave her an unsure look. "Did you tell her about us?"

"Yes." She typically told Kat everything. She could keep their relationship a secret from Mia, but Kat ... no way. "I didn't go into detail, but I told her there's been some kissing."

His gaze skated to the counter. "What did she say?"

Aw, he was nervous. How cute.

"What do you think she said, Jeremy? She's my best friend. She's known how I feel about you for a long time and she's married now. Sorry to burst your bubble, but I think she's over you. She was happy for us."

He looked relieved and then took a slow step toward her. Wrapping his arms around her waist he pulled her close and pressed his face into the curve of her neck. Her insides buzzed with tingling excitement.

"A long time, huh?"

"Don't act like you didn't know." Rolling her eyes, she playfully shoved him, but he only tightened his grip. "I'm sure you had a good old time towing me along for the past twelve months."

"I didn't 'tow' you along. I was waiting for the right moment."

"And that moment happened to be when I was all snotty and teary, having a breakdown in your Jeep?"

"Well, yeah, I picked up on some signals. Clearly, your yearning had driven you to a state of emotional delirium. It was that, and, I guess when you tried to break my nose. All serious come-hither moves on your part."

She laughed. "You're an ass."

His lips pressed to hers. "You like it."

It was true. His ass was very likable. "Feed me, Seymour."

"As you wish."

They had a quick lunch of deli sandwiches and chips. "I'm noticing a trend here. Your culinary skills are very bachelor."

He shrugged. "I can do the basics."

"One day I'm going to make you a real meal." First, she'd have to figure out some recipes, but the idea of cooking for him seemed domestically sexy.

After lunch, she, unfortunately, had to get ready

for work. She wanted to get in early to see if there had been any headway with her lab work. Her shift started in an hour and she used up an additional twenty minutes making out with Jeremy at the front door. It was the best goodbye she'd ever had.

"Call me when you're done work," he insisted.

"It'll be late."

He gave her a stern look. "Call me. As a matter of fact, stay with me again tonight."

Her smile trembled. "Yeah?"

He gave her a slow kiss. "Yeah."

"O—okay."

As she pulled away her heart fluttered like a leaf stuck in the windshield wiper of a speeding car. She was so gone for him. She truly hoped he was at least half as gone for her.

Twelve

KEYING in the last encoded link, Jeremy signed off the computer and stretched in his chair. After a fairly productive afternoon getting three case objectives checked off his upgrade list, he finally let his thoughts wander to Jade.

When he'd been in her apartment to fix the locks that morning he hadn't noticed anything out of place. However, her apartment wasn't an area he typically visited so he didn't know what qualified as normal. Usually, people's homes felt like the person. Her condo should have been warm, welcoming, cozy, and happy, but that wasn't what he sensed.

The building had been eerily quiet. He wasn't trying to be a stalker, but his protective nature insisted he check things out and take a tour.

A rinsed dish sat in the sink, her bed was unmade, and her clothing actually wore a fine layer of dust where they lay on the floor. The shower tiles were dry and a stale. Un-lived-in scents masked her softer fragrance. Homes usually smelled like food, soap, cleaning products, or pets. Jade's smelled ... empty.

Her locks were shit, with a hairpin catch and loose hardware. He'd replaced it with an industrial deadbolt and an inner/outer key knob. He also tightened up the weather stripping and replaced the bolts on the hinges.

If she still wasn't ready to go back, she could stay with him. He had no problem keeping her in his bed. But the real concern was with her vague explanations for her strange behavior lately.

Jade wasn't a skittish woman and something had really scared her. Losing a debit card didn't match the sort of anxiety she was showing.

Digging in his cabinets, he found a can of tomato soup and pulled out a pot, finding it sweet the way Jade left the lid right on top. It was odd having someone other than Mia in his house. He'd built it with only his daughter in mind. And every time he found a trace of Mia's presence a sort of warmth filled him. Now he was finding traces of Jade and he liked that just as much.

Jade teased him about his decorating, which really couldn't be considered decorating at all. If he saw something girlie, pink, and sporting a princess, he picked it up for Mia. Other than that, his color scheme was white and beige. Some walls weren't painted with anything more than primer.

His carpets were neutral and his furniture was selected with only necessity in mind.

Stirring the soup, he flipped his grilled cheese sandwich. He should probably get some more food in the fridge besides Mia's snacks, mac 'n cheese, and cold cuts. What did girls eat?

Retrieving a beer, he examined the empty shelves. Girls liked healthy stuff. Next time he went to the store he'd grab some yogurt and produce so she didn't think he was living off beer and takeout.

What would Mia think if she found out he and Jade were semi-dating? She'd go nuts. His daughter loved Jade and Jade loved Mia, yet something had him adamantly deciding to keep their relationship a secret from Mia for as long as possible.

People broke up because of dumb shit all the time. He couldn't risk Mia getting attached and things falling through. He wanted something monogamous with Jade, but as far as longevity ... he wasn't sure they could make this work.

Biting into his sandwich, he let his mind drift to the future. Maybe it could work. Maybe she was *The One.*

They had something good. Real good. Their chemistry was off the charts. She was girlie as hell, but not overly sensitive—aside from her little outburst the other night. She usually rolled with the punches and he liked that.

Then there was her beauty. Green, mesmerizing eyes that clouded with lust when she was aroused and bounced with laughter when she broke his balls. He could stare into those eyes for days.

He frowned, recalling how devastated she'd been the night of the wedding. Her eyes had been so vacant that night, deep pain hidden in the simmering depths. He wished she'd confide in him a little more, but they were still new and he shouldn't rush things.

Whatever had upset her, he understood it was a personal matter. Maybe something to do with her family? He wanted to protect her, fix whatever got her so worked up, but the most he could do was let her stay here, listen when she spoke, and replace her locks so she would feel safe in her home. It was a start.

For a guy who didn't relish drama, he sure was a sucker for Jade in distress. So used to her boisterous independence, seeing her sad knocked the wind out of him. It made her more ... human, less intimidating.

He hadn't spent the night with a woman since returning from Iraq. It was too risky. But with Jade, he wanted more than a booty call. He wanted to hold her and wake up beside her. So long as he woke up like a normal guy and not some PTSD tragedy.

Gasping out of sleep in a cold sweat, muscles tense, ready to fucking kill someone was not the guy he wanted to show Jade. Scrambled fucking dreams were not something men cry about, especially not in front of a woman who never seemed to flinch when life took a swing.

But seeing that she had her own demons to fight—whatever they were—gave him the confidence to chance her seeing him in that unfavorable light. Who wasn't a little broken at this stage of life? He had to remind himself that no one was perfect and if she did see the scars he hid inside, she might not flinch then either. He believed she wouldn't.

Jade was tough, but not invincible. Her sarcasm kept people at a distance. Having her open up to him, show a bit of her vulnerability the other night, enhanced his desire tenfold. It made him feel special, important, knowing she didn't share those sides of herself with just anyone. His protective instincts kicked in and the urge to shelter her from further distress hit hard.

Pushing his plate away, he looked at his watch. Only a few more hours until midnight. He liked having her in his home, in his bed. The house already seemed a little empty without her, but she'd be back soon.

His body hardened with anticipation. He needed to blow off some steam so he headed to the basement for a late night work out. Soon enough she'd be back, and for reasons he didn't want to identify just yet, that made him incredibly happy. Locks fixed or not, he liked having her with him.

Thirteen

LILY'S TEXT hit Jade's phone halfway through her shift.

Meet me in my office in 30.

With shaky hands, Jade placed her phone back in the pocket of her scrubs and tried not to throw up. Her lab results were obviously in like Derek promised they'd be by the end of her shift. But why didn't Lily just text her that everything was fine? How the hell was she supposed to wait thirty minutes?

She swung by the reception desk. "Hey, Rachel. Do you know where Dr. Bishop is?"

The intern referred to her chart. "Um... Oh,

she's down in the OR. She just finished a C-section and they're wrapping up."

Damn it. "Okay. Thanks. I'm going to take my break."

The minutes passed at an excruciating slow pace. She was starving—and anxious—so she destroyed three slices of pizza and tried to pass the time playing *Candy Crush* on her phone.

She tried to keep busy as long as possible, but couldn't take the waiting anymore so she took the elevator to Lily's office. Luckily, she was returning from the maternity ward just as Jade stepped onto her corridor.

Lily smiled. "Perfect timing. How are you feeling?"

She took the smile as a good sign and relaxed. "Much better than I was two days ago."

"Good." She shut the door and waved Jade to a seat as she settled in behind her desk. "Did you happen to visit that place we talked about?"

She shook her head. "I'm going to file a report after my shift."

"Good. Do you need a friend to go with you?"

One hurdle at a time. "Was there something wrong with my test results, Lily?"

She folded her hands and took a slow breath. "Well, I have some good news for you. All your labs came back clean as a whistle."

A gust of air blew out of her lungs in a full body exhale. The relief was immense. "Oh, thank God."

"However, I'd like to run an additional tests. It's probably nothing, but just to be sure—"

"But you said everything came back clean." Her back knotted with tension.

"You tested negative for all the STD screenings, but I noticed something in your blood work that needs a second look."

She sank deeper into the chair. "What is it?"

"You're perfectly healthy, Jade, but your hCG levels are a little high."

Her mind rapidly shifted through a mental glossary of medical terms. *hCG, hCG?* She was at a loss but knew she'd used the term before. Human Chemical, no, not chemical... Human Chorionic Guh, Gun, Gonadotrophin. Yes, that was it! Human Corionic Gonadotrophin.

Oh fuck... "*Oh Fuck.*" Her wide eyes stared at her friend. "You think I'm *pregnant?*"

"Like I said, it could be nothing. That's why I want to run a second test."

She couldn't breathe. "No. No, no, no, no. Lily, I *can't* be pregnant!"

Rounding the desk, she gripped her hand. "Jade, take a deep breath. You might not be. The blood work was done too early to be sure. I noticed a slightly higher level than normal, but not enough to be a true positive. We can take your blood right now and run it down to Derek at the lab. He can have your results in a matter of minutes. Don't stress yourself out until you have all the facts."

"Lily! What am I going to do if I'm pregnant?"

She was going to throw up. Jade bent over until her head was between her knees, swallowing great gulps of air that didn't seem to reach her lungs.

Her peripheral vision flickered as a tingly sensation chased over her skin. Her name vaguely registered in the distance as her ears made a strange wobbly sound.

Breathe—

~

Mmm, cozy.

She reached for Jeremy, but her hand gripped air. A tiny beep echoed in the distance. Did she have a voicemail? Where was her phone? Why were her eyes so heavy?

"Sweetie?" Whose voice was that? "I think she's coming around. Jade, sweetie, can you hear me?"

Who *was* that? Angelic. It was a familiar voice, soft and gentle, maternal, but not her mother's. It lacked that Jewish, Long Island twang.

"Jade, can you open your eyes?" The voice had the effect of a lullaby, making it harder to force herself awake. "Can you say something?"

Jade hummed. "Long Island is neither long nor an island. Discuss amongst yourselves."

"Is she high?" a male voice asked.

"Oh, do shut up, Derek. Jade, sweetie, open your eyes for me."

Her lashes fluttered and quickly shut them against the light. "Bright," she grumbled, trying again.

Lily leaned over her with a smile. "Good morning, sleepy head."

"Where am I?" Jade squinted at the fluorescent light.

"You fainted in my office."

"Oh God…" Jade moaned and rolled to her side. Pieces of her last conversation came hurtling back to her and she wanted to be unconscious again.

"Derek, can you give us some privacy?" Lily asked and a door clicked. "Jade, honey, look at me."

"I don't want to," she moaned into the cot.

"Have it your way then, I'll talk to your bum. While you were unconscious we ran some more tests."

At that, Jade turned to gage Lily's expression. Blank.

"Should I sit up for this?"

"No, I think you're safer lying down." A sympathetic curve turned her lips. "Jade, honey, you're pregnant."

Fourteen

"AND THAT'S how I ended up here with you," Jade told Trixie.

The beagle lay resting its chin on Jade's lap, sharing a pint of *Ben & Jerry's Cherry Garcia* in Kat and Tyson's bed. After Jade's second episode at the hospital, she was sent home. Well, not home. She didn't want to go home and Lily didn't want her to be alone.

Crises have a way of improving one's ability to bend the truth. Needing to get away from people in general, she looked her friend in the eye and lied, swearing she was going straight to Jeremy's and wouldn't be alone. Yeah, right. She couldn't face anyone, let alone him.

Jeremy expected her at his place around midnight, but that was long over. It was now two a.m. and she had three voicemails and several missed calls she had no intention of returning. She was hiding.

After leaving work, picking up the essential life crisis ice cream flavors and startling the hell out of Tyson's sister when she called about the dog in the middle of the night, Jade tearfully explained everything to Trixie. The dog didn't have any advice but was a good listener.

She was pregnant. She tasted the word right along with the ice cream, but bitter resentment soured the sweet flavor.

Dear God, what was she going to do? She knew nothing about the father aside from him being a psychopath that preyed on unconscious women. Not his age, ethnicity, background, not even his name. Not only was she carrying this asshole's child, but her hair sample showed traces of benzodiazepine, one of the main ingredients of Rohypnol.

It was all so wonderfully romantic one could puke. Which she had. Several times since getting the news.

Her phone vibrated. Glancing at the screen she moaned. How was she ever going to explain this to him? It was fun while it'd lasted, but sadly it was over.

The idea that she'd never get the chance to actually make love to him built a sob in her throat, choking her, shaking her body to the core. Throwing her face into the pillows she wailed in despair, punching her fist into the bedding.

Why was this happening to her? The pain in

her chest was unbearable. Gasping through her fear, every emotion wrung out of her in an excruciating exorcism of hopeless acceptance. She sobbed until her voice was hoarse and her strength was depleted.

Focusing on nothing at all, her mind slowly quieted as numbness set in. It was a fitful rest, one in which she cried throughout. With no memory of shutting her eyes, her body jerked awake as Trixie barked like a maniac.

Her heart pranced in her chest, pummeling her ribs as she drew a pillow protectively to her chest. What was happening?

Disoriented and startled awake, she recoiled at the rumbling of heavy thunder mixing with the dog's angered barking and squinted at the empty ice cream container next to the alarm clock. 4:28 a.m. Then the banging continued and she realized it wasn't thunder.

Jade sluggishly rolled out of bed and cursed as she stubbed her toe on the nightstand. "Fuck!"

She hobbled to the window. Her gaze landed on the Jeep parked at the curb. *Shit.*

Taking the steps at a zombie's pace, she unlocked the front door. Jeremy's hand stopped mid-knock and he scowled, looking furious and disheveled.

"Tell me you're okay before I freak the fuck out," he growled.

With zero emotion left, she quietly said, "I'm okay."

"Why didn't you answer the fucking phone? I was worried sick!"

He barged into the house and she shut the door behind him.

"What the fuck, Jade? You don't tell someone you'll be at their house around midnight and never show up and then not even have the courtesy to call or answer the fucking phone! I called the hospital and they said you left *hours* ago! *Hours, Jade!* Where the hell have you been all night?"

"Here," she answered in a small voice.

Feeling exhausted, selfish, and small, she lacked the energy to face his rage. He obviously hadn't slept. He had every right to be furious.

It shouldn't be possible to feel more horrid than she already felt, but seeing how livid he was dropped her several layers beneath rock bottom. If only his concern could save her from the hell she was living.

He angrily forked his fingers through his hair as he paced the hall. "If you didn't want to see me, you could have said so. I called the cops."

"You called the cops?"

"Yes! For all I knew you were kidnapped or in a ditch. It never occurred to me you would be hiding out here all by yourself. What the fuck, Jade?"

"Kat needed someone to watch Trixie. Gloria's husband's allergic," she explained lamely.

"You could've brought the dog to my house!"

"Please stop yelling," she said in a small voice, staring at the ground.

The empty house echoed with the sound of his breathing. "Why didn't you call?"

"I didn't want to talk to anyone."

Still angry, but no longer yelling, he snapped, "Why the hell not?"

"I had a really, really bad day."

The tension syphoned out of the house and he seemed to look at her—really look at her—for the first time since barreling inside and demanding explanations. His hand reached for her brow and she pulled back before he could make contact. He scowled. "I was just checking to see if you have a fever. You look..."

She didn't want to hear how she looked. "I'm not sick."

He took another step closer and she retreated, maintaining the same distance. His jaw ticked. "What's going on, Jade? You're not acting like yourself."

"I can't do this right now, Jeremy. I'm sorry." He had no idea how sorry.

"Is this about your apartment? Your wallet being stolen?"

"No, not really."

"But it's somehow connected? Jade, you have to tell me what's going on with you."

Knowing her opportunity for diversion had passed, she shut her eyes and accepted what she had to do. So overwhelmed with sadness, she was physically ill. "Jeremy, I want you to leave."

His head snapped up as his gaze hardened. "What? Why?"

She squared her shoulders. "Because I can't do this. Us." Her chest tightened as her vision blurred, but she kept her voice stern. "It's not going to work."

"What are you talking about? Jade, we just need to set some ground rules—"

"No," she interrupted. "There'll be no ground rules. There'll be no working this out. You don't have to worry about where I go because there will be no us."

His shoulders bunched and released with each labored breath. "Why are you doing this?"

"My reasons are my own business. I'm sorry, but I just..."

She'd wanted him for so long and in the short time she had him, she realized he was more amazing than she'd ever imagined. A sob lodged in her throat and she swallowed it back.

"I just can't be with you."

"Jade—"

"You have to leave." He took another step toward her but paused when she, again, took a step back. If he touched her, she'd shatter. "Please go, Jeremy."

He shook his head. "Why won't you talk to me? Jade, don't—"

She turned away and opened the door with an unsteady hand. "It's over, Jeremy."

His brow creased as his lips thinned. His voice

was reed thin as he stared at her, confusion filling his eyes. "Why are you doing this?"

Lowering her face to hide her tears, she waited for him to accept that this was the way it had to be.

Leaning close to her ear, he voice hardened into a cruel hiss. "You're a coward, Jade Schultz. You don't deserve my time if you can't even find the courage to be honest with yourself, let alone me. You want to keep secrets, play games, and alienate yourself from everyone who cares about you for anything more than a quick fuck? Fine."

Her eyes closed as she refused to argue with him. If only he knew how deeply his words stabbed her already punctured heart. Any more holes and it might stop beating once and for all.

"Have a nice life." He slammed the door and she flinched.

Tires screeched in the quiet night and she numbly slid her back down the wall, crumbling to the floor in a heap.

She held her belly, surrendering to the agony ripping at her perforating heart. She gasped and sobbed until her sides ached.

Her arms wrapped around her torso as if to cover the undeveloped ears of the baby in her womb as she howled every hateful word she knew toward the bastard who, in one depraved moment, derailed her entire life.

"I fucking hate you..." Tears and snot formed rivers down her face into the collar of her shirt.

"What did you do to me?" She moaned, the weight of her condition sitting on her chest like a grand piano. "You ruined my life." Her hand swiped at her eyes and nose, but there was no stopping her tears. "I ... hate ... you," she sobbed. "I hate you."

Fifteen

BY NOON THE FOLLOWING DAY, the only productive thing Jade managed to do was call out of work. Around one, she made some soup only to let it grow cold. She couldn't eat. She couldn't sleep. She stared at nothing in particular for hours on end. She was utterly numb.

When Trixie occasionally scratched at the door she roused from her comatose state with barely the strength to hold up her head. There was nothing to do. She was pregnant.

Around six o'clock she managed to climb up the steps and crawl into bed. She didn't remember falling asleep. She didn't remember dreaming. She awoke around eight the next morning and ran to the bathroom, where she immediately vomited.

The painful, unending bout of heaving turned her hollow stomach inside out. She cried as she hugged the cool porcelain to her clammy cheek. How had this become her life?

Forcing herself to drink some water and eat a few saltines she fumbled from one room to the other, often finding herself somewhere she didn't recall walking to. The pattern continued, much the same, until Sunday.

It was all a blur, minutes feeling like days, hours fleeing by but leaving no memories in their wake. Eventually, she had to return to work, but at the moment she could barely function on a personal level. How could she possibly take care of others?

All she could do was sleep, the numbing pull of unconsciousness an anesthetic to her soul. And no matter how long she slept during the day, by nightfall she was still exhausted. She gave up. She didn't want to cry and she didn't want to try to make sense of an ugly fucked up situation that couldn't be justified. She just wanted to pain to stop and she wanted to be left the fuck alone.

~

A soft whimper escaped in her sleep. It had taken him two days, but he finally found her. She hadn't been going to work. Why? Was she ill? Keeping to the shadows, he studied her face in the pooling moonlight as she slept, curled on her side in yet another bed. Her eyes were swollen and her cheeks bore the dry tracks of tears.

His head tilted as a peculiar emotion twisted

in his stomach. It bothered him that she was sad. His fingers itched under his leather gloves to touch her, but not with barriers between them.

What if he ran a hand over her hair? Comforted her? Would she be terrified to see him there in her friend's house? Better to stay back.

The other man wasn't here with her, which was a relief. She shifted and he stilled, holding his breath as she rolled to her back. Her flaxen hair tangled across the pillow and, again, he was tempted to move closer, touch her.

His mind replayed their night together. It had been so easy.

After endlessly observing her, she'd become a bad habit he couldn't quit. Walking her out of the bar that night was a breeze. She was out cold by the time he put her in the car.

He had to touch himself on the drive to her place because the simple task of tightening the seatbelt over her body and feeling around for her keys had left him rock hard. Those full tits and curvaceous thighs. Her pussy tasted like the sweetest nectar. Her skin rivaled the softest silk. And when he shoved his cock deep in her cunt... His eyes rolled back on a silent sigh, his dick twitching hard against his zipper.

He needed to have her again. He wanted to hold her to him as he forced his cock down her throat. Watch her eyes tear as she struggled to take all of him. Maybe she'd beg—for him to stop, for more, it didn't matter. The word *please* on her full lips would be enough for him to shoot his load. God, he wanted to cover her in his come.

He peeked into the hall. The beagle was still busy devouring the steak he'd brought as a distraction.

Biting off one glove, he slowly lowered the zipper of his pants, each little tooth coming undone letting a risky moan into the silence. His cock pulsed in his grip as his eyes devoured her. He'd give anything to trace his dick across those lips again. Maybe see her tongue skate out and sample his flavor.

The other night had been beautiful. His hands molded her body as his cock filled her, pumping hard and harder still with not even a peep of objection from her pretty mouth. He'd held her soft hair in his fist, yanking her head back so he could see her. Like a glutton, once inside of her, he couldn't stop. He'd filled her with come, painted her skin with what seeped out of her cunt, rubbing it into her tits and over her tongue.

He grunted, his hand jerking faster as he stood in the shadows. Almost there.

He locked his jaw, silenced his breathing as he leaned into the wall. His gaze zeroed in on the curve of her breast, as he longed to pinch it hard. It was amazing how an unconscious body could still respond.

His spine twitched and his balls lifted. He reached to the dresser and quietly swiped a tissue. *Yes...* He swallowed a grunt as he emptied his load into the tissue and quickly shoved the evidence into his pocket.

Letting out a jagged breath, he ran his thumb over the crown of his dick, catching one last drop seeping from the tip. He was a fool, but he couldn't resist. Hiking up his zipper, he moved closer to the bed. God, she was stunning.

His thumb slowly reached out. "You're mine," he whispered, pressing the tip of the digit past her full lips onto the hot tip of her tongue.

Her face turned away and she rolled on her side. Time to go.

He paused as her shoulder caught his eye, the nightshirt slipping down her arm. The branding had been the difficult part. He'd planned to leave the mark on her thigh but decided against that placement just before he stamped the hot metal into her lily-white flesh. He wanted other men to see it, to know he'd been there before them—wanted her to think of him every day she saw it.

As a successful man with multiple degrees, a beautiful home, and plenty of money, all he was missing was a good woman—her. One day she'd be his. He'd make sure of it.

As she evenly breathed, he lingered another minute. Keeping his motions steady and his touch feather light, his fingertip traced her eyebrow, followed the curve of her cheek, and coasted over her lips.

He *would* have her again. But this time he'd be smart. This time she'd be the one to come to him. It would only take a matter of time before he got everything he wanted. He always got what he wanted.

Shutting his eyes he breathed in her scent one last time, reaffirming the memory. Walking quietly down the steps, he passed the dog. It should be waking within the hour from his special treat. He pulled the door closed behind him.

Sixteen

TRIXIE BARKED, springing off the bed. Jade was so weak the jostling sent fissures of pain shooting through her body. The dog bolted out of the room.

"Jade?"

She opened her eyes but made no move to uncover her face from the blankets and pillows. The mattress dipped. Turning stiffly, she found Kat looking at her with concern and Tyson standing tall behind her, appearing worried as well. The dog raced around the room, howling with excitement to have her people back.

"Are you sick?" Kat asked.

No matter how much she wanted to put her troubles aside and lose herself in her friends' romantic adventures, there was no hiding the pain welling up inside of her. A tear escaped and rolled into her matted hair.

"Jade, honey, what's wrong?"

When she tried to talk all that came out was a raw sob. Kat pulled her into a hug, rocking and soothing much like a mother does with for her child, and Jade cried in earnest.

"Jade, what's happened? Do you need a doctor?" Easing her back, Kat looked into her eyes. "You're pale and your eyes are puffy. You're a wreck."

"I'm so glad you're home," she bawled and Kat continued to hold her.

The thought of having so much to explain exhausted her before she spoke a single word. There was nothing Kat could do to change her circumstances, but having her near was the most comfort she'd felt in days.

As her cries dwindled to shivers and shuddered breaths, she shut her eyes and rested against her friend's lap. It was a closeness she needed, one she couldn't get from anyone else.

When she awoke again, it must've been in the middle of the night. Kat was sleeping in a chair next to the bed and Tyson was gone. Numbness set into her hip and she forced herself to sit up.

"You're awake," Kat whispered. Her grim expression showed in the shadows. Jade's outburst had obviously scared her. "Do you want some water?"

She took the glass from Kat's hand and greedily swallowed its contents. When she finished, it was too late. "Oh, God—"

Stumbling from the bed, she bolted for the

bathroom. Her knees crashed down on the tile floor as she clung to the cool ceramic bowl and puked.

Minutes later, water was running and a cool damp cloth pressed to her brow as she rested her clammy face against the now warming seat of the toilet. She opened her eyes and found Kat kneeling beside her and Tyson standing at the door.

"Jade, I think you need to go to the hospital," Kat whispered.

"No," she rasped.

Kat looked at Tyson then back to her. "Ty, see if you can find some crackers and Ginger ale. See if we have tea, too. If we do, make a cup and add some of the soda to it."

Once Tyson left, Kat helped her stand. Jade braced her palms on the vanity of the sink and winced at her reflection.

Her hair was a rat's nest and her skin was paper white. Crescent shaped bruises hung like hammocks under her eyes and her cheeks were sunken in. No wonder Kat was so concerned. She looked half-dead and she smelled fully there.

"I need a shower," she croaked, her throat raw. She hadn't spoken more than a few words in days and her esophagus burned from bile.

Kat turned on the shower and adjusted the temperature. As the room filled with swirls of steam, Jade pulled off her pants. As she twisted her arm through the strap of her tank top she froze.

There, in the reflection on the mirror, was the stain of her predicament. The small, angry pucker was beginning to heal and she would be forever branded a victim.

She wanted to claw the mark from her flesh. *Fucking motherless whore—cock sucking, scum bag...* Her vocabulary failed her. There was no word vile enough to describe the monster that had done this to her.

The ever-present dip and swell that came with thinking of him turned her stomach. Like attempting to thread a needle when too blind to see the hole, she would never have the satisfaction of rightness again. There would be no closure, no justice.

She breathed through her teeth. No one could fix this. *No one.*

Kat held her arm as she stepped under the spray. Too exhausted to stand, she lowered herself to the floor. Kat adjusted the plug and switched the water flow to the bath faucet.

As the warm water filled the tub, Kat gently washed her hair, pouring a Cookie Monster cup over her shoulders and chest. When she rinsed the remainder of shampoo away she pulled Jade's hair behind her shoulders and stilled.

Her fingers tentatively touched Jade's shoulder and Jade flinched, her shoulders curling inward. A myriad of emotions played across Kat's face as she ran her fingers gingerly over the abused tissue.

Shaking, Jade whispered, "Do you know what it means?"

As her best friend shook her head a crushing

disappointment broke another part of her meager reserves. They finished her bath in utter silence.

A little while later, she sat at the kitchen table across from Kat while Tyson made coffee. It was time.

Jade took a deep breath and finally spoke the truth she'd been hiding from. "I don't want you to tell anyone what I'm about to tell you. If you can't give me your word, then I can't confide in you."

Kat nodded and looked at Tyson, who hesitated but also nodded.

"The night of your rehearsal dinner, Jeremy and I went to the Pink Lounge afterwards for a drink. I only had a few drinks that entire night and was by no means drunk. Jeremy left around nine o'clock, just after I got your text about picking up your ring. I was supposed to leave shortly after him, but I don't remember getting home. I can't remember anything after getting your text."

Kat frowned. "How did you drive if you can't remember getting to your car?"

"I don't know. The next morning I woke up in my apartment and knew something wasn't right. It didn't take long to realize someone had broken into my home. My purse was dumped all over the floor and my wallet was totally empty."

Tyson shifted closer to the table, his eyes as dark as storm clouds. "Did you call the cops?"

"That was the least of my concerns at the time. I knew someone had been there. My door was wide open and..." She took a deep breath, her voice seizing. "And ... I could ... I could feel them ... on me. In me. And then... They marked me."

Kat's head snapped up, her eyes lit with stark fear. If her friend said anything she'd lose her nerve to finish and she still had more to say, so she quickly continued.

"My only thought was to get clean. I didn't even think about ... about going to the hospital until it was too late. The day after your wedding I finally saw Dr. Bishop and had some lab work done. Luckily, all my results came back negative. They took a sample of my hair, as well, and found Rohypnol in my system, which explains why I can't remember anything."

"Jesus," Tyson hissed.

"In the meantime, Jeremy put a new lock on my door, but I only told him I was robbed. The funny thing is they only took what was in my wallet. They didn't touch anything else. It was like ... like they wanted a souvenir."

"Oh, Jade," Kat breathed, her eyes shimmering with unshed tears.

"I'm not finished." Jade took a shaky breath. "I thought... I thought if I was alive and I replaced all my credit cards, I could get over it like it never happened. I even spent time with Jeremy. I felt safer with him and memories of the ... attack faded when he was nearby, but my awareness of what happened never disappeared and it turns out I'm much more fucked up than I ever imagined possible. Aside from the mark on my shoulder, there's no real proof of it, certainly not in my memory at least. But my thinking is totally damaged. I'm not right. I don't know if I'll ever be right again."

"Oh, Jade..." Twin tears fell down Kat's cheeks.

"What mark?" Tyson's scowl pressed deep crevasses into his face.

Jade pulled her collar aside and he cursed.

"Is that a fucking burn?"

"You don't remember anything?" Kat overrode Tyson's question.

"I can't remember one single detail after Jeremy left and, *believe me*, I tried. I thought I could beat it, but I was wrong. Last time I was at work, Lily ran some more tests. All my blood work came back good, but she noticed something else. It turns out ... I..."

Jade couldn't get the words out. Trembling, tears ran unchecked down her face.

Kat took her hands in hers and squeezed. "Honey, whatever it is, we're here for you."

Letting the last of her boundaries fall, she whispered, "I'm ... pregnant."

Stunned, her friend's confidence visibly faltered. She pulled her into a fierce hug as they wept together.

"What am I going to do?" Jade whimpered.

Kat smoothed her hand over her hair and whispered, "It hasn't even been two weeks. Maybe it was a false positive."

"No, I saw my lab work. It's early, but I'm definitely pregnant."

"You don't have to keep it," Tyson said softly. "You have a choice in this, Jade."

"I have so much going through my head right now. I don't even know how I feel about that option." She wiped her eyes with the heel of her palm. The soft skin surrounding her lashes was chafed from crying so much.

"Did your doctor talk to you about your options?" Kat asked.

"She may have. I was in shock. I can't really remember what she said past me being pregnant. After that, I came here and went to bed. I've been sleeping for days."

"You haven't been out of bed since you found out? You should've called me."

"And what, ruin your honeymoon? No, this is my problem."

"That's bullshit." Kat swearing meant she was seriously upset. "We're your closest friends. We'll do whatever you need us to do. For starters, you can stay here as long as you need. Right, Ty?"

"Right. Did you tell Jeremy any of this?"

"No." The horrible empty feeling in her chest exploded as the last words he said to her echoed through her mind.

"Is it..." Tyson hesitated. "Is it possible the baby could be his?"

"No. We never slept together. Besides, Jeremy has nothing to do with this. After I came here we had a huge fight and broke up. I'm pretty sure he doesn't care about my problems or me anymore. He made that quite clear before he left."

Kat sighed. "I'm sure that's not true. Why don't you give Tyson your keys so he can pick up some of your things before he gets Mia? You can wear my clothes, but I'm sure you want your own. In the meantime, you have to try to eat something."

After forcing down a cup of broth and some crackers, Jade headed back upstairs. Kat insisted she use their room until she made up the guest room. As she walked the steps she paused and listened as Kat and Ty discreetly whispered.

"Jesus Christ," Tyson hissed. "The fucker drugged her, raped her, robbed her, and then felt the need to *brand* her? What kind of twisted fuck does that? Kat, you have to convince her to go to the police and talk her into getting an abortion."

"I am not going to press her, Tyson. About anything. It's her body and that baby is as much hers as it is the father's. Yes, how it got there is despicable and ugly, but I'm not going to try to convince her to do anything that'll add to the weight on her shoulders, including going to the police. Do you know how unlikely it is they'll ever find this guy? It'll just upset her more and she already looks like she's a tear away from a total breakdown. When she's ready, she'll go. But, right now, I'm not going to tell her what to do."

"She knows nothing about the father except the fact that he's a criminal and a predator."

"I don't care," Kat snapped. "When I was pregnant with Mia, Jade was the only person who respected my right to make up my own mind in the time frame *I* needed to decide. She deserves the same, and I, for one, will not take that away from her. Besides, she's been through enough. Ending a pregnancy is not a simple solution. It's complicated and extremely emotional. I'm not sure she could bear such consequences after everything else she's been through. I've never seen her like this before."

Tyson sighed and Jade couldn't listen to any more. She needed silence. Silence from their opinions. Silence from her thoughts. The only way to find that sort of quiet was through sleep. She trudged quietly up the stairs.

JADE TURNED the channel as a diaper commercial came on. A few minutes later she changed it again as a *Gerber* commercial played.

Have there always been so many baby commercials?

She needed to distract herself with television while Kat was on the phone—asking all the questions Jade was too afraid to ask her OBGYN.

When she returned to the living room with a pad of paper in hand, she sat on the ottoman across from Jade and muted the TV. "Okay, here are your options." She flipped back a page in her notebook.

That was Kat. She could divide and conquer the world, so long as she had a list to keep her organized.

"There's a Clinic about an hour from Parkside that performs ... that can make this all go away.

You don't have to make up your mind right now. You have about five weeks, longer even, but the longer you wait, the more *involved* the procedure becomes. I'm not suggesting you do that. I just want you to have all the facts. Whatever you choose, I'll support you."

"Did you ask Lily what it involves?" She wasn't leaning one way or another, but being informed about every option seemed wise.

"From what I understand, it's a fairly quick procedure and you can either be awake or asleep. The recovery's about two weeks and afterward, there's mild bleeding and cramping. Three weeks after the procedure there's a post-procedure check-up. It isn't uncommon to experience intense depression. Dr. Bishop gave me a list of counselors she recommends if you choose to do this, and one she thinks you should make an appointment with simply because of the trauma you've already suffered."

Kat paused, her eyes measuring Jade's expression. She couldn't guess what her friend saw because on the inside Jade was dead. "Go on."

Sighing, Kat flipped to the next page of her list. "Another option's adoption. There are basically three different types. You could go through Social Services, but the baby may have to live in foster care for a time and may never get placed with a permanent family. However, you'd reserve the right to change your mind for an extended period of time."

"What else?"

"You could go through a placement facility, like Christian Services, but they have final say in the family. The third is private adoption, where you use an attorney and select the family yourself. That option gives you the most control, but all options come at a cost. The placement service is pricey unless the chosen family picks up the expense, but we'll help you if that's what you want." Kat took a deep breath. "Do you have any idea what you're leaning toward?"

"You and Mia," Jade softly whispered. "You two managed to make it with nothing more than your promise to love and protect her. This baby ... it didn't ask for this any more than I did."

"No, it didn't."

"Who am I, Kat? I'm twenty-three years old, a nurse, I have an apartment, a car, over fifteen thousand dollars in the bank, the start of a decent pension, and I'm not in any sort of serious relationship. I have to cope with this no matter what I choose—that's become painfully clear. There's no easy way out. And ending the pregnancy might be the one thing that destroys me once and for all."

Reaching for a tissue, Kat blew her nose. "I'm so sorry we can't make this easier for you."

Jade blinked, a strange sense of numbness blanketing her. "I'll probably never be the same person again, regardless of what I choose. Maybe this baby is the one innocent thing in this whole ugly mess. Who am I to decide whether it lives or dies?"

Kat blinked, her damp lashes flickering, and

affectionately squeezed her knee. "You're the definition of strength, Jade. Whatever you choose, I know you'll come through this one way or another. Think about it a little longer and when you're sure, we'll be there for you. No judgment, just love."

"Thank you."

The front door opened and Kat stood as Tyson came into the living room, Mia running in after him. "Momma!"

Kat held out her arms and, as if she had wings, Mia flew into her embrace as she squealed with laughter. "Hey, princess. I missed you."

"I missed you more!"

Jade listened as Mia detailed her week at her grandparents' and asked what souvenirs they'd brought her. As Kat went to the kitchen to retrieve a bag of foreign treasures for her daughter, Mia gave Jade a hug she desperately needed and then climbed onto Tyson's lap and kissed his dark, bald head.

When Kat returned, she, Mia, and Tyson sat together opening gifts on the floor. The family moment unfolded with perfect chaos. Like a voyeur, she took vicarious pleasure in their joy, coveting the magic within their intimate family that outsiders didn't often see.

Tyson tickled Mia and she giggled, her musical laughter a balm to Jade's battered soul. "Tyson, can I call you Daddy now that you're married to Momma?"

"You can call me whatever you want, princess."

Mia smiled, gripping both his dark cheeks and pressing her brow to his. "Okay, Daddy."

In that moment all the puzzle pieces seemed to slide into perfect order. Here was Tyson, in love with not just Kat, but her daughter as well, making what seemed the perfect family. Yes, Mia's father was in their lives, but a year ago he wasn't and Kat still managed to find her happily ever after. Maybe there was a happily ever after for everyone, no matter what circumstances needed to be crossed to get there.

Her hand slowly slid to her abdomen, pressing ever so slightly as a sense of warmth enveloped her. That was her baby in there, no one else's. Years from now, no one would question her. She could just be another single mom. A strong mom. And, like Kat, she wanted to love and protect her baby better than anyone else ever could.

Kat's gaze connected with hers and she stilled. Jade slowly nodded and her friend smiled. Knowing she had her support solidified Jade's decision. She wasn't just pregnant. She was going to have a baby. Making that decision, feeling that she actually had a choice, was the most in control emotion she'd had in days.

Eighteen

OVER THE NEXT EIGHT WEEKS, Jade came to terms with her situation as much as one could expect. She'd notified her landlord that she would be moving and temporarily moved into Kat and Tyson's home while Tyson painted the cottage down the street. Kat's old rental property was the perfect location. It was in a good school district, the landlord was an old friend, there was a great babysitter in the neighborhood, and it was only two houses away from her best friend. It was the safest place she could go.

Jade took Lily's referral and was slowly working through her issues with Dr. Chloe Wolfe, a family therapist who specialized in post traumatic stress. Dr. Wolfe was a godsend with a natural gift for listening.

Jade expected the therapist to do exercises to

help jog her memory, but Dr. Wolfe wasn't interested in that. She was more concerned with helping Jade cope with the after-effects of the assault. The frustrating fragments of her memories would always be there. Sometimes they hit her with sharp, shocking force and other times they rested quietly in the background.

Dr. Wolfe was training her to prepare for the days ahead. And Jade found herself anxious to stop dwelling on the past.

Therapy helped Jade emotionally prepare for the many ways her life would change once the baby arrived. As a small baby bump took shape, her concern turned to her parents. Dr. Wolfe was also helping her find the courage to finally tell them she was pregnant.

They spoke a lot about anxiety, from that night, in regard to her parents, the inevitable approach of *becoming* a parent, but most of all they talked about Jeremy. The heartache she still felt from pushing him away never seemed to fade.

Living at Kat's created some awkward moments when Jeremy came to pick up or drop off Mia. The first time he stopped by, Jade hid in the shadows at the top of the stairs and listened—hoping he'd somehow come to forgive her for all the things he didn't understand.

"Is she here?" he asked Kat.

"Yes, but she's resting."

"What's going on with her, Kat? I'm worried."

"It's not my place to say, Jeremy. I'm sorry."

"Is she okay?" His voice cracked. "None of

this makes any sense."

"She'll be okay. She just needs time."

"I just... I just don't understand what happened. She didn't even give us a chance."

"Maybe she gave you all she could right now."

"Why, though? Why start something she had no intention of finishing? I need to speak to her."

Jade drew back and Kat hardened her tone. "Jeremy—"

"Is she up there?" The shuffling of his shoes whispered in the foyer. "Jade?" The echo of his voice set another crack in her heart.

"Jeremy." Kat repeated his name in her stern mother voice.

"I just want to know that she's okay. The things I said to her..."

Jade's hand covered her mouth as her chest ached. She wanted to go to him, but nothing had changed. She couldn't be with him and the idea of telling him everything that happened destroyed something inside of her. She didn't have confidence to spare right now and baring her soul to him might steal the last scrap of her delicate self-worth.

"She's okay, but you can't push her, Jeremy."

"I need to hear it from her. She won't even take my calls."

"I'm sorry, but this is how it has to be right now. You have to respect her privacy."

For as traumatic as her situation was, she was managing it—every day, every hour, it was baggage she never put down. The only thing she couldn't bear was the pain of losing Jeremy. It was an ache that consumed her heart and wouldn't heal.

The only distraction, aside from going to work, was the rapidly developing affection for the one person who would soon be her everything. Her child.

Her life had been overhauled by this pregnancy and she welcomed the simplicity of her new routine. Sometimes stillness was good, Dr. Wolfe had come to teach her. Jade embraced the still moments between work and the daily grind. And she seemed to be evolving on some fundamental level she didn't know she possessed.

Her job—now day shifts—had always been a satisfying part of her life, but it was no longer enough to fill the void of all the missing pieces. It was a great distraction, a place to build confidence and serve a purpose that helped others. But no one at work, aside from Lily, knew the battle she fought silently on a daily basis. Everything was changing.

She developed a serious aversion to poultry, had an unhealthy relationship with peanut butter, and found a new level of bliss in napping. Whenever there was a chance to sleep, Jade took it. Every night around eight-thirty, she took her prenatal vitamins, chugged a glass of milk, and headed to bed. It was perfectly acceptable because Mia was keeping the same schedule.

As she sat outside in the cooling autumn weather, enjoying the subdued sunlight while waiting for Kat to finish in the shower, Jade thought about Jeremy. Her mind always went back to him.

It was an indulgence she rarely allowed herself. She missed seeing his smile, missed his humor, his kisses, his strength, and his friendship. She missed *him*.

His calls came less and less often as the weeks passed, which was for the best. Along with the heartache of losing Jeremy, came the guilt for hurting him. Sooner or later he'd meet someone new and forget all about her—a gutting hypothetical that would eventually be reality.

But today was not the day to dwell on heartache. In a few hours, she was going to her first *official* OB appointment with Lily. She was going to hear her baby's heartbeat for the first time.

"You ready?" Kat asked as she opened the sliding door.

Jade glanced at her phone and frowned. "It's still early." Her appointment wasn't for another few hours.

"I know. I figured we could stop at that new maternity store before your appointment. I know you're picky about clothes, so I figured we better start shopping for your maternity wardrobe now."

She laughed. "You know me so well. I never turn down a chance for shopping."

They hit three stores, then a Mediterranean café for lunch. Jade was constantly eating or sleeping. Everything else came second. Her obsession with food replaced prior obsessions with shoes and purses, although, she did manage to snag a Coach diaper bag on clearance.

Just as she returned from the ladies room—peeing was also a new obsession—she noticed a shift in Kat's mood, which didn't make sense after such a delicious lunch and a morning of shopping.

As soon as she reached the table Kat gathered her purse and bags. "We're leaving."

"Are you okay—"

"Now," she snapped, tossing money on the table.

Jade grabbed her bags and followed her out the door. When they reached the sidewalk, a masculine voice called out. "Kat?"

Jade stopped, but her agitated friend continued briskly walking toward the car. The man called her name again and finally, Kat turned with fury in her eyes.

Whoa. Jade looked between the unfamiliar man following them to the sidewalk and her friend. "Kat, what's going on?"

Rather than answer, she tossed Jade the keys. "Do me a favor and wait for me in the car." Then she pivoted and walked back toward the restaurant.

Jade put the key in the lock and frowned. What was she, a dog? She wasn't waiting in the freaking car. Turning, she squinted at the man approaching Kat. He was average height, with brown hair, a neatly trimmed beard, and small, beady eyes.

In three charging steps Kat—a typically non-confrontational person—was in his face. *What the hell?*

"What do you want?"

Unsure what to do, Jade left the car and sped to her friend's aide. The man leaned back and held up his hands in surrender as Kat railed at him.

"Kitty Kat, what's the matter? I just wanted to say hello."

Jade's lip curled at the purr in his voice. Ew. Just ew. Who was this douche-canoe?

Kat's face distorted with rage and darkened. "Do *not* call me that! My name is Katherine, but you can call me Mrs. Adams! You and the pack of vermin you keep company with are nothing more than a group of criminals. I should have you arrested!"

He held up his hands defensively. "Whoa, Kat, what are you talking about?" He seemed genuinely concerned with her stability, as was Jade, at the moment.

Kat viciously swatted his hand out of the way and he scowled. In a waspish tone, she snapped, "You know exactly what I'm talking about!"

"What the hell's your problem?"

Jade took a step forward, unsure what exactly was happening. A car sped to the curb behind her and a door opened and closed, but her eyes were glued to Kat and the man about to be assaulted by a woman half his size. People exiting the restaurant gathered at the sidelines, but that didn't stop Kat from making a scene.

"You! You're my problem!" she shouted, crowding him again. "I know what you do! I know all about your secrets!"

"You're insane!" With a humorless laugh, he gave up the pursuit of a friendly hello and turned back to the restaurant.

Kat viciously grabbed the sleeve of his suit jacket. "Where are you going? Afraid someone might notice?"

"Get your hands off me, you crazy bitch!"

Suddenly all hell broke loose. Out of nowhere, Jeremy was there, pushing the man and growling in his face. "Watch your mouth!"

Disoriented by his sudden appearance, Jade turned and realized it was his Jeep at the curb.

"Who the fuck are *you*?"

Rather than answer, Jeremy shoved him. "Apologize to the lady."

"No! I just wanted to say hello and she went ape shit. She's a whack job."

In a flash of movement too quick to track, Jeremy punched him in the face. The man bent his head and cursed. Kat yipped and jumped back a step just as Jade took another quick step forward.

"What the fuck's wrong with you people?"

"Apologize!" Jeremy barked.

"For what? I don't even know what she's upset about!"

Jeremy looked at Kat and then Jade. Jade shrugged and looked at Kat. Her friend's hands were clenched in trembling fists at her side. Never in her life had she seen her so angry.

"Kat?" Jeremy asked, perhaps wondering if he'd just punched an innocent man.

"You remember him, don't you, Jeremy? When you first returned and we were at the market together?" Jeremy looked back at the man and recognition seemed to dawn. He glanced back to Kat. "What did he do to you?"

"Look," the guy said, wiping a dab of blood from his lip. "I have no idea what's going on. I just—"

"Shut up!" Kat snapped. "I know you know something!"

"Know *what?*"

Eyes wild, Kat marched to Jade, who flinched as she grabbed the collar of her blouse. "Hey!"

"You know about *this!*" Kat yanked the collar aside. "*Don't* you?"

Time stood still. Jade's knees buckled as bile rose. The man stood completely motionless, his stare fixed on the tiny brand. Insurmountable rage boiled in her veins, as transparent recognition registered on his face.

Jade's lungs tightened, making it impossible to speak above a whisper. "You know about this?"

His eyes darted to hers then quickly away. *Shame.* She saw it, brief, but undeniable.

He knows.

He took a hasty step back, shaking his head as he opened and closed his mouth like a fish out of water. In a low voice, he said, "You're all crazy."

"Hey!" Jade called as he pivoted and rushed around the corner. Sheer panic sprang her into motion and she sprinted after him. *"Wait!"*

"Jade!" Jeremy yelled, but she wasn't stopping until she got some answers.

Her feet pounded over the paved sidewalk as she chased after him, snagging the back of his jacket just as Jeremy caught up with her.

"Get off me!" The man snapped, yanking out of her reach. "I'm done with this. If you don't desist I'll sue you for assault. I'm a lawyer, I know my rights."

"Your rights?" Delirium struck. *"Your rights!"* Shoving him with both hands he stumbled back. "What about *my* rights? Do you know something about this mark? Tell me! *Tell me!* Was it you? Did you do it? Did you have fun with me while I laid there like a dead animal?"

"Jesus, no! It wasn't me! I don't know what you're talking about." Tiny beads of sweat gathered on his brow.

"Fucking liar!" She shoved him again. Hysteria took over. *"Tell me!"*

"I don't know anything!"

"Why did this happen to me?" Gripping the collar of his jacket, she shook him with all her strength and screamed as strong arms dragged her off the man. *"Who are you?"*

"Enough!" Jeremy barked, restraining her. "I'm calling the cops."

"Go ahead. She'll be the one arrested."

An unholy growl left her throat as she lunged, only to come up short as Jeremy restrained her.

"Jade! You need to relax."

Her entire body shook. Giving the man her most severe glare she growled, spit gathering on her drawn lips. "Well, I know something you don't. Your little game … you fucked up. You see, it didn't break me. As a matter of fact, you left behind a crucial piece of evidence, and in seven months you'll be caught." Her hand covered her belly. "I've got all the evidence I need. I've got DNA. If you or your friends *ever* come within a breath of me or my child, I'll show you what it feels like to be a victim and, I'll make sure they're *awake* for every second of my revenge."

The man's face paled white as snow as her words sank in. Good.

Jade pivoted and stilled. Jeremy, also pale, stared at her with wide unblinking eyes. Then there was Kat, still a furious shade of red and shaking with anger. Jade didn't have time for this. She marched around the corner to the car. *She* had a heartbeat to hear.

Sliding into the passenger seat, she cranked the engine on and turned the AC on high, rubbing her belly affectionately. "Sorry. It's all right now."

Staring out the windshield, Jade committed the man's face to memory, waiting for something to click. Nothing. She didn't recognize the sound of his voice. There wasn't anything distinguishing in his scent or the sound of his voice. Seeing him, jogged nothing as far as fragmented memories went.

She glanced at the rearview mirror. The guy was gone and Kat was speaking to Jeremy. Kat was visibly upset, pressing her hand to her forehead as Jeremy wildly gestured with his hands. Kat's shoulders slumped and she placed a nurturing hand on her own belly.

Jade's brow pinched. Looking down, she gasped as she realized they were each holding their stomachs in the same way.

Is she pregnant, too?

Staring out the front window, Jade tried to imagine all the ways that changed her situation. If Kat was pregnant, she wouldn't be so alone—

The door opened, Jade smothered her excitement as Kat gripped the wheel, still quite distressed. Offering her a moment to find her bearings, she turned and sucked in a breath. Jeremy stood on the sidewalk watching her, his eyes haunted, and his expression completely unreadable.

She lowered her chin, unable to make eye contact. "I know you're upset, Kat, but can we get out of here?" The car slowly pulled away from the curb.

They didn't talk the entire drive to the doctor's office. When Kat finally parked the car she turned to Jade and said, "I'm sorry."

"You don't have to apologize."

Her fingers tucked a strand of brown hair behind her ear. "I didn't intend for that to happen."

Jade looked at her phone. They were already ten minutes late. She was still processing the scene at the restaurant, wondering who that guy was, how Kat knew him, and how he could possibly recognize the mark on her body. But according to her therapist, she wasn't supposed to get lost in the spiraling vortex of *what ifs, hows,* and *whys,* so she shelved the issues to focus only on the *now.*

"Listen to me, a name changes nothing about my circumstances. I waited weeks for this appointment and I don't want anything to spoil it. We'll talk about it when we get home, okay?"

"You're not mad?"

She wasn't sure what she felt, mainly because she was focused on staying positive at the moment. "Kat, you've been my best friend my entire life. You were there when I peed my pants in Russell Fisher's shed and when I stole the fish from Mr. Simon's koi pond. Now, I'm not sure what animal came out of you back there, but being best friends means we accept the good, the bad, and the *fugly.* Whatever that was, it changes nothing. But I need my best friend now because I'm about to hear my baby's heart beat for the first time and *that's* what matters."

Kat smiled and her shoulders noticeably relaxed. Her hand gripped Jade's. "Let's do this."

Nineteen

THE PAPER SHEET crinkled beneath her as she eased back and focused on the poster of ducklings tacked to the ceiling. Lily smeared cool jelly on her belly and pulled out something that looked like a microphone attached to a walkie-talkie. She pressed the microphone onto the blob of jelly and slid it around her abdomen. At first, there was amplified friction, but then came the most magical sound in the world.

A fast pattern of waves swished like a propeller. *Shoosh, shoosh, shoosh, shoosh...*

She drew in a deep breath and smiled. Her baby's heartbeat.

Kat squeezed her hand and her eyes prickled. It sounded so strong for something so small. Jade grinned at Lily. "It's amazing."

Her friend nodded. "It sure is."

Jade scheduled her next appointment and

stilled when the receptionist said, "And Mrs. Adams, don't forget your prenatal booklet. Your first appointment's scheduled for next Wednesday at four."

"*I knew it!*" Jade shrieked and laughed, snatching Kat into a hug and dancing around the waiting room. "How long have you known? When are you due?"

"I took a test a few days ago and I'm not exactly sure of my due date yet, but I think it's a June baby."

"Oh my God! A little June bug. They'll be best friends! Does Tyson know?"

This news was so welcome, Jade could hardly contain her excitement. Everything was suddenly different. She'd have a pregnancy buddy, someone to order random take-out with when the cravings hit. Their children would have each other, just like she and Kat had one another. Jade was certain, for the first time in a long time, she'd been given a gift. No matter what brought her to this point, the fact that her best friend arrived at basically the same spot in life at the same time seemed like kismet. She was meant to have this baby.

"Ty knows, but Mia doesn't. We don't want to tell her until I'm farther along and showing. So don't give it away, blabbermouth."

"Oh. My. God. This is fabulous! We're going to be like two fat *Weeble Wobbles*. We can paint each other's toenails!"

There had been so many questions she assumed would never be answered. But knowing

Kat was pregnant answered a huge one. Had Jade aborted the pregnancy only to watch Kat go through one... It would have been the biggest mistake of her life. This was right. She'd done something right and it felt incredible to have that certainty back in her life, repairing so much broken confidence.

Her euphoria held the entire way back to the house until she spotted the Jeep in the driveway. She hesitated at the car door.

"Do you want me to send him away?"

"I don't know what I want."

Kat gave a sympathetic grin. "I know it's hard to see him, but maybe it would help to talk to him. He's a good guy, Jade. After today, I'm sure he understands a lot more about what you've been going through."

Jade nodded and they entered the house. Kat called for Tyson, but he didn't answer. Out back, Mia played with Trixie by the edge of the property. Jeremy and Tyson sat on two patio chairs angled toward the covered fire pit.

Jeremy's head hung between his drooping shoulders, his elbows braced on spread knees. As Kat slid the glass door open Ty looked up and scowled. Jeremy glanced at Jade and his expression was ... regretful.

Tyson walked to Kat, kissed her, and then spoke in a seething but controlled tone. "Do you mind explaining what in the world would make you attack Nathan Lithe on a sidewalk? In your condition?"

Nathan Lithe. That was his name.

Not wanting to eavesdrop on their quarrel, having decided to leave the past where it belonged, Jade walked over to Jeremy who'd returned his gaze to the ground.

"Hey." She nudged his knee with her own.

He eyed her solemnly. "Hey."

"I'm sorry you had to be there for that today."

"I understand a little more about why you didn't want to talk about what was going on."

Her stomach pinched. "Did Tyson tell you?"

"Some."

There was such sadness in his eyes, she couldn't shake the feeling that she'd somehow betrayed him. "Jeremy, I'm so sorry. I—"

"You're pregnant."

She wasn't sure if he was saying it to himself or her. She dropped her weight into a vacant chair.

"You were..." His hand closed in a fist as he stumbled over the explanation of her condition. "And now you're pregnant and you're keeping the baby."

Her protective touch drifted reflexively to her abdomen. "This baby is as much mine as anyone else's. I'd never expect everyone to understand that, but it's how I feel."

His eyes narrowed. "You wouldn't expect me to understand?" He laughed without humor. "You don't expect much of anything from me, do you, Jade? As a matter of fact, you set the bar so low I can't seem to slip under it and convince you otherwise."

"It's not that I think you couldn't understand, but why should you have to, Jeremy? This entire situation is fucked up."

He shook his head. "I'm too selfish to accept your condition, is that it? I'm too judgmental to understand, too superficial and cynical to see past it?" He scoffed and rolled his eyes as if he was giving up. "You don't know me at all."

"I don't think you're any of those things, Jeremy. I just didn't want you to be burdened by any of this. You deserve better."

"And *you* don't deserve better?" He forked his fingers through his hair. "Jesus, Jade, none of this would've ever happened to you if I saw you home that night. If I just—"

"Don't. Nothing good comes out of the *what if* game. Believe me, it doesn't change the facts."

"And the fact that I still care about you, does that change anything? I still want you and you won't even accept my calls. You took something that should have been my choice and decided for me. These last few weeks have been hell and I've been in the dark the whole time trying to figure out what I did wrong. And the things I said..."

"I'm sorry. I didn't think..." She swallowed hard. "Why would you want me, Jeremy? I'm damaged."

"You're no more damaged than I am."

Tears burned her eyes and she quickly swiped them away. "Fucking hormones."

His hands closed over hers. "I miss you, Jade. I miss your presence in my life. I miss your optimism, your silly work anecdotes, your laughter. I miss touching you and kissing you and waking up next to you."

His words washed over her, emotionally unhinging her resolve. "But we were only together for two days."

"Bullshit. This thing between us has been going on for over a year. I'm done with the secrets. I want everything on the table."

Her heart shifted and she couldn't catch her breath. He was actually admitting to wanting her all that time. "I... I don't want to rehash things from that night. I can't."

"At first, I was angry you wouldn't confide in me. I couldn't understand why. I get it now. No more avoiding me, Jade. I understand if you don't want a relationship right now, but I want my friend back."

His thumb made a slow drag over her fingers and she lost the battle against her tears. Sucking in a jagged breath, she let him pull her to his lap. His long arms enveloped her and she breathed in his familiar scent.

She pressed her face into the curve of his neck and he held her close. "I'll always be here for you, Jade. Do you hear me? I don't want to be in the background of your life. I want to be close enough to catch you if you fall."

Brushing the hair away from her eyes, he kissed her temple, her teary cheeks, her nose, and finally, her mouth. Like the sweetest kind of homecoming, the pain in her chest eased. Their lips pressed with gentle force. She closed her eyes and tilted into—

"Daddy, why are you kissing Kiki?"

Annnnd, moment's over.

Jade blotted her eyes and caught her breath. Stifling a snicker, she pushed off his lap. Her legs tangled with his and he reached to steady her.

Cheeks flush, he ran a nervous hand across the back of his neck. "Uh... Kiki was just ... telling me a secret."

Mia squinted at her father, tipping up her scrunched nose. She turned her suspicious gaze on Jade and grinned. "I like secrets."

Jade's mouth slowly opened. "Well ... the secret is..." Her mind blanked. "Your dad makes really bad coffee."

Mia frowned, not impressed. "When did you have Daddy's coffee?"

Jade stilled. "Um..." Time to bail. She cupped a hand to her ear. "Do you hear that?"

"Hear what?"

"I think your mom's calling me. I'll be right there!" She bolted. She had her own problems to solve. Let Jeremy handle that one.

~

The new living situation over here on happy street was really starting to piss him off. Yes, Jade was back to work, but her activities outside of that had dwindled to inside that house. Someone was always there, preventing him from getting in. If it wasn't the enormous black guy, it was her friend or the kid. And now, the guy with the blonde hair was back after weeks of not lingering for more than a few minutes. When was she going to go back to her apartment?

The dog barked at the fence where the little girl played. His eyes narrowed. While no one else noticed him parked under the oak tree at the edge of the street, that yapping little pain in the ass had spotted his car.

The kid's head turned as the blond guy approached the fence. His hand patted the beagle's head in a calming motion. The dog stopped its barking. As they turned toward the house, the guy glanced back, looking over his shoulder in his direction.

He held his breath. "Do you see me?" his voice whispered in the silence of his still car, his glare holding the other man's searching eyes. "No, you don't see me. But I see you. And if you touch her one more time I'm going to take her someplace you'll never reach her."

Twenty

THE IMPRESSIVE THING about having protective men in her life was that they were very helpful when it came to moving heavy things. The locks Jeremy had installed at her apartment were impressive, but no longer needed. However, he had all intentions of upgrading the locks at the cottage before she officially moved in. He was a worrywart about security and, although she teased him for it, deep down she truly appreciated the measures he took to make her feel safe.

On move in day, Mia watched a DVD in the living room of the cottage while Tyson and Jeremy transported the last of Jade's belongings from her apartment. Being that she and Kat were both pregnant, the men didn't want them overtaxing themselves, so they stuck to the bedroom—sorting and unloading Jade's personal items.

"I don't understand why someone who wears

scrubs to work needs so many clothes," Kat mumbled from deep within the closet.

Jade sat on the carpet stuffing jeans into random drawers. "Clothes are my one vice."

These jeans were never going to fit. Thank God there was a closet in the spare bedroom. Giving up, she huffed and stretched out on the carpet, leaving a clog of denim hanging from the dresser.

Kat classified her footwear by height and color scheme. "What about shoes? I've never seen so many. You have two of the same boots. Who needs two of the same boots?"

"I like them. It's good fashion sense to have them in two colors. It's all part of being a *fashionista* and don't be upset when I mix up whatever ROY-G-BIV rotation you have going on in there."

"I'm sure all my unappreciated organization will get destroyed the first time you go out."

"Ha! Like I'm going anywhere. I can't even get my fat ass off the floor."

Kat turned and twisted her lips, but Jade didn't pay her any mind. "We still have a lot to do."

"Seriously, Kat, why aren't you as tired as I am? I could hibernate for months if people would just stop waking me up. Trust me, I'm not missing my social life right now."

"That'll pass." She stepped over Jade, refolding the items wedged haphazardly into the drawers.

"When? And what's up with my stomach? I'm

bloated as hell, and I haven't taken a decent crap in weeks. I mean really, have you ever—"

"I found them," Tyson's deep voice called from the doorway.

Jade's cheeks burned. *Whatever.* Sometimes women had unladylike confessions.

Ty stepped aside as Jeremy carried a large box of books into the room. *Mmmm, the view was fine.* "Where do you want these, Jade?"

"Just stick them next to my bed for now. Thanks."

"Yeah, you probably want to hide some of those titles under the mattress." Tyson teased and Kat smacked his arm.

"Oh, actually, Kat wanted to borrow some of them. She said something about you needing pointers."

He gave her the finger.

"The rest of the boxes are by the table. Did you eat?" Jeremy asked, as he nonchalantly flipped through her box of novels. His eyebrows rose at a couple titles.

Jade shoved up on an elbow but remained on the carpet. "Do you have food?"

"Didn't you just have the last of the leftover pizza?" Ty asked.

She rolled her eyes and hitched a thumb toward her belly. "I'm growing a person here." Ineffectively and without much grace, she rolled to build the momentum needed to hoist herself into a sitting position, giving up after about two tries and plopping back on the floor. Her size did not match the amount of energy this pregnancy was draining from her. How the hell would she get around once she *really* started to show?

Sitting was overrated anyway.

Without a word, Jeremy took her hand and helped her stand. She smiled only to get a quick nod in return before he returned to the other side of the room.

They were trapped in this awkward hiatus. They hadn't had a private moment to discuss their relationship since Mia caught them kissing—the child now watched them like a hawk.

She had absolutely no idea what his intentions were. As far as Jade was concerned, when it came to Jeremy, she had very little self-preservation left. If there was going to be any sort of fling, they should indulge before she fattened up like a pig at the county fair.

Her stomach growled, effectively silencing the room. Her body was now a hostage of her condition. "Sorry."

Kat cleared her throat. "I'm going to take Mia home and make dinner. You can meet us there in an hour. How's that?"

"Sounds good." Kat's food was way better than her own cooking, which consisted of take out and dehydrated noodles.

"Any special requests? I can do fish on the grill or a meatloaf."

"Ooh, meatloaf!" Her fantasies turned from tasting Jeremy to eating ground beef. Pregnancy definitely changed a person.

Unsure if Jeremy planned to stay, she busied herself at the vanity, organizing cosmetics on a small glass tray. Their eyes met in the reflection of the mirror and he gave a hesitant smile.

Once they were alone, he drifted closer and picked up a miniature purple bottle of body mist, the bottle too dainty and delicate in his bulky hand. He inspected the label then sniffed the cap.

"This smells like you."

Replacing the mist to its place on the tray, he moved behind her and tentatively placed his hands on her shoulders, giving a soft squeeze. Pent up tension skipped about in her chest as she tried to relax into his attention.

His hands gently massaged her neck, his touch tender under his strong fingers. Her head lolled to her shoulder as he swept her hair aside, sending chills up her arms.

Warm lips pressed to the hollow of her neck. A shiver chased up her spine as his breath teased over her shoulder. His fingers traced down her arms, drifting along the sides of her breasts. The backs of his knuckles swirled over her abdomen as his gaze held hers in the reflection.

There were no words, but his intentions seemed clear as he acclimated himself with her condition, acknowledging the subtle changes.

"You're having a baby," he whispered, more to himself than her.

There was no judgment in his voice. His tone laced with admiration.

Sorrow mixed with hope as she reminded herself she was done regretting her circumstances. His wrist turned and he flattened his palm over her belly. She drew in a slow breath. Her hand closed over his.

His intense gaze turned predatory as he stared at her through their reflection. Her skin prickled as a different sort of hunger took shape.

Breathing deep, she pushed past the awkwardness. She still wanted this, wanted him.

Jade wanted to sleep with Jeremy for many reasons, but she wasn't quite ready. The next time she gave herself to a man—*gave* being key—it would be unlike every other experience because it would be significant. No more one night stands. No more meaningless encounters. She needed something real. Jeremy was real.

She stared into the smoky, green irises of his eyes, the golden flecks prominent in the filtered sunlight. His skin carried a familiar scent and she longed for the memorable taste of his skin. He made her brave, made her want things she thought she'd never desire again.

Pressing a knuckle under her chin, he turned her face and brushed his lips against hers. Oh, how she'd missed his mouth, so soft and warm, knowing exactly how to move with hers.

His tongue gently slid past the seam of her lips, silently beckoning. She teased back and a guttural, masculine moan echoed in his chest.

His hand grazed her breasts. Another sifted into her hair. She twisted. Her hand squeezed his hip as he deepened the kiss. His fingers pinched her pebbled nipples through her cotton shirt and she drew in a deep breath. It had been months since she'd had any sort of intimacy with him.

His fingers plucked at the hem of her shirt and her body tightened at his palm's contact with her skin. Her blood hummed with anticipation.

She deepened the kiss. "We have forty-five minutes until dinner."

"Then we better make it count. Stand up."

He pulled her shirt over her head in one swift movement. His lips returned to hers and he growled. "God, I missed you."

Using his hips, he corralled her toward her bed. The back of her knees bumped the mattress. Sifting fingers through his thick golden hair, she guided his mouth to a lace-covered nipple. He yanked her bra away and she moaned as his mouth closed over the sensitive tip.

Overwhelming pleasure had her knees trembling. He toppled her to the mattress caressing her curves, sucking, licking. Every touch, despite his intensity, carried a level of care. Even now he seemed protective of her.

She fumbled for the hem of his shirt, needing to feel his flesh. He reached behind his head and yanked it off, flinging it across the room. His lips sealed over hers in an penetrating kiss as he ground his erection into her hip. Her knees fell wide as she arched against him.

He flicked the button of her jeans open. "I need to touch you, Jade. Here."

Her heart fluttered with anticipation as her

subconscious battled the threat of an unprecedented meltdown. So long as they didn't go too far, and so long as she remained aware that it was Jeremy touching her, she thought she could handle this—hoped she could.

"Yes." She panted.

The slow, sultry glide of her zipper coming undone echoed through the room like a tribal drumbeat. Sturdy hands tugged the material over her hips and she lifted. His stare covered her exposed body.

"You're gorgeous."

Lazily dragging a finger down the center of her stomach, stopping at the lace below her navel, he gave her an intensely hungry look. "I've never touched you here before."

Mesmerized by the way he watched her, her heart fluttered in a frantic rhythm, building until it roared in her ears. Her panties lowered as he slowly dragged a finger under the material covering her hip. The delicate fabric stretched over the swell of her thighs.

His eyes shut and he breathed deeply, as if slowing his desire. When his focus returned to her, life stood still. Fingers skated up her thigh, hesitated a heartbeat, and then softly traced her folds.

The tip of his finger swept over her clit, teasing, taunting. What the hell was he waiting for? "Forty minutes," she rasped.

"Even if we had hours it wouldn't be enough time. Don't think about the time." His fingers delved with lazy, shallow dips into her slit and her lashes lowered. His touch was incredibly gentle, building her need for more without hurtling her too far ahead. His pace was perfect.

"Did you miss me, Jade?" He asked as though it were all part of the game, but something in his question resonated, seeking assurance.

"Yes."

"Do you think of me at night, when you lie awake in bed?"

If only he knew how much. "Jeremy," she breathed, pleading.

"Did you imagine me deep inside you? Here." His finger sank into her core and she moaned.

His thumb moved in delicious circles as his fingers slowly stroked in and out. Her back arched and he lowered over her body, taking her nipple in his mouth.

Teeth scraped over her sensitive flesh while his wicked fingers teased below. Faster, deeper, firmer, tighter, her body heated. She gripped his shoulders as her hips rocked against his touch.

Her muscles flexed taut as flutters formed into a steady thrum of pleasure. His hand rode out her pleasure as she clung to his strength, giving over to the intrepid wave of release as she sang his name through every breath. "Jeremy..."

As her trembling subsided, he lightened his touch and slowly withdrew his fingers. Peeking through her lashes, too exhausted to fully open her eyes, she hummed, her mouth forming a lop-sided grin. His lips gently kissed her jaw as he pulled her into his arms.

Blankets drifted over her naked body. Replete and sated, she lay wrapped in the warmth of the man she adored. An orgasm and a nap? She'd died and gone to heaven.

Sometime later, someone nudged her shoulder. *Why are people always insisting on waking me up?* She groaned.

"Rise and shine, sleeping beauty."

She grumbled and turned her face into the pillow.

"You missed dinner, so I brought you back a plate."

Food or sleep, which did she want more? "What time is it?"

"Eight-thirty."

Unearthing her face from the pillows, she squinted around the room. Sure enough, the house was dim. "Was Kat mad I missed dinner?"

"No. She said she understands. Her and Mia passed out on the couch right after we ate anyway." He pushed her hair away from her eyes and tucked it behind her ear. "Are you hungry? I brought you a slice of meatloaf, some mashed potatoes, and corn. It's in the kitchen, but your table's covered with boxes so I didn't know where you wanted to eat."

Jade smiled, lacing her fingers with his. "You're so thoughtful."

"I have my good points. You want me to bring you your dinner?"

"That would be marvelous." She stretched and he kissed her nose before leaving to retrieve her meal. The microwave hummed in the distance. A girl could get used to this.

Between his pampering and their pre-dinner lust filled foray, she wasn't sure what to make of their relationship. Were they *in* a relationship? They'd discussed being exclusive before she discovered her pregnancy, but then she took a little vacation from her senses and broke up with him. Or did she?

Was that a breakup or just a lengthy disagreement? Was there a timeline on things like that? Maybe they needed to revisit the relationship negotiations table. He probably—

"Do I even want to know what's putting that look on your face?"

He carried a steaming plate to the nightstand, filling her bedroom with the delicious scent of Kat's home cooking. There was something wrong with her. The fragrance of flowers she now found repugnant, but the aroma of beef... *Bring it on!*

Sitting up, she adjusted the pillows. He laid a napkin across her lap and handed her a fork before passing her the plate. "Wow, you found my silverware?"

"Kat put everything away in the kitchen for you."

"I swear that girl has O.C.D. I'm sure my dishes are all systematically classified by length and color."

He laughed but didn't deny it.

Shoveling a heap of corn and potatoes into her

mouth, she moaned. Jeremy left and returned a moment later with a large glass of milk.

She scrunched her nose and covered her full mouth with the corner of the napkin. "What are you doing with that?"

"It's important you drink plenty of milk in your condition."

His concerned comment caught her off guard and she laughed because, Toto, they certainly weren't in Kansas anymore.

"Oh yeah?" She hated milk. "And how do you know I didn't already drink a carton today?"

"Because Kat said you aren't drinking enough and gave me a firm order to make sure you have a glass with dinner."

Jade curled her lip and took the glass.

She ate in silence while he busied himself with collapsing the empty boxes littering her new bedroom. When she finished, she slid her dish onto the nightstand and wiped her mouth.

"That was delicious. Thank you."

He smiled and returned to the edge of the bed. Her contented belly roiled as she sensed him readying to say goodbye. She didn't want him to go. When would she see him again?

Without thought, she blurted, "Wanna sleep over?"

Regret flashed in his eyes, stinging her in a way that made her want to rescind the offer.

"I wish I could, but Mia would get suspicious if she saw my Jeep here in the morning."

True. Or was he using Mia as an easy out?

Attempting to appear indifferent, she smiled. "You're right. I have things to do tomorrow anyway."

"What kind of things?"

"I have work at ten and I have an appointment in the morning before I go in."

"A doctor's appointment?"

"Sort of." He was so accepting of her faults thus far. But confessing she saw a shrink twice a week might be too much crazy too soon after everything else.

"What do you mean, sort of? Is it a check-up for the baby?"

"No." She plucked at a loose thread on her bedspread.

He lifted her chin with a finger until she was looking at him again. "Be honest with me, Jade. No more secrets."

Honesty was tempting, but she was scared she'd frighten him away. She had a slew of issues to work through—not something men typically flocked toward. Most men preferred women with minimal drama. She had drama coming out of her pores and armfuls of baggage.

But he asked for honesty.

Taking a deep breath, she slowly exhaled. "Tomorrow I have an appointment with Dr. Wolfe, my shrink. I have a session twice a week."

"How long have you been seeing him?"

"Her," she corrected, measuring his expression for judgment, which she couldn't detect. "I've been talking to her since I found out I was pregnant. She specializes in posttraumatic stress and sexual abuse.”

“Well, that’s … good. Is she helping you cope with things?”

Her sessions with Chloe still mostly revolved around Jeremy. *Lots to share on Monday…*

But confessing she’d been obsessing over him in therapy was definitely a little too much truth. Better to keep it general.

“She’s trying. I never remember anything from that night, so most of the time we talk about regular stuff.”

“Do you talk about us?”

Her gaze darted to the floor. “You’ve come up a few times.”

“And what does this Dr. Wolfe have to say about me?”

“She thinks you’re a player.”

“What?”

She laughed. “I’m just messing with you. She doesn’t share her opinions. She mostly listens and asks questions.”

His fingers brushed over hers. “And how do you answer?”

She sighed. Some secrets took a little longer to confess than others. “That I want to find the courage to trust the good people in my life.” Meeting his gaze, she whispered, “I’m working on that.”

“Dr. Wolfe seems like she’s making a good impression on you.”

"I like her. She seems to understand me. She isn't pushy or judgmental."

His fingers laced with hers. "I'm really glad you're talking to someone, Jade. You've been through a lot."

At the mention of all she'd "been through" her mind recoiled.

Their fingers looked right intertwined. It was discrete, yet intimate. She wanted to trust that he'd hold on long enough for her to find normal again because she wanted *normal* with him.

"What are we doing, Jeremy? I mean, I know we talked about a relationship before, but everything's different now. I'm different. Come summer, I'll have a baby and you aren't the father. I mean..." She quickly tried to retract her words. "Not that I expect you to act like the father to my child or that you're in anyway responsible for my situation. I just..."

God, she was messing this all up. His brow pinched as he waited for her to finish.

"I'm having a baby. A baby I didn't ask for, but a child that's still very, very real. I'm going to get fat and my body's going to change. I'm going to be hormonal and scared and excited for things I can't expect others to understand. For the life of me, I can't figure out why that might appeal to you."

Her shoulders lowered as reality pressed heavily into her. Then came the fear. "I'm going to give *birth*. A child is going to actually come out of me!"

Flashes of labor, sweating and screaming skittered through her mind. Her skin was suddenly hot and she wasn't breathing so steadily.

"Newborns are like seven pounds. Seven pounds is a lot! That's like *four* meatloaves. What if it's bigger than that? Oh, my God, I can't have a ten pound baby!"

"Okay, breathe." Visibly hiding a smile, he moved closer and rubbed her back.

She sucked in one deep gulp of air after another. Holy Moses, how was she going to do this? Drugs, lots of drugs. Fuck that Mary in the manger with a rope shit. Yes, an epidural was definitely the Cadillac way to go.

Her breathing slowly returned to normal. "I might be a little nervous about labor," she mumbled into his shirt.

"I think that's normal when it's your first time." He moved his palm over her back in soothing circles. "I was scared and I wasn't the one giving birth. I wasn't there when Mia was born and I ran away from parenthood the second I saw her. I envy you for having the strength to embrace this. You're stronger than I was."

She scoffed. Jeremy was the epitome of strength in her eyes. "How can you say that?"

He shook his head. "Don't pretend you forget. I know you were there when I wasn't and I know there were times you cursed me for leaving every responsibility on Kat's shoulders."

He was right, but since coming home he'd repaired so much of the damage he'd caused, she instinctively excused his mistakes. "You were young."

"So was Kat. There's no excuse for abandoning them, so please don't make one. I know what I lost and I have to live with that for the rest of my life. Maybe being here for you the way I wasn't there for Kat will help me accept and forgive my past mistakes." He tucked a strand of hair behind her ear and smiled at her. "I'm okay with the pregnancy. I wouldn't be sitting here if I wasn't."

His acceptance jarred her, far exceeding anything she'd hoped to hear from him. "I don't know what to say. I thought it would be a constant reminder of things you wanted to forget."

"Does this mean I'm okay with what happened to you? Fuck, no! If I ever find the bastard that did that to you I'll gut him like an animal. But this is no longer about him. It's about you and your baby. Stop searching for obstacles. They'll come naturally, Jade, and when they do we'll figure out how to proceed from there."

His confession washed over her like a balm, soothing her bruised heart, and softening her tattered nerves. She leaned in and softly pressed her lips to his.

Twenty-One

"FLATULENCE IS YET another symptom you may experience during your twelfth week. A good way to relieve this embarrassing pregnancy symptom is to slow down your eating. Scarfing down food too quickly will cause pockets of gas to build in your already over-taxed stomach..."

"Wonderful," Jade mumbled dryly, as Jeremy read from the pregnancy guidebook. With her head on his lap, all she could see was the cover, a woman rocking in a chair looking wildly perfect and content. She didn't look like a farter.

In the last two weeks of her first trimester, her old self was now forgotten, replaced with a new body, overflowing with plenty of new, unattractive reflexes. When she wasn't vomiting, she was trying to poop, and when she failed at that she was grateful for the vomiting. At least something was leaving her body.

She had an obscene amount of saliva going on and often woke up in a puddle of drool. That whole glowing thing, she suspected, was a crock of shit.

Plagued by heartburn, headaches, fatigue, and dizziness, she was constantly coping with one bodily function or another. Her sense of smell evolved to that of a bloodhound. The fragrance of food she once loved now sent her dashing off to the nearest toilet.

While she was an exhausted, sweaty, hormonal mess, Kat—the bitch—was Donna Reed gestating. No one looked that good pregnant. The only symptom Kat suffered was her need to pee often.

She groaned and cupped her slightly swollen belly. "It's not fair. I have every gross symptom there is and Kat's running around looking like a woman in a shampoo commercial."

Jeremy laughed. "What are you talking about? You're beautiful."

"You *know* if farting's a symptom I'll undoubtedly get that too."

"A little farting never killed anyone."

"I'm getting fat." She pouted.

He rolled his eyes. "It says the baby's the size of a large plum now. I love your little pooch."

"Nothing fits."

"Then start wearing maternity clothes."

"I can't. I still haven't told my parents I'm pregnant."

"Well, that's a whole other issue I don't understand, but personally, I think you're glowing."

"Yeah, right. That's sweat. And according to that book, it's going to be at least another two weeks before my 'dry spell' passes. By the second trimester, we should be good to go."

For as excited as she was to finally be able to test out all her Jeremy fantasies in the flesh, her libido wasn't cooperating. Rather, it dried up like an old sponge. She had raging hormones, but they were the wrong kind.

"I'm sure you'll feel more like your old self in the second trimester." He paged ahead, probably trying to see when her sex drive was scheduled to return. Grunting, he turned a few more pages. "We'll just skip reading about week thirteen."

"Greaaaat." She adjusted the pillow at her hip.

"Here you go." His optimism only testified to his lack of uterus. "By week fourteen you can expect a decrease in fatigue. You won't need to pee as much, there's less morning sickness, and your breasts should be less tender."

"Thank God!"

"But you may get a congested nose and sound a little nasally."

"Man, I am just an endless supply of sensuality! How do you find the strength to resist me?"

He arched a brow. "Oh, it takes more strength than you realize."

Grinning, she batted her lashes. "You kiss me now."

With a low chuckle, he tossed the book aside and bent—There was a knock at the door.

Jeremy paused and frowned. "Are you expecting someone?"

"No."

He craned his neck toward the door. "There's an old, bald man and a short, chubby woman trying to see through your curtains."

"Oh, shit!" She struggled to sit up. "It's my parents. Hide that book! Are there any other baby things lying around?"

He helped her stand as she quickly scanned the area for pregnancy paraphernalia. The knock sounded again.

"Okay, behave and don't say anything about the baby. That's a conversation I can't have right now."

"Jade, it'll be fine. Just get the door. I'll be a perfect gentle—"

"I'm not worried about you! It's them. They don't have filters. I told you, they're nuts."

He rolled his eyes and she knew he didn't believe her.

"Just remember, I warned you."

She walked through the kitchen and unlocked the door.

"Jadinka!" her father yelled and pulled her into a smothering hug.

"Hi, Daddy."

Her mother elbowed them apart and bustled into the house, carrying a covered dish with a brown grocery bag on top. "Hello, Jade. Get out of my way, Larry. I have things in my arms."

"And I have our daughter in mine. Which do

you suppose is more valuable?" He winked at Jade and pinched her nose.

"Yes, well, if it wasn't for me you wouldn't even have that. And if we waited for Jade to invite us over we'd be dead before the invitation arrived."

Jade kissed her mother on the cheek as she unloaded her bundle onto the counter. "Hi, Mom."

Her mom huffed and placed her hands on Jade's shoulder, holding her at arm's length as she inspected her appearance. "Hello, baby. You look too skinny. Are you eating enough? Probably not. Here, I brought you Kugel. It's still warm."

At fifty-six years old, her mother had more vitality than the *Energizer* bunny. Her family was right off the boat from Italy and staunchly Catholic. However, when she married an out of practice Jewish man, she hung up her rosary beads and converted. It didn't take long for her to master passive, yet not so subtle, maternal guilt. If martyrdom were a sport, her mother would be an Olympic class gold medalist.

Her mother opened and shut cabinets and drawers, piling the counter with plates, napkins, and forks. She was on a mission to feed her family and when she got like that there was no distracting her.

Jade moved toward the other side of the kitchen. "Mom, Dad, this is Jeremy."

Her mother stilled as if just realizing there was another person in the room. She brushed her palms down the apron she wore over every outfit and turned with a smile. "Well, look at you. You're a tall one."

Jeremy extended his hand. "It's a pleasure to finally meet you, Mrs. Schultz. I can see where Jade gets her beauty."

"Oh, and smart too!" She ignored his hand and gave him a firm pinch on the cheek. Then, without missing a beat, swatted her husband's hand away from the foil covered dish. "Larry, get out of the Kugel and come meet Jeremy."

"Nice to meet you, Jake."

"Jeremy," Jade corrected, offering the man a handshake.

"A good firm shake, that's a sign of an honest man."

"Thank you, sir. Do you play?" Jeremy angled his chin toward the clarinet her father carried in his left hand.

Drawing in a slow breath, Jade rolled her eyes. Her father carried that damn instrument everywhere. No one knew why and they learned not to ask. No one ever got a straight answer anyway. Still, he never went anywhere without the clarinet. It even made an appearance in her portraits from the father-daughter dance back in high school.

Her father furrowed his brow, as if not comprehending the randomness of Jeremy's question. "No. Do you fish?"

Jeremy looked at her, his brows drawn together in incomprehension. She shook her head. This was the craziness she'd tried to warn him about.

"Enough about that," her mother interrupted, as she carried plates to the table. "We can discuss while we eat. Do you like Kugel, Jeremy?"

"I can't say I've ever had it before."

"Ah, not Jewish then. I suppose you're Catholic. I hope Jade's heritage isn't an issue for you. We, of course, are fine with a *shagetz.*"

He shot her a questioning look as her mother babbled Yiddish and heaped servings of the sweet noodle casserole onto their plates.

"Mom, stop." She turned to Jeremy and mumbled, "We're not Jewish and a *shagetz* is a non-Jewish male."

"Jade! *Vei is mir,* we most certainly are Jewish!"

"Really? Then why do you put pork in your meat sauce and why do we get a Christmas tree every December? Dad, tell her to stop."

"What do you like to fish for, Jake?"

Jeremy, obviously trying to follow the rapid conversation, ignored the fact that her father was calling him by the wrong name. "Anything I can catch from a boat, sir."

"Ah, a true fisherman then. Got yourself a pair of sea legs, do you?"

"I put no *traif* in my sauce! My sauce is kosher!"

"That's not what the butcher says," Jade grumbled and took a bite of the Kugel. *So warm.*

"While in the service, my favorite moments were those spent on the ships."

"Ah, a military man. This Jake is a good guy, Jadinka."

"What is it you do now?" her mother asked. "Are you still in the service?"

"No, ma'am. I work with computers and live in Parkside so I can be closer to my daughter."

Her mother raised a brow at the mention of a child and Jade cut in. "Mom, you remember Mia, Kat's daughter. Jeremy's Mia's father."

Her mother's eyes widened as her mouth opened and closed. Her father smiled and elbowed Jeremy. "Gotch' yourself a good *shmeckle* there, eh Jake? Nothing wrong with that. However, if my Jadinka here gets knocked up I'll be cutting it off and using it to poke you in the back all the way to the *chuppah*."

"Nobody's getting knocked up, Larry. And we should be so lucky. All my lady friends have pictures of grand babies posted on MyFace. What do I have on my wall? A picture of you."

"It's Facebook, Mom."

"MyFace, SpaceBook... I can't keep up with today's technologies."

Jeremy cleared his throat. "This is delicious, Mrs. Schulz. What exactly is it?"

Her mother beamed with pride and Jade was grateful for the change in topic. As she explained, in detail, all the different ways to make Kugel, Jade enjoyed the home cooked treat.

Once they finished eating, she walked her father around the cottage while her mother told Jeremy stories about God knows what. She held

Jeremy's large hand in a death grip between her two smaller, pudgy ones. He couldn't escape if he tried.

An hour later, as Jade walked her parents to the door, she thanked them for bringing her the Kugel. Her mother also brought her a jar of sugar and a small broom having to do with some Jewish housewarming custom. They hugged her and Jeremy goodbye.

As they pulled away Jade leaned her weight against the door and exhaled. "I warned you."

"What are you talking about? They're great!" He pulled Jade into her arms and kissed her ear. "I didn't know your father was in the CIA."

She laughed. "He wasn't."

Twenty-Two

DR. WOLFE'S office looked nothing like what Jade had initially expected a psychiatrist office to look like. The walls were a soft beach-yellow and the trim was glossy white. No pretentious certificates were displayed, nor a bust of Freud.

Rather, Dr. Wolfe's shelves were peppered with old apothecary jars filled with pearly shells, white buttons, and unique shards of sea glass. There was a shelf completely dedicated to vintage bears and another decorated with antique teapots, brass pocket watches, and broken bits of soapstone. Her photographs were sepia landscapes that told of a personal hobby done for pleasure more than natural talent, but their lack of mastery made them all the more beautiful.

Overstuffed chairs and ottomans draped with well-worn quilts were arranged in an intimate cluster at the center of the room. Her desk, more of an afterthought than a necessity, sat forgotten in the corner.

She burned autumn-scented candles and always served fresh coffee. It was the same kind Jade kept in her cupboard at home, but for some reason, Dr. Wolfe's coffee always tasted better.

Perhaps it was the warm terracotta mugs she served it in that made it more of an experience than refreshment. Sharing a cup of coffee with Dr. Wolfe took away the anxiety connected to needing therapy, and replaced it with the sense of sharing a ritual, like teatime with a friend.

She initially gave Jade the option of addressing her as either Dr. Wolfe or Chloe. At first, Jade used her formal title, but after sharing so many intimate details of her life she naturally shifted into calling her Chloe.

Chloe comforted Jade in ways she couldn't quite pinpoint. It was relaxing to vent to someone who was simply there to listen. She could easily pretend Chloe was a good friend rather than her shrink. The only giveaway that she was truly in therapy was the bill Jade paid at the end of the month. That and the fact that the conversation steadily centered on her own life and rarely touched on Chloe's. But there had to be a cost for curing one's soul and Chloe was slowly curing hers.

Facing each other, feet tucked under their legs and hands cradling their mugs of warm hazelnut flavored coffee, they continued to discuss Jade's issues with her parents.

"Do you think if Jeremy wasn't there you would have told them about the baby?" Chloe asked.

"Probably not," Jade admitted, heavy with guilt for prolonging the secret. "They know I've been avoiding them. My mom dropped plenty of unsubtle hints about how I neglected to invite them to see my new place. I have to tell them soon, though. My clothes are too tight and I'm avoiding a maternity wardrobe because that would be a dead giveaway."

"So why hesitate? Do you fear they'd blame you for what happened?"

"That's just it. I don't want to *explain* what happened. I could act like I just slipped up and got pregnant, but I know them. They wouldn't relent until they had a name. My mother would insist on meeting the father, and my father would want to hit him with his clarinet."

Chloe took a sip of her coffee, her eyes creasing with silent amusement at the mention of the instrument.

"Besides, where would that leave Jeremy? Once they found out he wasn't the father they'd assume he was standing in the way of my baby's family being together. Which is just too ridiculous to even contemplate."

"You could tell them the truth about what happened."

"No way. They'd be devastated. I'm their only daughter and they're a pain in the ass, but I know they only interfere in my life because they love me more than anything else. My father still calls me by my childhood nickname and my mother would spoon-feed me if I let her. It would crush them to know what I suffered."

Chloe placed her mug on the end table and folded her hands gently on her lap. "I think, perhaps, your parents underestimate how strong their daughter is. Yes, you suffered a horrific ordeal, but you also survived. You *are* surviving it everyday. You're thriving. Perhaps, trusting their ability to share this burden with you will work in your favor and shed some light on the strong qualities they instilled in you. Your parents may surprise you, Jade."

"I know. I think that, too, sometimes. They've always supported and loved me, but then I think about my baby. He or she has only been a part of my life for twelve weeks—twelve *short* weeks. In that short amount of time, I've realized a special kind of love that comes with a ferocity that scares me. Without even seeing my child's face, I know with absolute certainty that I'd lay down my life to save him or her from a moment's pain. I can only imagine that love intensifying overtime. My parents have loved me for twenty-three years."

Her eyes glazed under the sharp sting of tears as she experienced a wave of hurt similar to what they might feel. She couldn't hurt them and that was exactly what that information would do.

"I never want my parents to know someone did such a horrible thing to me. Grief would haunt them and it's nothing they can fix."

Chloe was quiet for several minutes as she reflected on her words. "You're going to be a wonderful mother, Jade. You're very wise and, while I don't condone lying, I must say that I respect what you've said. Your sacrifice to save your parents anguish is a testament to how much you love them."

Glad she'd conveyed her feelings clearly—something she'd been struggling to improve—she took a deep breath and sat back in her chair. "Thank you."

"It seems you need a way to announce your pregnancy without revealing the events leading up to it. I want you to start contemplating explanations for your condition, not only for your parents but also for others who will ask. Keep in mind that one day it will be your own child who's asking. I want you to be prepared when those moments arrive."

The sense of progress vanished as new worries arrived. Chloe was right. How the hell was she supposed to explain a monstrous father to a child that shared the same genetic makeup?

"I'm gonna need a solid explanation. It should be as close to the truth as possible—but without the ugliness."

"You can water it down for a child, because I assure you, yours won't be the first to ask 'how did I get here?'."

Another thing to prepare for. Parenthood came with tons of awkward conversations. The stuff that came out of Mia's mouth on a daily basis was insane. Kids were definitely curious little people.

"Think on that over the next few days," Chloe said, bringing their session to a close. "I'll think on it, too, and perhaps we can come up with something that neither divulges too much nor qualifies as a lie. You're making great progress, but I'm going to be honest. I'm still leery. We've been working on ways to prepare you for events that might set you off, but life's unpredictable and sometimes hidden triggers arise."

Jade wanted to think her moments of emotional breakdowns were over, but that was just being naïve. Motherhood was an endless challenge. She'd seen Kat lose it plenty of times and Kat was a damn good mom. But Chloe wasn't worried about Jade's parenting skills. She was warning her about the emotion backlash that came with being a victim.

"I know it's going to be hard."

"It's okay to relapse into grief, Jade. So if something happens to trigger a flashback, embrace it and use what you've learned. Sometimes we move backward in life and our new position offers a better point of view. If that happens, we'll reassess and revise the path forward."

Drawing in a deep breath, she confessed, "I know one day I might learn things I have no knowledge of now, but I almost hope that never happens, even if it means I'll never get revenge. I want to move forward, not backward. Sometimes ignorance *is* bliss. I just want closure—however I can find it."

"In your situation, flashbacks could be especially disorienting. Remember, pay attention to your memory if it tries to bridge the gaps, but don't forget your surroundings and those individuals here to support your progress. We'll cross that bridge together when and if we get there."

Chloe's words empowered her. "I always feel so confident by the end of our sessions."

"You should. You're making great progress." She glanced at her watch. "Unfortunately, we're out of time. Think about the suggestions I've made and next time we meet we'll see where things stand."

As Jade took the elevator to the lobby her posture felt a bit taller, her chin a notch higher. She was doing pretty well, considering.

Zipping her jacket, she crossed the breezeway onto the sidewalk, cutting a quick left into the underground parking garage. Her shoes clicked over the worn cement as she climbed the stairs, echoing in the silent space.

As she thumbed her key fob her alarm chirped and her headlights flashed in the distance. A black SUV with tinted windows idled at the end of the row of parked cars. The headlights were off—probably someone with an automatic starter. She should get one of those.

She turned toward her Lexus as the black SUV lights flashed. The shrill squeal of tires cut through the silence as the driver ripped out of the spot and down the aisle. Jade gasped and flung her back to her car, pressing her hand to her chest.

"Asshole!" she shouted as the jerk peeled around the corner. Her blood ran cold as her alert gaze snagged on the back of the SUV. "What the fuck?"

She took a staggering step forward, but the sound of screeching tires below told her she'd never catch up. Was she seeing things? A chill sank into her bones as her mind clung to the memory of the car speeding away, zeroing in on the decal of the rear bumper.

It had been there. She saw it. A scrolled symbol resembling a number four with flourishes. Her body shook with adrenaline as she lifted a hand to her shoulder. She'd seen it.

The garage silenced and she reached for her phone, her fingers shaking violently. She dug her nail into her key fob, setting her car alarm to panic. She needed to call someone, but first, she had to get out of there.

The horn of her Lexus bleated obnoxiously, muffling the sound of her frantic footfalls and labored breath as she raced back down the stairs toward the street. She burst through the doors onto the bustling sidewalk and pedestrians scrambled out of her way.

The sunlight momentarily blinded her as she cut right and raced back inside Chloe's building, sprinting past the reception desk toward the elevators. Her heart thundered in her chest as she was hyper aware of others nearby.

Jabbing her finger into the button, she impatiently waited for the doors to open. "Come on..."

The elevator opened and passengers stepped out, new passengers moving in. Jade pushed inside and stabbed a finger into the button for Chloe's floor.

A woman speaking on a cell phone stood to her left, a man reading the paper filled the back corner, another man sending a text message occupied the middle. She kept closest to the doors, her breath soughing out of her lungs as her mind replayed the image of the SUV on a continuous loop.

The elevator chimed and she shoved through the partially opened doors, running full speed toward the office. Propelling her body against the door, she panted as Chloe gave a startled yip.

"Jade?" Standing by her assistant's desk holding a manila folder, her serene expression tightened with evident concern. "Is everything all right?"

Breathing jaggedly, words rushed past her lips. "I saw it ... on a car ... the four... They tried to run me over!"

"I'll call the cops!" her assistant said, as she grasped the phone on her desk.

"*No!*" Jade shouted.

"Wait a minute, Jennifer." Chloe placed a hand on the secretary's shoulder. "Come into my office, Jade."

It was then she noticed who was likely Dr. Wolfe's next appointment sitting to her left, staring bug-eyed at the crazy lady in the office. She quickly followed Chloe and shut the door.

Chloe walked to her desk and pressed a button on her phone. "Jennifer, I'll have to reschedule my next appointment."

"Yes, Dr. Wolfe," Jennifer replied over the intercom.

She turned toward Jade and gestured for her to take a seat. "Tell me what happened."

Jade quickly explained as Chloe took notes. "You're certain you don't want to notify the police?"

"No, I want to call the cops. That asshole almost killed me! I just don't want to get into... other stuff with them."

"But this is more than a near hit and run. Are you ready for that conversation? I can sit in on the phone call with you—"

"Wait," she interrupted, her mind moving too fast to track. "Can't I just report what happened today?"

"Of course, but is this about reporting a bad driver or a bad person, Jade?"

She frowned, her breathing finally slowing. "But ... what if I just imagined it. What if I got scared and my mind was just playing tricks on me?"

"Do you think that's what happened?"

"No." It all happened so fast. "I don't know."

"Did you notice anything else about the car, aside from its coloring? The make or model?"

Damn it, she had nothing. "No. It might have

been a..." *Nissan? Mercury? Cadillac?* Shoulders shrinking, she mumbled, "No, I didn't notice anything else."

"Well, all is not lost. Do you still intend on going to work? I've canceled my last appointment for the day and I'd like to see if we could use that time to do some fact gathering."

Jade quickly ran through a list of co-workers in her mind, wondering if any of them would cover her shift. "I can probably call out."

"Okay, use the phone at my desk. I'll give you a few minutes. After you call your work I'd like you to call your support group. Kat, Tyson, Jeremy, and anyone else whom you're comfortable discussing your situation with honestly. Ask them if they're available to join us for an hour or so."

Jade nodded and Chloe stepped out of the office.

Several minutes later Chloe softly knocked and peeked through the door. Jade was just hanging up the phone with Jeremy, who was furious. Not with her, but with the idea that someone put her in danger—*again*. And possibly the same someone from before.

As they waited, Chloe handed her a large glass of water and moved some additional chairs into her office. Before long, they were interrupted by a ruckus in the waiting room. Jennifer shouted from her desk as the door to the office flew open.

There, fierce with the eyes of a predator, Jeremy filled the doorframe . His sharp gaze zeroed in on Jade, his steps carrying him to her side in two strides as he gripped her in a crushing hug. "Are you okay?"

"I'm fine."

"Jeremy, I'm Dr. Chloe Wolfe."

With only a quick nod, he turned back to Jade and ran his hands over her hair and shoulders. "Were you hurt? Should we take you to the doctor's?"

"Jeremy, I'm fine. Just a little shaken up and angry someone tried to hit me with a car. Sit down. Please."

After several minutes, she convinced him to take a seat, but he was pacing by the time Kat and Tyson arrived. Once everyone was satisfied that she was unharmed, Chloe had her explain what happened in full detail.

Jeremy's shoulders remained tense, his body ready to spring at any moment. He only needed the identity of his target and she had no doubt he'd be gone.

"Now," Chloe announced, retrieving her tablet. "I think it's in Jade's best interest to gather the facts before we move forward. She invited you here so that we could work together to make sure we don't leave out any important details. We need to form a comprehensive timeline of events including anything that relates to Jade's assault. Who would like to start?"

"I'll start," Kat announced, taking a stuttered breath. "A little over a year ago, Jade came over for coffee and as I was walking her back to her car I noticed a bumper sticker."

"What?" Jade asked, having no clue what this had to do with today. There was a niggling of familiarity to what Kat was saying, but she didn't know how it was related.

"You remember," Kat prompted. "You were pissed someone put a sticker on your car. I thought you put it there and it was some kind of trendy new symbol, like an awareness band or something. You ripped it off and threw it away. You blamed ignorant kids for vandalizing your car, so I never thought much else about it."

"Oh, my God..." Jade breathed. She remembered now. She didn't even really look at the design on the sticker. She was too busy being furious with the fact that someone defaced her property. But now that she thought about it, there was something familiar in the shadows of her memory. "Was it the four?"

Kat wavered. "I... I think it might have been."

Jade gasped, her fingers crawling over her arms and skin to fight the unnerving sense that someone might have targeted her. "What the hell does that mean, that I was tagged or something? I never considered that what happened to me as more than a snap decision. What if they were watching me all this time?"

Tyson cursed and Jeremy looked ready to kill someone, his hand tight in a closed fist as it bounced on his thigh. Bile swilled in her stomach as she struggled to breathe.

"Take a long, deep breath, Jade," Chloe advised. "Do you know what month that happened, Kat?"

"Um, I guess early September, because it was around my birthday the next time I noticed something."

"There's more?" Tyson snapped.

"Yes."

"I'm going to throw up." Jade moaned, bending over as someone handed her another glass of water.

"Do you need a minute, Jade?"

She shook her head, wanting to finish this.

"Continue," Chloe said to Kat.

"On my birthday I was at the salon getting a manicure. The girl doing my nails had a scar on her hand. It was the same stylized four."

Jade's head snapped up as tears swam in her unblinking eyes, clouding her vision. *"What?"* Why was this the first time she was hearing about this?

Kat shook her head, expression regretful. "Again, maybe I'm remembering it wrong, but all of this suddenly seems a little too coincidental. You're always covering the mark, Jade, so I never really see it. Sometimes I forget it's there. Maybe it's not the same."

"Maybe it is," Jeremy growled, jaw tight.

"Tell us what about the salon, Kat."

Kat took a deep breath. "I asked the woman about mark, but she got uncomfortable. After a couple of minutes she excused herself and another girl finished my manicure, saying something about the first girl double-booking or something," Then, in a smaller voice Kat whispered, "If she got it the same way Jade did, I understand now why she didn't want to talk about it."

"You think this girl was raped?" Tyson asked, appalled.

Jade cringed at the word *rape*. That word was so ugly, so vile. How could four little letters carry such a detrimental consequence?

Kat nodded and Chloe asked, "Do you remember the woman's name or the name of the salon?"

"I don't remember the manicurist's name, but the salon's called Trinidad's." She took a deep breath. "I never said anything, because I didn't know. There were weeks between each incident. I never suspected it was a way to mark victims. I would've said something if I thought anyone was in danger, I swear."

Tyson took her hand, holding her closer as he softened his deep voice. "They know that, kitten. It was trivial coincidences at the time, nothing else. I saw a blue jay yesterday and one the day before. You don't hear me telling everyone, do you?"

Jade couldn't bear the thought of Kat blaming herself for any of this. "He's right, Kat."

Bringing them back to the matter at hand, Chloe asked, "Jade, have you ever seen the four before?"

She shook her head. "No. I mean it was on my car, but I didn't even notice what the sticker said, only that I hadn't put it there. The first time I saw it was the day after the assault, but even then I couldn't make out what it was. It wasn't until it healed that I realized it was intentionally put there, a branded symbol of some sort."

"What about that guy? Nathan?" Jeremy asked, directing his question to Kat. "He knows something. What made you link this to him?"

"Nathan, the man Jade had a confrontation with before her ultrasound appointment?" Chloe clarified and Kat nodded.

"Nathan's a friend of my parents—"

"He's a prick," Tyson interrupted.

"Well, that too," Kat agreed. "I met him a couple years ago. He's a friend of Dawson's."

"Also a prick," Tyson added.

"Anyway, Nathan always made me uncomfortable. He's chauvinistic and self-righteous. The reason I assumed he knew something was because I ran into him at the market with Jeremy one time. I thought it was odd that he was in our neighborhood. When he pulled away I noticed he had the same four on his car."

Jeremy's eyes darkened. "I remember that day. I didn't realize that was the same guy. Do you think it could be some sort of gang?"

"I don't know. I totally forgot about it until we saw Nathan at the restaurant. As soon as he followed us outside I remembered and that's why I freaked out. I figured he had to know something, but he swore he didn't. Then Jeremy showed up and punched him in the face."

"I envy you, man," Tyson commented.

Jeremy only scowled in reply.

"You told this Nathan about the pregnancy, Jade?" Chloe asked.

Sitting back slowly, her mind replayed that confusing day on the sidewalk as her heart slowly sank into the pit of her stomach. "Yes."

The room grew silent and she felt the walls closing in. She hadn't meant to put herself in jeopardy. She only wanted to tell him off, take back the power. Afterward, she put the entire episode behind her, hoping she scared him enough to run in the opposite direction if they ever crossed paths again. With all the news of Kat's pregnancy and the excitement of her own, she didn't want to dwell on some lead that probably meant nothing.

"What if he's the reason that car came after me today? What if this is all some kind of game? What if they're still watching me? That guy knows I'm pregnant!"

"Shh, take a breath." Jeremy soothed, but even he clearly couldn't manage calm. His body was tight and coiled to spring into attack at any second. "This Nathan isn't going to come near you. I'll make sure of that."

"I don't want him involved in this," Jade protested. She didn't want any trouble.

"Jade, he already knows. I saw his face when he saw your scar. He knows what it means. We need to get ahold of him and get more information. I think we should go back to that salon, too, and see if the nail girl knows anything. We should be retracing all your steps as far as we can. There might be surveillance from the night of—"

"Stop!" Her heart beat too fast. "You don't get it, Jeremy. I don't *want* to know. I just want to live a normal life."

"Well, how normal is it when people are trying to run you over?"

"I was scared! What if I didn't even see the four and just imagined it?" She looked hopelessly to Chloe. "Like you said, our mind can play tricks on us and make us see things that aren't really there."

"Do you think that's what happened, Jade?" Chloe asked, her tone quiet and gentle.

Swallowing, her lips trembled as her vision blurred with unshed tears. This was too much. None of them understood how badly this was ripping her apart. She couldn't live her life in a state of constant fear and panic. "I just want my life back."

Chloe passed her a tissue as a tear fell. "I think we've done enough for today. Thank you, all, for coming. If you don't mind, I'd like to have a few minutes alone with Jade."

"Jade," Jeremy whispered, but she couldn't take her eyes off the floor or find the nerve to answer any more questions. Pressure built like a heart attack in her chest as she waited for them to leave.

Chloe shut the door and returned to her side. "Hey." She took her hand and chaffed it gently. "If you want to cry, that's okay. I've got time."

Face crumpling, she gasped on a sob and broke as Chloe pulled her into a hug.

"I know this is a lot." Chloe ran a soothing hand down her back. "It's scary and not what you want."

No words came out, only tears. She cried for what felt like days. She cried because she was scared. She cried because someone tried to hit her with a car. She cried because her pants were too tight. She cried because she hated feeling victimized. But most of all, she cried because this wasn't over and might never be.

"You have a great group of people out there who love you very much, and one in particular who's quite determined to protect you."

"Jeremy doesn't love me," Jade corrected with a sniffle.

"What makes you so sure? He's here. He wants to help you. And he's going against his very nature to do right by you when every instinct he has is screaming for vengeance. I wouldn't be so quick to dismiss his feelings."

Smudging her makeup, she rubbed the heel of her palm over her eye socket. "Why though? My life's one big clusterfuck."

Chloe laughed. "He's an alpha, Jade. He can handle it. Maybe you should trust him to take whatever you can dish out."

"I do trust him, but I know he wants to punish someone for what happened to me and I don't want anyone sniffing around sleeping dogs. I just want to let them lie and move on with my life. I can't handle anymore trouble."

"But you also can't spend your life looking over your shoulder. It's no way to live. Believe me. Why not let him help, so long as he's discreet? There's plenty he can find out without mentioning your name. Remember, the child who closes his eyes *feels* invisible and safe, but he's *safer* facing his fears with eyes wide open."

She sniffled and gave a half chuckle. "You sound like a fortune cookie."

"Well, if I had friends that looked like yours the last thing I'd do is close my eyes. How's that?" She laughed. "Do you think you're calm enough to go out there now? You have a very surly, handsome man willing to drive you home."

With a cleansing breath, she sat back and nodded. "Yeah."

"Good."

"Thank you for this, Chloe. I know you're my therapist, but ... sometimes you feel like a friend. Right now I really need friends that understand what I'm going through."

When Jade exited the office, Jeremy was pacing. His long legs gobbled up the small waiting area in two strides. Pivoting, he stilled as his gaze fell on her.

Timidly, she folded her hands, giving him time to—

He yanked her into another bear hug. "I'm sorry. I don't want to push you. I just worry and want you safe."

"It's okay," she whispered back, breathing in his familiar scent. Her eyes closed as she tried to lose herself in his presence. "Can we go home now?"

"God, yes." His lips pressed to her hair as his hold tightened and released.

Twenty-Three

MEXICAN MUSIC PLAYED SOFTLY in the dim lit restaurant. Jade felt the weight of Jeremy's stare through every bite of her fajita. "You're going to give me a complex if you don't stop staring."

"Can we talk about it?"

She rested her fork on the edge of the plate and sighed. She knew he wouldn't just let it go. "What do you want me to do, Jeremy?"

"I want you to go to the police."

"And say what? I woke up months ago, I have no recollection of what happened, now I'm pregnant, and I'm pretty sure the guy's a bad driver? How far do you think they'll get with a lead like that?"

His eyes narrowed. "How can you be so cavalier about all this?"

She scoffed. "Cavalier? Are you kidding me?"

"What if they can help you?"

"What if they can't?"

"But what if they can?"

This was getting nowhere. "Jeremy ... can you just try to think like a woman for a minute? That man, whoever he is, did something horribly repulsive to me and I was defenseless. I didn't get to defend myself or even protect my body when it happened. He took something from me I will never get back. Do you think he couldn't do it again? I'm not saying that will happen, but it's a fear I face every day. I literally pray it was a one-time thing and I make bargains with myself, promising if nothing like that ever happens to me again, I won't retaliate for the one time it did happen. Do you think that's the thinking of a brave person? It's not. I'll never be as brave as I was and you will never know what it's like to have a stranger inside of you without your permission."

"Men get raped, Jade."

"Look at you and look at me. Maybe if I was your size I'd be a little less timid, but I'm tiny. I'm scared. And I'm having a baby. I couldn't protect myself, but I *will* protect my child. The best way for me to do that is by moving forward and leaving the past behind."

"Then let me do some digging. I swear I won't use your name and I promise not to do anything to put you or the baby in danger."

"Jeremy... No."

He sighed, clearly not agreeing with her, but he no longer pressed her. They drove to his place after the restaurant and Jade needed to get clean. It had been one of those days that just made her feel dirty.

"Can I use your shower?"

"Sure. You know where it is."

Looking back at him, seeing the tension he now carried, she gave up. "You can't use my name."

He turned and frowned, and then he understood she was giving him permission to investigate. "I won't."

A nervous smile turned her lips. "And ... thanks. For caring so much."

His smile mirrored hers. "I'll always care about you, Jade."

She was starting to believe that.

As Jade pulled the shower curtain back, she reached for the towel Jeremy left on the vanity. Wiping the steam-coated mirror, she stared at her reflection, replaying their conversation. Her number one priority was keeping her baby safe and she didn't want anyone coming after her because they felt threatened.

Jeremy promised he'd do everything necessary to keep her and the baby safe. Discretion was key. Chloe was right. He was an alpha. As soon as she gave him permission to get actively involved, he seemed satisfied.

What else was Chloe was right about? Did Jeremy love her? She had a hunch that she very much loved him, but that was one of those pesky thoughts better left ignored for now.

Sleeping with Jeremy would confirm that she was ready to move on from her tragedy and reclaim her life. But the fear of an emotional crisis in the midst of intimacy made her hesitant.

Why did it have to be complicated? She wanted him. He wanted her. But more than anything, she wanted normal. She wanted to forget.

Staring at her reflection, she whispered, "You want to have sex with Jeremy Larson." Big shock there.

It shouldn't have to be complicated. Love didn't need to play a part in it. People had casual sex all the time. She could do this—*would* do this, because she trusted him.

He definitely took up a space in her heart. He was her friend—her super sexy friend. She *should* be sleeping with him. If her life hadn't derailed right before Kat's wedding, she'd be a seasoned veteran by now in terms of sleeping with Jeremy. There was no doubt.

But now ... now there were all these unexpected emotions clouding her perception. He was more than her hot friend, more than a body she wanted to conquer. In a way, he was her hero—always looking out for her and trying to protect her.

You're in love with him.

Shut up. Sex is sex. Don't make it out to be more than it is.

Her mind was made up. She was going to sleep with him and she was *not* going to mess everything up with big, four letter words like *love*.

Do not screw this up.

As she left the bathroom, she found a folded pair of Jeremy's sweats on the bed with an old T-shirt that said *Navy*. Yep, she was bagging herself a sailor tonight.

Making her way downstairs, she found him sitting on the couch quietly talking on the phone. She sat beside him and pulled the afghan over her feet. He smiled and pulled her into his side.

"You did?" He smiled and adjusted the phone. "Without falling once? Well, that's great. Hmm, maybe if you ask Santa he will bring you some ice skates of your own." He paused and laughed. "Well, then, you're just going to have to be extra good."

She gathered he was talking to Mia and re-membered she had a field trip this week to go ice-skating with her class.

"Okay, Princess. I love you, too. Be good for Mommy. Bye, baby."

As he hung up the phone she turned to him and asked, "Mia have her field trip today?"

"Yup. Now she wants to be an Olympic gold medalist. You look sexy in my Navy shirt."

"It's the first thing I've worn in weeks that hasn't cut off my circulation."

"Don't start," he warned. "You want to watch a movie? I won't hold it against you if you nap."

Love. Love. Love. Love.

"Then yes." She smiled while internally growling at her stupid subconscious.

Snuggling deeper into his side, she shut her

eyes as he selected a movie. She guessed it was a comedy by the way laugher occasionally rumbled in his chest, but she couldn't keep her eyes open long enough to be sure. A while later she stretched awake to find her face pressed into his hard abdomen.

"Have a nice nap?"

"Mmm, I forgot where I was. You're a good pillow."

"That's what I'm here for." He winked and brushed her hair away from her face with his fingers.

"How was your movie?"

"Sucked. Some people just try too hard to be Jim Carey."

"Yes, there are only a few of us who are naturally funny. It's a gift really." Shifting, she rolled to sit up.

"Where you going? I was comfy."

"I have to tinkle."

When she returned to the living room Jeremy wasn't there. She followed the clank of dishes coming from the kitchen.

"What do you have there?" she asked, spotting the heaping bowl of ice cream.

"Cookies and Cream, but it's all for me." He glided past her, holding the bowl out of her reach.

"I happen to know that if you don't give me that bowl, you'll get a very nasty sty."

"What?" He laughed as he dropped to the couch.

"It's true. The woman at my work told me. If

you deny a pregnant woman what she craves you'll get a sty. It's a fact."

"Really? Then I better give you *everything* you crave." He spooned a dollop of ice cream into her mouth and kissed her. "Mmm, delicious."

She licked her lips as he took his own bite, his gaze smoldering as he slowly pulled the spoon from his mouth. They took turns, chasing each bite with a kiss. The press of the cool spoon on her tongue, the weight of the metal in her mouth, the sensual way she sucked it clean and swallowed slowly; it was culinary foreplay at its best.

"Have I satisfied all of your cravings this evening, Ms. Schultz?" His husky voice reeked of implication as she placed the bowl on the coffee table.

Easing back, she tried to match his smolder. "You're getting warmer."

"Well..." Stretching over her, he pressed his lips to hers. "I aim to please. You taste like cookies."

Their bodies pressed together, molding to each other's contours, as he took her mouth. Their hands searched over one another. His palms gently cupped her breasts, respecting their new tenderness. Brushing her fingers over the bulge of his pants, he growled into her mouth.

She worked the button of his jeans free and he caught her wrist. "Let's go upstairs."

Lacing his fingers in hers, he stood and pulled her to her feet, only to kiss her again. Her arms wreathed his neck as he lifted her, cupping her ass.

"Wrap your legs around my hips." He nipped at her neck and her thighs tightened around his waist. He carried her toward the stairs, detouring to lock the front door and explore her throat with his tongue.

His breath tickled over the shell of her ear as her body pulsed and quivered. Her legs tightened around him to relieve some of the pressure. He groaned and carried her up the steps.

As they entered his room, he kicked the door shut behind them and lowered her to the mattress, his body covering hers like a blanket.

"Clothes. Off. Now," she panted between kisses, as she tugged at his T-shirt.

Pulling his shirt over his head, he tossed it to the floor. Undoing the drawstring at her waist, he slid the borrowed sweats off her legs and raised an eyebrow when he saw she went commando.

"I, too, aim to please," she remarked and pulled her shirt off.

His hands slid from her ankles to her knees, slowly pressing her thighs apart and exposing her sex. Heat caressed her folds with every breath. The first swipe of his tongue had her body pulling taut. His fingers pressed into the soft flesh at her thighs as his tongue deeply licked. Her fingers locked in his hair as the pleasure intensified, slamming through her. His mouth moved to the sensitive peak at the cleft of her sex and sucked, driving the waves of ecstasy higher.

Sweet euphoria took hold and she broke, shattering into a million shards of bliss. Breathy sighs sang his name as he continued to pleasure her through the tremors. Her muscles flexed and pulsed with each jolt of exquisite sensation.

He pressed an affectionate kiss on her tummy as his lips coasted to the underside of her breasts where he licked and teased.

"Tell me if I hurt you," he whispered as his mouth closed over her taut nipple.

The sensation was so extremely acute it nearly had her coming again. She gave a hoarse cry and he paused.

"No good?"

"Good, good ... don't stop..." she panted and he returned his wicked mouth to her nipple.

He gently sucked and nibbled as her hands roved over his muscular back, a masterpiece of chiseled bulges and dips. She longed to run her tongue over every hill and valley. She pressed at his shoulder.

He lifted, his face flush with arousal, and she nudged his shoulder. "On your back, sailor."

Sliding over his legs, she lowered the zipper. His arousal tightened the denim, but once she had his fly undone, she unceremoniously tugged his jeans off his legs.

"Eager?" he teased, as she yanked his briefs next.

She crawled between his muscular thighs. Gaze fixated, her lips parted. There was nothing disappointing there.

Moving his arms to the pillows, he folded them behind his head. His arrogant expression made her want to shatter his control all the more.

The hair on his thighs tickled her sensitive breasts as she leaned closer. She licked across his hips and he moaned, his cock twitching as she drew closer. Without using her hands, she nuzzled the swollen head of his cock with her cheek and then licked from the root to tip.

His stomach muscles jumped and another moan escaped his lips. She gave him a look of promise before she took him into her mouth, swallowing him to the hilt. Breath hissed through his teeth as his hands knotted in her hair, clamping her to him.

"Jesus, Jade…" Her scalp tingled and her eyes watered as his grip tightened. "I've had so many fantasies about your sexy fucking mouth. Yes…"

Her fingernails dug into his rigid thighs and he let her up only to lead her back down. Apparently, Jeremy liked control.

"Tighter. Fuck." His hips jerked, stabbing deeper, as he held her to him.

Her body tightened at the dominant show. Gazing up at him through glassy eyes, his expression was warped with pure pleasure. "Yes," he hissed. "Let me see those eyes."

He rammed his cock deeper, thrusting and using her mouth. It was scary and exciting and absolutely thrilling to see him so impassioned. Her thighs were wet, her pussy clenching with the need to be filled as he fucked her mouth.

"Enough." He flipped her to her back and

kissed her hard. Urgent energy coursed through the air, matching the burning need pumping through her veins.

She bit his lip and he playfully bit back. His hand moved to her wet pussy, where he quickly delved past her folds with two long fingers. Her hips bucked, meeting his frenzied rhythm. He added another finger as his eyes locked with hers.

"More?" He rasped and she nodded. This was it.

He reached into the nightstand drawer and pulled out a condom. "How will you be most comfortable? How do you like it?" Sliding the condom over his straining erection, he continued to tease her clit as if unable to stop touching her for even a second.

"I like it from behind, but maybe we should start like this."

She didn't know if sex would feel different now. Sure the baby was only the size of a peach, but that apparently was big enough to make her bladder feel like it was being crushed by an anvil, so who knew what else it affected in that region?

He spread her thighs and leaned into the cradle of her hips. His cock nudged at her opening but didn't penetrate. She waited for the dreaded panic to take hold but found nothing but eagerness in her mind. Resting his weight on his elbows next to her head, his eyes met hers as the world slowed to a stop.

Such intensity showed in his gaze, it was difficult to hold his stare. "I love you, Jade."

Before she could reply, time sped forward, seeming to move twice as fast and his lips pressed to hers in a soul-shattering kiss. His cock sank deep and their mouths slowed.

This was it. Jeremy was finally inside of her. It was a surreal moment. He gradually pulled back, his body lifting and steadily moving over hers, his gaze traveling back with increasing emotion hidden in the depths of his stare.

Despite his steady pace, her mind raced. He loved her? Tears welled in her eyes and she blinked them back, not wanting to get lost in the significance of the words. Maybe it just slipped out in the heat of the moment.

Wrapping her legs around his hips, urging him deeper, showing him she wouldn't break, she pulled him closer. His confident strokes pressed deeper as her mind and body tipped into an overwhelming sea of pleasure.

His chest, glistening with perspiration, skidded over her nipples as her center tightened and pulsed. She dug her heels into his ass and urged him on. Their bodies rocked together as they built momentum and the room filled with their moans and the scent of sex.

"Can you handle more?" he asked between breaths and he smiled when she nodded. He pulled out. "On your knees."

She quickly readjusted her position. He moved behind her, placing a kiss at the nape of her neck. A calloused finger trailed down her spine to the cleft of her ass.

Following the crease, he glided his finger over her rear and paused. "*This* will be negotiated later."

She shivered and he aligned himself with her sex. His hand gripped her flesh as he thrust. Slamming her body back into his, she moaned. Her eyes closed as she luxuriated in his complete possession. His hand slid under her body and found her clit, the dual stimulation her undoing.

She frantically rocked her hips as their bodies came together. The sound of their slick flesh colliding filled the room as did their needy cries. He pistoned in and out of her as his fingers rubbed her clit in tight little circles.

Sensation grew, tightening into a knot at her center. Her toes pointed as her calf muscles locked. The walls of her sex fluttered and constricted around his cock with such intensity her climax might have been an act of God.

His hands squeezed her ass as he slid forward, pressing his face into her shoulder. His chest shuddered as he panted her name. She collapsed to the mattress as he tumbled onto his back by her side.

"That was..." he breathed.

"Fucking ... amazing," she finished for him on a wheeze.

They smiled and laughed as they struggled to catch their breath, the moment taking on weight as the subtle levity passed, making room for something too big for her tired mind to contemplate. Suddenly shy, she shut her eyes and snuggled close to him.

No need to address his outburst. No need to ruin the perfect moment.

She awoke sometime in the middle of the night, needing to use the bathroom. As she quietly returned to the bedroom she paused to look at Jeremy. His sleeping expression was completely serene.

One arm draped across his chest as it moved with the slow ebb and flow of his breathing. His right leg was twisted in the blankets, his bare hip and left leg peeking out of the covers in the center of the bed.

Her gaze followed the length of his exposed skin as she moved around the bed, quietly climbing onto the mattress. A trail of scars peppered his thigh. Interspersed with the pale nicks and healed cuts, were larger markings. There was a jagged welt below his hip on his outer thigh and much straighter scars surrounding his knee, likely made by a surgeon's scalpel.

Her fingers drifted to the mark at her shoulder. Scars were funny little bookmarks of life. She had one on her knee from when her dad taught her to ride her bike without training wheels. That one made her feel proud. She had another on her hand from when she tried to be a hot shot chef in her first apartment. That one reminded her to be cautious.

Then there was this one, on her shoulder... No

matter what she told herself about being an innocent victim, that one only made her feel shame.

What did his scars remind him of? Leaning forward, she placed a kiss on the largest scar of his thigh. The linens rustled as his breathing changed. Glancing up, she found him watching her with curious eyes.

"Do you hate them?" she asked.

His expression remained unreadable, and she worried this wasn't something he talked about. "I did at first. Now, I don't even see them."

He scooted toward the head of the bed and she curled into the curve of his arm. His hand stilled her fingers as they traced the scar at her shoulder. She hadn't realized she was doing that.

"I hate this more," he whispered, gently touching hers.

"Does it bother you? To see it, I mean."

She hated that he might see part of her as disgusting, but she couldn't argue with that judgment. The sight of that curious little mark repulsed her too.

"It only bothers me because of what it represents," he murmured, placing a soft kiss on her temple. "In no way does it take away from your beauty, if that's what you're wondering."

"I despise it."

They lay silently for a long time in the dimly lit room, their hands tracing over each other's bodies, learning every nook and cranny. There was something so peaceful about lying in his arms, something she'd never felt with anyone else. It was real and real was always better.

"Jeremy?"

"Yeah, baby?"

"I love you, too."

Twenty-Four

JADE AWOKE TO DEEP, distant voices rumbling from the floor below. A gentle wash of disappointment had her frowning as her hand pressed into the cool side of the Jeremy's bed.

What time is it?

Turning to see the clock, she realized she'd made two grave mistakes. One, sitting up too quickly, and two, it was only seven forty-five. As she rushed to the bathroom, she wondered who the hell made house calls at this hour.

After a lovely bout of morning sickness and almost peeing her pants—because puking took precedence over peeing—she took a shower and vigorously brushed her teeth. Retrieving her borrowed clothes from the night before, she dressed and pulled her hair into a haphazard ponytail.

It was almost December and her feet were freezing from the early morning chill.

She found socks in a top drawer, exactly where she kept hers and snatched a pair. She also found something that should have been destroyed a long, long time ago—a tattered picture from high school of Jeremy, Kat, and herself.

He looked like he did now, only rail thin and too naive for his own good. Kat looked the epitome of innocence, which she was until she got pregnant a few months later. Jade smiled, her attention shifting to her younger self. She wore a cocky smirk like her shit didn't stink—*which it didn't.*

God, we were babies. Where did he get this?

Feeling like a snoop, she quickly placed the picture back at the bottom of the drawer and covered it with clothes. She pulled his way-too-large socks over her feet and padded into the hall. Pausing at the bottom of the stairs, she listened to the grate of baritone voices rumbling from the kitchen.

"I want it wired to all the windows and doors," Jeremy said. "None of that key on, key off bullshit either. I want it so that if a door's opened, it beeps until it's shut."

"Does she have any pets we need to work into the system?" A deeper voice asked.

"No, it's just her. And if someone breaches the system I want to be notified the same time as the police."

"You got it. A system like that isn't cheap though, Jer."

"I'll handle it."

Were they talking about her? The cottage? Feeling like she should be a part of this discussion, she stepped into the kitchen.

Jeremy was sitting with his back to her and a giant of a man was sitting across from him. *Holy Goliath Batman.*

She thought Jeremy was big. This guy could turn the chair supporting him into kindling. Every thread of his shirt looked ready to split as it stretched taut over his enormous, chiseled biceps. He was nothing but cut muscle.

Pitch black hair tucked behind his ears, dusting his shoulders, exposing a jagged scar down his neck which disappeared beneath the collar of his shirt. He was a gigantic broken beauty of a man—

"I can see why you'd want to protect her."

Jade's gaze snapped to his. Piercing blue eyes, trimmed with lashes so thick and dark they looked lined with coal, stared into her and she found it impossible to move.

Jeremy walked to her and brushed a kiss across her lips. "Hey, baby. Did we wake you?"

"No, uh, I was sick," she mumbled, looking back at the outsider.

"Do you want some toast?"

She shook her head and he followed her gaze.

"Oh, this is Trent. Trent, this is Jade."

The man stood, his head nearly clipping the

light fixture. He reached out a hand. "Trenton Cole."

"Jade Schultz," she replied as his hand swallowed hers. Pulling away, she took a seat at the far end of the table.

"Trent lived with me in Okinawa. He lives in PA now and specializes in security."

She glanced at Trent but had a hard time maintaining eye contact. His overwhelming size made her sit a little straighter and want to hide at the same time.

Jeremy poured a glass of milk and put bread in the toaster.

"Jeremy's been telling me a little bit about the problems you've been having, Jade."

She shot Jeremy a chastising look, but he had the nerve to appear unrepentant, pointedly arching an eyebrow at her as if daring her to disagree.

"He tells me you don't have an alarm system at your new place."

If she was going to be informing anyone about the inadequate security at her home, it certainly wouldn't be a guy who could smother her in her sleep with his pinky. Her roundhouse wouldn't even reach this guy's cash and prizes.

Jeremy placed a glass of milk in front of her with some lightly buttered toast and returned to his seat. "She doesn't have sensory lights around the perimeter either."

"I have locks," she grumbled, taking a bite of her toast and pushing her milk aside.

"She has privacy locks." Jeremy slid the glass of milk back in front of her.

"And this is a single home?" Trent asked.

"Yup, ground level too. Drink your milk, Jade."

"That really isn't a great set-up." Trent turned his baby blues on her. "I got my one sister all hooked up, mortise locks, night latches, sensory alarms, *and* a panic button."

"Is she expecting an invasion?" she joked, but no one laughed.

Jeremy gave her a reproving look. "This isn't a joke, Jade. You live alone and you're small."

"I have Tyson and Kat two houses away."

"How's that going to help if someone breaks in during the dead of night?"

"Oh, come on, you've heard me scream," she teased, trying to lighten the mood. Trent laughed. Jeremy didn't.

"I'm serious. You need to be prepared in case—"

"Look," she interrupted, not about to divulge her every vulnerability in the presence of a stranger. "I've already started my morning with puking. I'm sorry if I don't want to follow that up with a discussion about how defenseless I am to predators. You're going to do whatever you want anyway, so why even argue about it?"

Her voice cracked and she became painfully aware of Jeremy's enormous friend watching her. Did he think she'd object to a better security system at her home? She wasn't an idiot, but she also knew having the best alarm in the world still wouldn't make her feel safe. Nothing would.

"If someone wants to harm me badly enough there's nothing I can do about it. I'm small and uncoordinated and every day I become more and more pregnant."

"You're pregnant?" Trent interrupted.

"Yes!" *Why the hell am I crying?* "I'm a big, hormonal mess. So, if you don't mind, I'd rather skip the lecture. You don't need to scare me because I'm already terrified. Put whatever goddamn alarm in you want. Now, if you'll excuse me." She stood, jostling the table enough to spill a splash of milk over the rim of her glass, but she couldn't deal with that at the moment. "I need to go cry."

When she reached the living room, she sat on the couch and tried to calm down. She wasn't even that upset—not *really.* It was super sweet of Jeremy to have his burly security expert friend customize a security system for her home. What other guy would do such a thing? She should be thanking both of them for taking such an interest in her safety, but she couldn't stop crying. She wanted to bawl into a pillow and the fact that they'd hear her only made her want to cry more.

"Got yourself a feisty one there." Trent's voice carried from the other room.

"I don't know why she got so upset."

"Well, first of all, she's a woman. They're all nuttier than bat shit. Second, she's pregnant. She won't be normal until that kid's at least three. Third, we probably *did* scare her. No one likes to feel helpless and threatened."

"I should apologize."

"Give her a minute. It probably didn't help that I was here, a stranger."

Not wanting to hear anymore, she grabbed her coat and slipped out the front door. She needed fresh air and some privacy.

Trent was right. She was going nuts. But surely she'd be better before her child turned three. Right?

As she sat on the cool cement of the front porch—probably increasing her chances of finishing this pregnancy with hemorrhoids—the front door opened. Expecting to see Jeremy she turned, only to find Trenton Cole. The guy was seriously freak show tall, probably had carny ancestors.

"Hey, you okay?"

She wiped her now wind-dried tears from her face and nodded. "Sorry you had to see that."

"Got a lot of sisters. I've seen it before." He awkwardly folded his body and sat next to hers on the step. His booted feet stretched onto the pavement like leathered cinderblocks. "How far along are you?"

"Almost thirteen weeks."

"It's about to get a lot easier. My one sister, Phoenix, cried every minute of her first trimester. It was like she was possessed. We'd tease her and she'd start laughing hysterically, but still cry while she laughed. It was like she was leaking."

She giggled because she could relate.

"Then, when she reached her second trimester, the tears just stopped. My other sister, Bristol, she walked around half-naked the entire pregnancy. Said there wasn't a laundry detergent out there that didn't irritate her nose or skin. I figure you ladies are doing something almost godly, creating life and all. You do whatever you gotta do to get it done."

She smiled, beginning to like Trenton Cole. "Do you have kids?"

"Nope, can't. I was in an accident when I was a boy. Got this scar on my neck and my equipment was damaged."

She made a silent "O" with her mouth, not sure how to reply to something like that.

"Got eight nieces and nephews, though. I spoil the girls rotten and make sure all the boys know how to fight and curse. My sisters don't really appreciate that much, but boys gotta know how to be boys, you know?"

"You said your sisters names are Bristol and Phoenix? Are you all named after places?"

"Yup, Bristol, Phoenix, Ireland, Georgia, Brooklyn, Paris, Dallas, Austin, Brielle, Carlisle, Carolina, and Trenton Jr."

"Wow." She shook her head. "I didn't realize there were so many places that could be used as baby names. How did your parents pick them?" She needed to start thinking about names.

"Well, my mom was from Trenton and my dad

was from Bristol. She always wanted to visit Ireland and I don't know how they came up with Georgia. I guess they just wanted to stick with geography."

"What are your parents' names?"

"Bill and Nancy."

She chuckled.

"You got a name picked out for your little one yet?"

Placing her hand on her stomach she thought. There were names she liked to say, like Jebediah and Aurora, but they weren't the names she wanted to give her first-born. Maybe she should name the baby after someone she loved, like Kat. Katherine Schultz. No, that didn't sound right. She could always go with something nice and traditional, John, Kate, or Will, but that didn't feel right either. She wanted something good, something strong.

"I don't know."

"Well, you got time." He patted his denim-clad knee with a big bear claw of a hand. "And by the way, not that I'm suggesting anything, but just so you know, my equipment might have been damaged, but it still gets the job done."

Yikes, Way too much information. Time to change the topic. "So you're going to install my alarm?"

"That's what I hear."

He didn't intimidate her as much as he had five minutes ago. "Is that what you typically do, alarms and stuff?"

"Actually, no." He unfolded his legs and re-crossed them at the ankles. "I do all kinds of security, but mostly I work as a guard."

"Like a prison guard or like a Kevin Costner-Whitney Houston kind of shtick?"

He laughed and it practically rumbled the foundation. "I've done the bodyguard thing, but I'm better than Kevin Costner. I've also guarded valuable objects and celebrities' children and bounced a few private parties for politicians. And I teach self-defense."

That got her attention. "Really? Could you teach me some moves?"

"Sure. Want to learn some now?"

"Okay! We just have to watch the bean in the belly."

He laughed again as he stood up. "I promise not to harm the bean."

She stood and faced him with her legs apart and knees bent. Her eyes were level with his torso. "Jesus, you're big."

He laughed.

"What do you eat, antelope for breakfast?"

"Nah, too chewy. I prefer buffalo."

She smiled and tossed her coat to the steps. "Okay big guy, I'm ready. Let me warn you, I'm small, but I'm spry, so watch out."

"Settle down, Scrappy Doo. I'm just going to show you some quick defense techniques. Now, your most powerful weapon's your elbow. If your attacker comes at you from behind, make a fist, hold it with your other hand, and slam it as hard as you can into their solar plexus." He curved her hand into a fist and showed her the technique.

"Use your entire torso to throw your weight into the strike, but strike before he has a chance to grab your waist. Once he makes that grab, your mobility's limited and you lose force."

She cuffed her left hand over her right fist and jabbed her elbow back. "Got it."

"If he does get your waist, your next best weapon is your foot. Keep it low and kick as hard as you can. A clear cap to the knee can incapacitate an attacker, but it isn't always an option. Don't underestimate the power of simply slamming down your heel on someone's foot. And don't try to get fancy with round houses and *Karate Kid* shit. If he grabs your foot mid-kick, you're done. You want to move fast."

She nodded. "Kick low, aim for the knees. Got it."

"As soon as you strike, bring your limbs back into your safe zone. If he gets into your zone, you fight him out. This isn't a time to shy away from a little blood and gore. If you throw a punch, aim for the throat."

He pointed to his own throat and she again took note of the jagged scar there.

"It'll do more damage there and not be as hard on your fist as, say, a face. Remember, no one's expecting you to tackle, detain, and hog-tie your assailant. Your only objective is to escape."

She bobbed and weaved. "Got it. Heel, no face, elbow. What next?"

"Use your palm and slam it as hard as you can, upward toward his nose. If he bleeds, he'll be distracted. Don't be afraid to use your fingers to gouge out his eyes."

"Ew."

"You're defending your life. If you have nails, even better. Or a set of keys, but only if they're already in your fist, which they should be if you're walking alone. Don't think about it, just do it, and when you do, be prepared to run. People don't take kindly to losing an eye."

Blowing out a breath, she bit her lip and stopped bobbing. "I don't know if I can poke someone's eye out."

"You could if you needed to. You fight dirty. You pinch, scratch, and even bite if you have to. And if he gets you on your back, you drive your knee into his balls with all your strength. You ready to try out some moves?"

"What if I hurt you?" The things he just explained could seriously fuck someone up.

"You won't. We're gonna move slowly, no force. We're just doing a run through the motions to help you remember."

She nodded. "Okay."

He walked behind her. "Stay where you are. You're alone and walking. You have no idea you're being followed."

His warm breath clouded in the cool air of her peripheral. She shut her eyes, imagining the scene.

He grabbed her shoulders. "He's got you. What do you do?"

Making a fist with her left hand, she held it with her right and, in slow motion, slammed it into him.

"Good!" he said, as he dodged her shot. "You knocked the wind out of him. Now what?"

"Run?" she guessed, unsure.

"Okay, you run. Go ahead, go."

She took a step just as his long arms snaked around her ribcage, pulling her feet off the ground and she sucked in a startled breath.

"He's bigger than you. His reach is longer. Before you ran, you should have made sure you had a fighting chance. Don't be afraid to do a little damage." He lowered her to the ground. "Elbow him more than once while he's bent over. Why not go for the temple? You only need to deter him long enough to get away. Every distraction is to your advantage."

With each word, his warm breath fanned across her cheek. His grip remained on her upper arms, firm and secure.

"What the fuck's going on?"

Trent's attention jerked to the porch where Jeremy stood, brows low. She slammed the heel of her socked foot into the top of Trent's boot and he grunted, his arms instinctively loosening.

She spun. Her arm extended to his jugular,

halting a mere hair before making contact. "Throat!"

Opening her fist she held her palm up to his face as if directing traffic. "Nose!"

Grinning triumphantly, she made a peace sign with her fingers and pointed them at his face. "Eyes."

His smile was slow but proud. "Atta girl."

Beaming under his approval, she turned to Jeremy, raising her chin. "I just kicked his ass!"

Jeremy scowled and she pressed her lips together trying to hide her delight. Wasn't defense his big thing?

"Maybe we should ix-nay on the ighting-fay," Trent mumbled from the corner of his mouth.

She turned to Trent and then back to Jeremy. "Oh please, come on. Jeremy, *I* kicked *his* ass. He's, like, three times my size!"

The morning sun glittered across Jeremy's golden hair as he bent and reached for her coat. He walked over to her and wrapped the jacket around her shoulders, pulling it closed in the front. As she looked down she realized her nipples were stabbing against the shirt in the cold December air.

"You shouldn't over-exert yourself."

She frowned at him. "I didn't."

"Then why are you flushed?"

"Probably because it's cold out or because I was crying twenty minutes ago."

"You have hives." His thumb brushed over her cheek.

Trent tilted his head to examine her face.

"Huh, maybe you wanna go in and take a look at that, Jade."

"What?" She pressed a hand to her face. "Oh, *sonofabitch*! I get them when I exercise. I usually have to take a pill before my Pilate's classes, but I can't take them while I'm pregnant. It's nothing, really."

"Well, maybe you should go and splash some cool water on your face," Jeremy suggested.

"Yeah, right." She snorted. "And leave you out here so you can pee all over the spot I was standing on and be all territorial. Give me a break, Jeremy. We were just having fun. He was teaching me *self-defense*. I figured you'd be all about that."

"Really, man," Trent chimed in. "I didn't show her anything I haven't shown my sisters."

"Yeah, so stop being all possessive and weird," Jade tacked on, teasing.

"I'm not being weird."

But he was being possessive, which she sort of liked. There was such a sensitive man hidden under all that growl and gruffness. He wasn't fooling her, not when he always made sure she had enough milk and asked if she was warm enough. And if he thought she didn't know about him playing princesses with Mia, he was wrong.

Seeing he wasn't taking her teasing well, she gave him a hug. Nestling her cold nose into his warm chest. "I love you."

His arms tightened around her and he kissed the top of her head. "I'll catch you later, Trent."

His words sounded almost like an afterthought, as he shuffled her up the steps.

Trent laughed. "All right, man. Call me when you're ready to have that system installed. Nice meeting you, Jade."

"Nice meeting you, too," she called as Jeremy shut the door behind them.

He turned and locked the deadbolt, facing her with clear intentions. She stepped onto the first step and he slowly stalked her. Her position on the stairs put them almost at eye level.

"Did you like Trent?" His gaze locked with hers.

"Yes. He's nice. Are you jealous?" She stepped up another stair.

"Should I be?" His hand played at the tie of her sweatpants.

"No, but I think you are. You look like you want to mark your territory."

"Maybe I just don't like seeing your face all flushed from exertion while you're in another man's arms." He pulled at the string and the pants loosened, drooping around her hips.

Another step. "Maybe I don't like the *feel* of another man's arms."

The pants fell to her ankles, tangling at her feet. He moved his hand to her arm, securing her balance, as her other hand grabbed the railing.

"Still no panties," he rasped his focus now between her legs. Lifting his gaze, he watched her as he dragged a slow knuckle over the hood of her clit. ""Spread 'em."

Her feet stepped further apart as his finger slid into her wetness and her breath hitched. His gaze locked with hers as his finger slid deep inside of her.

"Will you use self-defense if I fuck you here on the steps, Jade?"

She loved the way he said her name when they were being intimate, voice thick with arousal. "Never with you."

She inhaled as he added another digit, cupping her pussy as he buried his fingers inside of her. "Careful." Reaching down, he moved the pants from around her ankles and tossed them aside, never taking his fingers out of her.

She stood before him in nothing but oversized gym socks and his too large T-shirt. He smiled as his fingers withdrew slowly, glistening as he brought them to his mouth. "Sit."

She lowered herself to the step as he kneeled before her on the foyer floor, pressing her knees apart. His gathered the extra material of the shirt in his fist and yanked it behind her, exposing her pussy. Leaning in, he dragged his tongue up her slit.

She arched backward, her fingers gripping the lip of the step as his fingers returned, pushing, teasing, stroking her into a fast frenzy. Her moans echoed through the empty house, reverberating off the rafters. He crooked his finger and she shattered, gasping his name as he made her come hard and fast.

"Beautiful." He kissed up her thigh, dragging

his tongue slowly over her exposed flesh until he found her mouth. Her arms wrapped around his shoulders as he kissed her softly.

He was the perfect lover for her. Tender when it counted, but feisty when the time was right. It was like they were made for each other. *And* he loved her. He actually loved her. His mouth moved to her neck as he drew her into a hug. She tightened her arms around him and started to, of course, cry.

"Hey, hey… Baby, what's wrong?"

Sniffling into his shoulder, she hiccupped. "Nothing. I'm sorry. I don't know what's wrong with me today. I just can't stop crying."

Trent was right. It was like she was leaking.

"Come here." He picked her up and turned, seating himself on the steps. She rested her damp check on his shoulder as she sniffled.

"Did something upset you?"

"No, I was just happy."

His lips pressed into a thin line as his eyes creased.

"Don't laugh at me. There's nothing funny about this!"

His broad shoulders quaked as he tried, unsuccessfully, to hide his amusement. "Maybe you should just let it all out."

"But I wanna have s-s-sex on the steps." Dear God, it was getting worse. She gasped and choked on an inhalations.

His laughter pealed from his lips in a deep gasps.

"I said it's not funny!" She shoved his shoulder, but he was so damn built he barely moved.

"I'm sorry." His words vibrated with laughter. "I really am..."

She leaned back and frowned at the top of his head.

He took a few deep breaths, small hoots of laughter slipping out in between. When he finally gained control, he blanked his expression and raised his head, keeping his face under control for about three seconds and then bursting into guffaws again.

"Oh, for God's sake!" She shoved off his lap and marched up the stairs.

"Wait, don't go!" he shouted, *still* laughing. "I'll stop... I swear..." He fell back against the wall, holding his stomach and yelled in a mock crying voice, "But we were gonna have sex on the steps."

When she got to the top of the stairs she pulled off her sock, balled it up, and pegged it at his head. He dodged it, the dick wad. "I hate you."

"You love me."

"No, I'm pretty sure it's hate."

His mouth twisted in a crooked smirk as his gaze turned challenging. "I'm coming to get you in two seconds. You better be naked on my bed by the time I get there."

She scoffed and then saw him start to move. With a squeal she pivoted and bolted down the hall, her own laughter now mixing with his.

Twenty-Five

IN COMPARISON to her previous mood, Jade was a little too chipper at work that week and people were starting to wonder about her. She tried to dial down the euphoria around her more despondent patients but gave up after about an hour. There was no use. It was as if she had extra teeth in her mouth and needed to grin.

And why shouldn't she be happy? She was in love, she hadn't had heartburn in two days, and she was about to tear into a huge *Tasty Cake* from the vending machine.

"You seem happy."

Feeding her last quarter into the machine she turned and saw Dr. Philips, a young, handsome surgeon from a floor she sometimes worked on.

"Hey, Bryan." She punched in the code for her chocolate fix. "I am happy."

As her snack fell to the bottom of the machine

she reached into the trap to retrieve it. Springing back up to face the doctor she smiled. He had one of those faces that could be in a catalogue, all American boyish charm in the shape of a man. His medical degree didn't hurt matters either, although he did have a bit of a chip on his shoulder from time to time. But with his grandparents funding an entire wing of the hospital and his father one of the most prestigious surgeons in the country, she supposed he was entitled.

She tore open the cellophane. "Life is good."

"I'm glad." He turned, holding a paper coffee cup under the spray of the cappuccino machine.

She shut her eyes as the caffeinated fragrance steamed from the cup. "God, that smells divine."

Reaching for the stack of cups, he held one out to her. "Want a cup?" No wedding band. Maybe she should introduce him to Lily if they didn't already know each other.

She bit into her cake and swallowed. "No. I can't. I'm trying to cut back on my caffeine. Thank you, though." She took another bite and moaned.

"Well, you know that Twinkie probably has more caffeine in it than a cup of coffee."

"Shhh, one step at a time, doc."

He watched her for a second and she sensed he was a little jealous. A kind person might offer him the other half. She was kind, but that half belonged to bean. "So good."

He chuckled. "I can tell."

She liked Bryan Philips and, again, wished

she could fix him up with Lily. Although they all worked in the same hospital, the two never really crossed paths. Jade, however, knew them both and thought they would make a nice couple.

"Are you dating anyone?"

He paused mid sip and met her stare. "Not at the moment. Why?"

She wiped her mouth and crumpled the wrapper in her hand. "I have a friend. She works here. You should check her out."

He frowned. "A friend?"

"Yeah. Lily Bishop."

"I know Lily."

"Oh. Good." He didn't seem too interested. "Do you not like her?" Everyone liked Lily.

He shrugged and leaned a hip against the counter. He looked good in a lab coat. He and Lily could have little junior practitioner babies that would be adorable with her Latin complexion and his strong features.

"She's nice. I never really talked to her about anything but work. I'm not sure she's my type."

"And what is your type?"

"Why this sudden urge to fix me up?"

She shrugged and dusted the crumbs off her fingers. "I don't know. I just figured... I'm always surprised you're single."

He gave her a slow smile. "Aren't you single? I'd find that more surprising."

"I was, but not anymore." Nope! She was happily taken. "God, that coffee really smells good."

Bryan frowned at his cup. "Why this sudden need to give up your one vice?"

"Ah, but I have many vices, shoes, clothes, romance novels. Coffee's but one and I'm merely trading it in for the next few months. I could never abandon caffeine completely."

"And what's in few months? Don't tell me you're doing that crazy cleanse all the other nurses are on."

"You just saw me devour a cupcake."

"True."

She tilted her head. In another month there'd be no hiding her condition. "Well, in six months I'm going to have a baby."

He coughed into his cup and quickly wiped his mouth. "You're kidding?"

"Serious as a heart attack."

He looked at her, his mouth open, but no words came out. "How far along are you?"

"A little over three months."

"Well, that's ... that's wonderful, Jade."

"Thanks. I didn't plan it, but I'm adapting."

"Well, you seem happy." His eyes studied her for a long moment. "I'm happy for you."

"Thanks. You're actually one of the first coworkers I've told, so you should feel very privileged."

"I'm truly honored." He theatrically bowed at the significant honor. "Who else knows?"

"Well, Lily knows, and my ... friends, but I'm thinking I can start telling the others now."

He nodded. "You aren't showing much yet."

She stretched her scrubs over her belly. "A little."

He stared at her stomach then looked at her face. "So, Lily... Did you mention my name to her?"

Jade's smile grew. "No, but I can. Do you want me to?"

"Yeah. I'll take her out and see how I feel."

That was the one drawback to Bryan. Sometimes he acted like his opinion was the only one that mattered. For the most part, he was cool with Jade, but she'd seen him act like a bit of a me-monster with some of the other nurses. She hoped Lily got the nice side of him.

"Lily's a good catch. I think you might like her once you get to know her outside of work."

"We'll see. I have specific tastes."

Ugh. She really didn't want him going into this with that attitude. "I'll let you know if she's interested."

He chuckled. "Find me when you do." He glanced at his watch. "I have a patient I need to get back to. Good luck with the ... baby."

"Thanks. See ya."

As soon as he walked out of the break room, she pulled out her phone and texted Lily.

Hey! What do you think of Dr. Philips?

Bryan Philips? IDK sort of a walking ego. Why?

. . .

Jade frowned. So Lily knew him well enough to know his flaws.

I think he's sort of cute. You should go out with him.

Maybe YOU should if you think he's that cute. Not my type. He's too young and a little entitled for my taste.

Okay, maybe his reputation was worse than she realized. He was always nice to her. Little quiet at times, but very attentive whenever she asked him anything. She texted back, asking Lily to just think about it. She hated the idea of her friend being alone over the holidays, which were rapidly approaching. She was happy so she wanted everyone to be happy.

Once Jade stuffed her phone back in her pocket, she bought one more treat from the vending machine as a snack for later. Checking her watch, she chugged the rest of her water, tossed it in the trash, and returned to her shift.

She'd done it. She'd told someone about her pregnancy and the world didn't crumble into pieces. Perhaps she could finally share her news with her parents.

Twenty-Six

JEREMY FINISHED up some routine paperwork so he could address more pressing matters while Jade was at the hospital. Closing out the program on his main computer, he opened his favorite search engine and typed in the number *4*.

His results showed nothing but a bunch of businesses with the number in their title. He switched to an image search and again came up short. The first twenty pages were simply the numeral in different fonts and colors and some pictures of people holding signs that said 'Vote 4 Change'. Not what he was looking for.

He tried using key phrases like, *the symbolism behind the number 4, definition of 4, clubs that identify with the number four,* but none of the results were what he needed. He wished he could draw the mark and somehow feed it into the search engine, but Jade hid the scar behind clothing and he wasn't quite sure of the exact detail. He couldn't very well study it because it was a sensitive subject and he didn't want to upset her. As things were going right now, he was just wasting time.

Frustrated, he grabbed his keys and headed for the door. As Jeremy drove out of Parkside, he hit up his Bluetooth.

"What's the address for *Trinidad's Salon* in New Castle, PA?"

The phone rattled off the street address and linked it to his GPS. Recalculating his route, he quickly turned left and headed toward New Castle.

The salon looked more like a boutique than a beauty parlor. Display racks of makeup and delicate hand carved boxes too small to keep anything in filled the entrance. Some beauty products were made completely from beeswax.

He frowned as he saw the prices. How did a little tube of something cost thirty dollars?

"Are you shopping for your girlfriend?" a woman dressed in black asked, giving a coy smile.

"Uh, yeah." Jeremy quickly grasped the opening. "Am I in the right place? I'm looking for *Trinidad's,* the salon."

"You're in the right place. Our salon's in the back. Were you interested in a massage today or perhaps a manicure?"

"I'm not really the salon type—"

"Oh, we have plenty of male clients who enjoy our spa. Sometimes there's nothing nicer than an intensive Swedish massage after a long day's work." She touched his arm as if they were old friends. "We also have lots of men who enjoy our buff no polish paraffin dip."

"What's a paraffin dip?"

"It's a manicure where your hands are dipped in warm liquid wax. It hardens and, as it's pulled off, it removes all the old follicles and dead skin cells."

"You ladies sure like to find uses for wax. Sounds painful."

"Oh, I don't know." She pulled his palm close and examined his fingers. "I'm sure a tough guy like you could handle it. You have rough hands. I bet you do a lot with them."

He politely retrieved his hand and took a step back. "Would a manicurist do this?"

"Of course." She giggled.

He wasn't sure what was funny, but smiled anyway, trying to remain friendly. "I don't have an appointment."

"Oh, I'm sure I could squeeze you in somewhere." Her lips twisted into a smile. "Come with me."

She sashayed to the counter where she typed something into a computer. The screen was hidden from the customer's view so he wasn't sure what she was typing.

"Last name?"

"Larson."

"First name?"

"Jeremy."

"Phone number?"

He rattled off his number.

"Birthday?"

"You need all this information to do my nails?"

"We like to send cards to our clients."

"Oh."

So outside his comfort zone he considered bolting, but then he thought about Jade and figured she was worth the sacrifice of his manhood for one afternoon. He recited his date of birth.

"And you've never been here before, correct?"

He had an idea. "No, but my friend goes here. She came for a manicure a while ago. Is there anyway you can set me up with the girl she saw?"

"Sure, what's your friend's name?"

"Katherine. Katherine D'Angelo. Or it might be under Adams."

The woman typed some more. "Here she is. Let's see... It looks like she's been here a few times in the past year. Would you like to see who she had her last manicure with?"

"I know she really enjoyed her first visit. Can I see who she saw that day?"

"Let me go back in her file. Oh, here it is. Hmm, that's weird. There are two names here."

Bingo.

"I'm not sure if she saw Caroline or Rebecca. Well, it doesn't really matter. Rebecca isn't here anymore. Would you like me to see if Caroline's available?"

"Yes, if you don't mind."

He was finally getting somewhere. Hopefully, this Caroline was the woman with the scar. He had other places to go today and hoped to get his nails buffed, grab the info he needed, and get going without being neutered in the process.

"Oh, you're in luck! Caroline has an opening. Have a seat and I'll let her know you're here."

While he waited, he was assaulted with random womanly questions about his preference in shades of lipsticks, what scent of perfume he liked best, and forced to sample lotions. Female shoppers didn't care who they talked to. By the time he was called back for his appointment, he was pretty positive his testicles had crawled into his stomach never to descend again. He seriously needed to wrap this up and go hammer some drywall or something.

He was escorted through a room of odorous chemicals he never smelled before and was seriously questioning how the hell something could smell that awful and at the same time make a woman pretty. As he sat in a cushioned chair at an undersized vanity, he noticed a drill with all kinds of pointed drill bits hanging to his left.

What. The. Fuck.

"Hi, I'm Caroline."

Pulling his gaze away from the display of torture devices, he looked at the woman taking a seat across from him. She was in her mid-thirties, had short brown hair, was of average weight, and disappointingly, had no scar on either hand.

Letting out a sigh of disappointment, he said, "Hello."

An hour later and about a hundred bucks poorer, he got back into his car and got the hell out of Dodge. His search, so far, had turned up nothing worth his efforts. He wasted an hour having his fingers soaked, picked, clipped, filed, and dipped in hot wax, all to learn that Rebecca, the manicurist with a scar in the shape of a four, had quit and moved to Florida eight months prior.

What a waste of a tank of gas, even if—cough, cough—his hands were softer than a baby's bottom.

Caroline was nice, but she didn't know much about Rebecca. She remembered she was in her early twenties and new to the area. From what Caroline could recall, the girl was always falling in and out of love and having her heart broken by various men.

She did remember the scar on the girl's hand but said she never talked about it. She once got upset when Caroline asked about it. That sounded right.

She was very helpful but politely refused to give him Rebecca's last name. He supposed if it was someone asking about Jade, he wouldn't want her name thrown around to curious strangers either.

Growling in frustration, he drove down Ninth Street. He needed *something*, some little detail he could use to find this prick.

What did the mark mean? Was it a game, a form of *tag, you're it?* All he needed was one clue to follow and once he found that thread he'd pull until the motherfucker completely unraveled. Then he'd kill the cocksucker with his bare hands.

He couldn't believe how well Jade was taking all of this. He didn't know if he should be grateful or skeptical. He worried it was a façade, that inside she was breaking. But the more time he spent with her the more he believed she was truly unbreakable. And in denial.

He tried not to think too hard about the details as he reached his next stop. Perfect timing, too, because he could really use a drink.

The Pink Lounge was a recently revamped bar attempting to bring the sophistication of New York to New Castle. It did okay, he supposed.

Years ago, it was a dive where his father and his reprobate friends wasted their days and paychecks boozing. Now, however, it served mostly top shelf liquors and was a place the locals could score a good martini. He wasn't sure when the new management took over. It must have been sometime when he was in the service, but it was a nice place for a date—or so he'd thought.

The lounge was dimly lit and voices were buffered with soft, trendy music. Red velvet booths made for a more intimate environment. The walls were papered with vintage *fleur de lis* prints and the moldings were painted glossy black.

He took a seat at the bar, the same place he and Jade sat the last time, and ordered a beer. The bartender behind the counter was a woman, not the man who served them the night of the rehearsal dinner.

He drank his beer and observed his surroundings. From his standpoint, the view was limited. He could see the people to his left and right, the bartender, but no one sitting at the tables behind him. Someone could have easily watched them the night they were there. Everyone could see who sat at the bar, but that left the patrons sitting there with their backs to everyone else.

Currently, there were only a few other customers present. He supposed Tuesday evenings weren't big bar nights.

"Can I get you another one?" the bartender asked.

"Sure." He gave her a friendly smile and she returned it. "So, you guys stay pretty busy here?"

She placed the beer in front of him and removed his empty. "We do all right. I used to work in the city, so it's nothing like that. I made better tips, but by the time you figure in the cost of gas and travel, it really isn't worth it."

"How long have you worked here?" He took a swig from his bottle.

"In February it'll be a year. Why, you looking for a job?"

"No, just curious. I remember when this place was the Tavern. It's changed a lot."

"Yeah, well, Frank's a stickler about keeping the clientele to a certain standard. If he could, he'd probably make it one of those bars where customers can't wear jeans or flip-flops."

"Is Frank the owner?"

"Yup."

"I guess you don't have many incidences with rowdy drunks here like they do in the city."

"No, not as much, but there's always your run of the mill asshole." She rolled her eyes.

"Every time I've been here I've never seen any bouncers or guards. It has to be nice to work somewhere you don't have to worry about fights breaking out."

She expertly sliced lemons and tossed them into a garnish tray. "Sometimes I guess that's true, but whenever there's an issue, if Frank isn't in the back, I have to remove the problem myself. It doesn't happen a lot, but when it does, it's a pain. It pulls me away from my customers and that means I'm losing money."

"Yeah, but there has to be security cameras in case anything gets out of hand," he hedged.

"You casing the joint?" She laughed. "We have cameras, but they mostly cover the exits and the offices."

Good to know. And footage he very much needed to see. "A buddy of mine specializes in security. He'd be more than happy to set you up with a better system and help out with security on your busier nights."

"Oh." Her expression told him he was discussing issues above her pay grade. "Well, I guess you could talk to Frank about that. Do you have your friend's card or something I can give him?"

So, Frank wasn't there. Damn. "How about I leave you my number?" He jotted it on a napkin and slid it across the bar with a twenty. "Keep the change."

"Thank you. I'll make sure Frank gets your number."

"Thanks. When's Frank usually here?"

"Every night, ten 'til closing and all day on Thursdays, Fridays, and Saturdays."

He'd definitely be back.

～

She should be coming out of the Emergency Room entrance any second. It had been the same routine since he first saw her. She always parked by the ambulance garage and went in and out through the ER. Sure, she threw him off a bit when she cut back her hours, but now she was back to work, back to her old habits.

He reached in his console and found a book of matches. Pulling a cigarette from his pack, he returned his gaze to the exit. Someone was coming.

Is it her? No, just another fucking patient.

Delicious adrenaline had his cock hardening in expectation. Just one glimpse was all he needed. He'd mastered her every routine, even her weekly visits to a shrink. That had been a close call the other day in the garage, but seeing her walking around so smug and fearless... He wanted to shake her up. Loved seeing her on edge. It wasn't often she could surprise him, but she recently took him out of his safety zone so it only seemed right to knock her out of hers.

Now, she was back to a routine and he was back to doing what he loved most—watching her. People were generally habitual beings. Jade was no different. Until recently.

He struck his match and inhaled deeply, the interior of his otherwise dark car momentarily glowing red. Where the fuck was she? He assumed she'd want to get back to her *boyfriend*.

Fucking jarhead.

She thought she was so smart, moving to her new place, screwing some military reject, just living it up over there on 100 Happy Street with her friends. Well, he had other plans.

He'd made it in and out without getting caught, wiped her car, wiped her memory, wiped her place. There was only one tiny complication.

The memory of her hand resting protectively over her stomach filled his mind. His fingers tightened on the steering wheel. Unable to leave any strings untied, he waited for more validation. Her apartment was a bitch to watch, but the little cottage she'd moved to had low windows and no neighbors sharing her walls. It would be so easy to—

There she is.

Chucking his cigarette, he hunched low behind the wheel. The silent car hummed with the slow pull of his zipper. The weight of his cock heated his flesh as his fingers wrapped around his length and squeezed, remembering her tightness.

"There's my little slut. What have you done, Jade? You've done something very, *very* bad." His eyes rolled as he squeezed his dick, stroking faster as the hiss of his breath filled the silent car.

She paused in the breezeway as someone spoke to her. The contour of her belly pressed against her coat as she turned, showing him once and for all that his fears were true. *Stupid fucking cunt.* She was spoiling everything. And why did she look so fucking happy?

As she took another step, he saw who she was talking to. It was that fucking doctor again. He wondered if the doctor knew what happened to her, wondered if Doc was working with Jade to piece together evidence. Well, they'd find nothing.

His fist pumped quickly, his harsh breathing fogging the glass. There wasn't much time. Staring hard at her tits, he gripped his cock almost painfully and grunted as he came.

Sloppy filth.

Yanking a tissue out of the side compartment, wiped himself clean, and tossed it behind him with the heap of used tissues he'd gone through in the past week. He should have her clean them up with her filthy whore mouth. Fuck, he was still hard. This was what she did to him.

He'd used protection the first time he fucked her, but a lot of fucking good that did. Damn her for lying there like a little fuck toy, those full lips open and silently begging for him. She deserved it again and again and he made sure she got it. This was her fault.

"Fuck!" He shoved his cock back in his pants and grabbed another cigarette.

Linking a bastard's DNA to an unknown suspect was improbable, but he couldn't have a loose end like that walking around for the rest of his life. One slip up, one mistake, and his info would be in the system. If she made a report—which she hadn't yet—they'd eventually find it.

It seemed like a tall order keeping his record spotless for the rest of his life. But he had connections, so there was always a way. Still... it was safer to simply get rid of any evidence now.

She hugged the doctor goodbye and walked to her Lexus. Zipping up his pants, he timed the turn of his key with her engine. Would it be the boyfriend's tonight or the new house? Time to find out...

Twenty-Seven

THE SUN GLINTED in his eyes as he dialed Jade. He was installing the new alarm system at the cottage with Trent and Tyson while she was at his place keeping an eye on Mia.

"Hello?" she practically gasped into the phone.

He frowned while fidgeting with the front door. "Why are you out of breath?"

"We're outside twirling. It's snowing!" She laughed, the sound mingling with his daughter's giggles in the background.

"I thought the snow wasn't supposed to come for a few more days." He squinted into the cloudy December sky and cursed. Snow was definitely on its way.

"I think we're supposed to get a blizzard or something early next week. I don't think this is it. This is just flurries. It's not sticking."

"It's just cloudy here." She was as free spirited as a kid at times. How could a little precipitation make someone over the age of twelve so happy?

"Is that Daddy? Ask him where my sled is!" Mia yelled in the background.

"Mia, sweetie, I don't think there's enough snow to actually go sledding."

"Please," Mia begged.

Jade laughed. "Mia wants to know where her sled is."

"It's in the shed. Tell her I'll get it out when I get home."

"And when will that be?"

He looked toward the other guys to see how things were coming along. "Well, we're wrapping up with the locks now. Trent's installing your alarm sensors and Ty's wiring your motion detector lights. I'd say I should be home by dinner. Is that okay?"

"That's fine. I told Mia we'd make Christmas cookies. I stopped on the way over and grabbed a tub of the frozen kind you slice and decorate."

"The *frozen* kind? That's cheating!"

"It counts! Besides, if I made them from scratch no one would eat them. This is really better for everyone."

"Kiki, come on!" Mia yelled. "We can play *Beauty and the Beast* and dance in the snow."

"Sounds like you're being summoned. I'll let you go. I should be home by five. How's pizza for dinner?"

"Great. I'll see you then."

"Love you." He snuck in the sentiment before she hung up.

She giggled and whispered, "Me too."

Grinning, he headed back inside the cottage.

Trent screwed a tiny sensor to the top of Jade's back door. Jeremy returned to installing the night latch on the front door. "I told the girls I'd be back by five. You think that's doable?"

"I'd say definitely doable. Ty's halfway done. He just needs to get up in the attic to run some wire to the other end of the house and set the timers to test the bulbs. After this, I gotta hit all of the windows and install the main control panel. Once that's done, you gotta run all your codes and shit to activate the system. I'd say another three hours tops."

Two and a half hours later they were right on schedule as Jeremy was screwing the last sensor on Jade's bedroom window. It had snowed briefly, but not enough to interfere with their work.

Tyson came through the front door and a piercing beep filled the house. It stopped as soon as the door shut. "We're good out back. The two front bulbs should wrap the house enough to cover all angles, but we won't be sure until it gets dark. I'll test them out tonight."

Jeremy's phone rang and the screen said *HOME.* Jade was probably getting hungry. "Hello?"

"Daddy?"

"Hey, baby. You making cookies with Kiki? I hope you saved some—"

"Daddy, something's wrong with Kiki," Mia interrupted, panic in her voice.

Holding a hand up to tell the guys to quiet down, he covered his other ear. "What's wrong?" She hadn't had morning sickness in a few days.

"I don't know. She won't come out of the bathroom."

"Okay, princess. Where are you now?" He tried to remain calm, not wanting to upset Mia further. Ty stepped closer.

"I'm in the kitchen. What should I do?"

"Stay calm. Can you go to the bathroom door?"

"Okay."

He listened as Mia stomped up the steps. Tyson and Trent gave him questioning glances, but he couldn't take his ear away from the phone until he knew what was going on. They thought she was past the puking stage, but the book said it sometimes returned.

He heard Mia knock. "Kiki? Kiki, Daddy's on the phone. He wants to talk to you." Her breath echoed in the phone as she knocked again. "She's not answering, Daddy."

"Does it sound like she's sick, Mia? Did she say she had a belly ache?"

"She said her back hurt."

"Put your ear to the door. Tell me what you hear. Does it sound like she's throwing up?"

Mia shuffled the phone against her clothing. "It sounds like she's crying."

He silently cursed. "I'll be right there. Wait for

me on the steps by the bathroom in case Jade calls for you. Keep the phone with you. Call me if anything happens. I'll be there in ten minutes, okay?"

"Okay, Daddy."

He hung up the phone. "Something's wrong with Jade. I gotta go."

Tyson grabbed his keys. "I'll follow you and get Mia,"

"I'll stay here and lock up. Hope everything's all right," Trent said, as they left the house in a rush.

As soon as Jeremy got in his car he dialed Jade's cell phone. It rang four times then went to voice mail. He dialed again only to have the same result. As he turned onto a straight run of road, he texted, *Call me.*

Too impatient to wait for a reply, he called her phone again.

"Fuck!" he yelled, as it went to voicemail.

As he stopped at a light Tyson pulled behind him, talking on his phone. He was probably speaking to Kat, telling her something was up. The light changed and Jeremy sped through the weekend traffic. About six minutes later he peeled into his driveway and ran into the house.

"Mia!"

"I'm here, Daddy." She stood at the top of the stairs holding the cordless phone in her tiny hands, her eyes huge in her pudgy face.

"Did she come out yet?" he asked, taking the steps two at a time.

"No."

Jeremy quickly pulled her into his arms. "Listen to me. Sometimes grown-ups get sick, that's all. You did the right thing by calling me. Now, I have to check on Jade. Tyson's on his way here. I want you to go sit at the kitchen table until he gets here. Okay?"

"Okay." She sniffled and he kissed her on the cheek, waiting until she turned down the hall to speak to Jade.

"I'm here, Jer."

Jeremy thought quickly. Whatever was going on with Jade, he didn't want Mia around. His daughter was already upset and he had to focus on Jade at the moment. "Take Mia home. I'll call you."

"You got it," Tyson yelled.

Jeremy jiggled the bathroom handle, which was obviously locked. "Jade?"

He listened but heard no reply. "Jade, baby, it's me, please open the door." Pressing his ear to the door, he listened again but only heard silence.

"Jade? Honey, I'm going to count to ten and then I'm coming in. One...two..." He heard nothing, not the running of water, or the sound of her breathing—no crying. When he reached ten he yelled, "I'm coming in, so move away from the door."

He took a step back and kicked at the knob. The door splintered from the frame and the knob hung loosely in its spot. He shouldered forward and the lock broke free. A chill raced through his body.

She sat on the toilet, hunched over, her arms wrapped around her middle, her face wracked with tears. She faced him and her mouth opened in a silent roar of agony. Her legs were buckled around the seat and her pants bunched around her knees.

He didn't understand. "Jade?"

That was when he saw it. Blood. It coated her hands and thighs like dark, horrifying oil. It was everywhere. *Jesus Christ, the baby.*

He staggered to her and fell to his knees. His hands pulled at her face, trying to get her to see him. She didn't seem to register his presence. "Baby. Baby, look at me."

Her torso and lap were smeared with crimson. There was just so much. His eyes prickled with tears as he pulled her into his arms, holding her as tightly as he could.

A brutal sob escaped her throat, taking him back to memories on the battlefield. Tremors shook her body as she moaned in agony. He rocked her back and forth as they huddled on the floor, his own tears mingling with hers.

"I've got you. I've got you..."

In a tortured wail, she moaned, *"Why..."*

Twenty-Eight

A MACHINE CHIRPED. That steady chirp was the only thing Jade could think about. *Chirp... chirp...chirp...* She lay on her side, hollow and vacant, listening to the beeps every few seconds. She knew they were there, Jeremy, Kat, and Ty, waiting for her to awaken. She didn't want to wake though. She wanted sleep, mind-numbing sleep.

The heater kicked on and she couldn't decide if she was warm or cold. Her pillow smelled of bleach. The fabric was coarse and starched against the slightest flick of her lashes. She stared at a half-occupied outlet and wondered if she lost her mind enough, if she could slip away into those tiny holes that sat empty, as hollow as she felt. She wasn't making sense, but nothing did.

She wanted to slip away. Just let go of everything. Escape. Break from the pain. Never come back.

Her peripheral vision caught sight of her wrist curled under her cheek. Her nails were dirty. There, wrapped around her arm, was a band telling her where she lay. A familiar place, a place she visited many times a week. A place she planned to eventually admit herself and leave as a mommy.

That was all different now.

She was a patient, but not in a way she'd ever expected. She wasn't there to be a nurse, and she wasn't there to become a mother. No, they brought her here to finish someone's ugly trick.

She lost everything.

Her baby was gone.

Her pillow moistened with tears and she wondered if she would ever blink again. *Chirp...*She was empty, too light to hold to this world, too vacant to cope, too processed to breathe. The door behind her opened and she quickly shut her eyes.

They wouldn't understand. They wouldn't grasp the pain, humiliation, or loss. There was no one who shared in this baby's life as she did, no one who could comprehend how real her child had been, how important to her sanity.

Footsteps moved nearer, then a soft whisper. "Is she asleep?" It was Kat.

"Yes," Jeremy whispered back.

"What did the doctor say?"

"He said she lost a lot of blood and needs to rest." His hoarse voice accompanied his touch as a hand coasted along her hair. He touched her as if she might break from the slightest contact. Too late, she was already broken.

"They wouldn't tell me anymore than that because I'm not her husband."

"I found a nurse named Heather. She said she contacted Dr. Bishop. She's Jade's friend and primary OB. She might give us more information. Did you call her parents?"

"No. They didn't know."

"It's probably best to wait, then," Kat said. "She'll get through this, Jeremy. She's stronger than anyone I know."

There was a long beat of silence.

"I didn't understand it," Jeremy whispered. "When I found out what happened, I couldn't comprehend why she'd want it, but now..." He took a deep breath. "Now, I can't imagine her without it. She loved that child to a fault. I couldn't understand how she saw past the evil that put it there, but she did. Everyday, I watched her adapt more and more. How's she going to get through this?"

"She'll get through it like she gets through everything else in this world, with integrity and blind courage," Kat promised. "I know it'll take a while, but I assure you, Jade will make it through this. I'm not saying it won't leave a mark, but she'll be okay. She *is* okay." Her eyes shimmered. "She's just ... heartbroken."

"God, I hope you're right, Kat."

～

Jade woke to the crushing realization that the nightmare she dreamt was, in fact, her life. Unable to deal, she fell back to sleep. A few hours later she awoke again to the same realization, only this time when she tried to escape it with unconsciousness, sleep proved evasive.

"Are you awake?"

She opened her eyes to find Lily sitting across from her.

"Jade, honey, I'm *so* sorry. I'm so sorry this happened and I'm so sorry I wasn't here to help you get through it. Dr. Zoll said there were no other options. Sometimes our children just aren't meant for our arms to hold."

Hot tears trailed down her face. Every word resonated with tawdry truth and she refused to contribute to such simple explanations for her pain.

Lily rested a hand on hers. "If there's anything I can do, please tell me. Are you thirsty?"

Was she thirsty? Her mouth was dry, but even the idea of the effort of quenching thirst exhausted her. Swallowing hard, she looked at Lily and said, "Sleep."

Lily took a deep breath. "The ache in your heart will still be here when you wake up. This is something that only time can heal, honey, not sleep or drugs."

She nodded her understanding but said nothing.

Finally Lily said, "I wouldn't normally do this." She stood and walked to the door, requesting a nurse bring her five milligrams of *Ativan*.

Returning to her seat, she whispered, "I'll do this for you one time, Jade. I know it hurts, but this type of pain isn't the kind you medicate. You need time. If in a few days you're still out of sorts, we'll talk about other kinds of prescriptions. These past few months have been incredibly difficult. I'll write you a script for bed rest and have Nancy start the paperwork so you can file for a temporary leave of absence. Not that I expect you to stay in bed or recommend it. I want you to keep yourself busy. Try to enjoy the holiday, maybe spend the New Year in Antigua. Take time to be sad, but then take time to realize all the things you have to be happy for. Doctor's orders."

She loved Lily, but she made everything seem too simple. That's how most people would treat her loss, like it didn't count. While they never saw her child, she felt it, heard its heartbeat, and in four more weeks, she would have seen its tiny face at her next ultrasound. Unable to prevent it, a sob escaped.

Thankfully, the nurse arrived. She took the pills and quickly swallowed them. It was just too much. She needed to make it all go away.

When morning finally came, Jade sat on the edge of her hospital bed feeling physically tender and emotionally hopeless. They were kicking her out, or 'releasing her' as they put it.

She didn't want to move. She didn't want to do anything, but apparently, her situation didn't usually require patients to be admitted longer than a day.

Whatever.

She just wanted to get out of there and find her own bed, away from the rest of the world.

"You ready?" Jeremy asked from the door, his voice gentle.

She nodded. The simple movement required more energy than she had.

After she signed all the release forms, Lily gave her a hug, and Jade was escorted to Jeremy's car parked by the visitor's entrance where Kat and Tyson waited. Jeremy was very attentive, supporting her weight, speaking in soft tones. He seemed to think the slightest movement or noise would shatter her into a million pieces. He was probably right.

They all scrutinized her, waiting. For what, Jade didn't know.

Kat's brow creased with worry. She stood by the fender of Jeremy's Jeep, wringing her hands in front of her slightly swollen belly. Jade had to look away.

Jeremy helped her into his car and fastened her seat belt. Before he closed the door Kat came to Jade's side. Her friend couldn't look her in her eyes, so she just looked toward the ground as she wrung her hands.

"We'll be there when you get home. I went to the store and got your favorite DVD's. I also charged your cell phone and left it by your bed, so call if you need anything. I'll bring you something to eat in a little bit, okay?"

She wanted to tell Kat she didn't need to do all that. She wanted to tell her she was okay, but all she could manage was a nod.

As she shut the door, Jade shut her eyes. She was a terrible friend, incapable of seeing past Kat's condition, seeing everything her friend still had in comparison to all Jade had lost. She couldn't seem to stop her envy from swallowing her whole.

When they pulled into her driveway, Jeremy again helped her to the door. He unlocked the door and a shrill, repetitive squawking pierced her eardrums. She jumped and the tight pull of her abdomen was like an emotional explosion in her brain. Jeremy cursed and quickly typed a code into a panel on the wall.

"Sorry."

She silently nodded.

He got her settled into bed and brought her a glass of iced tea. Once he put in one of the DVD's Kat had picked up, he told her he'd be back in a few minutes. "Call me if you need anything. I'll be right next door."

As he left, she rolled to her side, shut her eyes, and cried.

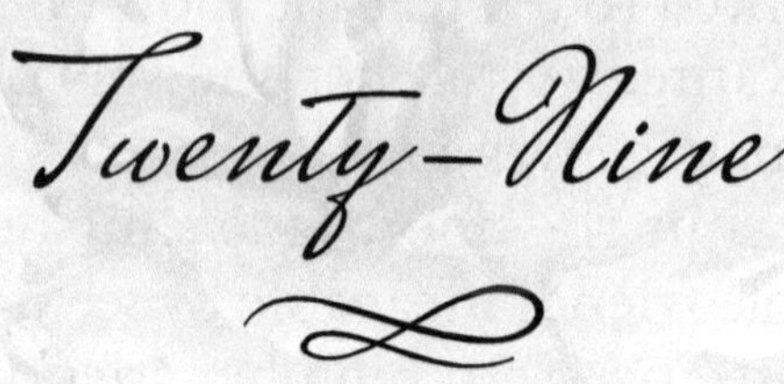

Twenty-Nine

"HOW IS SHE?" Kat asked as Jeremy walked into her kitchen.

"The same." He took the beer Tyson offered, exhaustion settling in every muscle of his body.

Kat frowned. "Ty, it's eleven-thirty in the morning."

"Let the man have a beer, Kat. He hasn't slept in thirty hours." Tyson pulled out a pitcher of iced tea for himself.

"Fine, but don't forget you have to pick up Mia in a few hours."

"Do you see me drinking?" Tyson snapped and Jeremy worried he'd walked into something he shouldn't be a part of. The fridge slammed and, without another word, Ty left the kitchen.

"Sorry," Kat said, her voice trembling. "We just had an argument. He told me I coddle Jade and I got a little defensive."

Jeremy didn't want to get involved in their argument so he took a sip of his beer. He just wanted to get Jade's lunch and get back to her. He didn't like leaving her alone.

"Maybe I do," Kat said, apparently satisfied with having a conversation with herself. "It's just, Jade did everything she could when I was pregnant. She was always there when I was scared and alone."

He tried not to wince as guilt sliced through him. Kat would have never been scared or alone if he had manned up and acted like a father from the start.

She sighed. "I remember, right after my parents kicked me out, I didn't budget my money well enough and my electric was going to get shut off. Jade loaned me the money. And when Mia was an infant, she got sick. I didn't have a prescription plan and the antibiotic the pediatrician prescribed cost over a hundred dollars. Jade picked it up and never asked for the money. She got me all the papers to apply for a government medical plan after that."

"She has a good heart," he said, stating the obvious.

"She's always helped out any way she could. She picks up Mia when I can't be there, takes her overnight. She's so good to our daughter. She's stuck by me through every bump in the road and convinced me I was strong enough to make it through and now..." Her voice cracked as she gave in to her tears. "Despite my hopeful words at the hospital, I don't know how to get her through this."

Jeremy tentatively rubbed a hand across her shoulders and Kat turned into his arms. "I feel incredibly selfish for being pregnant while she's going through this."

He hugged her, wishing Ty would come back so he could return to Jade. But maybe this wasn't Ty's mess. Maybe it was his.

"Kat, that's crazy. You can't feel like that. Jade would never hold your pregnancy against you. She loves you. She's happy for you and Tyson. Just give her time before you start asking her opinion on baby names. She'll get through this just like you said. We have to be patient while she adjusts. It'll take time, that's all." He hoped his words were true.

"I know you're right." She wiped her eyes and took a step back. "But I'm not going to stop taking care of her. So, if you or Tyson or anyone else has a problem with that, they can just ... eat shit."

Jeremy laughed. Kat never learned how to use swear words with the right confidence to back them up. The girl could be in the middle of a catastrophe and the vilest thing she'd utter would be somewhere along the lines of *fiddlesticks*.

"You do whatever you think helps. She may not appreciate it now, but I'm sure she will in the long run."

There was one more thing he needed to read-dress, something he should have made clear a long time ago. He took a deep breath.

"Kat, I was wrong to leave. I know I said it before, but maybe I don't say it enough. No matter how hard your situation was, you proved to be one of the most incredible mothers I've ever met in my entire life. I'm eternally grateful you loved our daughter when I didn't know how. I was selfish and wrong and I can never apologize enough for abandoning you and Mia."

She smiled and wiped the tears from her eyes. "Our daughter has two good fathers now. That's all that matters, Jeremy. Even if one was a little late, he showed up and hasn't missed a day of her life since. That's what counts, Jeremy. That's what she'll remember."

As he walked back to Jade's with a covered bowl of chicken soup, he saw Kat hugging Tyson in their backyard. When he entered the cottage, he quickly shut the door and punched in the code so the alarm wouldn't disturb Jade. He opened a drawer, retrieved a spoon, and grabbed a napkin, heading into her room. She was asleep again.

Placing the bowl on her dresser, he covered her with a blanket. As he sat in the chair beside her bed, he recalled the days after his buddy Josh died in Iraq, how all he wanted to do was sleep. Those were some of the worst days of his life, the kind he didn't have the strength to face ever again. He figured there wasn't any harm in letting her rest a while longer.

~

Jeremy's concern grew over the passing days. Jade had only left her bed to use the bathroom, had uttered nothing more than a simple yes or no answer, and slept for hours on end. She wasn't eating and when she was awake her eyes looked vacant and haunted. Needing to do something, he flipped through the contacts in her phone until he found the number he wanted.

"Dr. Wolfe's office, this is Jennifer. May I help you?" the receptionist answered.

"Hi, this is Jeremy Larson, Jade Shultz's boyfriend. May I please speak to Dr. Wolfe?"

"Oh, hi, Jeremy. Jade missed her appointment today. Is she feeling okay?"

"Well, that's why I'm calling. Is Dr. Wolfe available?"

"She's with a patient right now. Would you like me to have her call you when she's finished?"

"Yes, please." Jeremy gave the receptionist his number and returned Jade's phone to her nightstand.

When the doctor finally got back to him he explained what had happened. She was, of course, concerned and very upset to hear that Jade had lost the baby. Jeremy explained how much she was sleeping and how little she was eating and communicating. Dr. Wolfe agreed to stop by to see her later that evening.

~

Jade woke up to the sense that someone was watching her. She opened her eyes and found Jeremy sitting beside her on the bed.

"How you feeling?"

She shrugged, lacking the energy to pretend otherwise.

"You have a visitor."

She cringed. She didn't want company. She wanted to be left the fuck alone.

Over the past couple days, when she wasn't crying, she was suppressing the urge to cry and claw the walls. She wanted to kick at the furniture and slam things and punch anything close to her until her knuckles bled.

"Who?" she rasped and winced, her throat hoarse from disuse.

"Why don't I let you see for yourself? I'm going to run next door and see what Mia's doing. I'll be back in a little bit."

She wanted to object. It wasn't that she cared if he left, she just didn't want to be left alone with company. Before she could voice her protests, he kissed her on the head and said, "Call if you need me."

As he left the room, Jade sat up and frowned at the door to her bedroom. *No visitors.* Why was that so fucking hard for people to understand?

Chloe entered her room, and her anger washed away with relief. Her grief faded for a millisecond, replaced with gratitude, and then every emotion tumbled through her in an avalanche she couldn't handle. Jeremy figured out the one person Jade didn't mind seeing.

Unrelenting emotions slammed into her, and, as if a trigger was pulled, she broke beneath the weight. Letting out a sob that was more like a war cry, she moaned as her shoulders quaked.

Chloe was by her side, pulling her into her arms in a matter of seconds. "Oh, honey. Let it out."

Jade flung every broken word she knew. She sobbed and wept and pleaded and crumbled while Chloe sympathized through it all. When she finally calmed down, Chloe tried talking to her.

"I know it hurts, Jade. It's going to for a while. I can't imagine the loss you're suffering right now, but it isn't healthy to let it destroy you like this. Like I said before, sometimes life takes us on unpredictable turns and we scrape our knees along the way, but we have to keep moving. This is one of those turns. You need to take a moment to look at your path, accept the detour, and figure how you want to move on. This is not a life sentence. I know you loved your child. No one's taking that away from you."

"How can anyone bear this much pain?"

"It's an unfortunate part of the miracle of life. Look at this as a sad experience you survived because you are strong. And you learned a bit about yourself, too. Now you know how much pleasure being a mother could bring you, no matter what the circumstances. I'm not telling you to run out and get pregnant. No child will ever replace the one you lost. But you need to keep in mind that your days of becoming a mother are not over."

"But that one's gone. I'll never hold him or her. I never got to give all the love I felt."

"You gave everything you could, honey. You're young. You're healthy. All that love will find a place to go. You just have to hold onto it a bit longer than you expected."

"I just feel so empty." Jade wiped her eyes. "I feel like there's a hole in my heart and a gaping void in my womb. It's like an amputation. I reach for my stomach to connect with my baby, but then I remember nothing's there and I want to scream and punch something."

"It's okay to be angry, expected actually. You've been through one traumatic ordeal after another and perhaps, after all this, you're coming to terms with everything you've suffered. There are stages of grief. Anger's one of them, but your friends aren't the enemy here."

She was tired of being blindsided by life. "What are the stages of grief?"

"Well, there's denial, anger, bargaining, depression, then acceptance. I'd say you're passing over the first stage and entering the second. Most people bounce back and forth, in and out of stages for some time after a trauma."

"I don't understand how bargaining's a stage. It isn't like I can make a deal with God to bring back my child."

Chloe gave a sympathetic smile. "Perhaps the loss of your baby isn't the only thing you are grieving. What have you consistently said since our first session, Jade? This baby was the one beautiful thing out of an entirely ugly experience. I think the baby was a shield for you, something you focused on to cope with what you went through. The baby's what got you through the stage of denial, a bargaining chip for your initial loss. Now that shield's gone and you're probably realizing some lasting affects the baby helped you ignore."

"Chloe," she said, shaking her head in shame. "I'm so incredibly angry." She pressed her lips together and frowned. "I've never felt like this before. I feel like I have poison in my veins that needs to be bled out. I can't stomach their happiness when I'm so very sad. Kat has Mia and she's having another child when I have nothing. Isn't that the most wretched jealousy you ever heard? I'm disgusting for even admitting that. If you could hear my thoughts you'd be appalled. I'm a horrible person and an even worse friend. But where's the fucking balance?"

"And there's your bargaining. What you just did is the grieving equivalent to counting your cards before placing a bet. You see, it isn't about what's fair. It's about what's real. Good or bad, this is the life you've been given. You can accept it and try to make the best out of a horrible situation, or you can spend your days complaining about all the things you didn't get.

"But that's not you. You're too smart to let life

pass you by. I know it hurts now, but, with time, it'll hurt less. It'll become a memory you hold in your heart and think about from time to time, but what you will eventually remember most, is not how sad you feel now, but how hard you fought to survive that sadness, how much love that baby filled you with in the short amount of time you had it."

Tears silently fell as she nodded, taking in everything Chloe said. "Thank you."

"You know I'm always here. Tell me what you want and, together, we'll figure out a way to reach your goals."

She sniffled. "I want to be happy again. I want my life back. I want to stop feeling victimized, like I'm the result of someone else's actions. I want control of my own life."

Chloe smiled. "Good. Well then, I'd say the first thing to getting back to your old self is getting out of this bed and taking a shower. Put on some makeup and do your hair. Even if you just want to lie around and watch movies all day, do it with confidence. Put on jewelry and perfume and re-member who you are—start acting like the woman you want to be. Before you know it, you'll find her again. What else do you want?"

"I want a martini," Jade said and laughed. She hadn't had a drink in months.

"I think we can arrange that."

She looked at Chloe and, with absolute calm and determination, said, "And I want to find the person who derailed my life and make it so I never have to feel threatened or victimized by him again. I want justice."

Chloe's smile was replaced with absolute understanding. She nodded tightly. "Okay, Jade. Then we'll move in that direction."

Thirty

"YOU'RE SURE ABOUT THIS?" Jeremy asked as he held a bottle of chilled *Patron* and a bowl of oranges.

"Absolutely." Jade smiled as she sat across from him on her couch, legs tucked under her as she bounced with anticipation.

She'd done exactly what Chloe advised. She'd gotten herself out of bed and slowly but surely started acting more and more like her old self. Jeremy had been relieved to see the change in her mood and was now convinced Chloe was a magical person akin to the Easter Bunny or Merlin the Magician. Jade kind of thought the same.

Although she still suffered from severe moments of sadness almost too heavy to survive, she pushed the melancholy thoughts away and focused on the positive. She allowed herself time to cry, alone in bed at night, but maintained as normal of a life as she could manage during the waking hours of her day.

It was a battle. Acceptance started when she stopped expecting others to understand her experience the way she did. Every day she reminded herself not to penalize her friends for their lack of trauma, which was the spiral she'd almost fallen into. This was no more her friends' fault than her own and it was ludicrous to misplace the blame. Thanks to Chloe, she understood that now and was progressing toward a balanced, hopefully normal, state of mind.

Jeremy poured the smooth, crystal liquid into two tiny shot glasses and passed her an orange. "What should we toast to?"

"Life. That we never let the ugly parts overshadow the good."

They raised their glasses and clinked them together. The fiery liquid tickled her tongue as the silky, cool flavor of tequila ran down her throat, seeping deep into her belly, warming her from the inside out. Her face puckered and she laughed as Jeremy flinched at the taste.

Her teeth sank into an orange, the juicy fruit soothing the delicious burn. With jagged motions, Jeremy did the same and gasped. "That's terrible."

"Only the first one," she promised, tipping the bottle over their empty glasses. "The second shot's easier and the third's a breeze."

As a self proclaimed beer and whiskey man, Jeremy did his best to abide the tart selection, keeping pace with her shot for shot. Tonight was about meeting her resolution to get very, very drunk.

As the evening progressed, their coordination suffered. Her worries faded with the passing of her inhibitions, and laughter fell from her lips, cleansing her soul as she reacquainted herself with old pastimes.

Sliding to the floor, she flipped through her iPod. "Oooh! Beyoncé!" Cranking the stereo, she jumped to her feet and clutched her microphone —a.k.a. the half empty bottle.

Her blood pumped as she gyrated to the fast beat. The world blurred and her lips stretched over her grin as she mouthed the words to *Crazy Love*. She let go.

Somewhere in the midst of their mortifying dance-off, she had a moment of hope. Jeremy still loved her. Not every relationship could survive such excruciating circumstances, but theirs had.

Twirling and giggling, she stumbled into his arms. He caught her and laughed as the music changed to yet another great song. They talked, danced, ate, talked some more, but most of all, they laughed, which was perhaps the medicine she needed most. It had been too long since she truly let herself go and it was magical, traveling there with Jeremy.

~

Jeremy chuckled as she swung her tight, little ass in his face. Parking the bottle on the coffee table, uncaring of the orange peels that littered the floor, she turned the volume up and reached for him.

She danced like a cat on speed and he perfectly content to be her scratching post. Fisting the neck of the bottle, she tipped it to his mouth. Adjusted to the sour taste, he swallowed back a swig. The song changed, this one heavy and fast, rattling the dainty decorations she'd posed on a shelf.

"Do you know how much I love you?" she shouted.

It couldn't be more than he loved her. "How much?"

"Like this much." She held out her arms and stumbled, but he caught her wrist and pulled her flush to his front.

Tugging her closer, he held her ass and brushed his lips to hers. "That so?"

"Oh, it's so," she slurred and he laughed.

Scooping her into his arms, her legs wrapped around his waist. "Well, I love you more." He stole the first passionate kiss they'd shared in ages, as the rhythmic music filled the room.

Liquor-diluted blood thrummed through his veins and his body swelled. "I've missed you."

Half lidded eyes studied him as he drew back and swayed at a pace incongruent to the fast song playing. "That's why I love you, Jeremy. You only *miss me* when I'm gone. You never give up on me."

Giving a slight shake of his head, he promised, "I can't give up on you, Jade. I care too much that you're happy."

Her forehead pressed to his. "You make me happy."

"You make me happy too."

As an old Elvis classic came on, he chuckled. "And here I thought you only had shitty music on your iPod."

She gasped. "My music is *not* shit. You take that back right now."

"Fine. But this—*this*—is what I consider music." He swayed, holding her to him, his focus drowning in her gaze as her legs clung to his hips.

"I can't help falling in love with you, Jade Schultz," he whispered.

"I was always afraid of falling," she confessed, her breath ticking his neck as she rested her head on his shoulder. "But with you, I know you'll catch me."

"If you fall... I'll always catch you."

She hummed and pressed a kiss just below his ear. The romantic tune ended and some fast nightmare blared. He winced.

"What. Is. This?"

Her shoulders shook as she laughed and slid down his body until her feet touched the floor. Swaying as if the horns played for her the way a snake charmer plays for its serpent, she became a siren, a temptress, a woman he'd never be able to resist. He smiled as she pulled him into the rhythm, easily the sexiest girl he'd ever watched dance.

"You know what I want?" she yelled.

"What?"

"Bacon."

Snorting, because that was *not* what he expected her to say, he laughed. "You want bacon? Now?"

Holding her hand over her mouth as if divulging a big secret, she shouted, "I only eat it when I'm drunk. But it's soooooo good. We should make some bacon!" She cranked the stereo to the max volume, took his hand, and they congaed to the kitchen.

Thirty-One

JADE AWOKE and immediately wondered if a blind person had given her a haircut with a dull axe. Opening her eyes, she winced as the bright morning light flooded her room. Something heavy was crushing her ribs.

"What did we do last night?" she groaned, giving Jeremy's arm a shove. "You're crushing me." She nudged him again

His unbuttoned shirt only covered one arm and his pants were gone. *Such a cute ass.* Giving him a strong shove, he flopped to his back.

In the distance, Zeppelin was playing. That meant she'd played through almost all of her tunes.

Wiping her eyes, she eased into a seated position. Squinting at her clock there was a half eaten plate of—bacon?—yes, bacon, sitting on her nightstand.

Oh, God. The 'secret' drawer of her vanity, where she kept her toys, was open and a varied array of items hung over the edge. Her leg brushed something cold and solid. Lifting the blanket, she bit her lip, one empty bottle of tequila and one—definitely used—bottle of lube.

Well, mission accomplished.

Stumbling to her feet she hissed and bent to pick up whatever she'd stepped on. It was a tiny house from the *Monopoly* game and several more littered her floor.

Jeremy let out an unattractive snore and she raised an eyebrow. Tiptoeing through the minefield of plastic game pieces, she shuffled to the bathroom. Memories from the night before pieced back together in scattered disarray. But they were there. She made a choice and had control of her actions enough to recall at least the basics of the evening.

A long shower restored a bit of her equilibrium and she found herself smiling as she remembered some of the stupid shit they'd done last night. They were wrecked.

When she entered her room Jeremy was lying with his arm draped over his eyes. "Why's it so bright in here?"

"I feel your pain. I was going to make some toast. You want some?"

"Shh." He moaned. "I need coffee. Lots and lots of coffee."

Jade paused. *Mayday.* "Umm, I think I'm out of coffee."

He released the most pathetic man-cry. *"Whyyyy?"*

Slipping into her pants, she slid onto the bed and kissed his belly. "How about I make breakfast and you get dressed and pick up coffee?"

His hand lazily dragged down her hair. "Tell me you at least have aspirin."

She smiled. "Aspirin I can provide. Go get showered. You smell like the day after spring break in Punta Cana."

Jeremy dressed and headed out the door for coffee. The alarm shrilled and he cursed as the noise stabbed into his skull harder than an icepick. Blinding white light pierced his corneas and he flinched, squinting at the drifts of heavy white snow that weren't there yesterday. Before he had time to process that they'd gotten the blizzard forecasted, his eardrums were shattered by an exhilarated scream from the sidewalk.

"Daddy!"

Looking past the mountain of snow that was his car, Mia, rosy-cheeked and dressed like a Christmas card, trudged toward him. Her pink hat and snow pants popped against the white hills with each trudging step.

"Did you come over to play in the snow?"

"I, uh, came over to dig out Jade's car," he fibbed.

Mia frowned at the two snow covered mountains in the driveway. "Your car's all snowy too?"

"I got a ride," he lied again.

Thankfully, Tyson shoveled himself within earshot and tossed him a life vest. "Mia, why don't you see if Mommy's out of the shower? Ask her if she wants me to make breakfast and tell her to look and see if we have the ingredients for hot cocoa."

"Hot cocoa!" Mia yelled and quickly turned, bounding toward her house.

"Long night?" Tyson asked and Jeremy shook his head.

"Do you guys have some coffee we can steal?"

Tyson laughed. "Already brewed, and you're welcome to take some. You two want to come over for breakfast? You look like you could use something solid in your stomach."

"You have no idea," Jeremy said, glad he didn't have to shovel out his Jeep in his condition.

~

Jade helped Kat finish up some Christmas shopping online, while the guys watched the hockey game in the living room and kept Mia occupied. Her headache had morphed from the hatchet scenario into a dull throb.

Shopping always cheered her up. Although the mall was preferable, the blizzard limited them to Internet spending. While Kat worked on Ty's computer, piecing together Mia's Christmas list,

Jade used her iPad for some of her own holiday shopping. So far she'd purchased a shirt for Jeremy and a dress and some new earrings for herself, and a cute kitchen sign for her cottage.

Every few minutes the guys yelled at the television in the other room. Jade laughed. "I guess Jeremy's head's feeling better."

"What did you guys do last night?" Kat scrolled down a list of toys. "And where the heck is this doll she wants?"

"I'm not sure there's anything we didn't do, but it's just a blur of fun in my mind, so I'm okay with not recalling every detail." This was definitely different than waking up and recalling nothing at all. "What can I get Mia this year?"

"You want to get her this doll that doesn't exist?"

"No."

Kat groaned and shoved the mouse away as she eased back on the chair. "I need a break. Should we order Chinese for dinner?"

"Sure."

"I'll go tell Ty to call." She left the room and Jade snatched Mia's list off the desk.

Before she moved on to the rug rat's gifts, she checked her email to make sure her last order processed. As she skimmed through her inbox, one message, in particular, caught her eye. The email address of the sender wasn't one she recognized, but in the subject line were two words that made her blood run cold. *The 4.*

"What the hell?" She scowled and clicked the message.

J.,

I believe I can help you, but I'll do so only if our communication is kept completely confidential. I don't want any trouble from your friends. If you're interested in what I have to tell you, email me at this address. If I have somehow tracked down the wrong email address and this is not J., please disregard this message.
Sincerely,
N.L.

Sitting back, she exhaled. *N.L.* had to be that guy Nathan. What was his last name? Lake? Leithe? How had he gotten her email address? And why would he suddenly want to speak to her? Was this a trick? Only one way to find out...

N.L.,

How did you find my email address? What information do you have?
-J.

As she contemplated hitting the delete key and tossing the entire message into her spam folder, Kat walked in and asked her if she wanted chicken or shrimp with her rice. Startled, Jade meant to minimize the screen but accidentally clicked *send*.

Turning, she hid her dismay and said, "Chicken."

Jade was convinced she'd lost her mind. She didn't receive a response to her first reply until late Sunday evening. At first, their correspondence was brief.

J.,
Please verify that it is, in fact, you. We share a mutual acquaintance. Who is she?
-N.

Jade wrote back.

K.D. now K.A.

His reply only took a few minutes.

J.,
Do I have your word that what passes between us will be kept in the strictest confidence? The information I have is no doubt something you'll find useful, but I'm reluctant to share it unless I have your

word that you agree to my terms. No one can ever know we spoke. Is that acceptable?
    -N.

Guaranteeing him complete anonymity left her at risk. After much deliberation and a pretty solid plan to protect herself, she finally wrote back.

N.,
    You have my word. However, in the event that anything should happen to me, I've made arrangements to expose you. If I'm unharmed, the evidence of our communication will be destroyed before anyone sees it. I am doing this to secure my safety and feel it's a fair stipulation to our agreement. Let me know if you can abide by these conditions.
    -J.

Nathan took longer than usual to respond to that email.

Agreed. Meet me this Wednesday, 12:00pm, at the coffee house outside of New Castle on the corner of Barkley and Clearwater.

She corresponded with Nathan for five days before finally agreed to meet him. She was taking a huge risk, meeting him without letting anyone know where she was going or what she was up to, but his conditions were unchanging. And her need to know what he knew was keeping her up at night. Her gut told her to meet him, something inside of her saying he wasn't her guy, but he might have the key to finding the bastard she was after.

Presently, sitting in said coffee shop, she sipped her skinny half-caf with shaky hands. She'd been waiting for over an hour, an absolute nervous wreck.

Before she left, she'd written a note on the stationary Kat gave her a while back. In her recognizable handwriting, she penned,

With Nathan Lithe. Call police if you do not hear from me by the time you read this.

After slipping the note into Mia's backpack, which Kat emptied every night around dinnertime, she felt a little more secure in her choice to meet Nathan alone. When she made it back unscathed, she'd simply sneak over to her friend's house and remove the note. If she didn't...

Well, she had visions of swat teams swarming Nathan's home, wherever that might be.

The door to the coffee house opened and her spine stiffened. Without a doubt, Nathan gave off a sinister impression. His beady eyes and well-kept beard and thin mustache did little to hide his lack of scruples—at least that was the impression she got.

Scanning the area, he smirked. Was his smile creepy because of everything she heard about him or was it creepy because he was a rapist and possibly a serial killer?

Please don't let this be the part where I get crammed into a trunk and dragged off to some dilapidated cabin in the woods. Remember what Oprah said. Do not let them get you to the next location!

His gaze found hers and he slowly pulled out the adjacent chair. "Hello, Jade."

She should leave. She should stand up and leave. Just get the fuck out of there. This was a bad idea.

Lowering himself into the chair, he flipped over a small menu and pushed it aside. "Were you waiting long?"

She swallowed. "No," she lied in a barely audible voice.

"Can I get you another coffee?"

Eyeing her drink, inspecting every last froth of foam, she pushed it aside. "I'm not thirsty." Even breathing the same air as her possible assailant terrified her.

He sighed and folded his hands in his lap, perhaps a purposely passive move on his part. "I didn't come here to harm you."

She scoffed, finding his words anything but comforting.

He fidgeted, his gaze skittering to the glass

window and back to her. He flattened his palms on the table. "You don't believe me."

His nails were tidy—the kind that told of little manual labor. "Not even a little."

"But you're here." He looked at the surface of the table as if unable to look her in the eye. "I can't say I blame you. Certain incidents make it difficult to trust others." His gaze finally found hers. "I should know."

Blood running cold, she gripped her purse at her side. If she left, would he follow her?

"May I see your scar?"

Her thoughts jolted as a terrifying sort of paralysis took hold. Everything inside of her stilled except the bile rising in her throat and her heart beating out of control. "Excuse me?"

"May I see your scar?" He repeated.

This was insane. "Yeah, you know what? This was a mistake. I have to go." She lifted her bag.

He grabbed her hand across the table and she froze. She didn't know whether to scream or hit him.

"Get your fucking hand off of me before I scream. I could have the cops here in seconds."

"Please," he beseeched, loosening his hold.

She snatched her hand out of his grip. *This was a no touch zone.*

Lowering his voice, he whispered, "Jade, I want to help you, but I can get into a *lot* of trouble for what I'm about to tell you. These aren't people you fuck with."

He knew who they were. They? Wavering, she scanned the café. Plenty of witnesses and this time she was sitting in the view of a very obvious surveillance camera.

Relaxing by small degrees, she slowly lowered to her seat. "You don't touch me. Ever."

"My apologies. It won't happen again."

She nodded, keeping her hands on her lap, her chair now drawn back from the table. "How is it that you know about... About what happened to me? Did you—"

"No. I swear it."

"Don't be offended if I don't take your word at face value, Mr. Lithe." She wanted to make sure that was his last name so she used it to see if he'd correct her.

"Understandable. But still, if you want me to lay my neck on the line, you're going to have to show me your scar. The day I saw you in New Castle was chaotic and I want to be certain it's what I think it is before I explain what I believe will help you a great deal."

She needed to know what information he was hiding. "Fine. But we're going to do this quid pro quo. And if you go Hannibal Lector on me I swear to God..." She'd what? She thought of Jeremy and is enormous tree of a friend, Trenton Cole. Ty was a big guy too. "I know people. Scary people."

He nodded. "I don't want any trouble."

She took a deep breath and yanked the collar of her sweater aside, turning her head, exposing her branded shoulder. "Satisfied?"

"Yes."

She readjusted her collar and crossed her arms over her chest, sending him an impatient look. "Your turn."

He, too, took a deep breath. "Do you speak Latin, Jade?"

She shook her head.

"No? Okay. Well, there's a group. No one knows who they are or when the group originated. It's a society of sorts, a brotherhood. From what I understand you can't request entry or be grandfathered in. Every member's hand-selected.

"I have no idea how one's nominated, only that I was selected. I don't know what qualifications I had that got their attention. I mean, I went to an Ivy League school, belonged to a fraternity, played some sports, but I was never told such a club existed. It wasn't until I was up for review at my firm and being considered for partner that I was notified about my eligibility."

"Who contacted you?" She was intrigued in spite of herself.

"It's not that simple. I was in my office, just a random afternoon when my secretary brought me the mail. She usually opens the mail and shreds the envelopes. There's a lot of confidentiality in the law business, so we don't like paper lying around."

She arched a brow. "Of course not."

"I found something that, at first, I thought was a social invitation. It was in a heavy, pristine white envelope, the kind you find inside a wedding invitation. On the lip of the envelope was a wax seal. It was embossed with a stylized number four."

Okay, now he really had her attention.

"When I opened the message, I realized it *was* an invitation, but not to an event. It was an invitation to join an exclusive group of professional men. They made it seem like an honor, to be accepted into this society. The letter explained that the group admitted only five members a year. It guaranteed entry into certain circles and seemed an appropriate invitation at that point in my career, but a little too good to be true. I researched it on the Internet, but I found nothing. They weren't asking for a donation or anything along those lines, just proof of my loyalty."

"Proof?"

She highly doubted something revolving around social prestige connected to her assault. Disappointment seeped in as her small flicker of hope faded, telling her this meeting was nothing more than coincidental symbols between her scar and a freaking stamp on a seal.

"Yes, proof. The order was called *Postestas Adimpleo Postestas Quattuor,* which is Latin for the *Authority to Perform the Power of Four.*"

Thoroughly unimpressed, she humored him. "The power of four? What is this, like a math thing?" This was a total waste of time.

"Sort of. The number four has a lot of symbolism. It signifies completion, stability, and predictability. It also represents all earthly things. The logic of the number four flows from the previous three numbers. *One* represents the male principle. It's raw energy and creativity."

She rolled her eyes, but he continued, ignoring her.

"In the creative process, it's the initial flicker of an idea, a scheme, perhaps, to form a secret society. *Two* is the feminine principle, the yin to one's yang. It's the gestational period in which ideas take shape, the earth into which the seed is sewn and impulses grow. *Three* is the synthesis of *one* and *two*. It's the ideation and articulacy of one's plan, the foundation itself, the finished idea. To put an idea to paper, it shows intention. An idea becomes a commitment and is somehow irrevocably made real."

It all seemed too calculated and rote. Too practiced. Yet, now she was listening intently, curious to know the meaning of four.

He looked her directly in the eyes. "*Four* is the material manifestation of *three*, the *physical* fulfillment, the tangible achievement of the idea. It's what happened to you, Jade. You were selected, studied, and conquered with such comprehensive preparation you never suspected a thing."

Holy fuck. Her skin pulled as her blood turned to ice. Her throat tightened, but she couldn't swallow back the lump of dread choking her.

What happened to her had been spontaneous —that's what she'd told herself from the beginning. Her mind didn't allow space for other possibilities. There was no deliberate, coherent plan. It had been nothing more than impulsivity.

She gripped the table and shut her eyes, trying to level out her breathing. Her skin tingled as though a thousand voyeurs watched her, their gazes crawling over her like spiders, each one with multiple eyes. She closed her arms over her chest, shrinking into herself. If what he said was true, there wasn't a single sacred place left for her to hide. She'd been fucking stalked, chosen for some fucked up ritual. And... *My God, they ruined me.*

Nathan weighed her reaction. "Shall I go on?"

She nodded, unsure if she could hear much more.

"*Four* represents mastery. It's a self-righteous and narcissistic belief when applied the way it is to *Postestas Adimpleo Postestas Quattuor.* It's the freedom of life, to do as one pleases as if by the will of God. It's absolute power. Then there is the Negative meaning."

"You don't consider everything you just said negative?" Jade asked incredulously.

"I'm speaking numerically. Of course, I find this entire notion despicable and vile. I know you don't think much of me, but I'll tell you how contemptible I find it in a moment. First, I want to make sure you comprehend how intricate that simple symbol on your shoulder is. The meaning of a negative four is stagnation, fossilization, paralysis, rigidity, or stubbornness. Were you awake?"

"No," she quickly answered. "I was drugged."

"So you can understand how the negative is relevant then."

"I don't understand any of this." Her voice

cracked and she fidgeted to avoid making a scene. She fought the urge to scream, to clear the table of its contents with a swing of her arm, anything to change this reality.

"There's one more factor. That tiny slash above the four on your shoulder changes its meaning from that of a number to a character that can be traced back to ancient times, a character that defines the ultimate violation of a female."

His brow creased and something shifted in his eyes. Regret? He glanced at the table and Jade lost her patience. "Look at me and tell me what it means."

His jaw ticked as he swallowed. "It's the ancient character for rape."

This time it was her who had to look away.

They sat in silence for a long while, neither able to make eye contact. That was it in a nutshell.

Some old boys formed a club, recruited a bunch of men who had God complexes, then they formed an idea, a way to demonstrate the ultimate show of power and authority in their minds. Each member selected a victim, studied her, learned her, and brought their plan to fruition when they finally attacked her.

She reached for her cup but saw how badly she was shaking and curled her fists in her lap instead. She wanted to rail at every despicable man who ever contemplated taking what they wanted without asking.

Her vision narrowed as she lifted her gaze and glared at him, seething. Voice low, a volatile mess of emotion swirling inside of her, she prepared to attack, quite certain she could seriously murder someone in that moment. "Are you a member?"

Backing up as much as his chair allowed, he rapidly shook his head. "*No.* I swear. I was telling you the truth. I have nothing to do with them. I—"

"Then why were you invited to join them?" she snapped. "How do you know all of this?"

Self-consciously scanning the café, he leaned in and whispered, "I don't know why I was invited to join. They only told me only the basics in the first letter, nothing about what was expected. I filled out a form that added up to a resume of sorts and sent it back in the enclosed self-addressed envelope provided. There was no mention of anything besides prestige in the first message."

"Where did you mail it?"

"It went to a P.O. Box in Upstate New York and, like I said, my secretary had already shredded the outer envelope of the original message."

"Original? So there were more."

He nodded. "About a month after that, I received another letter. I told my secretary I no longer wanted her to shred the envelopes until I saw them, but the outer envelope had no return address and came as certified mail, sender undisclosed. That letter told me I had to reach step four to ensure my membership, but they didn't say what that entailed. I was instructed to identify a desirable female. I didn't know why. I thought they were asking me to pick someone I thought would make a suitable wife, just to see what kind of choice I'd make, but I'm a divorce lawyer. I wouldn't get married if my life depended on it."

"So you didn't pick someone?"

"Not a real person. I lost interest in joining the group, but my curiosity was piqued. I couldn't find even the thinnest evidence to prove the society existed and that intrigued me even more. The letters were coming from somewhere. So I sent back my reply with a made up name. I had to give a description of what she did, where she lived, whom she was associated with, and how well I knew her. I made it all up."

"Did they respond?"

"About a month after that, I received another letter. This one had a package with it. That's when I was given a seal. I guess even organizations dating back however long as this one does, still modernize. It was just a sticker. It all suddenly seemed silly and juvenile. I was told to place it on the woman's home or car. But there was no woman, so I put the seal on my own car. I was curious and didn't realize the final outcome of the test."

She drew back, her blood running cold as her muscles tensed as chills rushed from her ankles to her shoulders. "Son of a bitch." Her entire face numb. "Someone put one on my car last year."

He rushed on as if he wanted to leave as much as he wanted to finish his confession. "A month after I received the seal, another letter arrived. I was to wait anywhere between six and eighteen months. Time, I was told, to learn her routines, her quirks. I was to make no move until I became a master. Once I was ready, I should then send them back another envelope telling them I studied the woman and was prepared to *complete* stage four without the chance of error.

"I still considered this all some hokey way to measure a man's respectability, as if all of this was for the purpose of finding a suitable wife, someone to accompany me during social gatherings and such. By no means did I consider ever actually marrying someone to be a part of a club."

"But it was never about marriage," she supplied, hating him, hating that he was the only person she could trust to help her understand what had happened. He seemed to pick up on her increasing hostility.

"Jade…" His eyes turned pleading. "I also never considered it might revolve around brutalizing another human being. If you believe anything, please believe that." He leaned forward and whispered, "I know I'm a prick. I'm a lawyer for Christ's sake. But I also love my mother and my sister and would never purposely hurt a female or anyone for that matter. I could never do what they wanted and never would've gotten involved had I known what would eventually be expected of me."

"But eventually they told you. Somehow you figured this out. How?" He had to know something. Gritting her teeth, she said, "Tell me the part that will actually *help* me."

"Six months later I got another package. It included very specific instructions and a small metal stamp. The second I understood what was actually expected I cut all ties. I tore the seal off my car and shredded all evidence of ever having an association with such despicable people.

"They tell you, in the first letter, the group's not for the meek. They use words to describe themselves as above common law. They consider themselves demigods who are not to be dicked around, pardon my French."

Touching her cup, but not bringing it to her lips, she fidgeted. "They said that?"

"It was implied. Any man willing to accomplish all four stages and provide proof of the crime proved to be a member capable of entrusting the brotherhood with a piece of their soul. Somewhere out there, there's the coordinator of all this, and he holds enough evidence to incarcerate each and every member and destroy their lives. He also, I imagine, holds enough evidence to blackmail his members into assisting others and that's why there's so much influence that comes with the affiliation. With a simple note, he can demand one member do whatever needs to be done to get another member out of trouble. It's absolute power."

Dropping her gaze to the table, she covertly counted the men in the room. There were seven, including Nathan. There were only three women and one was herself. As improbable as such a society seemed, it also made strange sense. There were probably lawyers, police officers, politicians, government officials, and more involved in this boys' club. Each one obligated to anonymously help the other members in exchange for omnipotence.

It was absolute corruption of power. There was no way of knowing how many of them were out there pretending to be members of polite society. She could go to the police and end up reporting her assault to an actual member, who could ultimately be the man who raped her, who could then send another member to finish what was started and kill her.

As if he read her thoughts, Nathan said, "They're dangerous, Jade. You need to understand that. I feel for you, I do. But the best thing you can do for yourself is nothing at all. If you start sniffing around for clues, they'll find out and they *will* retaliate. Forget what happened. Just worry about protecting yourself from here on out. When your baby comes—"

"There is no baby."

His focus shot to her face, his eyes wide and his mouth trembling. "I thought—"

"I miscarried three weeks ago."

His expression shifted from puzzled to empathetic. "I'm sorry, Jade. You already suffered so much. I ... there's no excuse for what they did to you. I'm sorry."

Jade swallowed, forcing back her tears. Hurt gripped her chest like a vise, strengthening her resolve. Shaking her head, she rejected that forgetting what was done to her was her best option.

"I'm not going to just walk away. I'm not going to let fear control me. Yes, your story scares me, but not enough to run and hide. When I lost the baby I promised I'd do everything in my power to—"

"Jade—"

"No," she cut him off. "You were on the other side. You have no idea what my side feels like, what I've been through physically *and* emotionally. I'm not going to let some old boys' club scare me into silence."

Panic contorted his face. "You're making a mistake getting involved with these people."

"*Why?*" she hissed. "For all we know those letters came from one sick fuck. You don't know for sure how many members are out there."

"No, but I guarantee you there are more of them than there are of you. They. Will. Hurt. You."

"They already did."

His insistence faded as his gaze lowered in resignation. "Remember how I told you about the symbolism of negative four?" His voice suddenly sounded riddled with shame. "Well, consider yourself lucky, Miss Shultz. I was not unconscious when they found me. I was beaten to a point that I thought I'd never be curious again. As far as victimization is concerned, we have more in common than you realize."

"What are you talking about?"

He looked to make sure no one was watching and slid his tie to his shoulder. His fingers moved to the buttons of his shirt, loosening the top four as he pulled his shirt apart.

Her breath left in a whoosh. There, on his chest, was a branded four, about six times the size of hers.

He closed his shirt, quickly fastening the buttons and lowering his tie. "I didn't come here to help you catch them. I came here to protect you from making the same mistakes I did. Don't underestimate their power. Put it behind you and try to move on."

Her vision blurred. Glancing at the table, a tear splattered on the smooth surface. "I can't."

"Then I can't help you," he said, regret clear in his voice.

Seeing his mark didn't have the effect he likely expected. It only proved she was not alone. How many more times would this happen to some unsuspecting woman if no one ever tried to stop them? "Sometimes doing what's right takes precedence over common sense."

Shutting his eyes, his shoulders lowered. "You can't use my name. I'm sorry."

She met his gaze and recognized genuine regret in his eyes. He was afraid and she had to respect that, no matter what. "I'm sorry too."

~

He sat in his black SUV parked just around the corner from the café and watched as Jade got into her car. He was still reeling from the relief that she had lost the baby. Sometimes life just worked out favorably on its own.

With all loose ends now tied, he should walk away, but he couldn't stop himself from watching her. She had a way about her. Perhaps it was the glimpse of fierceness he caught every time he heard her speak or perhaps it was the vulnerability that swiftly followed.

Originally, he'd thought she was nothing more than a ditzy blonde. Sure, she was a nurse and that took some brains, but outside of her job, she was a clumsy little kid with big tits who laughed at everything and took nothing seriously.

However, in these past weeks, he discovered a side of her he hadn't known existed. A side he grudgingly respected. She was strong, stronger than he'd assumed. Her short-winded displays of strength titillated him. She had a fire in her belly where their child had been. She was a feisty little mouse and he wanted to get her under his paws again.

The game had changed and he wasn't finished with her. This time, he'd go about it differently.

He'd maintained very limited contact with her up until recently, but now he was ready to show her how perfect they could be together. He'd play his cards right and, slowly but surely, cement himself in her life.

Every day he was making progress toward the inevitable outcome. Soon enough, she'd be his.

Thirty-Two

JEREMY WAS GOING to kill someone. Last he spoke to Jade she was getting in the shower and heading to bed. That was almost fifteen hours ago. She said she had some errands to run today and he assumed she meant last minute shopping. He never thought for a minute she would be doing something as reckless as running off with the asshole who may or may not be the man who attacked her.

What was she thinking? Was she thinking at all?

He'd been wrapping Christmas presents when Tyson called around noon. At first, he couldn't even wrap his brain around what the guy was trying to tell him. When he realized Jade was missing, he immediately called her cell phone, but it went right to voicemail.

It did the same thing when Kat called, which

she'd done the minute she found Jade's note in Mia's bag. What Jeremy couldn't understand was how such a thing ended up in his daughter's backpack. It didn't make any sense.

They each questioned Mia, asking if she found the note and hid it in her backpack, but she promised she never saw it before and was now convinced she'd done something wrong. Of all the places to hide a note like that, Mia's bag seemed absurd.

Why even write a note? How about fucking communicating for once? For all he knew, she'd been kidnapped in the middle of the night.

Kat used her father's connections to get Nathan's phone number, but his secretary said he wasn't expected back until the following Monday, after the holiday. Furious, Tyson called back and demanded the secretary contact Nathan and have him return their call. The man was quite intimidating when his wife was upset, but no amount of intimidation made any of their phones ring.

Trent approached. "I checked the cottage and found no evidence of forced entry. After keying through the electronic log it shows she left around ten a.m."

Jeremy frowned. "Mia leaves for school before then." He looked at his watch and cursed. "She's been gone for hours."

Trent laid a heavy hand on his shoulder. "She'll turn up eventually with an explanation. Try to relax."

He was crawling out of his skin. If that motherfucker harmed even a single hair on her body he'd murder him. He'd aged thirty years in the past three hours, every passing minute taking its toll.

Just let her get home safely. Please.

Kat was speaking to the two police officers who'd been dispatched to the cottage. Jeremy couldn't repeat himself anymore. He needed something to happen.

Kat wrung her hands. "I always go through Mia's bag before dinner. She knows that. She put it there on purpose."

The officer glanced at the sky and frowned. "But you found the note this morning?"

She nodded. "My daughter had a half day. It's Christmas break. I was going to wash her schoolbag. That's when I found it."

"I see."

Jeremy grit his teeth. Kat was meticulous and, knowing her as well as he did, he had no doubt she'd emptied Mia's bag last night around six or seven. That meant Jade had slipped the note inside sometime after that. That also meant she knew full well she was doing something reckless and didn't plan on telling anyone, which made him livid.

Not only did he plan on kicking the fuck out of Nathan Lithe, he was pretty sure he was going to lay into Jade—once assured she was safe. How could she do something so stupid?

Pulling out his phone, he called her again, but there was no answer. He continued to pace, letting his anger seep into every step so his fear didn't consume him.

He needed to hear her voice—something —*anything*—so he knew she was safe. Any minute now he was going to snap.

Where is she?

~

Jade parked around the corner from her house, trying to comprehend all she'd learned. She now had some of the explanations she wanted but wasn't any closer to finding the cocksucker that did this to her. She truly believed Nathan wasn't her assailant. While he still wasn't someone she fully trusted, she now shared an undeniable—if distasteful—connection with him.

Glancing at the clock on the dashboard, she forced herself to put her newfound information on the back burner. There would be plenty of time to process later. Mia would be getting home from school soon and she needed to get the note out of her backpack before Kat stumbled across it. After everything Nathan confided, she owed it to him to hold up her side of the bargain. No one could ever know they met.

Putting the car into drive, she distracted herself by going over her mental shopping list. Despite her Jewish upbringing, she loved the magic of Christmas, mostly because Mia made it so much fun and there weren't anymore little kids in her family to spoil.

As she pulled onto her street—"What the hell?"

Two cop cars were parked outside of the cottage. Jeremy paced her sidewalk like a caged panther and Trent, the giant, was on her porch talking to Tyson who looked furious. Kat was rocking in the rocking chair beside him with her face in her hands. Was she crying? Jade spotted Mia and everything clicked.

"Oh fuck," she whispered. "Fuck, fuck, fuck." She parked at the curb, her mind frantically thinking up one faulty alibi after another.

Jeremy jerked open her door before she even shut the car off. "Are you okay? Tell me you're okay. I swear to God, if that son of a bitch did something to you I'll kill him!"

Her adrenaline spiked. She never saw him so frantic. "I—"

"*Goddamn it, Jade!* How did you even get in contact with Lithe and why the hell would you leave a note like that without telling anyone?" The volume of his voice rose as his relieved expression darkened and contorted. "*Do you have any idea how dangerous he is?* Christ, Jade! He could have kidnapped you! *How could you have done something so stupid?*"

She jerked back as he screamed the last question in her face. Shock wearing off, she returned his scowl. Before she could respond—and oh, she *would* respond—a police officer approached. He looked to be in his mid-thirties and she found no comfort or security in his presence after everything she just learned from Nathan.

"Ms. Shultz, would you mind stepping out of the car so we can ask you a few questions?"

"Yes, I would mind. This has been a big misunderstanding and you may all leave, now."

"Ma'am, we can't leave without a statement. Please step out of the car," the officer insisted.

Feeling cornered by not just the officer, but her irate boyfriend, she flung her seatbelt off. "Here's my statement. I'm fine. I was finishing up some shopping and now I'm home."

The officer didn't look impressed. "Who were you shopping with?"

"None of your business!"

"Jade," Jeremy warned and she shot him a cutting glare. "We found your note. We know you were with Nathan Lithe. You specifically requested we call the cops if—"

"Well, what do I know? I'm just *stupid*!" Flustered, she hopped out of her SUV and slammed the door. "You have my statement. Now, I'd appreciate if you leave." Turning back to Jeremy she snapped, "*All* of you."

Barreling up the steps, overwhelmed by the scene, she avoided eye contact with the others. As soon as she unlocked her door, the alarm shrilled. "Goddamn it!" She punched in the code and threw her purse on the table. Turning to the window, she found Tyson and Trent staring at her like she was crazy. "What are you looking at?"

Kat peeked around Ty, her expression matching the others. Letting out a frustrated breath, she sighed and opened the door. "Are you coming, Kat?"

Kat nodded and quickly slipped around the men. The moment she was in the house, Jade slammed the door. "He called me stupid!"

"He said *meeting with Nathan* was stupid, Jade, and I can't say I disagree with him. What were you thinking?"

"You weren't supposed to know that!"

"Then why did you leave that note? You scared the hell out of us!"

Taken aback by her friend's hostility, she deflated. This was a disaster. "It was a precaution, in case something happened. You weren't supposed to find it—at least not until tonight and by then I would've been back and destroyed it."

"Mia had a half-day and I was going to wash her bag."

Jade slowly shut her eyes, understanding dawning. "Shit."

Kat gaped at her. Then she shouted, *"You could have been killed!"*

"Well, I wasn't, okay? I'm sorry I scared you." She rubbed her face and growled. "God, I should have never left a note!"

"Why would you want anything to do with that guy? I don't understand this. *Please*, help me understand, Jade. What would possess you to meet with someone who might have attacked you?"

She really should have thought of a back up story before she got home. "He didn't do it! Okay? He didn't." She'd completely broken her word. This was bad. "Look, just forget about all of this. I'm absolutely fine. I know this was my fault and I'm sorry I scared you, but I'm okay."

"How do you know he didn't do it?"

"Because I just do. I can't tell you the details, but I know."

"Why, because he denied his involvement? Jade, Nathan Lithe's a lawyer. He lies for a living. Why would you believe him?"

"I gave him my word and I've already betrayed him. I can't—"

"*Betrayed* him?" Kat scoffed. "For what? What do you owe him? This makes absolutely no—"

"Kat," Tyson interrupted from the doorway.

Great, more people to judge me.

Tyson stepped into the kitchen and gently shut the door. "Why don't you come home and cool off." He sent a withering glare in Jade's direction.

Great, just great.

"We're just talking," Kat said, crossing her hands over her belly.

"No," he corrected. "You're fighting. Jade obviously doesn't want our help with whatever's going on right now, so I think you should come home. This afternoon's been a nightmare for you and, while your friend may not realize it, getting this upset isn't good for you."

Okay, that hurt.

Guilt filled her stomach as she hung her head. "Kat, I'm sorry. I'm sorry I worried you. I shouldn't have done that. Please, don't be upset. For the baby's sake, go home and rest. Ty's right. I need to handle this by myself. I'll call you later."

Kat slowly nodded. "I wish you would just tell me what's going on."

She walked to her friend and hugged her. "I'm sorry. Please don't be mad. I'll come talk to you in a little bit. Right now, though, I need a minute to think."

Kat wiped at a tear that escaped her lashes and nodded again. As she left, Tyson stepped in front of the door, scowling down at Jade. "I know you've had a rough past few months, Jade, but you ever put my wife through something like that again and yell at her for caring, you and I are going to have a serious problem. You get me?"

Feeling about two feet tall, she nodded. "Yes."

The door closed. She walked to the front window and everyone was gone. Even Jeremy's Jeep was nowhere to be found. She had so many apologies to make and didn't know where to begin.

Pulling out her phone, she emailed Nathan with her phone number and asked him to call her as soon as possible. Her phone rang shortly after.

"Jade? It's Nathan. Is everything all right?"

Jade exhaled. "Um, we have kind of a situation. They know I saw you."

"Who's 'they'?"

"Kat, Tyson, and my boyfriend, Jeremy."

He let out a humorless laugh. "Jeremy must be the *gentleman* who hit me in the face."

Jade grimaced. "Yeah, that's him."

"Should I expect a visit from him? Are you warning me to lock my doors?"

"No, nothing like that." She hoped she was telling the truth. "See, I took precautions in case something happened with you. They found out before I could get back to retrieve the information."

"What was the information?"

"Uh…" Jade bit her lip. "That's not really important. The point is, when I got home, they were all here. I told them you had nothing to do with what happened to me and that it was none of their business why I met with you."

"Did they believe you?"

"Um, not really, but that doesn't matter. I won't tell them anything, Nathan. I know you weren't involved and I … I trust you." It sounded weird even to her own ears, but she wasn't lying. She did trust him on some strange, fucked up level. Maybe because they were victims together.

When he finally spoke he seemed not angry, but relieved. "I'm glad you trust me, Jade. I like you. I want to help you. I wish there was more I could do, but, like I said, the best thing for everyone is to forget about what happened and move on."

She took a shaky breath. It was strange, speaking of something so personal with a virtual stranger. A stranger she disliked, until a few hours ago. Funny how common tragedies forged bonds between people when they had little else in common. "I know where you stand."

Thirty-Three

JEREMY NEEDED time to cool off after being asked to *leave* Jade's property. He could tell when she hid behind a facade and fought to keep it together. That wasn't the case. If she was frazzled at all, it was due to everyone's concern—concern she provoked by leaving a note and electing to meet with someone no one trusted.

He had absolutely no answers and he was still furious. Nathan, the little prick, had yet to return a single voicemail. Kat said he was a lawyer. Was he consulting for Jade? No, Jeremy knew it was something to do with the rape. That creep knew things. Did Jade now know what he knew?

He had so many questions, but he wouldn't get a single answer until he worked things out with her. He wasn't going to apologize for his outburst when he spent half the morning worrying she might be dead.

Of course, she wasn't stupid. Her IQ trounced his. That didn't mean she couldn't make stupid decisions. This assumption that there was good in everyone was going to get her seriously hurt—more than she'd already been.

Gritting his teeth, he stepped aside as a couple crept closer to the display he was blocking.

"Pardon."

The mall was a thousand degrees. How fucking hard was it to pick up something he'd ordered weeks ago? The last thing he expected was to be in a fight with his girlfriend the day before Christmas.

This disagreement could ruin their holiday—it could ruin everything—so of course he'd apologize for shouting in her face, but that didn't mean he'd change his point of view.

This was ridiculous. They were past keeping secrets. He didn't understand why she couldn't tell him what had transpired yesterday. The girl was a vault and he was locked out. It fucking hurt.

"Sir." The salesman finally returned and Jeremy pulled out his wallet and signed the necessary paperwork.

As he left the jeweler, last minute shoppers hastily scurried around like a cluster of ants under a kid's magnifying glass. He should have done this yesterday, but of course, yesterday he had to wait with the cops for his girlfriend to safely return home—totally normal.

As he made it to his Jeep, parked the length of

three football fields from the exit, he stuffed his bag in the trunk and drove to Jade's.

She wasn't expecting him, which was clear the moment he walked into the cottage and found her sitting in a mess of paper, wrapping Mia's presents. Her hair was a disaster and she was in sweats.

"I thought you weren't coming until later," she said by way of greeting.

Sliding his keys on the counter, he tried for calm. "I thought we should talk."

Snapping off a piece of tape, she secured the end of the wrapping paper. "Oh? About what?"

"Jade, this is ridiculous." She unrolled another length of paper and he stepped forward, stilling her hand before she could reach for the scissors. "Stop."

"What do you want, Jeremy? I have to get this done."

"I want you to take me seriously. I'm sorry I hurt your feelings yesterday but do my feelings count for anything to you? I was fucking scared and all you can do is give me the silent treatment and get upset that—"

"You called me stupid."

"I said meeting with a man none of us trust without letting anyone know was stupid. There's a difference and you know it. I didn't call you stupid, so don't act dumb and try to get out of this on a technicality. You owe it to me to explain what's really going on."

Sitting back she sighed. "Fine. Meeting with Nathan wasn't the smartest move. I'm sorry I made everyone worry, although I'd think you'd be pleased I took precautions."

He nodded, glad to see she was at least realizing it was a dumb move, even if she didn't sound one hundred percent remorseful for going at all. "Why did you meet him?"

She fidgeted. "He said he had information for me."

"And you *believed* him?"

Her gaze cut to his. "Yes, and he did have information."

"What was it?"

"I can't tell you."

"Jade—"

She held up a hand. "Jeremy, I'm serious. What he told me, he told me in absolute confidence. The only reason anyone even knew I was with him was because *I* screwed up. No one was ever supposed to know I spoke to him. It could put people in danger." She truly wanted to protect Nathan, and somehow doing so made her feel more protected, but that might not make any sense to anyone else.

Tension knotted his shoulders as his molars locked. Taking a deep breath, he turned and mumbled, "I can't do this."

"Do what?"

"*This,*" he snapped, facing her. "I can't sit here and act like everything's normal when yesterday...

I don't want a relationship built around lies, Jade."

Her body staggered back as fear cinched tight around her heart. "I'm not lying to you. I told you I was with him. We met at a café in New Castle. We talked and he told me some things I needed to know, but it changes nothing. He told me for my own peace of mind and I can't take that information anywhere, so there's really no point in talking about it. I just want to—"

"Have a normal holiday," he finished. "Jade, you can't have normal unless you're honest with me."

Her mouth tightened. "Is that what this is, then? An ultimatum? Either I tell you what he said or we break up?"

That was the complete opposite of his original intentions, but now he was tempted to see which side she'd choose. "No, but what if it was?"

Her resolve hardened before his eyes, her shoulders drawing up and her chin lifting. The vulnerability she'd battled so hard to cover over the past few months was gone, vanished as though it never even existed. This was the strong woman he fell for and part of him celebrated her return. But a bigger part feared she might actually walk away because of whatever secrets she shared with Nathan fucking Lithe.

"One day you'll appreciate how strong my word is, Jeremy. I made Nathan a promise and I'm not going to break my word. I'm sorry if you can't accept that. I wish you could because I don't want this to change our relationship. It has nothing to do with us. It has to do with Nathan. It's his secret to tell and he told me, not you, not Kat. *Me.*"

Letting out a slow breath, he accepted she wasn't going to budge, not where Nathan's personal business came into play. "Was yesterday the first time you met with him?"

"Yes."

"How did he contact you?"

"Email. He looked up my professional profile online."

Meeting her gaze with a harder one, he let her see how seriously he took her safety. "This is the last time you pull a stunt like this behind my back, Jade. I know how determined you can be, but if you ever sneak off and knowingly put yourself at risk again, we *are* going to have a problem."

"Okay."

"Okay?"

"Yes. I told you it wasn't my smartest decision. I won't do it again. I'm sorry I scared everyone. That was never my plan."

He exhaled, supposing that was a better apology than her first attempt.

She stood and wrapped her arms around his neck. "Believe it or not, it means something that you worry about me."

He leaned back and tipped her face up so he was looking into her eyes. "Woman, you owe me. That was more than worry. You scared the shit out of me."

Her brow pinched and she lowered her stare. "I'm sorry."

And he believed her. "I know. It's over. Let's put it behind us."

Thirty-Four

AFTER JEREMY LEFT, Jade finished wrapping the last of her friends' gifts. Though she didn't celebrate Christmas, a sense of loss crept in as she stared at the towering pile of gifts for Mia.

Sliding open the drawer of the hutch, she tucked the tape and scissors away, pausing to brush her fingers lovingly over the silver menorah still sealed in its original packaging. It was the first investment she'd made in her future and it hurt knowing next Chanukah she wouldn't be sharing her family traditions with a little one. Sighing, she closed the drawer.

She wasn't allowed to dwell on the could-have-beens. She needed to live in the present and presently, she had a mess to clean up.

Selecting a small gift from the top of Mia's pile, she grabbed her coat and went to fix a few wrongs. Ty opened the front door as soon as she knocked, but for the first time ever, he didn't step aside and invite her in.

"Jade."

She hated how awkward she'd made everything. "Hey, Ty. Can I come in? It's cold out."

"Kiki!" Mia's voice rung from the rafters, as she bounded down the stairs and shoved Tyson's towering body aside. "Who's that present for?"

"Well, I have *so many* to carry over for Christmas, I figured I might as well bring one now." She held the small wrapped box out for Mia and she snatched it right up, giving it a firm shake.

"Can I open it, Daddy?"

Tyson pretended there was a debate, but everyone knew he could deny her nothing. "Go ahead. What do you say?"

"Thank you, Kiki!"

Jade smiled. "You're welcome, munchkin."

Mia took off, gift in hand. "Momma! Kiki brought me a present!"

Kat appeared at the end of the hall, wearing an apron with gingerbread men dancing on the front and a distrustful expression.

Jade raised a hand. "Hey."

"Hey."

She looked at Tyson and back to Kat. "Can you give us a minute, Ty?"

He hesitated, then turned and went in the direction Mia had gone, kissing the top of his wife's head on the way and whispering something in her ear that Jade couldn't say.

Jade shifted her feet as she stood in front of the door. "He's mad at me."

"He doesn't like seeing me upset."

"Neither do I. I'm so sorry about the other day, Kat. Everything got so messed up and it was my fault. I shouldn't have made you worry like that."

"You shouldn't have put yourself in a dangerous situation. Any one of us would have gone with you."

"Tyson would never let you go with me to meet Nathan."

"No, but if it was that important that you see him, he would have gone himself. Or Jeremy. Jade … you have to be careful."

"I was. That's why we met in a public place and I left a note. I never meant to upset everyone. Please don't be mad at me anymore. I can't take it. I love you, Kat."

She sighed. "I love you, too. If anything were to ever happen to you…"

"I promise I won't do anything stupid like that again." She waited for Kat to meet her gaze. "Hugs?"

"Hugs." They crossed the distance and squeezed each other tight. "Am I ever going to know what you two talked about?"

Jade rested her head on her friend's shoulder, not quite ready to let go. "I think you can figure the gist out. I wish I could say, but I can't. It's private and sad and I don't want any more ugliness touching the holidays. Just know, I went there prepared to call the cops on him and left ninety-three percent sure he wasn't my guy. He was trying to help me, Kat."

She made a disbelieving sound in the back of her throat and pulled back. "I don't think people like Nathan Lithe know how to help anyone but themselves."

"That's why I said trying. Everything he told me... It changes nothing and doesn't get me any closer to finding justice."

Letting it go for now, Kat gave her a remorseful smile. "How about some cookies? I have fresh ones coming out of the oven in about a minute."

"This is why I need you in my life. Lead the way."

Christmas was a wonderful distraction and she planned on losing herself in the excitement with her friends, rather than focusing on what she'd lost. Jeremy returned to load the gifts to take to her parents while she finished getting dressed, her mind trying very hard to push her unsettling thoughts aside for a few days.

She and Jeremy were still on shaky ground since his hypothetical ultimatum, and deep down she knew she would have told him everything to keep him in her life, but principles were involved and she was trying very hard to keep her word to Nathan. The man, after all, gave her a little more clarity on the situation if nothing else.

When they arrived at her parents' it was typical pandemonium. *Just an average day at the Shultz home*. The house was lined with blue twinkle lights, and a menorah sat in the front window of the house. The hall smelled of her mother's cooking and Elvis crooned from the stereo.

"There's my angel!" Her father greeted as he pulled her into his arms. He turned to Jeremy and stuck out a hand. "Jake, nice to see you again."

"Jeremy, Daddy," Jade corrected.

"Nice to see you again, sir. Happy holidays." Jeremy shook her father's hand.

"Is that them?" her mother called, as she bustled out of the kitchen. "There's my beautiful girl!"

Releasing Jade from a smothering hug, she turned and embraced Jeremy, her small body dragging him down to her stout height so she could squeeze his cheeks. "Jeremy, so glad you could join us. Larry, take their coats." She brushed some flour off her apron. "I've been cooking for two days straight. Dinner should be ready in about an hour. Jeremy, why don't you make yourself at home while Jade helps me set the table?"

"Is there anything I can do?"

"Aw, *bubeleh*, what manners you have. No, you sit here and relax while we get everything finished. I'll have Jade bring you something to drink." She bustled Jade into the kitchen. "What a nice boy. I hope you appreciate those manners. Your father has *none*."

Pots bubbled over and mismatched casserole dishes lined the counters. "I appreciate him."

"He's a nice man." Her mother poured a glass

of iced tea from a pea green pitcher that dated back to the seventies. "Handsome too. You think he'll marry you?"

Dear God. "Mom, don't start. We've only been dating for a few months."

She clucked her tongue. "But imagine the babies you two would make. They'd have his height and your striking features. I get *verklempt* just thinking about it. Don't you want me to be alive to see my grandchildren?"

She rolled her eyes and took the glass of tea out to Jeremy, struggling not to let her mind splinter at the mention of children—or marriage, for that matter.

Jeremy sat on the couch next to her father discussing various types of—batteries?

"You know, the generic ones hold up just as well as the pricey ones, Jake. What makes no sense is the packaging. They're batteries. Yet a light bulb comes wrapped in tissue and loose cardboard. I need to carry a Swiss army knife to open things nowadays. You own a Swiss army knife, Jake? A few weeks ago, I purchased scissors and do you know what I needed to open them? Scissors! How am I supposed to open scissors when I clearly purchased scissors because I don't own any? Makes no sense!"

"No, sir, it doesn't." Jeremy winked and took the glass from her.

"That's some dress you have on there, Jadinka. You better ask your mother for an apron so you don't spill anything on it."

Ah, the loony bin, we have arrived. "I will, Daddy."

Turning back to Jeremy, her father said, "Hey Jake, did you ever wonder why we drive on *park*ways and park on *drive*ways? Makes no sense!"

After dinner, the four of them shared cocktails in the living room and were entertained by her father's explanation of the *Lights* and an in-depth account of ancient practices. Jeremy was wonderful. He laughed at all her father's corny jokes, complimented her mother on her cooking, and even helped do the dishes, which nearly gave her mother a coronary.

They left around nine o'clock and Jeremy called Mia on the way home to tell her good night. It was nice the way he, Kat, and Tyson could all work together to give Mia a nice Christmas. Not many split families were so lucky.

She and Jeremy planned on exchanging gifts that night so as not to interfere with Mia's morning. He helped her carry her bags into the house and they made some coffee—well, Jade did.

As she settled on the floor by the tree, decorated in pink *Disney* Princesses ornaments, she slipped off her heels and waited as he found Christmas carols on the radio. When he finally joined her on the carpet she handed him a small wrapped box.

They took turns opening one present at a time. He seemed to like all the gifts she purchased for him. He, however, had some things to learn about shopping for a girl.

"Do you like it?" he asked, grinning expectantly.

"It's a ... jar opener."

He nodded. "Because you're always asking me to open things for you."

"I love it," she pushed the words through a forced smile. *Where's the receipt?* Next year he'd be going out with a list.

Next year. The thought sobered her. Would they be together next year? She hoped so.

Glancing down at her jar opener, new shoehorn, and various other odd presents, she genuinely smirked and chuckled.

"What's so funny?"

"You. I love them. I'll never forget our first holiday together."

He brushed a kiss on her cheek. "There'll be many more."

Around midnight they headed to bed. Halfway up the stairs, he turned to her. "Can you check if I turned the coffee pot off?"

"I shut it off."

"Can you just check?"

"Sure."

She was right. The coffee pot was off. But while she was down there she set the timer and filter for morning so they wouldn't have to wait or chance Jeremy getting up first and brewing a batch of sludge. On her way back up the steps, she paused. A piano solo of Silent Night played from inside the bedroom. She slowly pushed open the door and gasped.

Golden flickers danced up the wall as candles covered every surface. Smiling widely, her gaze fell on Jeremy who slowly lowered on bended knee.

Jade staggered back, her heart falling into a wild and unsteady beat. "What is this?"

A white satin box filled his hand, glimmering in the golden glow of candlelight. Her arms prickled with goose bumps as the gentle tinkling of Silent Night filled the air. "It's for you."

Her vision blurred, her voice shrinking behind the pressure in her throat. "You did this for me?"

"I love you, Jade. I never knew I could love someone the way I love you. No one's ever made me feel the things you do. When I'm with you, I'm alive. And when we're apart, I feel like every breath is my last. I want to be with you, not just now, but forever. Will you be my wife?"

He opened the box and there sat the most beautiful ring she had ever seen. It didn't matter what the cut was or how clear the stone. She couldn't see it through her tears anyway. All that mattered was that this man loved her enough to want her forever.

She wanted forever with him, too. Taking a shaky breath, she laughed and rasped, "Yes."

∾

Jeremy stood on shaky legs and pulled Jade into his arms, kissing her. "I love you," he whispered against her lips, clumsily taking her hand and sliding the ring onto her petite finger.

Lacing her fingers with his, she pulled him close, held his face and pressed her lips to his. "I can't believe this. You really want to marry me?"

Was she insane? "Of course I want to marry you. You mean everything to me, Jade."

She sniffled and laughed. "I thought you seriously gave me a jar opener."

He laughed then frowned. "Wait. You don't like the jar opener?"

Shaking her head, she smiled. "I think I'm the luckiest girl in the world."

He pressed his mouth to hers, gently coaxing her lips apart. Soft piano notes swathed them in a timeless moment. His fingers gently pulled the tie of her dress until the fabric fell away.

He unwrapped her like a present, her velvety skin glimmering in the candlelight. Stepping back, he slid her dress down her arms as it puddled on the floor. A vision of exquisite beauty, the woman he loved, his future wife, the mother of his children to come.

He placed his hand over her soft belly. "Here," he whispered, looking into her eyes. "Is where our love will grow, Jade. I want to give you everything."

She rested her hand over his as a tear trickled past her lashes, her chin trembling as she met his stare.

Moving slowly, he pulled the thin strap of her bra down her shoulder, pausing to kiss the scar at her shoulder. His tongue gently traced the curve of her shoulder to the tip of her ear and she shivered. As he nibbled on her neck, his fingers reached between her shoulder blades and unclasped her bra, releasing her breasts.

She stood before him in nothing but a wisp of white, lace panties as his fingers unknotted his tie. She slowly unbuttoned his shirt, her eyes full of love and promise.

She pressed her lips to the center of his chest and whispered, "I love you. I might not always say or do the right things, but I know you're right for me, Jeremy."

Caressing the flare of her hips, he bent to kiss the side of her breast. He leisurely pulled her panties to her ankles, exposing her sex. She lifted first one foot then the other as she stepped out of the garment.

Running his fingertips up her inner thighs, a spattering of goose bumps appeared in the wake of his caress. He nudged her legs apart and gently swept his tongue over her clit as she trembled. Her head rolled back as she held his shoulders. Her long, blonde hair fell like a silk cape as he slid a finger deep into her pussy and softly stroked.

The first taste of her arousal was a promise for more. He stood, scooping her into his arms, and carried her to the bed. Her hair fanned over the middle of the mattress, an exquisite sight that stole his breath.

He ran his finger down the valley of her breasts, shucked the last of his clothes, and climbed over her. Her body was perfection. Every lush curve and sinful dip. He spent an hour simply making her cry out his name. Her pleasure was his and he loved seeing her come apart under his touch.

Gripping her legs under the knees, he pulled her closer. Suited up with a condom, he nudged her wet folds with his cock, his body thrumming with anticipation.

"You're so beautiful," he whispered.

Her eyes only partially opened. "That's my line," she teased.

Resting her calves against his shoulders, he took himself in hand and stroked his cock along the cleft of her sex, and her hips rose. He rimmed her folds, teasing her until she begged.

"Please..." She lifted her hips, trying to force him inside and he pulled back. "You're teasing me."

"Tell me you want me," he whispered, prolonging the torture.

"I don't want you, Jeremy. I *need* you."

She was the sexiest woman he'd ever known. There was no denying her now. Leaning forward, he slid deep. "I need you, too."

Waves of pleasure wracked his body as he continued to drive into her. Their voices filled the room with incoherent pants and nonsensical words. A thousand tiny shards of pleasure splintered as they came apart, holding each other close, never letting her go.

Rolling to his back, he pulled her to him, belly

to belly, chest to chest, as he shivered and kissed her. She sighed as he brushed the hair from her eyes, finding a soft smile on her lips. The poignant moment seemed to sharpen like a dream just before dawn and he feared this might be just that, a dream.

Pressing her forehead to his, her smile turned shy. "How do you feel about a fast wedding?"

"What are you doing tomorrow?"

She snorted. "Tomorrow's Christmas, but my schedule's pretty wide open for the rest of the week."

"I think I can pencil you in." He playfully bit her shoulder.

"Use marker, because I'm not changing my mind."

~

Jeremy awoke some time in the middle of the night to find Jade sitting cross-legged at the edge of the bed. "Hey," he said in a sleep-roughened voice.

She turned and smiled at him over her shoulder. "Hey."

"What're you doing all the way over there?"

"Looking at my ring. It's beautiful." She shyly smiled at him. God, she was gorgeous.

He sat up and joined her at the edge of the bed. "Do you like it? If you don't we can take it—"

"I love it," she said cutting off his words with

a kiss. "As a matter of fact, I'm pretty sure I'm never taking it off, so I hope you're sure about this."

"I'm sure." He lifted her hair from her shoulder and kissed her neck. "Are you serious about not wanting a big traditional wedding?"

She reclined and pulled the covers over her body, nestling close to him. "Well, I was thinking about it. At first, it sounds fun. You know, every girl's dream and all, but it's also a lot of work. I'm sure Kat would do most of the planning, which I don't know if I'd end up appreciating or using as an excuse to beat her to death with her clip board. She'll start organizing things the minute she finds out."

"Well, what do *you* want?"

"I want to be your wife. It doesn't matter how it happens, so long as that's the end result. But I also don't want to rush to the finish and regret not taking the time to enjoy the journey."

"Then we'll have a traditional wedding. You can register for flatware, linens and a coffee pot that actually makes good coffee, all that girlie stuff, and I can have a bachelor party."

Jade snorted. "First of all, I'll be registering no matter what kind of wedding we have. No one's taking away my right to go on a shopping spree with a scanner gun. Second of all, your coffee pot makes fine coffee. It's you who screws it up. And third, you can have your bachelor party so long as I get a bachelorette party."

He pressed his lips together. "You know what?

Bachelor parties are so cliché. I'm already over the idea."

She laughed and then sighed. "I don't know. I like the idea of having a traditional wedding, but it's so much money and I really don't want to wait a year to be your wife. I have this beautiful picture in my head of me in a perfect couture gown, Mia as my flower girl, and Kat as my maid of honor, but all those expectations for perfection add up to a lot of stress that I don't want. No matter what, my mother will insist on handing out *yarmulkes* to all the men and my father will walk me down the aisle holding a clarinet."

He laughed. "What's with the clarinet? I'm gonna be family now. I feel like I should know."

"I don't know. He came home with it when I was in junior high and it's been around ever since. I think he thinks he's Teddy Roosevelt or something."

"Well, if you want to get married under a *chuppah* we can. We can even step on a bottle if it makes you happy."

"I think I'd actually prefer getting married somewhere exotic. We wouldn't have to wait, we could hire a wedding planner, and my parents would be limited to seventy-five pounds of cargo, so there wouldn't be room for my mom to over-pack tacky accents."

"I like that idea. I could see you in some billowy white dress on the beach with your hair blowing and your feet bare. As a matter of fact, I find that image very sexy."

She blushed. "Yeah?"

He nodded. "And I like the idea of not waiting. I know you just moved, but I really hate living apart. I want you here, and now that we're getting married, there's no need to hide our relationship from Mia anymore."

Her smile bloomed as she let out a quick breath. "Then let's just do it. Let's get married."

"What are you doing for New Year's Eve?"

Thirty-Five

JADE AND KAT descended in a puddle jumper that practically crash-landed on the white beaches of Negril and Jade dutifully held back Kat's hair as she puked. They took an early flight to meet with the resort's wedding coordinator. Jeremy, Tyson, and Mia were arriving the following morning and the rest of the guests, namely her parents, were scheduled to arrive the morning after that. She and Jeremy would be saying their vows at sunset on New Year's Eve.

After sharing the news with their friends Christmas morning, there had been a whirlwind of excitement. Apparently, only Americans thought weddings took a year to plan, because here in the world of Jamaica and OCD best friends, things were moving at light speed.

As soon as Kat washed her face and adjusted to the heat, she put on her control freak hat and immediately started giving orders. Their bags were delivered to their hotel rooms and the next thing Jade knew, they were meeting with the event coordinator to synchronize their agendas.

Jade wasn't quite sure what was on the schedule. Her focus was solely on finding out if her dress had arrived. She'd ordered it online and paid a fortune to have it shipped in time.

After Kat had made it clear to DeMont, the resort coordinator, that she was in charge, they went to the front desk to pick up Jade's gown. A shuttle took them into the village where a seamstress lived. Kat was a little skeptical when they arrived at the dilapidated hut with a near-starved dog roped to a bush out front, but DeMont had promised the woman was the best seamstress around.

The seamstress, Necie, was in her seventies and looked weathered to the bone, but the woman could sew a straight seam faster and neater than most people could write. When she finished, Jade stood in front of a bronze-tinged mirror and smiled. It was perfect.

The dress was the softest silk and slipped into place over her curves like it was made for her body. The natural train ran a few inches behind her and the back was cut into a deep V. As she studied her reflection, her finger slipped under the halter and traced the raised skin of her scar. She looked the picture of normal. And despite what others couldn't see, she felt normal. She was truly happy.

Once they were back at the hotel, they had

lunch and arranged another meeting with De-Mont to survey the site for the wedding. They would be saying their vows under a white *chuppah* on the beach, swathed in fuchsia lilies and ivory orchids.

After their meeting, they visited the salon for some necessary pampering. As the gossamer drapes danced in the breeze from the marble balcony of the salon, she sampled fresh fruit and drank from a coconut a native carved into a cup using a machete. Yes, she was in paradise.

The following morning, they awoke well rested and acclimated. While waiting for the others to arrive, Jade, again, sampled the rum being offered in the lobby. Several shuttles arrived as they looked for the guys and Mia. The longer they waited the more Jade consumed. Around her third pina colada, she spotted them.

"Momma!" Mia exclaimed as she saw Kat.

Jeremy walked to Jade and pulled her into his arms, delivering a slow, teasing kiss. "Mmm, coconut. You look like you're enjoying yourself."

Her drunken exuberance was impossible to hide. "I'm so glad you're here. Jeremy, it's so nice here. The water's so warm and clear. You can see starfish at your feet and the rum's delicious!"

He laughed and kissed her nose. "I missed you."

She hummed, pressing into him. "Do you think we can sneak away to our room before Kat sends you and Ty away on a *groomission*?"

"*Groomission*?"

"Yeah, a mission for the groom."

He frowned. "What do we need to do? I have Mia's dress and I have our wedding bands."

"Oh! Can I see them?"

"You can see mine, but I'm holding onto yours until we say I do."

"Well, I still think we should try to escape for an hour or five." Her fingers played at the exposed skin of his throat. "Our suite's unbelievable."

He growled. "Let's go—"

"Okay, guys," Kat announced, coming to their side. "We have an appointment with the officiant in about forty minutes, so that's just enough time for you to drop off your bags and change before we head to the beach."

"Who invited her?" Jade muttered under her breath.

Jeremy chuckled. "You."

The following evening, after the rehearsal, Jeremy walked Jade to a secluded hammock on the beach. The beaches glowed like jewels under the starlit sky.

As they swayed beneath the sheltering trees, he teased at the hem of her sundress just above her knee. "Tomorrow, we're getting married."

"Mmm... It's nice having a minute to ourselves." It must have been all the fresh sea air that put her so at ease. Well, that, and all the rum.

Wrapped in a tight cocoon of limbs and canvas, she curled her leg over his thigh. Although they were out in the open, with the hammock curving around them and the canopy of palm leaves blocking the noise from the hotel, they were hidden from the world.

He glided his hand up her thigh and under her dress until his fingers found the lace seam of her panties. Ever so lightly, he traced his finger along the edge and hooked the fabric with his fingertip. Jade lifted as he pulled the material away.

"I'll hold onto these," he teased, stuffing the panties in his pocket.

Slowly, Jade turned and maneuvered her way on top of him, careful not to flip the hammock. She straddled his waist and opened his pants, their exposed parts hidden under the skirt of her dress. Reaching beneath the fabric, he guided himself into her as she slowly rode him.

His blond lashes appeared almost silver in the moonlight. His expression eased with pleasure as she sensually moved over him. The hammock swayed with their languid pace, a relaxing escape from the rest of the world, just her and the man she loved.

They made love under the inky blanket of the sky, luxuriating in the freedom to touch and play with each other.

"I can't believe I can have you like this for the rest of my life," he whispered and she was thinking the same.

Leaning low, she kissed him softly. "I'm pretty sure I'm the lucky one."

"We'll see." He pulled her hips tighter to his. "Our bodies fit perfectly together."

Her heart raced as he brought her to climax,

her cries lost in the breeze. When they finished, she curled into his side and kissed his neck.

"Maybe we should stay here forever. We could live in a hut on the beach and sleep in hammocks all day, making love only when we woke at night."

He moaned in agreement. "Wouldn't that be nice?"

She wasn't sure if it was the chaos of wedding plans, the excitement of the island, or the contentment that came with marrying Jeremy, but her mind hadn't strayed to depressing thoughts in days. Of course, life couldn't always be so perfect, but the idea of maintaining the illusion was tempting.

"Unfortunately," he whispered, "I was supposed to have you back to your room an hour ago."

"Says who?"

"Your matron of honor."

"More like my Gestapo of honor." She could only imagine if she'd had a big wedding.

His eyes crinkled as he silently laughed. "I'm told you have a big day tomorrow."

She sighed and smiled. "That's true."

"Why don't I walk you back to the room?"

"Fine, but once we're married I'm revoking Kat's clipboard."

It wasn't easy leaving her fiancé that night. It would be the last time they slept apart and somehow saying goodnight was more excruciating than all their prior goodbyes. As she lay in bed, her mind wandered over pictures of their future. She wasn't sure what the next several decades would bring, but she truly believed they'd be happy.

The next day unfolded as if it had been planned for years. Delicious anticipation ran through her veins, passing every minute with a wave of giddiness. The women at the salon polished, buffed, waxed, and styled her to perfection.

Her hair was done in loose waves swept up on one side of her face. She used Kat's feathered lily pin in her hair as her something borrowed. Her something new was, of course, her dress and her something blue was a pair of sapphire earrings. Her mother had provided her with something old, a delicate pearl bracelet that was a family heirloom.

After the salon, she and the other women had lunch and relaxed until it was time for the photographer to arrive. While Jade was sitting on the balcony, the door slid open. She turned and saw Mia, her nails painted a pale shell pink, her hair loosely pinned up in curls and secured with a fuchsia ribbon headband.

"Hey, princess."

Mia climbed onto her lap. "Kiki, when you marry Daddy, will that make you my mommy?"

Ah, so that's what that look was about. "Well, I'll be your step-mommy, but your mommy will still be your mommy. Just like Daddy's your daddy, but Tyson's also your daddy."

"Sometimes I call Tyson Daddy."

Jade pulled back and studied her angelic face, noting the worry in her eyes. "Honey, I'll still be your Kiki." It was a nickname Mia had given her when she was just learning to speak and Jade loved knowing she was close enough to earn a one-of-a-kind endearment.

"Can I call you Mommy, too?"

"You can if you want."

"But no one else has a Kiki."

Jade smiled and kissed her nose. "Well, then I say we stick with Kiki. You know what's really cool?"

"What?"

"I'll still be Kiki, but now you'll be my step-daughter."

Mia smiled and hugged her tight. "I'm glad you're marrying my daddy."

~

Jeremy waited at the edge of the beach, where the banks were damp. His white linen shirt rippled in the breeze as the ocean teased his feet. His chest filled with anticipation as the ceremony began.

Tyson stood beside him, dressed much the same. A white *chuppah*, wrapped with bright splashes of flora popped against the backdrop of the turquoise sea. Fading shades of pink painted the sky under the setting sun as a native Jamaican softly played the steel drums.

Kat approached from between two arched palm trees, followed by Mia, an angel on a cloud of white sand. Then the music changed again and his heart jolted as he recognized the song *Somewhere Over the Rainbow.*

Jade stepped out from behind the trees, her arm linked in her father's, and stole every last breath from his lungs. More than exquisite, her beauty humbled him.

Her dress shimmered, shades of pearl kissed with hues of pink from the setting sun. In her hands, she held a cascading bouquet of berry colored lilies. As she approached the altar, her father kissed her cheek, and Jeremy shook his hand. This was it.

The officiant began the ceremony, but his attention was completely devoted to Jade. She smiled at him and took his hand in hers. When it was time to exchange vows, Tyson passed him the rings, and he turned to Jade.

"My beautiful Jade, I've known you for years, but feel as if I've loved you for an eternity. My love for you is written into my bones. I promise to love, honor, and respect you from this day forward. I will always place your needs above mine, your comfort above my own, and your happiness above all else. I promise this to you, forever and always. From this day forward, I will always catch you if you fall."

He slid the ring onto her finger as she gazed up at him, tears shimmering in her green eyes. "Jeremy, you're a unique work of art amongst a tarnished world. You're loyal, loving, and selfless in everything you do. You're gentle and kind. You've given me courage when I had nothing left to give. You've taught me to hope in moments of loss and given me strength when I needed it most. You accept me for who I am, make me laugh when I want to cry, and mend my soul when it's broken. I promise to do the same for you from this day to our very last. I promise to be faithful and love you for the rest of this life and in my next."

She slid the band onto his finger and every part of his being seemed to slide into place. The officiant said a few closing words and grinned. "You may kiss the bride."

She smiled, such genuine joy lighting her eyes as he pulled her close. "My beautiful wife."

Thirty-Six

WHERE WAS SHE? It had been seven solid days, *a full fucking week*, since he'd seen her. At first, he thought she was shacked up at the boyfriend's house, but no. There was not a single trace of her or her friends. It was as if everyone simply vanished into thin air.

He spent some time observing her home security system. They sure did do a thorough job. There wasn't a place within fifteen feet of the house one could walk without being bathed in light. Every window was locked with a sensory mechanism. The endless precautions were really starting to piss him off.

It had been too long since their last conversation. They weren't making any progress. At least not in the sort of progress he wanted. Where the fuck was she?

This was absurd! People didn't just disappear.

Last he saw her was Christmas Eve, her silhouette defined through the drapes as she spent the night letting that son of a bitch put his hands all over her. Like the little slut she was, she probably loved getting fucked. He'd teach her a new meaning of the word.

He was going to have to get rid of the boyfriend, and soon. He'd hoped she'd have come around and they could have built a better foundation for a future together by this point, but the whore was hardly ever alone anymore. That left little time to press his purpose.

He could kill the guy, but murder was messy and he wasn't a criminal. He didn't like violence. Was it too much to ask that she spend a little more time with him? He was doing everything he could to make her see him as a trustworthy friend, but the bitch was too wrapped up in other things.

He had friends in the legal department. Perhaps he could put some added stress on the guy's life? The more he thought about what an inconvenience her boyfriend was, the more enraged he grew. She shouldn't act like a whore. She was his. *His!* And it was time she understood that.

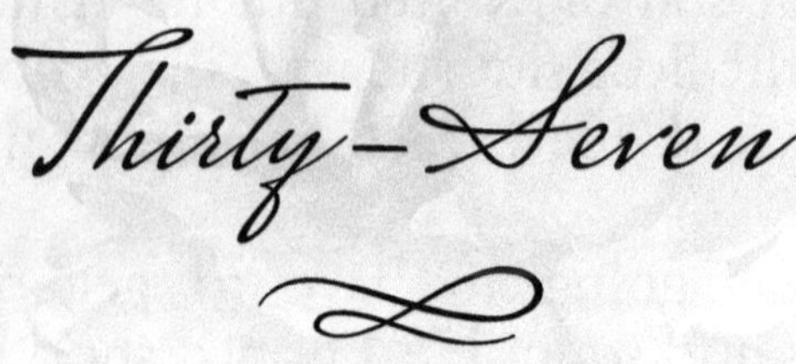

Thirty-Seven

AFTER A MAGNIFICENT TEN days in Jamaica, they waited for their luggage at baggage claim and Jade sighed.

Jeremy arched a brow. "Problem, Mrs. Larson?"

She smirked. "I miss it already."

"Jamaica?"

"Yes. I'm not sure I can live without room service anymore. And it's cold here. I wanna go back."

He chuckled and rubbed a hand over her thick coat. "We can go back."

"When?"

Knowing she didn't want to wait to start a family, he hoped to squeeze in as much adult time as possible. "Maybe in the summer."

She sighed again.

"Just think," he offered. "Now that we're home, you can register."

Despite essentially eloping, Jade still planned on hosting a reception at their home. He didn't know anything about weddings or etiquette, but Kat also insisted a reception was necessary, so he didn't argue.

"I can't believe I have to move again."

He pulled their luggage off the belt. "Because you did all the heavy lifting the last time?"

She swatted him in the arm. "Hey, I packed."

"You're right, dear, that's the hardest part."

She gave him a sour look and stuck out her tongue. "Don't pick on me." She adjusted the handle of her suitcase as they wheeled their way toward the exit of the airport.

"Look, all you have to do is put things in boxes and write what room of our house you want me to drop them in. They'll magically appear and we'll have Kat put everything away."

"I like that plan." They pushed through the exit door into the frigid January cold. "Oh, fuck this weather."

He laughed and hailed a taxi.

An hour later they pulled up to her cottage so she could grab some necessities and they could give Mia some souvenirs they'd purchased. Jade unlocked the door and piled her mail on the counter.

"I'll just be a minute. I want to grab some clothes to take to the house and my..." She frowned at his expression. "What's wrong?"

"The alarm didn't go off." His eyes scanned the cottage, finding nothing out of sorts at first glance. "Stay right there."

He checked each window to see if any of the sensors were disturbed. Everything was as it should be, but when he unlocked and opened a window, nothing buzzed.

"Maybe Tyson shut it off for some reason?"

At the kitchen door, he flipped the switch. Nothing. "I'm going to check the breaker."

"Um, okay."

"Wait in the kitchen."

At the box, he flipped each switch. There was no hum of activity anywhere in the house. The lamp on her nightstand did nothing as he hit the switch. "Shit."

Coming back through the kitchen he said, "I'm going to see if something's up with the meter."

Out back a lock box held the main controls for the security system. There should've been a small metal lock on the outside of it, but there wasn't. Lifting the panel open, he saw why. Wires were sliced and pulled from their places, cutting off all power to the house. There was no rationale behind the selection of wires cut that he could see. It was a mess, clearly not done by a professional, but by someone determined to dismantle her security.

His jaw locked as he cursed and slammed the box shut. He pivoted, almost crashing into Jade as she stood a foot away from him, silently trembling. He didn't want to scare her more than necessary. "Jade?"

"He was here," she rasped, eyes wide. "He was in my home. *Again!*" She shook like a leaf and his blood ran cold.

"How do you know?"

"My ... m—mirrors..." She was a mess, barely able to talk.

"Okay, listen to me, go to Kat's. Tell Tyson to call the police then have him come over here. I'll—"

"I'm not leaving you here!" Twin tears trickled down her cheeks. "What if he's still in there?"

"No one's in the house, Jade. I'm trained at searching people out. I would've seen him."

"You didn't see the mirror."

Only because it was dark and he wasn't looking for anything beyond an intruder. "Please. Just do this for me."

Stiffly nodding, she turned and headed toward Kat's.

Jeremy pulled out his phone and texted Trent.

Situation at the cottage. Alarm cut.
Calling police. He was here.

As he walked back into the house, he used his cell as a flashlight. He looked everything over once more, trying to spot something he might have missed before. Turning the corner into her bedroom, he saw the mirror and immediately wondered how he could've missed it.

WHORE was scribbled across it in what appeared to be lipstick. The writing was crude in itself. With the letters poorly formed, it was almost difficult to make out the offensive word. He turned and stilled, cold dread icing over his veins. On the wall behind her bed was the word, *MINE.*

~

While Jeremy showed the cops what had transpired, Jade lay on Kat's couch with a cool cloth over her eyes waiting for her headache to ease. The front door opened and she pulled the fabric off her eyes, noting the apprehension in his.

He sat on the edge of the sofa, picking up her hand and rubbing her cold fingers. "How you doing?"

She shrugged weakly and he took a deep breath.

"Jade, I told the police that you probably wouldn't offer a statement, but I think you should. I think it's time you told them everything. This isn't over and pretending it is will only leave you more vulnerable. You need to tell them what happened."

"Why is this happening?"

"Jade..." His Adam's apple made a slow bob as he glanced away. "I wish I knew. Right now, we need to find the fastest way to make it stop. The cops aren't going to look at this as an open case unless they understand how dangerous this person is, what he's capable of."

"Do they have anything to go by?"

"They found traces of latex by the security box and a partial fingerprint on your drawer."

She cringed. "Do I even want to know what drawer?"

"No."

"I can't do this." She moaned, covering her face with her hands.

"Baby, I know this is difficult and I don't want to push you too hard, but I have a feeling if you don't offer all the information now and they catch this guy later, you'll be compromising your case, because you didn't give all the facts when you had the chance."

"Are you saying that I can't amend my state-ment? Did they say that?"

"I'm saying I don't know. What I do know is that if they catch this guy and he gets away with just being charged with breaking and entering and some vandalism, I'm going to go ballistic and land *myself* in jail."

She was seriously hanging on by a frayed thread that should have snapped months ago. "I don't want to do this now."

He kissed her fingers. "I know, but I think it's best. I'll go with you."

It didn't seem right that she had to divulge her ugliest secrets to a stranger in a uniform. She wasn't ready. "I need to know what my rights are.

Someone was in my home. Who cares what else happened?"

If they caught him, she'd press charges for everything, but at the moment she was too overwhelmed to dredge up her past. But maybe she needed an open file to be taken seriously. What she needed was advice.

"I know it's hard to talk about—"

"I feel like I'm drowning." Maybe she needed a lawyer, someone to advise her on how to proceed. At the moment she felt cornered and scared. "I think I should call Nathan."

Jeremy immediately stiffened. Angrily, he hissed, "Jade, why would you call him?"

"Because he's a lawyer."

"A divorce lawyer," he snapped. "For all we know, he's the one who did this. There is no way—"

"He didn't do it. I told you, Nathan wouldn't hurt me."

"How are you so sure?"

"Because I just am. He knows stuff, stuff he wouldn't tell me if he was out to harm me."

"He knows stuff because he's a creep and maybe he just told you things so you would think the way you're thinking now, which proves he's manipulative."

"Jeremy, we know nothing about my rights and I'd rather not divulge every painful part of my past if I don't have to. Nathan knows what I should tell the cops and what my rights are, plus he—"

"There's no fucking way I'm letting you—"

"*Letting* me?" she snapped. "I'm an adult. You don't have to *let* me do anything. I don't need your permission."

"You may be an adult, but you're also my wife and there's no way I'm permitting someone like Nathan Lithe—"

"Excuse me, Mrs. Larson?" They both turned to the door where a police officer stood, holding a notepad. "Sorry to interrupt, but we'd like to ask you a few questions."

Jade quickly sat up. "In situations like this is it okay to have a lawyer present?" she asked before Jeremy could say another word.

"Uh..." The officer blinked. "A lawyer isn't necessary, but if having one present makes you more comfortable, feel free."

"Thank you." She slid her cell phone from her pocket and gave Jeremy a reproving look.

"Jade," he said, pleading yet at the same time warning.

She thumbed through her contacts and hit send. The phone rang a few times then went to voicemail. "Nathan, it's Jade. Please call me back. It's important."

Jeremy, clearly furious, stood and shook his head. "Good luck getting a call back from that asshole."

"He'll call back."

"We'll see—" His words cut off as her phone rang.

She left the room to take the call, which came

faster than expected. Nathan listened, digested the key points, asked if she was okay, and promised to be there as soon as possible.

She returned to the den two minutes later. "He'll be here in about twenty minutes. After speaking to my lawyer I'll answer your questions. You can wait around or leave your card and I'll contact you when I'm ready."

The officer left his card and Jeremy left the house without uttering another word.

Slamming the door, Jeremy paced Kat's front yard, his breath steaming out of him with every step. The door opened and he turned to find Jade shivering on the front step. He was too angry to face her right now. "Where's your coat, Jade?"

"Inside. If you're done having a tantrum, we can go in where it's warm and talk."

"I am not—"

She held up her hand, cutting him off. "I am not arguing about this. You ask me all the time to trust you. Now, I'm asking you to trust me. You can either accept that Nathan's coming here in a few minutes or you can leave and I'll meet you at home. I'm not talking to anyone until I'm sure of my rights."

"It's *him* I don't trust. Do Kat and Ty know you're inviting this guy into their home?"

"They do and they said that was fine once I

told them that if it wouldn't be okay I'd just speak with him somewhere else."

"Well, that's sure as fuck not happening."

"I'm scared, Jeremy."

He stopped talking for a second and looked at her, pleadingly. He was scared too, which was exactly why he didn't want this guy anywhere near his wife, his daughter's home, or their life.

"I don't want this guy here, Jade. You're my wife. This is Mia's home. Doesn't that mean anything to you?"

"Yes. Does it mean anything to you that I think he can help me?"

"What makes him so qualified on the subject? He's getting all this insider information somewhere and it's not the Internet. Do you think I didn't search myself? He knows shit because he's a part of this..."

"It's not like that." Her arms crossed over her chest as she shivered. "I'm giving you my word that he isn't dangerous."

"That's a guarantee you can't make and you know it."

"Okay, but it's a gamble I'm willing to take."

Gritting his teeth, he glared at his trembling wife and growled, "When he gets here, don't expect me to leave you alone with him for one second."

"I wouldn't expect anything less."

He opened the door to get her back in the heat before she got sick. "Come on. Your teeth are chattering. We need coffee."

When Nathan knocked at the door, Jeremy followed her to greet him. The piece of shit actually had the nerve to touch her, clasping her shoulders like they were old friends and asking if she was all right.

Jeremy sent Tyson a sidelong glance, spotting equal disgust in his friend's eyes. Kat remained upstairs with Mia, as she had no desire to see Nathan Lithe.

"Nathan, you remember Jeremy and Tyson," Jade said, her fingers wringing.

Nathan extended his hand, but Jeremy only nodded, leaving his arms crossed over his chest. That guy could eat shit before he would shake his hand. Tyson did the same.

"Right." Nathan received their message loud and clear. "Is there a place we can talk?"

"The kitchen's this way."

Jade led the way while he and Ty followed. Nathan looked a little surprised that they'd be having their discussion with an audience, but apparently thought better of objecting.

"Tell me what happened," Nathan said, as soon as he and Jade were seated.

She told the story and Nathan listened without interrupting. When she finished he asked, "Did the police find anything?"

"Yes, a partial fingerprint and traces of latex."

Nathan raised his eyebrows at that. "Really?"

"That scare you, Lithe?" Jeremy sneered and Jade gave him a sharp look.

"No, it doesn't. It just doesn't seem—" He

appeared to rethink his words. Looking at Jade, he lowered his voice. "Perhaps your friends could give us a little privacy."

"Not happening," Jeremy growled. "And for the record, I'm not her friend, I'm her fucking husband."

His beady eyes widened. "Her husband? Since when?"

Jade mouthed *stop* to him as she returned her attention to their unwelcome guest. "Since New Year's Eve. We were coming home from our honeymoon."

"I'd congratulate you, but I'm not sure I'd be telling the truth," Nathan mumbled, scowling over his shoulder at Jeremy. Good, let the prick hate him. Jeremy wasn't here to win friends.

"How about you get to telling my wife about her rights?"

"How about you back off?" Nathan snapped.

Jeremy took a step forward and Tyson caught his arm. "Don't make me kick your ass, Lithe." Then he added because it was true, "Again."

"All right, that's it!" Jade slapped her palms on the table. "Jeremy, you're not helping. Either shut up or leave."

"He's the one—"

"No, he's not! Now, if you can't act civilized, we'll go somewhere else. I just want some legal advice and you're making an already difficult situation worse. So either be quiet or I'm leaving."

Jaw locking, he scowled. Jade slowly relaxed her shoulders and lowered herself into her chair.

Ignoring him and Tyson, she looked at Nathan and said, "I'm sorry. Continue."

In a low voice, he said, "I just find it odd that they left a trail at all. It doesn't fit. I got the sense that once... I mean ... once what happened, happened ... that was the end of it."

"Are you saying you don't think it's related?"

"It's clearly the act of someone who singled you out. Unless you have other enemies I don't know about, I'd say it's related. But the guy isn't following protocol. He's off the reservation and they'll retaliate if they find out. Unfortunately, that means I'm going to give you the same advice I did before. Don't get involved. He's seriously unwell, Jade."

Jade's eyes softened in a show of vulnerability. Jeremy wanted to go to her but sensed she needed space at the moment.

In a nearly inaudible voice, she said, "Nathan, with all due respect, this maniac drugged me, raped me, robbed me, tried to run me over with a car, and has now broken into my home, touched my personal items, and vandalized my bedroom. He clearly doesn't want to be ignored, regardless if he's off the chain. Whether you agree with me or not, I'm going to talk to the police. My question is, how much should I tell them? I need to know what the statute of limitations is for sexual abuse and if it will jeopardize my case if they catch this guy and I wait to tell them about the rape."

Pride welled in Jeremy's chest as she pushed through the undeniably difficult statement. It also eased his concern that she wasn't blindly accepting this guy's advice.

"I'm asking you to be my friend, Nathan. Save me the legal fees of asking another lawyer and advise me as a friend, even if you don't agree with what I'm doing. We have some things in common."

Nathan tilted his head and Jeremy didn't understand what the fucking dilemma was. After a beat, he finally said, "The statute of limitations in the state of Pennsylvania for sexual assault cases is twelve years in your case. However, if I were advising you as my client, I'd advise you to disclose all information from the start. It'll draw more attention from the department and no one will question the change in your statement later on."

"Thank you," she whispered, slowly stretching her arm across the table and clasping his hand.

Nathan withdrew it. "There's one favor I like to ask in return."

"I know what you're going to ask and you don't have to," Jade said. "I won't mention any of it. I promise."

"Thank you."

Jeremy didn't know what the fuck was going on, but things were getting a little too intimate for his taste. He wasn't going to relax until the prick was gone and his wife was safely in his—*their* —house.

It didn't matter that Jade trusted the guy and apparently liked him. He didn't. Something about him just didn't sit right. Sure, he played the sensitive professional today, but the guy was a lawyer. He knew how to win a crowd. Jeremy was far from convinced.

"What do you think?" Tyson asked, stepping beside him as Jade walked the sleaze to the door.

"What would you think? Would you let him around your wife?"

"The only way a guy like that is getting near my wife is if he can take me out of the equation first. And that, my friend, isn't happening."

Thirty-Eight

THE FOLLOWING two weeks were surprisingly quiet and therefore nerve-racking. Jade had her interview with the police, an emotionally grueling experience that would likely scar him for life. So many horrid details put into words... It had a way of carving each syllable into his heart. For now, he was content not to broach the subject for a while, finally understanding why Jade always seemed to avoid the topic. Everything she went through... It was simply too much to process in days or weeks. Maybe even years.

He and Jade, in search of a distraction, went to register. She quickly became preoccupied with invitations, caterers, and paint samples. Giving her *cart blanche*, as far as decorating the house went, seemed the right move at the time, but now he wasn't so sure.

She constantly wanted his opinion on fabric

swatches and paint colors, asking him to choose between something called Mountain Dusk and another called Morning Dew. Whatever happened to good old dark blue?

He couldn't complain though. All the excitement of their reception party and the redecorating of the house kept her mind off the break-in. She had yet to return to the cottage for any of her personal things and Jeremy doubted she ever would.

She didn't like to talk about the things left behind and got defensive whenever he asked about moving some of her furniture to their home. When he made mention of her iPad, she purchased a new one the next day, stating her old one had a cracked screen, which was a lie. Knowing someone had intruded on her personal space and desecrated some of her items, but never knowing which ones, left both of them with an unsettled feeling, so he understood she'd be replacing everything she could.

Work also kept her positive. Had it not been for the break in, there'd be no reason to complain. But there had been a break in and there still was a threat to his wife, so things were far from perfect.

She came into the living room carrying the binder where she kept guest lists and menu samples—the binder that scared him. She slid onto the couch, tucking her feet beneath her knees. "What are you smiling about?"

"You," he answered honestly, thinking of how incredibly resilient she was.

"Aw, that's sweet." She kissed him on the

cheek. "But you still have to help me address invitations."

And that was why he hated the binder...

They sat addressing envelope after envelope to people Jeremy never heard of before. "Who's Hetish Patel?"

"Oh, he's a nuclear tech that works with me."

He nodded. "Is this supposed to be Francis with an *I*? You have it down as Frances and Joan Banning."

"No, that's right. Fran and Joan. They're both women."

"They're married?"

She nodded. "I work with work with a lot of lesbians, so don't be surprised if you see two women dancing together at the reception."

He tensed. "We're having dancing?"

"Well, not a dance floor, but you never know."

Were they inviting the entire hospital? They already had three stacks ready to mail and were only halfway though her list. His attention was snagged on the invitation she was addressing. "What are you doing?"

Without stopping her pen, she said, "Addressing an invitation."

"I see that. Why are you addressing one to him?"

She exhaled and put down her pen. Facing him, she drew in an irritated breath. "Are we really going to do this again? He's become my friend, Jeremy."

"I don't want him in our home, Jade."

"Fine! Then we'll just stop wasting our time and cancel everything."

"Because I said Nathan can't come? You're being ridiculous!"

"No, *you*'re being ridiculous. Why do you find him so threatening? Do you think if he had anything to do with what happened to me he would've told me to include so much detail in my statement to the cops? This is absurd. He isn't the guy everyone thinks he is. You're all wrong about him and I don't know how to prove it—"

"Because you don't know!" Jeremy barked. "You just believe the best in people and then you get hurt."

"I know with Nathan!" she shouted. "I've seen proof. How many times do I have to say so before you actually believe me? Every time we have this argument, it only amplifies how little you trust *my* judgment."

"What proof?" He raised his own voice. "Proof is finding the person who actually did it. Until you have a different suspect, you can't say for certain he isn't lying."

"Do you know how twisted that is? Why would Nathan go to such extremes to convince me otherwise? That's crazy!"

"Jade, do you think sane people rape women?" He regretted his words the moment they left his mouth.

They had referred to what happened to her as many things, but only in necessary situations, like when speaking to the police, did they use the word *rape*. The simple presence of that word destroyed her.

All visible anger melted into shame. Her shoulders sagged and her eyes lowered. He was an idiot. "I'm sorry."

"You're right," she whispered, refusing to look at him. "A crazy person would lie. What kind of judge of character am I anyway? I'm the one who got myself into this mess. I'm too trusting." She stood. "Invite whomever you want. I'm going to bed."

He stood. "Jade."

She kept walking, not even bothering to slam their bedroom door.

Easing back on the couch, he sighed. He hadn't meant to upset her, but every instinct he had told him to keep that man as far away from his wife as possible. She was so sure he could be trusted, but without knowing why, Jeremy was reluctant to trust her judgment in this case. And there was the crux of it all.

He didn't fully trust her. He did in thought, but not in action. He trusted her with his daughter, his money, his home, and his heart, but when it came to her safety, he was a control freak. He didn't trust anyone to look after her the way he could.

Until they had her attacker, stalker, whatever, behind bars, everyone was suspect. Nathan was a prick who he hated all the more for causing all this strife between him and his wife.

He grimaced, unable to get past his initial gut

feeling about the man. Based on what Kat told him, he slithered his way to the top social circles, objectifying women. He drove a car that was a testament to his little dick. And he was a sleazy divorce lawyer, making a living off others' misfortune. What redeeming qualities could he possibly have?

Staring at the ceiling, knowing they could not continue to have this same tired argument, he went against every good instinct he had and addressed the last invitation to a Mr. Nathan Lithe. He'd mail it tomorrow and, so help him, God, if that guy tried anything out of line in his home, Jeremy would make sure he regretted ever being born.

~

He could smell her on the paper, soft linen and a hint of some floral fragrance he now identified with her and her alone. How quaint, a reception to celebrate the newly married couple.

When he first heard the news, he had to force himself to remain calm and not strangle the life out of her. Others had been present and that meant playing the supportive friend.

How could she do this? It was too fast. This wasn't supposed to happen. She was supposed to fall in love with *him*. Marry *him*, and have *his* children!

He lit another cigarette to calm down. This wasn't the end. It was supposed to be the end, but

Jade was more than a mere conquest. No matter how stupidly she'd been acting, he wanted her forever.

Now that she was home again things would return to normal. Although she wasn't living at the cottage anymore, she was back to work and following her usual routine.

He'd find other excuses to make appearances in her life, ways to drive a wedge between the happy couple. He'd talk to her, comfort her, and in turn, she'd look to him as someone she could trust.

Women left their husbands every day. Who was to say Jade wouldn't get tired of this guy and look for someone more successful, someone with more than one degree and some prestige, someone with their name on an office door?

He held the invitation to his nose and breathed deeply. Progress. *Invited* into *her* house.

Pulling out the response card, he checked off the *will attend* box and licked the envelope closed. Perhaps he could persuade Jade into a dance at her little soiree. The question was, if he held her in his arms again, would he possess the strength to let her go?

Thirty-Nine

THE DAY of the reception started with frightening calm. Fifty-five guests were scheduled to arrive and Jade's phone had not rung once. Kat really was an asset to her sanity.

From up in her bedroom Jade could hear the clanking of silverware being set out and the caterer instructing his staff. The scuff of furniture being moved mixed with music samplings as the speakers were installed.

Another six inches of snow fell the night before, and a voice yelled for someone else to wipe his or her feet. Yet, no one needed her help.

Around five o'clock Jeremy finally came up to shower. His cheeks were flushed from the cold and he smelled like snow. Jade stood in front of the long mirror in the master bathroom adding the finishing touches to her hair.

"Well, don't you look pretty." He placed a kiss on the back of her neck.

She jumped as his cold hands pressed against the thin fabric of her gown. "You're freezing!"

"Now, I'm not sure what the etiquette books say about such situations—I may need to reference the binder—but I'm pretty sure we get another honeymoon after all this." He nibbled at her neck and her nipples pressed against the silk of her gown. "Why, Mrs. Larson, are you not wearing a bra?"

Moaning, she leaned into him. "You can have your second wedding night, but not until the party's over."

"Ah, but you see..." His hands spanned her waist, inching up the material covering her legs. "You're already my wife. I can have you whenever I want—at least that's what you promised the other night, all tousled and thoroughly fucked."

Exposing her white lace panties, he pressed them aside and slid a chilled finger into her heat. She gasped and her head lolled onto his shoulder.

"Look how beautiful you are."

Swallowed, she peeked through her lashes as he worked his fingers in and out of her. The erotic reflection quickened her breath.

There she stood, in four-inch satin heels, legs spread and quivering, while her sexy husband pleasured her. Her immaculate gown was an absolute contrast to his black army boots, patterned fatigues, and a fitted charcoal thermal.

His muscles flexed with each thrust of his

wrist, his fingers jabbing deep and hooking close to her G-spot. He kissed her neck, sending jolts of pleasure through her entire body. He played her like a fine instrument.

"You'll wrinkle my dress," she moaned, with little conviction.

"I would never." Unclasping the halter, the fabric peeled away, exposing the sharp slopes of her breasts. "All I have to do is move my hand, and the dress is no longer an issue."

"We'll mess up my hair."

"Not if I fuck you standing up," he whispered into her ear, teeth scraping deliciously. "What do you say, Mrs. Larson? Can you spare your husband a few minutes before the guests arrive?"

As soon as she nodded he withdrew his hand, and her gown fluttered to the floor. He quickly reached down and picked it off the floor, tossing it over a chair.

"Come with me." He pulled her into the bathroom and shut the door. "Hands on the counter," he ordered as he released the catch of his pants and turned her to the mirror over the vanity.

Placing her palms on the counter, she adjusted her footing and he slid deep. She gasped as he thrust hard, causing her breasts to sway. The room filled with her sensual cries and the echoes of flesh slapping flesh.

His hand moved over her curves, plucking at her nipples and squeezing her hips. His hand slid to her front and she cried out as he pinched and teased her clit. His hips snapped into her hard enough to loosen some wisps of hair from her twist. His fingers worked over her, driving her to a point where she could no longer stifle her cries.

"Come with me, Jade," he said, rubbing faster, a shock of pleasure shooting to her pussy so fast screamed.

His hand covered her mouth as he kissed her neck. "I love hearing you scream." He licked over her thrumming pulse. "But there are other men in the house and those screams are for me and me alone." He thrust hard, underscoring his possession with each emphasized jerk of his hips.

She moaned against his fingers, sinking into his possessive hold. She loved how he touched her, how demanding he was and how completely he owned her when they made love.

His fingers slapped over her clit and she jerked. He smiled at her through their reflection in the mirror. "One more. I want you to squeeze my cock so tight I come with you. Come on, baby."

He rubbed and drilled into her, her cries muffled against his hand as she came undone. He legs trembled, but he supported her. Her pussy clamped around him as his release pulsed inside of her.

"God, I love you." His body trembling as he placed a kiss at the nape of her neck. "My beautiful wife."

Forty

"JEREMY, I THOUGHT THAT WAS YOU." Jade's friend Lily approached with a man at her side. "This is Bryan Philips. He also works with us."

Jeremy held out a hand. "Nice to see you." Jade had so many co-workers it was a blur who he'd met before and who he hadn't.

The man shook his hand firmly. "I believe we met briefly when Jade was ... Well, it's nice to see you again, during happier times." He quickly covered, clearly not wanting to bring up the miscarriage in mixed company and Jeremy vaguely placed him from that horrible day. "We're glad Jade's back at work. You're a lucky man."

"I couldn't agree more." Jeremy nodded.

"What do you say we find the groom a drink, Lily?"

"I'm only helping if you plan on finding one for me too."

There was a tickle at the back of Jeremy's collar as Bryan and Lily headed toward the bar. Turning, he found Jade behind him.

"Wouldn't they make an adorable couple?" she whispered. "I've been trying to convince Lily to go out with him for months."

"Are you telling me to keep an eye out for other signs that you're turning into your mother?"

Jade opened her mouth and scoffed. "You know what? I'm going to find my mother right now and tell her you said that."

"No!" He grabbed for her and she slithered out of reach, sticking out her tongue as she looked back, laughing. He cursed and shouted, "I love your mother!"

"Ah, I remember those arguments," a man with a familiar voice, but a face he could not place, said from beside him. He was older, likely in his seventies, and had silver hair and smiling eyes.

"I'm sorry, you seem familiar, but I can't recall your name," Jeremy said, facing the gentleman.

"Dr. Stevens. Katherine works for me and I own that there cottage your wife rented. We spoke on the phone a few times before you had the alarm installed."

"Oh, right. How are you, Dr. Stevens?"

"I'm well and yourself? Ah, don't answer that, boy. Anyone married to Jade couldn't be anything but well."

~

Jade looked stunning—a bit too stunning, as men were watching her from every corner. It was a tossup who was watching her closest, him or her husband. The man never let her stray out of his sight, always turning from conversations to see who she was talking to and who was making her laugh. He was a fool for letting her dress like that in the company of so many men.

She greeted him briefly when he'd arrived, her surprise at seeing him evident, but he wasn't satisfied. He was in her home at *her* invitation and needed to make it count. He was determined to find a keepsake from the evening.

Placing his glass on a table in the hall, he surveyed the room and casually walked up the stairs. By now, the majority of guests were too drunk to realize who was who, and he'd seen others use the stairs. The trick was acting entitled, that way no one questioned you.

Guests were saying goodbye at the front door and if he wanted to take something of hers, he would have to make it quick.

He passed a room that clearly belonged to a child. He approached another door and found a linen closet. A door down the hall opened and a woman walked out. He looked inside and saw it was a bathroom. That left one more room. Her bedroom.

He turned the knob and slowly pressed the door open. On the other side was a huge tree of man, and a woman. He'd clearly caught them in the middle of something.

Uncaring about their embarrassment or need for privacy, he stepped into the room. "I'm sorry. I'm looking for my wife's bag."

"Well, thank you for helping me find my coat, Trenton," the woman said, scurrying from the room. The man shot him a hard glare as the woman fled.

Undeterred, he sifted through the coats on the bed until the guy left. Once the room was empty, he closed the door tightly. Returning to the bed, he picked up a pillow and breathed in her scent.

"Jade..." His cock twitched.

Once he had had his fill, he quietly perused her drawers, sniffing her personal items and—*Someone's coming.*

He gently closed the drawer and slipped into the master bathroom. *Well, well, what do we have here?*

In the corner of the room, just below the hinges of the door, was a tiny wisp of white lace. Crouching low, he scooped the lace off the floor. Brushing his thumb over the crotch of the garment, a rush of blood flooded his cock. Traces of her left the fabric damp. He pressed it to his face and breathed deep.

Heaven.

Sensing company, he pocketed the lace and flushed the toilet. Running the water, long enough to appear to be washing his hands he took a quick peek around the room for any other souvenirs worth keeping. Shutting off the water, he hummed as he left the bathroom.

A woman sliding into her coat smiled. "Oh, I'm sorry. I didn't realize anyone else was in here."

"Quite all right," he said. "Just using the facilities."

He continued to hum as he traveled down the steps to rejoin the party. His glass waited for him as if he had never been gone.

~

Jade was distracted from her conversation by the sound of Mia crying. Following the whimpers, she found a tired Mia holding her elbow in the hall.

"What happened, honey?" The poor child had bags under her eyes. It was *way* past her bedtime.

"I got a boo-boo," she sobbed, showing Jade a scrape on her elbow.

"Oh. How did that happen?"

"I tripped."

"Does it need a kiss?"

Mia nodded and Jade examined the injury. It was only a little scrape, but it was bleeding.

"Excuse me, Jade?"

She turned from her crouched position on the floor at the sound of Nathan's voice. "Are you leaving?" she asked, maintaining Mia's hand in hers.

"Unfortunately, yes. I'm in court on Monday and I have a ton of paperwork to look over tomorrow, but I wanted to thank you, again, for inviting me. It really does mean a lot."

"Let me walk you out."

"What about my boo-boo?" Mia asked and Jade apologetically looked back at Nathan.

"Who has a boo-boo?" another voice asked. Jade turned as Bryan approached. "Oh, my," he said, crouching low. "That *is* a boo-boo. You know, I'm a doctor. I could have that fixed up in no time."

Mia smiled and Jade relaxed. Bryan was apparently charming to all age groups. He stood. "Where would I find Band-Aids, Jade?"

"Upstairs bathroom, second shelf on the left."

He turned back to Mia and smiled. "What do you say we fix up that boo-boo?" Mia took his hand and followed him up the steps.

"Friend of yours?" Nathan asked.

"Yeah, we work together. Come on, I'll walk you out. I could use some fresh air."

Jeremy watched Jade leave with Nathan and politely excused himself from the conversation. At the door, he stared through a narrow window as Nathan dug in his pocket for his keys. When he finally retrieved them he said a few words to Jade, smiled, then leaned in to kiss her on the cheek.

Jeremy tolerated it, simply because the man was leaving and, hopefully, they wouldn't have to be in his presence again for a long, long time.

Once Nathan crossed the street, heading toward his car, Jade turned and walked up the path to the house. Earlier, cars had lined the block, but now there was only a spattering of those who still remained. Nathan disappeared from view and Jeremy opened the door for Jade, startling her.

She paused and accusingly looked him in the eyes. He didn't care if she knew he was watching her. It was for her protection.

Straightening her shoulders, she brushed past him and said, "You can relax now. He's gone."

~

Jade took the stairs to check on Mia, hoping Bryan found the Band-Aids in the few minutes she'd been gone. Of course, according to her husband, two minutes was too long unattended when it came to Nathan Lithe. But she refused to let old issues upset her on such a special night.

She didn't know what else she could say on the subject. They were simply never going to agree when it came to Nathan Lithe. She didn't like having unresolved issues in her marriage. But so long as there were no other incidents revolving around her assault, she couldn't see Nathan's name being incorporated in many conversations between herself and Jeremy.

She might as well let the dispute rest and focus on better and brighter things. Considering how much her husband disliked him, that was probably a good thing.

As she reached the top of the stairs, she saw Bryan leaving Mia's room. "How is she?"

He placed a finger over his lips. "She's out cold," he whispered, stepping aside to show Mia sleeping in her dress under a princess blanket. "She's fine. It was just a small scrape. Shouldn't scar or anything."

"Wow, Bryan, if I didn't know better I'd assume you were in pediatrics."

"Nah, I prefer all the excitement of the ER. Besides, it's sad seeing a child hurt, you can't make fun of them like you can the big people." He nudged her in the arm. They did see some strange things in their line of work.

Lily's voice echoed up the steps. "Bryan, you up there?" Oh yes, Lily was drunk.

There were only a few guests left, Kat and Tyson being two of them. Jade could hear the lingering company saying their goodbyes. This was the point of the night where she could finally stop playing hostess.

Lily stumbled up the steps. "Wha're you guys doin' up here?"

Jade laughed. Her friend rarely drank more than a glass of wine.

"I've been lookin' all over for you," Lily shouted.

Bryan shushed her as Jade quietly closed Mia's door.

"I thing I'm drunk," she loudly stage whispered, resting her elbow on Bryan's shoulder. "I thing yer gonna have a drive me home, *Philips*!"

She enunciated his name and giggled, letting out a hiccup. In the next second, she shut her eyes and let out a not so feminine snore right there on his shoulder while still standing up.

Jade sighed. So much for her match making. "Do you want me to help you get her to your car?"

"Sure."

After retrieving Lily's coat and helping Bryan feed her arms through the sleeves, they each took an arm over their shoulder and carefully ushered Lily down the steps.

Surveying who was still there, Jade saw Kat napping on a chair in the corner, her hand gently cradling her belly. Jeremy and Tyson's voices echoed from the kitchen. It seemed the rest of the guests had left.

As they maneuvered Lily through the front door, she moaned and both Bryan and Jade laughed. She was completely out of it but still able to semi-lurch her way down the path.

They shuffled her down the now vacant street to Bryan's car. He was about a block away from the house and, again, Jade wished she'd put on a coat before coming outside.

Shivering, her teeth chattered. As they hefted Lily along, Bryan made small talk. "So how do you like married life?"

"I love it," she admitted and he grunted in reply. Lily was now completely unconscious and nothing but dead weight.

He fumbled in his pocket for the key and the alarm disengaged as the lights flashed in the darkness. Struggling to keep Lily upright, they quickly shuffled her into the backseat. Once she was inside and safely buckled, Bryan shut the door.

Taking a step back, Jade rubbed her now freezing arms. She needed to get back inside before she froze to death.

"You're shivering."

Her teeth continued to chatter. "I'll be fine. I really appreciate you taking Lily home. She doesn't drink often, but when she does, she forgets how to pace herself."

"It's no problem."

Tilting his head, as if he wanting to say something, he instead reached in his pocket and pulled out a brass Zippo and a pack of cigarettes.

"I didn't know you smoked."

He couldn't possibly expect her to wait out here, chatting, for the length of a cigarette in nothing but a silk gown. She took another step back, slush touching her toes and making her hiss as the icy water saturated her satin pump.

"Careful." He steadied her and dropped his lighter.

"Oh." She bent to pick it up for him and her body went completely numb.

The world slowed as her stomach rolled, ice suddenly filling her veins as her heart ground to a painful stop. Her entire being froze as her wide eyes focused on the very small, but very clear number four engraved in the side of his lighter.

He cursed and her heart exploded in her chest, pounding back to life. *He drives a black SUV!*

Stumbling back, she looked at him, disbelief making it impossible to accept as fear clawed at her frigid insides.

"Jade—"

Spinning on her heel, she bolted.

"Wait!" Her body jerked as he gripped her gown, shredding the back wide with a tug.

"*No!*" Her voice echoed down the empty street.

He dragged her back to him. "Don't scream!"

Palming her fist, she slammed her elbow into his ribs and he grunted. "Get off me! *Jeremy! Help!*" Her screams broke into sobs as he struggled to detain her.

Frantically, she squirmed, trying to break free of his grip. His cold hands snaked around her waist, her feet lifting off the frozen ground. She elbowed him again and screamed, but he was too close.

"Stop fighting," he growled through gritted teeth.

Twisting in his arms, she clawed at his neck, her dress bunching around her legs. Her heart pounded furiously as she pressed her palm into his face, her fingernails gouging into the fleshy parts of his cheeks. The moment his grip slackened she stumbled free and kneed him in the balls, but he predicted her move and locked his knees around her legs.

The world spun and her back slammed against the frost-covered car, her head snapping back as sharp pain radiated through her shoulder, ripping the breath from her body. "No! *No! Help!*" Her shrill screams echoed in her ears as panic overwhelmed her.

"Stop screaming!" He jerked her shoulders and shoved her harder against the car.

The frozen exterior burned her skin as she pushed at him with all of her strength. Her weak attempts made him seem incredibly strong. *"Help—"*

He slammed her against the car again, her skull smacking against the glass. Pain flashed white behind her eyes. She was going to throw up. Her vision blurred as he shoved a hand over her mouth and gave her head a hard push.

She whimpered as all sound washed away to a droning hum. His lips moved beneath his angry eyes and she frowned, unable to hear him or anything over the ringing in her ears.

He jerked her shoulders again, shaking her until her teeth rattled. Terrified she was going to pass out, she begged, "Please... Don't... Don't hurt me..."

But her words clumsily fell from her lips, not making sense to her own ears as her vision winked in and out. Something jabbed into her side and her strength waned.

"Why..."A sharp, metallic scent filled the air as everything went black.

Forty-One

"I BETTER WAKE KAT UP," Tyson said as he poured the remainder of his drink down the drain.

"Yeah," Jeremy agreed. "I better go check on Jade. I think she's mad at me for being rude to Lithe. She went upstairs to check on Mia."

Music played throughout the empty house, repeating the songs that had started the evening. The night had come full circle. Glasses, discarded cocktail napkins, and dirty plates littered every surface.

Ty turned into the living room to wake Kat as Jeremy took the steps. His bedroom door was closed, as was Mia's. Peeking in on his daughter, he pulled the covers to her chin and kissed her forehead.

As he approached the door to his bedroom he took a deep breath. Hopefully, his wife wasn't too upset with him. He didn't see Nathan being much of an issue anymore, now that had no reason to see him again—he hoped. Steadying himself for the oncoming lecture, he turned the knob and opened the door.

"Jade?' The room was dim and empty.

The bathroom door silently opened as he pressed against the wood. Empty. Confused, he left the bedroom and checked the hall bathroom. Also empty.

A heavy ache took shape in his stomach as he moved downstairs, where Tyson was helping a groggy Kat into her coat.

"She's not up there." He walked to the cellar door. The basement had been closed off for the night. The stairs leading to his office were dark. "Jade?"

The uncomfortable feeling in his gut tightened. "Where the hell is she?"

With clipped movements, he walked out the backdoor of the kitchen. "Jade!" he yelled, but the yard was pitch black and there was no answer.

He cursed and turned back to Tyson. They frowned at each other.

"Could she have walked someone to their car?" Ty asked.

"I saw her maybe ten minutes ago. She walked Nathan out and then went upstairs. I didn't see her go back out."

"I'll go check if she's out front," Ty offered, turning toward the front door.

Kat followed Jeremy into the kitchen. "Try calling her cell."

Jeremy pulled his phone out of his pocket and pressed a button. Soft buzzing on the counter filled the eerily quiet house. Kat walked over and picked up Jade's phone.

The front door opened and Tyson returned, his brow tight. "Everyone's gone."

They stared at each other, sheer panic reflected in each other's eyes. Jeremy bolted out of the kitchen and ran up the stairs, taking them four at a time. Tyson and Kat searched through the downstairs, calling Jade's name over and over.

He went into his daughter's room and gently shook Mia's shoulder. "Mia. Princess, wake up."

She grumbled and squeezed her eyes tight shutting out his insistent voice.

"Mia, sweetie, open your eyes."

Slowly she opened her eyes and balled her fists, rubbing her knuckles in her sleepy sockets.

"Mia, have you seen Kiki?"

"She's downstairs," his daughter whined, shutting her eyes again.

"Mia, when was the last time you saw her?" he asked, trying to keep her awake. He needed to know who was still at the party before Jade went missing.

She let out an annoyed whine. "I got a boo-boo and the man with Kiki helped me get a Band-Aid."

"What man? What did he look like?"

She tilted her head and thought, seeming a

little more coherent now. "He had black hair and a picture like Kiki?"

"A picture? What do you mean a picture?"

"Know how Kiki has a picture right here?" She pointed to her shoulder.

Jeremy swallowed, dread seeping into his blood. "Yes," he rasped.

"After he put my Band-Aid on, he washed his hands, and I saw the picture on his arm, right here." She pointed to her forearm. "He was a nice man, Daddy. He kissed my boo-boo and made it all better. See?"

Jeremy stood. Had Nathan come back into the house? He'd seen him walk off but didn't see him drive away. "Go back to sleep, baby." He shakily kissed his daughter's head and rushed out of the room.

Tyson and Kat waited for him at the bottom of the steps, both looking apprehensive. "Mia said before she fell asleep a man with black hair and a mark on his arm matching Jade's scar helped her clean up a scrape she got."

Tyson cursed and Jeremy looked at them with sheer panic. "He's got her."

The phone in Kat's hand started buzzing and everyone stilled. Kat looked at the display screen then at Jeremy. "It's Nathan."

Time stood still. The fucker had somehow done it. He never should have let him near her. Snatching the phone out of Kat's hand he brought it to his ear. *"Where is she, you fuck?"*

"Whoa!" Nathan yelled, his car noisily down-shifting and accelerating in the background.

"I swear to God, if you harm one hair on her body, I'll fucking *slaughter* you, you piece of shit!"

"She isn't with me, asshole!"

Jeremy froze.

"When I got to my car, the door was iced up. It took me a while to jimmy it open. Then I had to let it warm up. That's when Jade came out with some guy and a girl who looked wasted."

"What guy?"

"I don't know who he was. I saw him at the party, though. You seemed to be chummy with him. The girl was tall and thin with dark hair and olive skin. She looked exotic, maybe European or something. They put the girl in a black SUV. Jade looked like she was about to return to the house, but something scared her. She turned and tried to run but he grabbed her."

"Why didn't you fucking do something?" Jeremy raged.

"I tried! I was over a block away. I jumped out of the car and rushed toward them. She screamed and there was a scuffle. Before I reached them he threw her in the back of his car and sped off. I'm following them. It looks like he's heading toward Ben Franklin Highway."

"What's the plate number?" Jeremy yanked a pen and paper out of a drawer.

"Looks like SUPDOC. Is this guy a doctor?"

"Oh, my God. You said he was with a tall

brunette?" His wide eyed gaze drifted to Kat. "That's Lily. It's fucking Philips! *He fucking works with her!*"

Nathan cursed. "I think he knows I'm behind him. I don't think he has any weapons, but Jeremy," he paused. "He roughed her up a bit. I don't know if she's conscious."

He dropped into a chair. Fear, worse than anything he ever experienced in combat took hold.

"You have to call the cops," Nathan continued and Jeremy worried he'd missed something the guy said.

Shaking away his dread, focusing on getting her home safe, he went into survival mode. "Keep your phone in your hand and don't lose them. I'll call you right back."

"You got it. And for the record, I never—"

"I know." God, he'd been so fucking wrong. "Just ... don't lose her." Ending the call, he looked at Ty. "Philips has her. Call 911 and tell them it's a black SUV plate S-U-P-D-O-C."

"On it." Tyson's phone was already at his ear.

Jeremy dialed Trent. He answered on the first ring.

"It's not Lithe. It's Philips, the doctor she works with! He's got her. They're heading toward Ben Franklin and Lithe's following them. He's got her friend Lily in the car with them, too."

"Is Lithe on our side or his?" Trent asked, catching up with no additional explanation like the security guy he was.

"Ours." And wasn't that a kick in the nuts to

admit.

"You call the cops?"

"Ty's on the phone with them now."

"Okay. I'm on 422. I'll pull over and wait until I hear anything. What's the vehicle ID?"

"Plate, SUPDOC." He spelled it out. "It's a black SUV."

"We'll get her, Jer. We'll get her."

Forty-Two

THE WORLD ROCKED and Jade heaved a dry sob as nausea churned in her belly, her head ponding with the rapid beat of her heart. She couldn't breathe the second she regained consciousness. Fighting the urge to vomit, her eyes registered shadows moving over her skin and the vibration of her surroundings.

Am I in a car?

Her last moments of consciousness came hurtling back. She was in Bryan's car, sprawled out in the back where a third row of seats would normally be. *Oh, my God, it's Bryan.*

It didn't add up. How had she been so blind? He was so convincingly charming, yet the look in his eyes when she'd spotted the seal on his lighter told her she'd made a grave error in judgment.

She pressed up on her elbows, the carpeted upholstery abrading her skin. The speed of the SUV was nauseating, each turn making the contents of her stomach swill. Unconsciousness tempted as her vision wavered.

Keeping her head low, she peeked through the tinted glass and looked for a street name or mile marker. Everything was moving too fast. Her eyes struggled to track, but the motion sent a spike of bile up her throat. Her vision showed like a funhouse mirror. A sign for the New Castle Municipal Airport flashed in the distance and she collapsed, catching her breath.

Fuck.

Lowering her head to the floor she breathed through her teeth, fighting the urge to puke. Did she have a concussion? Peeking around the headrest, she repetitively swallowed as she tried to focus.

Bryan hugged the wheel as cigarette smoke siphoned through the crack in the driver's side window. Streetlights illuminated the interior in drifting flashes and Jade gasped as she spotted a silver high heel. Lily. Her friend's hand swayed into the space between the back seats, as she lay hunched over and unconscious.

Creeping forward, Jade searched for Lily's purse. There, on the floor. Stretching her fingers under the car seat, she tried to navigate the obstacle of bars and gears. She couldn't reach.

Try again. You don't quit. This isn't a game.

Her arm pressed along the side, her fingers stretching. She shut her eyes and tried to extend her reach as far as possible. *Come on.*

The car hit a bump and something sharp scraped her shoulder. She winced and swallowed the pain. Gritting her teeth, she silently reached as far as she could. Her fingers brushed the leather strap and she blindly clawed for the bag. Her middle finger hooked on what she hoped was the purse and she pulled.

Her arm would fit through the seat's under-carriage, but not the bag. Feeling around, she found the zipper and tugged it open one jerking motion at a time. When her fingers closed around sleek glass, she sagged with relief. Fisting the cell-phone, she extricated her arm and folded her body back to where she was when she first awoke. She caught her breath.

Lying on her side, holding the phone deep in her lap, her fingers locked around the device, sweet relief making her dizzy, as she pulled it to her face. She shakily pressed the first digits of Jeremy's phone number but winced and stilled as the phone faintly beeped.

Smothering the phone against her chest, her attention jerked to Bryan. He stared ahead, appar-ently not hearing the beep.

Wrapping the phone in her gown to muffle the light, she slid her thumb over the silence switch and dialed. As she entered the last number, she pulled the phone to her face, shading the light with her palm.

Muffling the phone in the crease of her neck she hit send. The phone hardly rang and Jeremy answered, voice frantic, *"Hello?"*

She breathed a sigh of relief so intense her eyes glazed with tears. *Now what?*

Her mouth opened and she stilled. She couldn't talk without chancing Philips hearing her.

"Hello? Jade, is that you?"

She whimpered quietly.

"Baby, are you all right? Tell me you're all right!" He spoke in a panicked voice she never heard him use before. "I know Bryan Philips has you. Please tell me you aren't hurt. If you can't talk press a button."

Jade pressed a key and Jeremy gave an audible sigh of relief. "Okay, baby. Good. You're doing good. We're coming for you. The police know he has you. He won't get far. But you have to stay calm. Press a button if you're still in the car."

She pressed a button again, her thumb lowering the volume as much as possible.

"Okay, listen to me, baby. The cops are on their way. Nathan's following you. You were right about him. I'm so sorry I didn't trust your judgment."

Just then the car swerved and a phone rang on Jeremy's end. He cursed and Tyson spoke Nathan's name in the background.

Ty's deep voice spoke fast. "He's taking the jug handle to Route 376. Nathan's still on him."

"Good, tell him not to lose him," Jeremy said to Tyson. "Jade, you still with me, baby?"

Jade pressed a key.

"Good. I need to pull up Trent's number in

my phone. Don't hang up, okay?" As soon as she pressed another key she heard Jeremy fumbling with his phone. "Kat call this number and tell Trent they are heading north on 376. You still there, Jade?"

She pressed a key, just as the driver's side window closed and the car was submerged in unnerving silence. Her heart rate accelerated.

"Do you know where he's taking you?" She couldn't answer and had no answer to give, so she remained silent. "Are you injured?"

Her head hurt and her dress was torn, but she had no mortal wounds, so she stayed silent again.

Just then Bryan said, "We're almost there, my love." She froze, terror piping through her blood like poison.

"Was that Philips? Is he talking to you? Can he see you?" Jeremy frantically shouted into the phone, "Jade? *Jade!*"

Bryan's eyes reflected in the rearview mirror, a frown flashing on his lips. "Are you awake back there?"

Panicked that Bryan would overhear, she instinctively did the only thing she could do to protect herself and disconnected the call.

Forty-Three

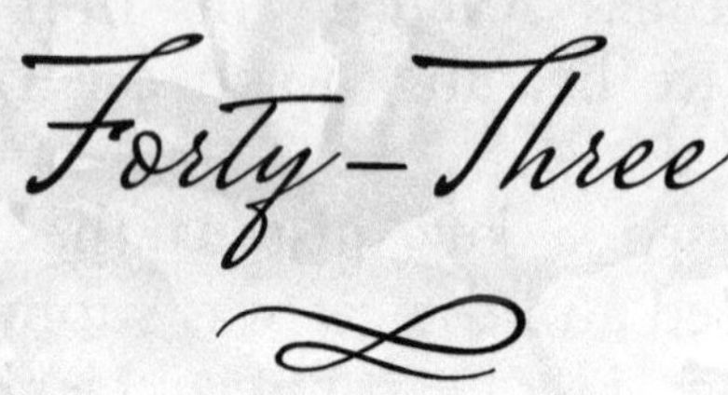

"FUCK!" Jeremy roared as he shut the phone. He dialed Nathan.

Without saying hello, Nathan answered, "He's slowing down. It looks like he's taking a road called Polaski."

"She's awake." Jeremy's heart thundered painfully in his chest. "She called me, but she couldn't talk. I don't think she's hurt too bad, but she's scared. Do you hear any sirens yet?"

"Nothing yet. Fuck, it's starting to snow again."

"A friend of mine isn't far behind you. Big guy. Trenton Cole. He'll be driving a beat up, blue pickup. If you see him, stay out of his way. He'll most likely try to shoot the fucker on the spot."

"Definitely would like to make it home without any bullet holes in me. Shit, he's turning again. I didn't catch the street name, but there's an old white church on the corner."

"Which way did he turn?"

"Left."

"All right, I'm calling Trent. Keep your phone on." Jeremy disconnected the call and dialed Trent.

"I'm on 376 now," Trent answered.

"They turned onto a road called Polaski. They were only on it for a minute or so before turning left. We don't know the name of the road, but there's a white church on the corner."

"I'm seeing signs for Polaski now. Should be there in about sixty seconds. How's our girl?"

"She couldn't talk without him hearing, but I think she's okay. Just scared."

"We'll get her, man."

Nathan shut off his headlights and rolled to a stop about fifty yards away from where the SUV parked. A cluster of evergreens at the curve of the driveway hid his car.

Turning off the engine, he quietly exited the vehicle. His dress shoes crunched over the brackish leaves, the leather soles sliding with the fresh dusting of snow. Pushing branches aside, he crept through the trees and walked toward the house.

It was a large chalet, with a peaked front window formed from several smaller windows, each glass surface angling toward the roof. Pine needles littered the ground, protected by the canopy of evergreens, but the drive hadn't been plowed from the last snowstorm, which told him this wasn't the good doctor's central residence.

Hugging the frosted trunk of a pine tree, he watched the guy exit the vehicle and approach the side door.

"What are you doing?" Nathan whispered, squinting as Phillips removed a bag and balanced it on his knee.

He rummaged through the bag and held something between his finger and thumb, angling it toward the interior light of the car. He reached back in the bag and raised something to his lips, spitting away part of whatever he held. The moonlight glinted and the motions were familiar as the doctor popped the two things together. The action resonated. A syringe.

Nathan stiffened as he leaned into the car. The passenger door slammed and the doc rounded the back of the vehicle, his hand still holding the syringe.

Nathan's phone vibrated, distracting him for a split second, but he couldn't chance answering the call. His eyes watched, unblinking, as the doc reached for the tailgate.

Jade's small body catapulted out of the SUV. The syringe fell to the snow, catching the moonlight as she kicked him and bolted in a flash of white silk.

"*Bitch!*" Philips cursed, snatching the syringe and trudging after her on the icy drive.

She made it about fifteen feet when he roughly tackled her. Her scream bounced off the trees and Nathan tensed as she hit the ground hard.

His legs bunched, ready to spring, but he hesitated. Jeremy said a guy was coming—with a gun. Nathan wasn't trained in combat and could hardly throw a punch. He wouldn't be much help to Jade—not yet. He had to be smart and keep his presence secret until the opportune moment.

"Get off me!"

Her panicked cry made him weak. He had to help her, but how? Glancing in the shadows, she searched for anything that might work as a weapon. A branch, a rock, he couldn't see shit.

His posture faltered as the sound of a fist smacking flesh silenced Jade's voice. The bed of snow reflecting the moonlight defined their figures. Arms flailed as their breath echoed.

Philips jerked her to her back and straddled her kicking legs, pinning her smaller body in the shadows of his much larger one. "Stay still! I don't want to hurt you!"

"No—"

Everything stilled and the doctor eased back, one hand closed around her jaw. Jade's form lay motionless beneath him in the snow.

"Stop fighting me or I'll gouge this needle in your throat and you won't wake until dawn," Philips threatened and she whimpered. "Are you going to cooperate?"

She whimpered again.

"Good girl. I just want to talk. Cooperate and

I won't hurt you." Slowly, the doctor rose from the ground. Jade remained perfectly still and Nathan wasn't sure if he'd changed his mind and drugged her anyway.

"Up." The doc reached and tugged her off the ground. She stood, but wobbled and nearly fell back into the snow.

Retaining a tight grip on her arm, he tugged her back toward the car. She didn't go easily, but the doc had her in too tight a hold and gave her no choice but to follow. The tailgate slammed, leaving nothing but dappled moonlight to cast inky shadows in the dark.

Holding her wrist, he led her toward the house. She looked toward the woods and Nathan crept a step closer.

"This way."

Her body jerked as the doc gave a hard yank on her arm. She stumbled under his prodding but didn't fight. Then they disappeared inside.

Nathan crept closer to the house. Reaching in his pocket as his phone continued to vibrate and lights illuminated the home. "I'm here," he hissed quietly.

"Where the hell were you?" Jeremy bellowed, irritation and panic evident in his voice.

Breath coming fast, forming clouds of vapor in the cold winter air, Nathan didn't waste time. "They're in a house. He drugged the other woman, but I think he only threatened to drug Jade. She's cooperating and he took her inside. He said he just wants to talk to her."

"Fuck!" Jeremy yelled. "I'm getting in the car. Where's the fucking house?"

"Just off a street called Norman Drive, about two miles after the church. It's woodsy here, secluded. The driveways are hidden. My car's at the edge of the property. *What should I do?"*

Jeremy was quiet for several seconds. "Trent should be there soon. Approach the house. I'll tell him to look for your car and meet you there. See if you can see what room they're in, but don't go inside. I don't want him to know we have him cornered until Trent or the police get there." He exhaled into the phone. "But Nathan, if he ... if he does anything..."

"I won't let him hurt her." He cursed himself, unsure how he could help without making things worse and also for not intervening sooner.

Sliding the phone into his pocket, he rushed along the drive, staying close to the trees on the property line, keeping his footprints hidden in the shadows. Approaching the edge of the home, he crept around the perimeter, peering into windows and spotted Jade shivering on a couch in a large room. Her dress was wet and torn, with splotches of dirt marring the once pristine white silk.

Her small form trembled, cold and clearly terrified. Her hair was a mess and there was either a bruise forming or dirt smudged on her cheek. He searched for Philips but didn't see him.

Her eyes scanned her surroundings as if looking for a way to escape. Taking a risk, Nathan tapped lightly on the window and she flinched.

Their gazes met and she quickly looked over her shoulder to see if anyone was watching. He held up a hand. It was the only way he could think to comfort her and try to warn her to remain calm.

Help was on its way. He wished he could somehow tell her that. Hopefully seeing him there told her others were close. Her shoulders shook as tears trickled down her flushed cheeks. Her pain became his as he held her gaze and they waited.

~

Bryan stood anxiously in front of the stove as the water heated. He needed to think. *Fuck!* It wasn't supposed to happen like this. She was supposed to come to him. She was supposed to love him.

If she wasn't such a fucking whore, running off and eloping, things could have been different. Then she'd gone and tried to fight him. He didn't like when she ran from him, but there was something to be said for her struggles. When they were rolling in the snow, his body pinning hers... His cock had started to throb. Yes, having her conscious was definitely preferable to the other option.

The last time he'd held her she hadn't fought at all. Her body accepted him beautifully. She'd been lax and malleable, nothing like the clawing bitch she turned into tonight. Yet... His cock swelled. She should be disciplined and he would enjoy every second of dishing out her punishment.

His eye twitched, a ripple of tiny muscle

spasms convulsing down to the corner of his mouth. He hadn't meant to hurt her back at the house, but she wouldn't stop screaming. She should be quiet. She was quiet now. Maybe a little too quiet.

He stepped away from the stove and glanced into the open living room. Her back was stiff as she sat exactly where he left her. "I'll be right there, my love."

Hmm. No reply. She'd come around.

All she had to do was leave her husband. He would give her a good life. She could still work at the hospital. He liked seeing her during his breaks. She hadn't been married that long. A divorce would be easy. She could marry him and he would give her back the baby she lost. That would make her happy. She just had to listen.

The kettle whistled and he removed it from the burner. His mother's heirloom teacups waited. As he steeped the tea, the steam from the kettle moistened his fingers.

He wanted to fuck her. She would fuck him. She just had to listen.

His jaw tightened as he looked at his watch. They didn't have much time. Someone would eventually start looking for her. If she didn't listen, he'd knock her out and take her away from here.

He had a place in Maryland. This time of year the shore town was practically dead. He could take her there and tie her to a bed and force her to listen—force her to do other things too. Eventually she'd learn consent would work in her favor.

He wanted her to *choose* the things he had to offer, but he had methods of swaying her. It would be a pleasure seducing her, showing her how things could be—teaching her what happened when she was bad.

He adjusted his cock and picked up the teacup. Jade would like his tea. She would like his mother's cups. She would like his baby in her womb. She just needed to listen. His eye twitched again as he left the kitchen.

Forty-Four

SHE WAS GOING TO DIE, or worse, live through something her mind would never heal from. She looked around, frantically trying to find a phone or a place to hide.

She was freezing and her back burned from the snow, the numbness fading into a prickling burn. Blood trickled, heating the back of her shoulder where Bryan tackled her against the rocks. Wet filth seeped from her dress into the cushions of the sofa she'd been told to wait on, but none of that mattered, because she was going to die.

Her mind mourned all the things she had yet to experience in life, holding her own child, watching Jeremy feed their son or daughter when he or she woke in the middle of the night, making love for hours on a Sunday with her husband while it rained outside, seeing Europe and going wine tasting through the vineyards of Spain. She'd been married for a mere month and her life was being stolen from her before it even began.

She thought of Jeremy, his grief at losing her and a whimper slipped past her lips. She needed to get out of—

A tapping sound caught her attention and she froze.

Her gaze jerked to the door Bryan had disappeared through and slowly scanned the room. The tap sounded again and she gasped as a face showed on the other side of the frosted window. Was that Nathan?

His breath fogged up the glass, his eyes looking panicked and relieved at the same time. Jade's heart stopped. They'd found her. Relief shook her to the bone as her shoulders quaked with renewed hope. He held up his hand in a reassuring gesture as if he could actually touch her. Strangely, it was incredibly soothing and she felt a tear slip free.

Don't be naïve. You're far from safe.

A floorboard creaked and she tensed. If her muscles pulled any tighter she feared her bones would start to snap.

"I'll be right there, my love." His voice slithered through the silence like an eel.

The man was certifiably insane. How had he managed a career thus far? She recalled his influential lineage, his grandparents and parents that had made obscene donations to the hospital. It all made sense. This was the prestige Nathan had told her about, the power that came with being a member of some twisted secret society. She wondered if they were aware one of their members were running rogue? She didn't know exactly how it worked, but she was almost certain taking a hostage was beyond even their screwed up policies for acceptable behavior.

Bryan walked in holding a mug and she held her breath, unsure what would come next.

"This should warm you up."

She took the mug, not trusting what was inside. She didn't need to drink it. The heat of the contents seeped through the porcelain and warmed her hands.

"I don't come here much, so it'll take a while for the heat to kick on."

She didn't respond because she wasn't sure how lucid his thinking was at the moment and she was terrified saying the wrong thing might make him snap.

He scoffed and she flinched as he snatched the mug from her hands. "There's nothing wrong with it," he snapped. Like it would be so unfathomable for him to slip something into her drink. He took a sip and handed it back to her. "See? Just tea. I told you, I am not going to hurt you if you cooperate."

"W-why are y-ou d-d-doing this?" Her teeth chattered uncontrollably, making her words skip out of her mouth with an uncontrollable stutter. She wanted to appear calm, but her body's natural response to the last hour was overpowering her will.

He sighed and ran a frustrated hand through his hair, leaving it standing on end. "This wasn't how things were supposed to go."

Maybe she could reason with him. After all, he said he only wanted to talk. She could pretend this was normal and they were friends, burn some time before help arrived. Nathan being here had to mean others were coming.

"Bryan—"

"*You weren't supposed to marry him!*" he snarled, his voice so venomous she flinched, fearing he'd hit her again. "He was supposed to be a fling! I was supposed to be the one you chose in the end!"

Fucking. Crazy.

Staring up at him as spittle clung to his lips she met his rage with forced composure. Her hands trembled as she brought the tea to her lips and lowered her gaze, buying time. Pretending to take another sip, she mentally counted how long it would take for help to come.

Her anger surged as a sort of realization struck with dull awareness. This entire situation was bizarre and she now had a target to blame, a face to accuse, and a mark to aim all of her pent up fury toward. This was *his* fault. Everything that happened to her, all of her heartache and tears, they were his doing.

Her teeth clamped tight as she fought back the impetuous urge to throw her scalding tea in his face and attack him. But she wouldn't win. He was bigger and stronger and a fuck load crazier.

She had to play it smart. Yet, she couldn't resist picking at the first vulnerability she found.

"He'll know I'm missing. He'll call the cops. They'll find you. If you let me go, you might not go to jail."

He gave a humorless laugh. "I have ways to handle the police."

That's what the society does... They cover up for each other. He knows other men who will help him, men who should be helping her!

Fear choked her so her focus turned to anger.

He touched you. He branded you. He's the reason you suffered. Without him, you never would've had a baby to lose!

She needed to knock him off balance before she clawed that cocky look off his arrogant face. "Ways like *Postestas Adimpleo Postestas Quattuor?*"

His eyes momentarily widened, registering shock. A mask of calm slid over his expression. "You bumped your head, my love. You're confused."

She was not confused and she certainly wasn't his *love*. Every time he called her that she wanted to scream. He was the confused one. She had more clarity than she had in the past six months.

"I know about your little club. I know that you watched me for months before you followed me to that bar and drugged me. I know about how they promised to protect you and get you out of trouble. But the police tell me that'll change the second you're put in front of a female judge." Her mouth curved, matching his cocky smirk from earlier. "I have connections too," she bluffed.

No comment from the sociopath in the room? Interesting.

She continued to push. "They'll betray you, Bryan. They'll leave you to hang because you broke the rules, and I happen to know for a fact that they don't take kindly to that."

His eyes moved frantically as if he were doing some sort of complex calculation in his head. She was hitting a nerve. His breath came quickly, setting a pulse to the silence.

Empowered by his show of fear, she sat a little taller. "Do you know what they do to men who draw unwanted attention to their club?"

He glared at her, his unease evident in his twitchy eyes. Clearly, he hadn't thought this through and was flying without a parachute.

"They'll find you and they punish you the same way you punished me. They'll seek retribution. And as they hold you down, you'll know the true meaning of victim, because you *will be* awake. And when you struggle, they'll laugh. They'll desecrate you in every possible way and then they'll brand you for the despicable animal you—"

Her head snapped back as the back of his hand whacked hard against her cheek. The teacup shattered across the floor. Pushing the pain aside, she met his glare, tasting blood. "How's it feel to be scared?"

"*Shut up!*" he snapped. "You made me hurt

you! And look what you did to my mother's china!"

His head jerked toward the door and then back to her. He snatched her arm in a bruising grip, yanking her from the sofa.

She yelped as he dragged her across the room. "Wait!" Struggling to break his hold, she lost her balance, but he pulled her toward an old desk, ripping open drawers and rummaging through papers.

A sheaf of thick white documents, still creased from where they'd been folded caught her eye. On the edge, there was a broken wax seal with a familiar number four.

Snatching the papers out of view, he stuffed them into his pockets. She grunted as he yanked her to the corner where a fireproof box sat.

He turned the dial of the safe and cursed when his shaky hand refused to cooperate. His skin wore a sheen of sweat and his grip was loosening. When the safe finally opened, he pulled out a wad of money and she yanked her arm out of his grip.

"Don't move." A small silver handgun pointed at her face from his trembling hand.

Oh, shit.

Her bravado faltered. He gripped her arm again, this time with an unbreakable hold and dragged her toward the front door. Her focus was glued to the handgun, knowing just one wrong move and her life could be over. Where was Nathan?

Did he have the foresight to slash his tires?

What about Lily? Was she awake yet? Oh, God... this was all going to end and Jade was no longer sure if she'd make it out alive.

An unexpected calm washed over her, numbing fear climbing into every organ and cocooning all of her bones. Surrender. She knew then she'd do anything to live. And that was how bad guys won, because she was now terrified enough to negotiate her life—at least long enough to remain alive and find help.

Life slowed as she considered all she'd lost and how glad she was she hadn't let her grief topple her in her last minutes. She was strong. She'd fought to the very end and didn't let sorrow swallow her. A silent rage boiled her blood. It was over, but she wasn't ready to give up.

She would *not* forfeit the game until she took her last breath and she was still fucking breathing! This was *her* life. She refused—*refused*—*to* let this maniac win.

Her thoughts pranced wildly through her head. Jeremy, glimpses of him making love to her, dancing with her, laughing with her, holding her when no one else was brave enough to come near her. She recalled an image of young Kat holding Mia, so frightened but determined to beat the odds. She imagined Jeremy rushing for cover, holding his friend Josh's body as bullets whizzed by. Tyson holding his baby sister as she passed on. They were all scared, but they all fought through the fear and survived.

Her feet tripped up a step as he yanked her to

the door and reality came crashing in. She hefted her weight in the opposite direction he was dragging her and jerked her arm. "*No!*"

Turning, his glare lit with impatience and rage. "Do. Not. Fight. Me."

Her foot dug into the area rug as her other one slammed into his Italian loafers. He cursed, catching her by the forearms and gouging his nails into her tender flesh. Her palms slapped his face and squeezed the flesh, her fingernails stabbing into the soft skin around his eyes.

"*I'll never stop fighting!*" she screamed.

"*Fucking bitch!*" He jerked back and she charged, throwing all her weight into his stomach as they slammed into a table.

A vase crashed to the floor, shattering on the hard marble. Her knee slammed painfully to the ground, something sharp gouging into her flesh as his weight fell on top of her. Limbs tangled as her fingers scratched away soft skin. He wrestled her hands away from his face and pinned her to the floor.

No! Shards of broken glass punctured her as he held her down. "*Get off of me!*"

She spit in his eye and yanked her wrists free. Grabbing a fistful of hair, she jerked his head down and bit his cheek until she tasted blood.

He roared and suddenly she couldn't breathe. Pressure threatened to collapse her windpipe as his grip tightened around her throat and lifted over her, his weight crushing her throat.

Her eyes watered as her palms slapped at his

arms. She tugged at his sleeves, but he didn't let go. Words mouthed in silent pleas flung, his vacant eyes staring down from his bleeding face.

"I didn't want to hurt you." The gun cocked back and slammed into her temple.

Pain exploded behind her eyes and her vision blurred. The warm trickle of her blood dripped into her hair as she gasped for oxygen, weightless and, perhaps, dead.

"Get up." He yanked her to her feet, but she could barely stand. "We have to go."

Her knees bucked, her dead weight collapsing back to the floor. Her eyes were barely open, and she couldn't make her body more. She was losing consciousness. Her fingers tingled as warm blood clotted in her left eye. Her throat was raw, her voice broken.

"*Get up!*" He caught her in a headlock and opened the front door.

A flash of movement caught her eye as a tall figure blocked her view of the outside. Sucking in a razor sharp breath, she winced as the raw tissue of her throat grated. Blood smeared her vision.

"Time's up, motherfucker." The barrel of a Glock aimed at her face.

"*No!*" she screamed as the blast echoed into a deafening hum and the world went black.

Forty-Five

EVERYTHING HURT. Her hand instinctively rose to the throbbing ache at her temple, but something gently caught her wrist.

"No, no, sweetie, I just stitched you up."

Syphoning in a deep breath, Jade wheezed and struggled to open her eyes. Bright lights and blue padding. A robust black woman in an EMT uniform leaned over her.

"Where am I?" She coughed, her throat battered, each word painful.

"You're in an ambulance. I'm almost done. Try to stay still a minute longer."

Cool air nipped at her toes. A coarse blanket draped over her body. She tilted her chin to her chest. The black sky flickered with flashes of red. Then she saw Trenton Cole.

A smile stretched above the jagged scar at his jaw. "How you doing, Scrappy Doo?"

Throat ravaged, she frowned and rasped, "Did you shoot me?"

"Course not." He laughed. "I don't make those kinds of mistakes. Shot that doctor, though, right between the eyes."

A tumultuous mix of emotion raced through her at the pace of a tidal wave. "Bryan's dead?" A few hours ago, that would have been devastating news.

"Yup." Trent winked. "Told you I was better than Kevin Costner."

She laughed and winced at the pain ricocheting through her skull. *I'm alive.* Tears welled in her eyes. "Jeremy?"

"He should be here any second. You rest and let the EMTs finish patching you up."

Her eyelids closed and she gave into the pull of sleep. Sometime later, maybe a minute, maybe an hour, gravel crunched and pinged as a car skidded to a stop. An officer shouted something she couldn't make out and her body tensed in response, fearful her safety was just a dream.

"I need to see my wife!" Chills shot through her body as Jeremy's voice thundered.

Trent peeked into the ambulance. "That'd be your husband."

The doors of the ambulance jostled as Jeremy shoved Trent out of his way and climbed through the opening, eyes frantic and hair disheveled. He was still in his tux, but the tie was gone and his collar was undone.

When their gazes connected he let out a deep, shaky breath. *"Jade."*

He fumbled his way closer to the gurney and grasped for her hand, pulling her scraped fingers to his lips with a trembling hold. "Thank God, you're all right." He sighed as his hands coasted over her body checking for injuries.

He scowled at the bruise he found on her arm and kissed the cut at her temple. His eyes welled with tears as her carefully traced a finger along her throat. She could only imagine what he saw on her neck.

"Did he...?"

"No," she croaked.

"I'm so sorry, baby. I'm so, so sorry. Tears flooded his green eyes. "Never again, baby, never again."

Slowly, she lifted a hand and caught a tear chasing down to his jaw. Running a trembling hand along his face, hating to see him so tormented, she forced her words out. "I'm fine, now. I fought." Her own tears choked her. "The worst part was fearing I might never see you again, fearing we'd never have our life together."

"I love you," he said fiercely, gripping her hand in his and ignoring the medic warning him to be gentle.

She smiled. Her husband didn't do gentle in moments of passion. She didn't mind. She needed him holding her, needed to know she was where she was supposed to be, where she never wanted to leave, held safely in his arms.

"I love you, too."

His arms pulled her close and she shut her eyes. She was finally safe and could breathe again.

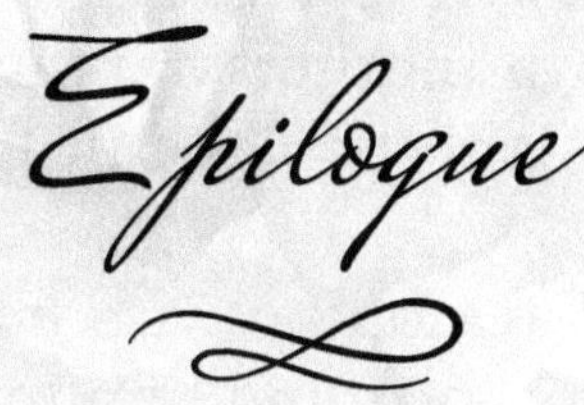

Epilogue

TEN MONTHS Later

"That's it! I can't walk anymore. My sciatic nerve is killing me and no one's giving out any good candy." His wife had definitely reached her limit.

"We've been to four houses," Tyson foolishly teased.

Jeremy sighed as Jade shot their friend a look of death. "I will kill you, Tyson."

Ty held his hands up in surrender. "Come on, Mia. Let's go knock on that door."

It was Halloween and Jade insisted they go to Tyson and Kat's to see the kids in their costumes. Mia was a witch and four-month-old T.J. was a pumpkin.

His wife had been miserable for weeks, sixteen days to be exact. Her mood declined from euphoric, to anxious, to downright angry ever since she'd passed her due date. According to Jade, she was the only woman alive who didn't go into labor early when carrying twins. Lily told her it was quite common for mothers of twins to go late, just like mothers of single babies, but Jade told Lily she was a liar.

Jeremy tried reasoning with her, but that only sent her on a rant, blaming him for her condition. He could swear she asked for this, but what did he know?

Now, he simply nodded and said a lot of *yes dears* while trying to make her as comfortable as possible. Being a military man, he was secure enough to admit he was a little scared. He hoped, for everyone's sake, that his children arrived soon. Either that or he was going to have to move.

"Do you want to go home?" he asked as she wobbled after the group.

She was ridiculously pregnant. Her belly swelled like a beach ball and swallowed her tiny legs. She hadn't been able to put on her own shoes for months. Her breasts were enormous—not that he was complaining—and her back was always aching. It should be unnatural for a woman to carry that much extra weight in her womb.

"No, I do not want to go home," she sneered. "I just want to rest for a minute. This has to be the hottest October ever!"

He hid a laugh. This woman, his amazing Jade, his beautiful wife, ensured there was never a dull moment in their lives. After the kidnapping, they had many sessions with Chloe, who now came to their home for events that had more to do with friendship than anything else. Jade had made remarkable progress and was slowly coming to terms with the prior year. He envied her recovery because he still struggled to accept all that had happened.

She survived what should've broken even the strongest person. She was his rock and she would be an unstoppable momma bear once she gave birth to their cubs.

Her determination to live life to the fullest and chase down her dreams made her unlike any other. No matter how much she complained about the pregnancy, she was happier than she'd ever been. Happy and scared. And when she was scared she got feisty. That's all this was.

The closer the babies came to being born, the more hopeful she became, but it also meant she had more to lose. He understood her fear, which was why he endured her moods.

She was a fighter. She would always be a fighter. Jeremy had no doubt she would have prevailed the night Philips had her if Trent hadn't arrived in time. The issue was, Jade sometimes put herself at risk to conquer her demons. If he could, he'd slay every obstacle in her way from this day forward. But his wife liked to do things for herself and hated being told something was out of reach. So, they continued to trick or treat.

They paused as the group walked to another house to knock for candy. "We can go back to Kat's and wait for everyone there," he offered, knowing she'd reject that idea. "There's ice cream."

"What's the fun in that? I don't want ice cream. I want to see my stepdaughter trick or treat. Is it too much to ask for everyone to just slow the hell down? I'm nine and a half months pregnant! My feet are swollen, my back is—"

She paused mid-sentence and Jeremy followed her gaze to the ground.

"Oh shit," she whispered, her hand grasping her protruding stomach. Her stare locked with his and her expression softened from irate pregnant banshee to terrified first-time mom.

He smiled. "Is it time?"

She nodded, her brow pinched and her lips pressed tight.

He turned and shouted, "It's time!"

"Thank God!" Ty barked as Kat clapped her hands, quickly ushering them back toward the house.

Jade's expression contorted and her breathing grew labored. Jeremy passed Jade's hand to Kat. "Stay with her. I'm going to get the car."

~

Jade gave a royal wave as she was wheeled into the maternity ward at Parkside Memorial and the nurses cheered. Her bitchiness over the past few weeks had earned such a welcome from her co-workers. No doubt they were glad to see her at the finish line.

She was scared to death of the pain and wanted everything to be over as soon as possible. Then she would have her babies and everything would be perfect—as perfect as life could be with twin newborns.

"Is my epidural ready?" she asked as Debra, one of the maternity nurses, escorted them to a delivery room.

"Dr. Bishop's already spoken to the anesthesiologist and he's on his way up."

Once she changed and had her epidural in place her mood was marginally better. Lily came in and checked her progress and informed her it would be very soon.

Whatever the hell that meant.

Her contractions decreased from sharp spasms to dull throbs. When everyone finally cleared out and gave her and Jeremy privacy, she reached for his hand. "I'm scared."

He tucked her hair behind her ear and smiled. "I'm scared, too. I hate seeing you in any kind of pain, but everything will be fine. The last miles always the hardest, but it leads to a lifetime of happiness. By the end of the night, we'll have our babies."

His promise came true just before midnight. She held a bundle of blue in her left arm and a bundle of pink in her right. Jason and Julia, the two most precious gifts she was ever given.

They gazed at their children, both fighting tears of joy and remarking how perfect they each were. With matching tufts of blond hair and tiny little features, they were a combination of both her and Jeremy.

She breathed a sigh of absolute satisfaction and bliss. "Everything I've ever fought for was for this very moment." Her gaze found her husband's and she smiled. "Thank you. Thank you for loving me through the good and the bad. Thank you for believing this sort of happiness was possible."

He kissed her temple. "Life's long, Jade, and it's far from over. But even when we're old and gray, I promise to always catch you when you fall."

With all she'd been through, she understood that more than anything. Jeremy was never letting go. He was hers and she was his, forever, a family. "I'll catch you, too."

Holding her children in her arms, staring into her husband's eyes, she felt the happiness of her life sink in. It warmed her heart and she knew, without a doubt, the bad times would never matter as much as the good. These were the moments of living that truly healed the soul.

THE END

Want more New Castle?
Read Something Borrowed (New Castle
3) Now!

Claim your FREE book when you subscribe
to Lydia's newsletter!

<u>Click here to sign up for Lydia Michaels'
Newsletter.</u>

Are you follow Lydia Michaels?
Stalk her on <u>TikTok</u>, <u>Instagram</u>, <u>Facebook</u>,
<u>Goodreads</u>, and <u>BookBub</u>!
<u>TikTok @LydiaMichaels</u>
<u>Instagram @lydia_michaels_books</u>
<u>Facebook @LydiaMichaels</u>
<u>Goodreads</u>
<u>BookBub</u>

Show Your LOVE
*If you enjoyed this book, please don't forget to <u>leave a
review</u>.*

LYDIA MICHAELS' READING ORDER

<u>MCCULLOUGH MOUNTAIN</u>
<u>Almost Priest</u>
<u>Beautiful Distraction</u>
<u>Irish Rogue</u>
<u>British Professor</u>
<u>Broken Man</u>
<u>Controlled Chaos</u>
<u>Hard Fix</u>
<u>Intentional Risk</u>

<u>JASPER FALLS</u>
<u>Wake My Heart</u>
<u>The Best Man</u>
<u>Love Me Nots</u>

<u>Falling In</u>
<u>Breaking Out</u>
<u>Coming Home</u>

STAND ALONES
<u>La Vie en Rose</u>
<u>Simple Man</u>
<u>Sugar</u>
<u>Breaking Perfect</u>
<u>Hurt</u>
<u>Protege</u>

About Lydia Michaels

Lydia Michaels is the award winning and bestselling author of more than forty titles, a certified life coach, and transformational speaker. She is the consecutive winner of the 2018 & 2019 *Author of the Year Award* from *Happenings Media*, as well as the recipient of the 2014 *Best Author Award* from the *Courier Times*. She has been featured in *USA Today, Romantic Times Magazine, Love & Lace*, and more. As the host and founder of the *East Coast Author Convention*, the *Behind the Keys Author Retreat*, and *Read Between the Wines*, she continues to celebrate her growing love for readers and romance novels around the world.

In 2021, Michaels released the groundbreaking, non-fiction series, ***Write 10K in a Day***, to commemorate her career in the publishing industry. She looks forward to many more years of exploring both fiction and non-fiction writing, teaching about the craft, and learning from the others in the author community.

Lydia is happily married to her childhood sweetheart. Some of her favorite things include the scent of paperback books, listening to her husband play piano, escaping to her coastal home at the Jersey Shore, cheap wine, *Game of Thrones*, coffee, and kilts. She hopes to meet you soon at one of her many upcoming events.

You can follow Lydia at www.Facebook.com/LydiaMichaels or on Instagram @lydia_michaels_books

Read By Mood
Billionaire Romance
Falling In | Sacrifice Of The Pawn | Calamity Rayne | Blind

Contemporary Romance
Wake My Heart | The Best Man | Love Me Nots | Pining For You |Almost Priest| My Funny Valentine | Side Squeeze | Almost Priest | Beautiful Distraction | Irish Rogue | British Professor | Broken Man (LGBTQ) | Controlled Chaos | Hard Fix|Intentional Risk

Emotional Favorites
La Vie en Rose | Simple Man | Wake My Heart | Sacrifice of the Pawn | Crush
Romantic Comedy
Calamity Rayne

Erotic Romance
Breaking Perfect | Protégé | Falling In | Sugar

First in Series
Almost Priest | Falling In | First Comes Love | Wake My Heart | Crush | Original Sin

Paranormal Vampire Romance
Original Sin | Dark Exodus | Prodigal Son

LGBTQ+ & Menage Romance
Broken Man (MM) | Breaking Perfect (MMF) | Crush (MMF) | Hurt (Non-Consensual) | Protege

Sexy Nerds & Second Chances
Blind | Untied
Teacher Student, Workplace, and Age-Gap
Love Affairs... Oh my!
British Professor | Pining For You |Breaking
Perfect | Falling In | Sacrifice of the Pawn

Single Dads & Single Moms
Simple Man | Pining For You | First Comes Love |
Controlled Chaos | Intentional Risk

Dark Tortured Hero Romance
Hurt

Non-Fiction Books for Writers
Write 10K in a Day: Avoid Burnout